In the Footsteps of Iskandar

Dan Silberman

To Trish

Hope you'll enjoy this
Book *[signature]*

Black Rose Writing

www.blackrosewriting.com

ISBN: 978-1-61296-246-7

PUBLISHED BY BLACK ROSE WRITING

www.blackrosewriting.com

Printed in the United States of America

In the Footsteps of Iskandar is printed in Perpetua

This book is dedicated to my wife Jackie.

Special Thanks

A number of patient and generous individuals assisted me with advice in the course of writing this book. I wish to particularly thank Jackie, my wife, for her unstinting effort in making this book readable. Special thanks to my daughters Gabrielle and Leah for their invaluable advice and their multiple reads of the manuscript. I am indebted to my editor at Black Rose Writing, Reagan Rothe and to his team of professionals.

In the Footsteps of Iskandar

Chapter One

Of Lice and Men

Paris, 1973

As dysentery cramps tormented my guts, I stood and scratched absently at the lice crawling in my long matted hair and filthy clothes. I hindered the purposeful scurrying of well-dressed, cologne-smelling, pink-faced passengers like a clog in a sewer pipe, forcing them to flow around me as they hurried to the luggage carousels at the far end of the Orly air terminal.

I noticed a six-foot-two, darkly tanned, black-bearded emaciated stranger staring at me. It took me longer than it should have to realize that I was looking at my reflection in the floor-to-ceiling windows. My sunken, bloodshot, brown eyes looked dazed and shocked as my befuddled brain attempted to process the facts: I was back in Paris. I felt ill and for a nineteen-year old, I looked like shit.

The sterile atmosphere of the terminal had the faint grassy scent of industrial freshener and made the smells of Bombay emanating from my unwashed body and clothes almost tangible. My clothing, a frayed, faded red cotton tunic, filthy, once-white pajama pants and Indian sandals made of tire-rubber soles with leather straps was well-worn, almost never laundered and retained the malodorous reek of car exhaust fumes, hot dust, urine and fecal matter. I thought wryly that I resembled the ubiquitous holy men of Maharashtra in Bombay, a city I had left scant hours ago, although even wearing these sad rags, I was still better dressed than the mostly-naked Sadhus. What little I owned fit into a beat-up hemp shoulder satchel.

A sudden disorienting sense of alienation and vertigo overwhelmed me and I staggered up to a French notion of a bench - an assemblage of chrome tubes and white leather straps — and sat down with my eyes closed until the surge of dislocation receded. Six hours ago I was in Bombay, a city, which took me an eventful year-long, overland odyssey to reach. And now, with almost no transition I sat in these air-freshened, climate-controlled, quiet glass-and-chrome surroundings. Instead of the clamor of innumerable rickshaws' put-put engines, the unceasing honking of horns, the cacophony of merchants hawking wares at the top of their voices and the constant din of countless transistor radios blaring Indian music all I heard was the occasional announcements on the PA system and the muted conversations of passengers.

By using deep breathing techniques, I regained a modicum of inner balance and rose to follow the luggage-toting herd moving towards the double glass doors leading to the main concourse. Cousin David leaned casually against the wall as he waited by the doors scanning the arriving travelers. I'd lost almost forty pounds and looked like a derelict, filthy hobo, so I was unsurprised when his gaze slid over me without recognition.

"Er... Bonjour, cousin," I said stopping in front of him.

David, a stocky, balding Frenchman in his mid-forties peered at me, his eyes widening in disbelief. He straightened up and squeaked, "Danny?" Clearing his throat he repeated in his normal voice, "I mean, is that you, Danny?" Astonished, he scrutinized me and took shallow breaths as my distinctive eau-de-Bombay stench hit his nose.

David was about five-foot-six-inches tall, had a healthy glow and was always impeccably dressed. He was wearing sharply creased grey slacks, suede hush-puppies shoes and a sport jacket over a pale shirt matching his lively blue eyes. His sparse sandy hair - combed from side to side in a futile effort to hide his balding pate - framed a tanned face with an easy smile.

"You have any luggage? No, I guess not." He glanced at my satchel and I followed him to the parking lot where we retrieved his gleaming Peugeot sedan. I sat in the car and stared through the windshield, racking my stalled brain trying to come up with small talk.

"How are you?"

"Oh, fine thanks. Before I forget, your mom is very worried about you... Please call her first thing tomorrow."

"Um... David," I stammered, looking at the floor mat. "Thanks a lot for paying for the flight. I'll repay you as soon as I can."

"Tut, tut. Don't mention it. Did you get checked out by a doctor at the embassy before you left?"

"Yeah, I did. He said I have dysentery and gave me some pills. He also suggested a visit to a clinic as soon as possible."

"I'll book you an appointment with Doc Roche," David said as he maneuvered the sedan with skillful competence into the busy stream of traffic on the freeway.

"Thanks David. Um… One other thing; I sort of have lice in my hair and need to see a barber." I hastily grabbed a handhold as David threw the car into a steep left turn in his reflexive attempt to put as much space as possible between us. He recovered immediately and, accompanied by strident, angry horns, steered the Peugeot back into our lane.

I fell asleep on the way to the apartment and the last thing I remember from that bewildering first day was having a long, hot shower, that couldn't cleanse me completely of India, before crashing on the guestroom bed at David's place.

* * *

The next morning I awoke befuddled by the unfamiliar surroundings. The sensation of luxuriating on a soft mattress on a firm spring box for the first time in months seemed almost decadent. I noticed a louse crawling on the pillow and absently crushed it between my fingernails as memories of last night flooded in. I was back in Paris, staying at David's apartment, check. A wave of despair engulfed me as I remembered the horrific events that preceded my flight from India. I calmed myself by inventorying the room. The guest bedroom with its distinctive large Persian carpet and the queen-sized bed was pretty much as it was when last I stayed here. A tall, mirrored double-door armoire flanked by dressers lined one wall while a couple of red upholstered Louis-something chairs, on either side of a small, graceful round table, completed the room's furnishing.

I stood up, padded to the window and pulled the curtains aside. As I scratched at bites on my neck, I gazed out upon a sea of steeply angled slate-shingled roofs interspersed with a multitude of TV antennae and terracotta-colored chimneys like a bizarre alien forest extending as far as the eye could see. The sun, high in the morning sky, shone from a bright blue dome dotted with a few white, fluffy clouds. By craning my neck to the right I could just see the Eifel tower seemingly wreathed in diamonds, its second-floor restaurant's windows sparkling as they reflected the early sun.

I searched for the filthy rags I'd thrown on the floor the previous night as I undressed and found instead a neat pile of folded clean clothing on one of the chairs. I donned a pair of jeans that fit too wide in the waist and left the room in search of David.

Did I mention that my cousin was loaded? He owned a number of stores in the heart of the fashion district and lived in a huge penthouse-apartment in the sixteenth arrondissement, one of the more exclusive Parisian quarters.

I found an old acquaintance, Asunción, the Spanish maid, polishing silverware in the dining room.

"Hola, Asunción," I smiled, happy to spot a familiar face. "Come va, me Corazon?"

She shook her head and gave me a patronizing glance. "I told you many times before, you're no speaking Spanish. That's spaghetti western talk!" Asunción was a short, wiry, energetic woman of undetermined age who applied little makeup and kept her gray-black hair in a tight bun. She had been with David's family since he was a small boy - I remembered her from my own childhood when we lived in Paris - and was one of thousands of Spanish refugees who fled after Franco and his fascists took over their country.

"You look terrible! Go wash up, Danny. Then I make you breakfast."

"Sure, man. What happened to my old clothes?"

"Ayee. They were full of bugs. Yuck! I threw them for burning. I loan you David's old stuff." She shooed me to the guest bathroom. I showered again, soaping and scrubbing with the luffa until the water sluicing down the drain changed from a grayish-brown color to just murky. I repeatedly shampooed and watched impassively as lice writhed on the shower's tiled floor on their way to Paris' sewers, Shiva the destroyer, me!

After the shower, I shaved off my scraggly, wispy beard with a safety razor I found in a cabinet over the sink. I examined the scrawny naked body reflected in the tall mirror with a critical eye. The ribs, collarbones and hipbones protruded clearly, stretching the skin. My stomach had sunken enough to show the outline of vertebrae and my limbs resembled long, thin sticks. Overall, I looked like one of the starving people from Bangladesh. Clean and dressed, I rejoined Asunción in the kitchen and perched on a stool at the center-aisle counter.

She poured me a coffee and handed me a sheet of paper wrapped around a few currency notes. The note from David confirmed an appointment with the hairdresser and the address of the salon, while the bills, about twenty bucks worth of francs, were a loan to buy clothing. I ate a light meal of dry toast and weak black coffee, mindful of the microbial parasites plaguing my guts and headed out.

* * *

Paris is at its most beautiful in early spring when shy new-growth peek from the sun-kissed wakening gardens. Flowers bloom everywhere, filling the air with sweet fragrances and the trees wear faint emerald halos as new leaves emerge.

Christophe's Unisex Salon occupied the ground floor of a building at the corner of two busy avenues. The long and narrow shop, shaped like a V contained a dozen barber's chairs facing the floor-to-ceiling windows and the sidewalk. Behind each chair, a wheeled cabinet supported a high mirror from which hung an assortment of electric clippers and hair dryers. Black, thin, combs and gleaming stainless steel scissors stuck out of tall jars full of pink fluid, a nightmarish bouquet of sinister stabby flowers.

"May I help you?" asked the languid receptionist without looking up from the fashion magazine propped on a small desk. He wore a fishnet shirt showing more of his pigeon chest than I wanted to see; his coifed dark hair cascaded to his shoulders in waves and he reeked of strong, spicy cologne.

"I'm Daniel. David made an appointment for me…"

"Oh, yes. Davy. He's a dear, let me check…" The man scanned the page of a book-sized planner and raised his eyes to me. He squeaked in shocked surprise, scrambled backwards in his wheeled chair hitting the back counter loudly and caromed back toward the desk. The place went quiet as everyone stared at us. A chubby man wearing tight colorful clothes waddled in a semi-run towards us.

"What's going on Mario?" he shouted, waving his hands in agitation.

"This… Er, that…Person has an appointment, Christophe." Mario pointed with a shaky manicured finger. The owner of the salon scanned the planner and confirmed the sad fact.

"Monsieur David is one of our best clients. And, when he called for a slot, even though there was nothing available for three weeks… God help me." He studied me for a moment and, still muttering under his breath, led me to the hair-washing stations ranged along the wall.

"Go on. Get back to work," Christophe urged the dozen hairdressers and their customers who, eyes wide, stared mutely at me. Activity resumed as I sat in a chair and reclined my head into a sink. I should have guessed that David would only frequent a top-notch, fashionable and expensive hair salon. Well, I thought, they are going to earn their money this time.Christophe ran his fingers through my matted curls, shook his head and mumbled in despair. Suddenly, he jerked his hand away, cursing in an utterly non-fashionable gutter French.

"Ah, merde alors. What the fuck is this?" he swore peering in horror as one of the Bombay hitchhikers crawled up his wrist. He paled and I feared he was having a coronary but he recovered and rinsed off the offending louse with a jet of water. He patted his hands dry with a small towel, gave me a long calculating look, most likely deciding whether David was indeed worth the indignity to his chic salon and came to a decision.

"Martin. Yoo-hoo, Martin, where are you?" He searched the back of the salon.

A slim young man about five-feet-five tall and wearing a blue tunic over bell-bottomed jeans slouched towards us through a bead curtain at the back of the salon.

"Oui, mon oncle?" he replied. The youth looked about seventeen and projected an indefinable androgynous image underlined by a couple of earrings in each ear, wrist bracelets and rings on the fingers of both hands.

Christophe slammed the edge of the counter. "Stand up straight, Martin. Nom de Dieu." He pointed imperiously at my curls. "This man has lice. I want you to wash his hair with the special shampoo. Do it three times, you understand?" Martin, unfazed, repeated the instructions. Christophe, shaking his head, left to rejoin the receptionist at the front of the salon.

"What's your name?" Martin asked, turning the water on and adjusting the taps for the perfect temperature.

"Call me Danny," I said as he ran the nozzle over my hair.

"Where did you catch lice?" He snapped on a pair of thick rubber gloves, the kind used for handling toxic materials and poured a measure of viscous liquid reeking of industrial chemicals from a plastic bottle. I noted a bright orange skull-and-crossbones warning on the upper part of the label. He spread the shampoo throughout my curls and massaged it deeply. The chemical tingled coldly as it penetrated to the scalp and stank of DDT overlaid with a hint of fake citrus fragrance.

"I just got back from India," I said.

"India, wow! How long were you there?"

"I was in Bombay for three months but it took almost a year to get there from London. And only six hours to get back," I replied bitterly.

"I'd love to travel!" He rinsed my hair, running his fingers through the tangled curls, teasing the strands apart. "Go to India, see Nepal, you know?"

"Good for you." The continuous, maddening, itching and crawling I'd felt since the lice first colonized my head stopped abruptly and the relief was almost orgasmic. Martin racked the water nozzle and repeated the shampooing procedure a second time.

"How much money does it take to get to India?"

"Well, the way I traveled was inexpensive. But, you can't be in a hurry." I described how drifters earned money by doing odd jobs, making and selling sidewalk jewelry, panhandling and busking to name just a few.

"How about smuggling dope?" he whispered.

"Too dangerous these days. In the east you can smoke locally as much as you want but don't try to cross borders with narcotics. Have you ever heard of an American named Billy Hayes? Three years ago, in 1970, he taped bricks of hash to his torso and tried to smuggle the stuff out of Turkey. They caught him at the airport and threw his ass in jail. In fact, as we speak, the poor shmuck is still rotting in prison."

Suitably impressed, Martin completed the third and final soaping. He rinsed and wrung the sopping mass of curls, wrapped a large fluffy towel around my head and led me to a barber's chair. Christophe walked over, pulled at a wet strand, checked the scalp, nodded and directed Martin to give me a haircut. He also instructed me to repeat the shampooing every day for a week because the poison only killed hatched lice and not the eggs.

I left the salon looking, if not good, at least presentable. I bought a pair of jeans, a shirt and no-name trainers at a discount store, asked the clerk to remove all the tags, changed into the new clothes and returned to David's flat. Sitting at a desk in the library, I pulled out my tattered journal, a dog-eared diary I'd carried for a year, and removed the fat elastic band that kept photos, postcards and loose notes between the covers. I flipped through the bulging notebook noting how the edge of the leather binding had worn thin and peeled back in spots. A faded stub, torn in half, reminded me of the long train ride from Quetta to Karachi and I could almost smell the spicy fragrance of chicken curry we ate during the trip.

I wrote about the previous few days while the memories were still fresh and raw. When I finished, I returned to page one and, reading from the beginning, recollections of my yearlong journey came back.

* * *

Chapter Two

I have the Gaul

Israel: 1971/1972

In Context:

- The Maharishi Mahesh Yogi, who popularized transcendental meditation, announced his "World Plan"; to establish thirty-six hundred centers, each with a thousand teachers apiece. The plan never comes to fruition.
- Hundreds of guests at a wedding in New Delhi drink bootleg liquor composed predominately of rubbing alcohol and paint varnish, More than a hundred die of poisoning.
- President Nixon reveals that Henry Kissinger is secretly negotiating with North Vietnamese leaders, and announces "a plan for peace that can end the war in Vietnam" The proposal is reject by North Vietnam the day after the announcement..
- The 1972 Iran blizzard ends after seven days. As much as twenty-six feet of snow buries villages in northwestern, central and southern Iran. An estimated four thousand people die.

* * *

"Kibbutz… a voluntary collective community, mainly agricultural, in which there is no private wealth and which is responsible for all the needs of its members and their families."

(Encyclopedia Judaica)

In the late 1960s' and early '70s, young people from all over the world came to Israel to work in the kibbutzim. They were called *volunteers* and toiled for little more than room and board and the opportunity to participate in a uniquely Israeli experience: the Kibbutz lifestyle. In exchange, they introduced us Sabras to the hippie counterculture of rock'n'roll, drugs and casual sex. My fascination with the overland journey to India started in the fall of seventy-one at Kibbutz Tel-Galil where I met Gerard, a thirty-something French volunteer from the city of Quimper in Brittany.

Although five-foot-eight-inches tall with wide shoulders, he had emaciated, thin limbs and a sunken barrel chest. On the homeward leg of a trek to Nepal via Iran, Iraq and Jordan, Gerard stopped in Israel for much needed rest and recuperation. He planned to stay at Tel Galil through the winter and resume his travels the following spring. The once burly Frenchman wore his long, wavy, dirty-blond hair in a ponytail tied with a leather strap. A strong Gallic nose dominated a tanned and lined expressive face with pale blue eyes, battered ears and drooping mustache reaching below a shaved chin, all of which reminded me of Asterix the Gaul.

"'ard work and good food, Danny," Gerard said in his native Breton accent. "That's the best way to bulk up and get healthy."

We were chatting during the scorching afternoon as we finished our chores in the long milking barn. Outside, the merciless sun ruled a cloudless turquoise-blue sky and hammered the upper Galilee into lethargic stupor. A large dial-thermometer nailed on the shady side of the barn's wall indicated thirty degrees Centigrade. Apart from the two of us and an entourage of buzzing flies happily dive-bombing the fresh manure, it seemed as if all of creation was taking a nap.

"To drift around the world, you must be 'ealthy and in good shape," Gerard continued as he guided a wide squeegee driving a liquid mixture of cow shit, spilled milk, water and urine towards the drain.

At his side, I waved the nozzle of a water hose, liquefying the lumps of manure. "What do you do when you get hurt or sick?"

He leaned on the long wooden handle and stared at me with intent. "If you get injured or very ill go to the nearest legation. They'll look after you."

We finished washing the concrete floor, forced the manure mixture from the gutter to a retaining basin, hosed off the squeegee and our gumboots and racked the tools.

"When you drift as a Freak, you must jump on opportunities and free resources."

"You mean like the embassy?"

"The legations, charitable institutions, shelters… I once panhandled a monk."

I stared at him and chortled, "What did he give you, a blessing?"

Gerard had a faraway look in his eyes and a slight smile. "That and a meal. Then, he gave me a ride to the next town in the monastery truck."

I admired and respected the French drifter who traveled the world on an endless journey. He'd held a multitude of interesting jobs from deckhand on a tramp freighter to lorry driver in Brazil. Like so many other drifters, he financed his travels by taking temporary gigs ranging from fruit picking, panhandling and busking, to washing dishes in exchange for food.

At school, we'd studied Arian and Plutarch's histories of Alexander the Great. The young Macedonian conqueror and his travels from Greece to India fascinated me. I'd longed to travel along that same road and Gerard's stories rekindled my determination to head out on a road trip of my own. As per his advice, I purchased a sturdy notebook the size of a paperback novel and made copious note of what he and the other volunteers taught me that fall and winter. I faithfully recorded their suggestions, contacts and comments about "going to India." Jotting every bit of road wisdom, I created a priceless, indispensable guidebook of the trek from Amsterdam to Bombay.

Gerard delighted in mentoring me, broadening my education and passing on his hard-won knowledge and lore. He genuinely enjoyed educating me on the finer points of road etiquette as well as innumerable clever survival tricks. During one of our regular trips to Tiberias, the nearest city, I bought a number of books my mentor recommended and spent evenings reading Jack Kerouac, Ken Kesey and Hesse's Siddhartha.

The Frenchman's lessons included a wealth of practical Freak counterculture skills such as a comprehensive pharmacopeia of recreational drugs. I learned the various methods to prepare and smoke weed, hash and oil. He patiently demonstrated how to roll perfect three-papers tapered joints, small single-paper spliffs and the endlessly entertaining means to convert household items into a pipe. I practiced using chillums, water pipes and bongs. There is a diagram, in my notebook, of a single-puff-double-carbureted toker made of cardboard tubes, plastic bits from Bic pens and packing tape. We built a prototype and proved it performed as advertised.

I absorbed my friend's encyclopedic knowledge of Freakdom like a sponge, filling pages with his pithy and useful wisdom. The journal became my travel Bible.

* * *

By late February '72, as winter relinquished its hold on the Galilee, Gerard, in good health once again, was restored and fit thanks to the wholesome kibbutz lifestyle. He prepared to resume the last leg of his journey, from Israel to Brittany via Tunisia, Algeria and Morocco.

A week before his departure we were whiling away the afternoon in the volunteers' quarters, drinking Kibbutz coffee and leafing through the latest American underground comics. It was a rainy, cold, gray day in the Galilee with wind gusts pelting raindrops on the windows and rattling the doors. A portable kerosene heater squatted against the wall and hissed softly as its heating coils glowed brightly orange, the room smelling of wet clothes and unburned fuel.

Gerard tossed a Dr. Atomic magazine at me and said, "Come with me as far as Haifa when I leave for the airport. We'll shop for your travel gear and I'll buy some souvenirs." I had turned eighteen at the end of January and planned to fly to London in March, the first step of my trip to India.

"That's a good idea," I replied. The crappy weather and the thought of my friend departing depressed me. Adding to the melancholy, a transistor radio played James Taylor's *You've Got a Friend*.

"Cheer up, man! You're leaving in a couple of weeks. You now know most of the basics of the open road. It's all in that goddamn book of yours." He smiled, pointing at my notebook lying on the small table.

The day of Gerard's departure dawned cold and sunny. The kibbutz lawns were soaked with dew and a chill breeze blew from the Sea of Galilee. We took the four-hour autobus ride to Haifa (including a transfer at Tiberias) and around lunchtime, arrived at the downtown central station. The terminal was a sprawling conglomeration of roofed-over platforms thronged by a milling crowd of passengers carrying everything from suitcases to string-tied card boxes and bales of goods. White on blue buses continuously filled the terminal with diesel fumes. Roaring engine noises and a cacophony of voices vied with a constant barrage of PA announcements.

Outside the station, lining the curbs, a multitude of stalls, carts and kiosks offered a wide selection of fast foods such as falafel, shwarma, kebabs, deep-fried fish, and assorted local favorites. Others sold freshly squeezed orange juice, ice creams and a variety of fruits and nuts. A bluish haze from smoldering charcoal and grilled meats floated above the sidewalks like delicious smog. Israeli and Arab peddlers hawking their wares at full volume added to the overall din of radios blaring atonal Arabic music, braying donkeys and the horns of the snarled street traffic.

We bought two bulging pitas full of fatoush (a finely chopped vegetable salad) and falafels dripping with tahini sauce and strolled down the street looking for an army surplus store. Gerard carried his well-travelled rucksack with its distinctive faded Swiss red cross stitched on the pocket flaps and we both wore, courtesy of the kibbutz's commissary, army-surplus, olive-green, field jackets that had probably last seen service by the U.S. forces in the Korean War.

Three blocks from the bus terminal, we found a large army surplus/camping emporium packed to the rafters with racks of khaki and olive-colored clothing, boots, sleeping bags, army-type musettes of every conceivable shape and size and empty ammunition crates. A long display counter ran along a wall, offering a collection of knives, compasses, watches, utensils and regimental unit flashes.

A tall, thin, middle-aged orthodox Jew standing behind the cash register by the door nodded his welcome and answered my query by pointing at the back of the shop where various backpacks filled shelving units. Always the teacher, Gerard thoroughly checked every bag for wear, tear and functionality, explaining the relevant features of each model. He finally suggested a tall, green nylon backpack reinforced by a scuffed aluminum frame with enough straps to attach additional gear. The "previously-owned" pack was in excellent shape, had three separate internal compartments and half a dozen pockets on the outside.

I also bought a sleeping bag and a pair of Pataugas hiking boots — considered, by the French military, at the time as the best all-purpose footwear. From the display counter, I selected a knock-off Swiss-Army knife, which had a variety of clever attachments. After haggling vigorously, the shopkeeper and I agreed on a mutually acceptable price well within my budget. Back outside, I shouldered the backpack, adjusted the straps for maximum comfort and wriggled my shoulders to test for stability and comfort. A pleasant anticipatory trepidation surged inside me. Although I was still two weeks away from my own departure I felt as if I'd taken the first step of the journey.

At an adjoining tourist store, Gerard bought a selection of hand carved olive wood rosaries for his mom and aunts. For himself he picked up a white marble chillum.

"How do you explain the pipe when you cross borders?" I asked.

He flipped the six-inch-long tapered cone, narrow stem pointing up, and said, "I tell them it's an incense burner."

"The border guards buy that?"

"They sometimes give me the hairy eyeball, but I carry a packet of joss-sticks (incense) and they let me keep the chillum."

It was time to leave, he had a plane to catch and I had to return to the kibbutz with the last bus of the day. Unable to delay the inevitable any longer, we returned to the station as the sun set over Haifa's harbor. Choked with emotion, eyes stinging and a lump in the throat I followed my friend to the ticket booths. We bought our tickets and strolled through the terminal towards our respective platforms.

"We'll meet in Amsterdam at the end of May, yes?" Gerard confirmed.

I nodded, looking at my feet. We planned to attend a Pink Floyd concert before I embarked upon my eastward trek to India. He punched me lightly on the shoulder. "Don't forget to leave me a note at the American Express office and at the Paradiso in Amsterdam. I'll do the same as soon as I arrive there."

Unable to speak, I simply hugged him tightly and walked over to my platform while Gerard headed for the Tel-Aviv bus. The flip side of drifting, as I would learn on frequent occasions in the following years, was the painful separations we experienced as we traveled along our individual paths.

* * *

A fortnight later, waiting for a bus, I viewed my home one last time. Kibbutz Tel-Galil perches on a strategic hilltop in the northeastern Galilee between Lake Kineret (the Sea of Galilee) and the foothills of the Golan Heights. The village, home to a couple hundred people, is a collection of white, single and two-story buildings surrounded by green lawns, bushes, flowerbeds and shade trees. The housing units are interspersed with communal utility and service structures such as nurseries, kindergartens, a large laundry, and a well-equipped infirmary all interconnected by a network of meandering concrete and gravel paths. The Heder Hochel (dining room), the social heart of the kibbutz, dominates the village from the top of the hill and commands a spectacular view of the distant lake.

At the base of the Tel (hill) and reached by a spider web of macadamized and dirt roads: horse barns, milking sheds, chicken coops, corrals, haylofts, garages and machine shops surround the settlement. Looking to the south, a patchwork of fields and orchards form a quilted pattern of greens, yellows and browns that roll gently down to the Sea of Galilee. To the north, purple-colored alfalfa fields and four long, rectangular fishponds reflecting the Galilee sun like giant glittering fractal mirrors, run to the horizon. Narrow, lush, grassy banks, home to otters, frogs and wading birds, separate the ponds. To the east, cattle pasture and no-man-lands climb to merge with the slopes of the overlooking Golan Heights.

I was going into the unknown, an exciting but daunting situation for an eighteen year-old country boy. I grabbed my backpack and boarded the bus. The first verse of Elton John's song *Daniel* was playing over and over in my head on the long trip to the airport.

* * *

Chapter Three

Finding the Right Kombi-nation

London, March 1972

In context:
- -Lisa Minnelli wins the Academy Awards for best actor for her appearance as Sally Bowles in the film version of the Broadway musical Cabaret.
- -United States immigration authorities revoke the visa of John Lennon
- -TWA Flight seven from New York to Los Angeles notified that it has a time bomb on board, lands back at JFK. The bomb, made with five pounds of C-four is defused with only twelve minutes to spare.
- -The maiden voyage of the *Mardi Gras*, the first for newly established Carnival Cruise Lines, departs Miami for an eight-day cruise. It runs aground on a sandbar and after being dislodged, continues on its way.
- -The last Indian troops from are withdrawn from Bangladesh, whose independence was secured from Pakistan in December.

* * *

Strapped to a towering backpack, I walked out of Heathrow airport and looked for transport to the city. London welcomed me with typical stabby spring weather of gray clouds scudding across a pewter sky and intermittent cold drizzles accompanied by icy gusts of wind that rippled the surface of rain puddles. I chose London as a starting point because of its prominence in the European counterculture movement and its influence on my generation's music. The greatest rock bands had played here and spurred alternative lifestyles that, in turn, spawned a thriving underground media and a flourishing drug culture complete with psychedelic art and fashion.

London, a melting pot of maturing talents, had launched the British

Invasion throughout the globe in the sixties and was now quickening a new genre that would become Punk Rock – our younger siblings' music. As an Age of Aquarius teen, I spent countless hours nightly, my ears glued to a cheap, plastic, Japanese transistor radio, straining to listen to the UK Top Charts' tunes fading in and out of the interference-laden ionosphere. Here at last, realizing a longed-for dream, I strolled the West End through Carnaby Street, past the notorious straight and gay Soho clubs, the outré fashion stores, the basements cafés and the pubs where legendary bands such as The Who and the Stones would hold impromptu sessions.

By 1972, the Street's boutiques had evolved from selling avant-garde, mind-blowing fashions to tourist traps displaying dubious quality kitschy products. Clearly, the counterculture had moved on. Notwithstanding the area's disreputable fall from grace and despite the crappy weather, a steady stream of shoppers imparted a sense of purposeful energy as people went in and out of the stores, restaurants and cafés. Fascinated by the throng of passersby and entranced by the ultra-short mini dresses worn by gorgeous, long-legged women, I almost tripped over a busker playing the guitar.

The slim, tall man, sheltering from the intermittent drizzle under a shop's awning, was strumming and singing a Bob Dylan classic, *Just Like a Woman*. He wore a floppy beret over long, shoulder-length sand-colored hair and an army style olive-green jacket over denim shirt and pants. Various pins and buttons on the jacket's breast proclaimed popular slogans like 'Keep on trucking' and 'Make Love Not War'. Hoping to compel contributions to the few coins in his guitar case, he vainly attempted to establish eye contact with the passing pedestrians.

I stood to one side and waited until he finished the song. "Hi man. Sorry about almost running you over. My name is Daniel." I offered to buy beers if he would point us to a decent pub.

"Hallo, Danny. I'm Trevor, call me Trev." He gathered his meager earnings and stowed his instrument. "I know just the place. Let's go to the Ship, it's a pub on Wardour."

As we walked under a store's awning, Trev spotted a long cigarette butt lying in a cranny, picked it up, wiped the filter end on his sleeve and lit the stub. The Ship, located on the ground floor of a corner building on Wardour Street, smelled of wet clothes, tobacco, stale beer and fried food. Framed pictures, drawings and daguerreotypes hung on walls made of polished red wood. On the left, a wooden bar, propping up a dozen patrons, ran along one wall. On the right, most of the tables and chairs were full and a group of drinkers stood watching two men playing darts. The background din was almost loud enough to mute a radio playing Carol King's *I Feel the Earth Move*.

Trev, using his guitar case as a ram, opened a path through the milling patrons and led us to an empty table in one of the corners. He perched on a stool, waved at a passing server and asked, "So where are you from?"

"Israel. What about you?"

"I'm a Scouser from the Pool." He noted the blank stare and added, "You know, Liverpool? Do you have any smokes?"

I fished out a pack of duty-free Camels I'd bought on the plane and a Zippo lighter. Trev helped himself and I followed suite. I sang softly, *Ferry cross the Mersey*... He grinned and nodded. "Hey. Yeah. Damn right! Gerry and the Pacemakers. They're from Liverpool."

"Let's not forget the Beatles, the Fourmost and the Searchers."

"Fuck no, man. Let's never forget the Beatles!" he repeated piously. "You know your music!"

A cute waitress in a red mini dress appeared and took our order for pints of bitter and meat pies. Trev noticed my admiring glance as I turned to watch her tantalizing, swaying ass and long shapely legs as she wove her way back to the counter. "First time in London?"

"No. In the mid-sixties, we lived in Paris for a while and I came here in sixty-seven on a school tour. We spent three days sightseeing: museums, Trafalgar... The usual tourist crap."

"Do you speak French?"

"You bet. Both of my parents were born in France, immigrated to Israel after WWII, met, and married in a kibbutz they pioneered. As a result, I have dual citizenship."

"How many languages do you speak?"

"Three. Hebrew, French and English."

"Cool! I can only speak English. So I guess you won't be visiting Buckingham Palace, the London Tower or Big Ben sort of thing?"

"Been there, done that. This time I want to do the Rock tour."

He raised his eyebrows so I explained, "I'd like to see the clubs, cafés and bars where UK rock'n'roll started."

Our waitress returned with two pints of amber brew and a distracted smile. I'm not a fan of room-temperature beer but, since this early in the year the pub's cellar kept the kegs on the cold side, the ale went down smoothly. Trev talked about the West End stoner scene, adding that John Lennon and Keith Moon used to frequent the Ship. He laughed when I turned around and scanned the patrons.

I nodded at the posters on the wall. "I envy you. Living in London, you get to go to performances and happenings..."

"More than most people. My mate Ian and I do odd jobs with some roadies we know, like help set up concerts, that sort of thing."

"No shit! How did you break into the business?"

"Thanks to Ian. He's studying woodwinds at the Royal Music Academy. Only, he meets many performers - like Ian Anderson - and stage managers."

"You mean Anderson of Jethro Tull?"

"Yeah, the same. So, anyway, one thing led to another and we got to know Rudy, a stage manager. He calls us when he needs extra help doing grunt stuff, load, unload, fetch and carry sort of thing. We make a few quid and get free tickets to the performances."

We talked about bands playing in Soho and the West End clubs, concert schedules and, inevitably, the conversation turned to drugs: prices, quality and availability of hashish and pot.

"The best and cheapest dope in Europe is in Amsterdam. Here we get Pakistani shit, blow for the rich and the usual psychedelics."

"My next stop after London is Amsterdam. There's a Pink Floyd concert in May."

Trev snapped his fingers. "Yeah, I'm thinking of going there, man. Check out if all those stories are true."

Our server brought two deliciously fragrant plates and napkin-wrapped cutlery. "Refills, love?" She pointed at our almost empty mugs. Trev and I nodded in agreement and tore into the pies.

"So, how far are you traveling, overall like?" the Scouser mumbled swallowing a large mouthful of the savory pie.

"I'm going to India, man. I follow the road in the footsteps of Iskandar."

"Who's Iskandar?"

"That's the eastern name of Alexander the Great. Alexander, Iskandar.... Sixteen-hundred years later, by Marco Polo's time, the trail was known as the Silk Road and now parts of it are called the Hippie Trail."

He gave me a wondering look. "How long is that going to take, then?"

As we sat in the pub that rainy afternoon, I could not have foreseen that the journey would take most of a year; drifting through Europe and Asia before I reached India. The trip, more than the destination, lured me, adrift on an endless voyage of discovery: The Freak lifestyle, meeting other travelers, strange and exotic foods, diving into native cultures and sampling local drugs.

Trev smirked. "Going to join an ashram, then?"

"Fuck no! That's not my thing. I'm as spiritual as a die-hard soviet. I just want to see the world, man."

The spirituality of a quasi-mystical India left me mostly indifferent and after reading books such as Hesse's Siddhartha and Kerouac's Dharma Bums (among others) I realized that I sought a cultural rather than transcendental journey of discovery.

"As for how long it's going to take, I don't know." I shrugged. "But it will be fun and a hell of an adventure!"

We chatted and drank beer most of the afternoon and I realized that Gerard had been right. Freaks from such diverse backgrounds as Trev's and mine were still Freaks and we had much in common. We shared an encyclopedic knowledge of the music we loved, we were cynics and sarky and our outlook on life was as irreverent as it was humorous.

Trev had a wonderful sense of humor, in a dry English way, and spoke with ease about any subject from chicks to the latest sci-fi book. He was almost twenty and at a crossroad. Busking, panhandling and doing odd jobs had been a lot of fun the last two years but now he was restless; searching for something, feeling the need to wander, to leave the UK and hit the road.

"Here, are you looking for a place to crash?"

I nodded. "Also for some dope."

"Let's head to my pad, you're welcome to sleep on the couch. We'll drop off the guitar and your pack and go look for hash."

* * *

It was late afternoon when we left the pub. The sky was gray and turbulent with low hanging clouds. The streetlights turned on in a weak effort to augment the waning daylight, the drizzle had stopped and the damp air stank of exhaust and wet dog shit. Cars zipped past us, their tires whooshing on the slick pavement, the temperature was falling and, though I wore a warm jacket, I was glad as we clambered down the steps to the Tube station. We rode the train for twenty minutes, climbed back to street level and shortly after arrived at our destination.

I followed Trev into a six-story apartment building, one in a long row of similar structures. We took stairs, covered by a faded red and gold runner, to the third story. The aroma of curry, cabbage and lemon floor polish filled the stairwell and I could hear TVs playing through the thin walls. Trev knocked on the second door on the right and, after a moment, a stunning brunette let us in.

Her name was Gina, a beautiful short, slim woman who at five-feet-three might have weighed ninety pounds if her clothes were soaking wet. She had shapely legs and large breasts, a heart-shaped face, lively blue-gray eyes, a pert nose and a wide, exquisitely shaped, smiling mouth. Her long, brown hair, pulled up in a ponytail, reached the small of her back. She was wearing a thin sweater over a pair of tight jeans highlighting her magnificent ass.

"Hallo, Gina," Trev said looking sheepish. "I forgot my key. Meet Danny, an Israeli Freak. I invited him to crash here for a few days. That ok with you?"

"Welcome, don't mind the mess," she said and offered her hand.

Spellbound, I gently shook her adorable small hand and followed Trev into the apartment hallway. On the left I could see three bedrooms and a bath. To the right, the corridor led into a living room filled with an assortment of mismatched, shabby furniture. A sofa, a couple of armchairs, a coffee table and assorted shelving were scattered around the small room. A wall unit supported a small TV and the components of a high-end stereo system. I detected the fragrance of incense wafting through the room; a cassette recorder was playing Cat Stevens' *Miles from Nowhere*.

"Is Ian back from the Academy?" Trev asked, propping his guitar case against the wall in a corner. I leaned my backpack by the sofa and reassuringly fingered the soft leather pouch (where I kept passport, fake student ID, driver's license and the two hundred bucks I had saved) safely tucked under my shirt.

"Not yet, he should be coming home soon. I have to get ready for work." She retreated down the hallway and disappeared through the last door on the right.

"She works in a restaurant," Trev said as he slumped in one of the armchairs. "Gina's Ian's cousin and we're sharing the apartment. Incidentally she's not my girlfriend, yeah?" He waggled his eyebrows.

The cassette stopped. Trev selected an LP from a long row on a shelf, extracted the vinyl disc, centered it on the record player's platter and lowered the arm with a precisely assured motion. *Come Together*, the first song of The Beatles' Abbey Road album, filled the room.

Trev and Ian were childhood mates, had attended school together and moved to London at the same time. Ian, who studied and performed music, auditioned for the Academy and won a student slot. Gina, who was four years older than her cousin, had preceded them to the city and offered to share the apartment.

Ian's talented Trev explained. He played woodwinds, the flute and the oboe, and composed music. Whenever possible, the two men busked at the better locations in the West End performing a medley of popular songs including challenging tunes from Jethro Tull's *Thick as a Brick*. Ian did a brilliant imitation of Anderson's trademark flute playing while standing on one leg.

Apparently Londoners were a jaded audience and only parted with money when buskers performed well, displayed talent and provided entertainment. Trev tried to line up a few gigs at local pubs but so far had limited success.

Gina emerged from her bedroom ready for work. She looked dazzling with skillfully applied make up, eyeliner and bright lipstick. She wore a thin, pale mango-colored V-neck pullover with a black miniskirt, showing most of her sexy thighs. Leather calf-length boots with modest heels and a colorful yellow plastic Macintosh completed the ensemble. She looked fashionable and highly desirable.

"Wow! You look spectacular..." I blurted. She gave me a sidelong stare and blushed turning an endearing shade of pink, grabbed her purse and headed out.

"Shit, man, I've never seen her flustered so easily," Trev muttered, shaking his head.

Ian entered the apartment shortly after Gina left. Trev introduced us and we took an instant liking to each other. Slim, five-foot seven Ian wore his long ash blond hair tucked behind elfin ears making him seem younger than his twenty years. His complexion was pallid from lack of sun but he had an easy smile and was dressed quite stylishly in a black leather jacket over a paisley shirt and bell-bottom jeans. He was carrying a bulging shoulder bag from which a thin, long wooden case stuck out. He carefully laid the instrument on a shelf before folding down on the sofa.

Trev brought three beers from the kitchen, told Ian that Gina had left for work and asked if there would be any dope at all lying around. Ian reached for his bag, fished out a flat tobacco tin and extracted the better half of a joint. He lit it up, took a drag and passed it to me. I sucked on the spliff, suppressed a cough from the harsh weed and handed it to Trev.

Ian wheezed, exhaling smoke. "That's all I had."

I looked at Trev. "Can we score some hash?"

He nodded. "I know a couple of guys in the West End." So, we finished our beers and left the apartment.

"We'll grab a bite on the way," Ian said. "It's been a long day at school and I'm starving."

"How do you like the Academy?" I asked as we strolled through the darkened neighborhood. The cold air smelled of incipient rain, the puddles reflected streetlights and a chill wind tugged at our clothes.

"It's hard work but very rewarding. And, there's this Scottish girl in my class…"

Trev hooted and punched his friend in the arm. "There he goes again, always chasing the impossible."

Ian gave Trev two fingers. "I think I'm making progress. I mean, she's only seventeen. She agreed to go for some Vindaloo next week after school." He stared dreamingly. "She's gorgeous and has a beautiful contralto voice. That girl will be a seriously good singer someday."

Trev chuckled and ruffled Ian's hair. "Well. So, we'll get to meet your mystery lass."

We reached a circular plaza with a statue in the center. A lone cart parked on the perimeter sold chips sprinkled with salt and served piping hot in a newspaper cone. The fries were delicious and we made short shrift of our portions as we clattered down a set of stairs to the Tube station.

The Bag O' Nails was a notorious club in London's rock scene and was famous for having hosted stars such as Clapton, Hendrix and Jagger. The place had mellowed out since the heydays of the sixties but it was still rocking and a popular spot to score dope. Powerful speakers throughout the club pounded out The Stones' *Satisfaction*. Gyrating couples packed the dance floor and a dense, colorfully dressed mob stood in front of the long, neon-lit bar. Strobes and spotlights lit the chrome-and-vinyl booths ranged along the walls while colored beams caromed off the chromed railings.

Ian and I remained near the entrance and watched couples push through the crowds as Trev shouldered his way into the club's innards looking for his connection.

"Fuck, but it's loud," I shouted in Ian's ear, shaking my head.

Ian smiled and hollered back "You should be here during weekends, it rocks!"

Trev reappeared and joined us by the wall. "How much hash you want to buy?"

I handed him a twenty-dollar bill. "Will that do?" Trev grinned and slipped among the throngs. The tall Brit returned as Rod Stewart's *Maggie May* started playing. We left the club and walked towards the Tube station at Oxford Circus. Trev handed me a cube wrapped in cigarette-pack foil measuring an inch per side, I squeezed the soft contents and sniffed the sweet aroma confirming the freshness of the hash. "It's a gooli, about a quarter ounce of Pakistani black," he said.

I nodded in satisfaction. "Feels fresh, man."

"Yeah, there's so much of this shit moving through here, it doesn't have time to get stale."

Back at the apartment, with the stereo softly playing *Mr. Bojangles,* I rolled a three-paper tapered joint, gratified that my companions had never seen or smoked a spliff of this size. Ian extracted his flute from its case, assembled the two halves and played a few trills. Trev grabbed his guitar and tuned the strings. "Do you play anything?" he asked me.

"The Blue's harp," I replied showing him my trusty C-tuned Horner's

Marine Band harmonica. Ian launched into a rendition of the Stones' *Ruby Tuesday*. Trev had not exaggerated Ian's proficiency with the flute, the man played at a professional level far above our aptitudes. We tried various tunes, refining our harmonization to the extent that my two companions believed we could busk on the sidewalks without shame. Later that evening, after a last goodnight toke, Trev and Ian withdrew to their bedrooms and I stretched out on the sofa.

* * *

The front door opening at two a.m. woke me up as Gina returned from work. She hung her Mac on the coat rack, kicked off her boots and stepped into the living room.

I rose on my elbows and whispered, "Long shift?"

"Hi, Dan. You don't have to whisper, the blokes sleep like rocks. Hmm, do I detect the smell of hash?"

"You sure do. I'll load a toke." I got up bringing the dope and a small brass pipe to the dining table.

Gina walked into the kitchen and rummaged through a cupboard pulling out a bottle of whiskey and two teacups. "A bedtime snort?" I nodded so she sat across from me and poured a couple of shots. She looked tired yet remained very attractive and my heart skipped as I peered at her face. I filled the pipe and handed it to her with the lighter.

"Ta," she ignited the hash. She took a long puff then passed it back. We smoked in agreeable silence and sipped from the ceramic mugs.

"Trev said you're from Israel? Did you live in Tel Aviv?"

"No, I lived in a kibbutz in the Galilee"

She refilled the glasses. "Oh, I heard of those."

"It's like a large communal farm," I replied making a heroic effort to raise my eyes from her exposed thighs as her mini dress rode up when she shifted in her chair, but not without a pause at her breasts on the way. The woman was gorgeous.

"Naughty..." She laughed, noticing my appraising glance.

"How did work go?"

"Terribly busy, good tips though. I'm glad I'm off tomorrow."

"What do you do on your days off?"

"Oh, a bit of shopping for the house," she waved in the direction of the cupboards lining the kitchen walls. "Check for sales in the boutiques, sort of things. You and Trev should come with me and help carry the bags."

"Be glad to," I answered.

"Well…I'm for bed." She groaned stretching her arms above her head working the kinks in her neck and shoulders, her braless tits stretching her sweater. "Are you going to hang around here for a few days?"

"I'd like to, if that's ok with you."

"I think I'd enjoy that," she said walking down the hallway to her room.

I took that as positive encouragement with delicious possibilities. Gina at twenty-four, was six years my senior and although she seemed well grounded and a bit sarky, I sensed, in her heart, she had an untapped capacity for tenderness. I certainly hoped so as I planned to mount an all-out campaign to get into her bed. With these pleasant thoughts, I fell asleep.

* * *

I woke up early, refreshed and eager to explore. Before retiring the previous evening, Ian lent me a key and sketched a simple map outlining the nearest Tube stations. I walked through the neighborhood searching for a cup of coffee and found a tiny café next to a newsstand. I bought a tabloid and, while sipping on the brew, read with amusement the latest scandals. That reminded me of a cartoon I once saw depicting a Freak on acid, sitting in front of a TV watching the news. The caption said, "What an imagination I have!"

On the way back to the pad, I stopped at a Sainsbury's and picked up breakfast supplies. The previous day's clouds had dissipated and although still on the chilly side, the sun shone from a pale blue sky. I walked along a boulevard lined with big chestnut trees, craning my neck to follow the antics of two black squirrels chasing each other in the branches. Back at the flat I noticed that Ian's shoes were gone and guessed he'd left for school.

I unpacked the shopping bag and prepared breakfast, chopping onions, garlic and tomatoes. Trev popped in the kitchen, made a beeline for the kettle so I took a break from cooking and sat at the table to roll a thin spliff. We smoked in silent companionship until interrupted by the whistling teakettle. The racket must have woken Gina who appeared wearing a baggy Tee shirt, her hair tousled but still looking very endearing. I whipped up a large omelet with ham, tomatoes, onions and cheese and dished out three portions with sliced bread, butter and jam. We tucked in and for a while the only sounds were munching, slurping, clinking and sighing.

"Now that was a grand breakfast," Gina sighed, mopping her plate with a slice of buttered toast. Trev, still chewing nodded in appreciation.

"I'm glad you liked it. It's pretty much the only thing I can cook," I admitted, thrilled at her happiness. Later, the three of us went to Soho where they played guide as we strolled along the crowded sidewalks and Gina window-shopped at the funkier boutiques. Like the rural hick that I was, I watched with delighted amazement the "beautiful" people dressed in outlandish fashions coming and going.

We popped into the Intrepid Fox, the Scots Hoose and the Flamingo, pubs where several famous bands and musicians started their careers. Lost in thought, I ran my hand over a battered piano, on which Reg Dwight - better known as Elton John - had debuted years ago and wondered what stories those ivory keys could tell. We had coffee in a dingy basement café where, back in the sixties, Long John Baldry, Rod Stewart and other rock stars hung around. The songs, which had influenced my adolescence, originated in this part of London. The lyrics, at times so poignant they left the soul aching, had been composed at these battered tables and the tunes performed on the scuffed stages.

We ate supper in a tiny bistro on Wardour Street and then went clubbing. Trev pointed out some of the gay bars and clubs sandwiched between sex shops. During the day, a subtle sexual tension built between Gina and me: knees bumping under tables, thighs pressing against each other, holding hands as we weaved among the crowded sidewalks, lingering glances and the evening held promise.

At the Marquee club, one of the best-known rock bars with a rich history, Trev said, "You just never know who will show up, man. Lots of musicians who started here and became famous return for an occasional visit."

Gina nodded and added, "Last month, Procol Harum performed on stage." We shouldered our way through a crowd of people into the packed club. The Flying Hat Band, Glenn Tipton on lead guitar, played that night; Tipton would eventually join Judas Priest and release *Rocka Rolla*.

Trev bumped into a friend and they were going to meet some of her mates. He shouted in my ear and asked if he could have a chunk of hash. I broke off half of the remaining gooli giving it to him with my best wishes. He smirked at me, glanced sideways at Gina who swayed to the music and, raising two fingers like a priest, blessed us both.

I leaned over to talk to Gina, close to her ear, just as she turned her head and our lips met. I'd guessed correctly that her mouth would be soft; the first kiss lit me on fire. Gina, feeling the same jolt, laughed, grabbed my hand and dragged me out of the club. We hurried back to the apartment, kissing and touching at every chance, offending a couple of old biddies seated near us on the short ride in the tube. I knew Gina was as turned on as I because her nipples were in danger of poking holes through the knit sweater she was wearing.

We necked in the hallway leaning against the apartment door and almost fell as Ian, on his way out, pulled it open. Gina slipped giggling past her startled cousin and skipped to her bedroom. Ian gaped, started to say something, thought better of it, shrugged his shoulders and left.

I closed and locked the front door and dashed into Gina's room. It was fragrant with the scent of strawberry incense and hints of patchouli; scented candles stuck in wine bottles flickered casting dappled shadows on the walls and the semi-naked goddess reclining on a queen-sized waterbed. The undulation of the bed made her perfect breasts thrust toward me with hypnotic rhythm. I stood beside the bed enjoying the view until Gina grabbed my shirt and pulled me down.

We kissed deeply, our hands trying to grope and undress each other, the bounciness of the waterbed working to thwart us. She ground herself against my erection as I nibbled her firm pink nipples jutting from roseate areolas. I managed to remove her lacey white panties opting to bunch up the miniskirt rather than remove it but neither of us could gain enough purchase to get my pants down. The bed's rocking and bucking forced me, in frustration to jump off, tearing at my clothing like it was on fire. "Give me a second, let me get my clothes off." I panted,

Gina caught my hard-on as it was freed, guided it into her and commanded, "Less talking, more fucking." So we did, repeatedly.

* * *

Someone once said there are two kinds of Londoners. One type arrives in the UK for the first time in his life, lands at Heathrow, rides the tube to the center of town and takes to the city like a duck to water from day one. The other type, a Londoner by birth, endures an interminable childhood and can't wait to migrate out of the country to the sunny shores of the Med. I was, without a doubt, of the former type as I realized with surprise that I loved the dowdy, gray city.

The next day set the pattern for the remainder of my stay in London: Breakfast late in the morning after which Trev and I would drop off Gina at work if she was on the early shift then off to Covent Garden to find a good spot to busk or panhandle until we earned enough cash for beers and smokes. Trev strummed his guitar and sang the lyrics while I accompanied him with the harp and joined in the chorus. He performed well and his repertoire included folk and rock tunes from both sides of the pond.

Ian met us after school and added the sweet trills of his flute to our efforts, boosting our performance to new heights, a sentiment shared by passersby as coins and bills accumulated rapidly in the guitar case at our feet. One evening, he showed up accompanied by a shy, attractive blonde Scottish young woman who was also studying the flute at the Conservatoire. She was seventeen years old, had a lovely voice and when she laughed at one of Trev's jokes she surprised us with her absurdly contagious contralto laughter which soared in volume, bringing a smile to anyone within hearing distance.

Trevor, smitten, launched into a rendition of The Who's *Behind Blue eyes* and we all joined including Ian's young companion who astonished us with her beautiful, unforgettable voice, after which Ian and she moved on.

Most evenings, we grabbed supper from a street vendor's stall and then hung around the west-end with a variety of Freaks and drifters, sitting in small plazas, weather permitting, or in cafés if it drizzled. I spent a number of gloomy, wet evenings in various coffeehouses reading copies of London underground papers like Friendz, Oz and old issues of It that had stopped publishing early that year. We regularly scored hash and speed and on two memorable occasions bought hits of microdot acid, which we promptly dropped. Tripping in Soho is a unique experience because of the mind-blowing variety of people ranging from knobby-kneed guys with five-o'clock shadows in drags to gorgeous women wearing super short minis.

When Gina worked late, I picked her up at the end of her shift and we went to a party or returned to the apartment and made love. People who toil in restaurants and clubs tend to hang out together because of their odd schedules. Gina and her co-workers slept during the day, started their shifts at five pm, worked until two in the morning and socialized into the wee hours. I managed to share her lifestyle as well as Trev's with judicious use of bennies: crashing exhausted, one night in three.

I had the unfortunate habit of falling heads-over-heels in love with any female I slept with and I was hooked on Gina. She was a sweet, uncomplicated young woman and the quintessential middle-class Brit who talked and acted tough but was soft and pillowy when intimate. I enjoyed acting old-fashioned and chivalrous by opening doors or holding her chair for her at the table because I knew she appreciated the attention and it made her blush.

Our unrestrained physical intimacy allowed for a raw honesty between us and I garnered a rare glimpse of the typical, working-class life in the UK. Gina grew up in Kirby, a burb of Liverpool, her dad eking a living in a steel mill and her mom raising three kids, cheek-by-jowl, among her working-poor neighbors. My lover painted a vivid, bleak image of a tough community, uprooted and placed by an uncaring local authority in a dreary estate with no facilities or services, suffering high unemployment and racked by vandalism and teen pregnancies.

Gina, like many of her contemporaries, moved to London after school to escape from what she perceived as a stifling drab future. I met some of her friends at parties and realized that London was full of these twenty-something borderline middle-class refugees desperate to break the cycle of poverty and trying their luck at life's lottery in the City.

At the beginning of my second week, Ian returned from classes and informed us about an upcoming job working a concert. "I spoke with Rudy this morning. He needs help with a gig at the King's College."

Trev looked up from a magazine. "Who's playing?"

"A band named Queen, used to be Brian May's Smile."

"Yeah, I watched Smile in sixty-nine at PJ's. I remember a song called *Step on Me*. Did Rudy say how many guys he needs?"

"Yeah, all of us." Ian turned to me and asked, "Are you interested?"

"You bet, man. What does the gig pay and when is it?"

"We'll get a fiver each. The concert is on the tenth and Rudy wants us there early."

So on March tenth, Trev, Ian and I rode the Tube to Covent Garden where a scruffy panhandler accosted us just as we alighted on the platform.

"Spare some change?" The vagrant was filthy and hirsute and held up a grimy palm while his bulging eyes seemed to stare at his ears. He reeked of spilled beer and piss and commuters detoured around him in disgust. I reached in a pocket and fished all the coins I had, about two quid, and dropped them in his hand.

"Thanks Guv," he mumbled. His right eye focused on me for a moment and he staggered towards the stairs. Ian, I noted, had also avoided the wino and looked at me shaking his head in mock despair.

"Pay it forward, man. I'm sure I'll have my hand out before too long."

We walked to the King's College Medical School where we met the crew of six roadies at the loading docks in a narrow back alley. Rudy, the stage manager, was a short, energetic, wiry man in his mid-forties. He had nicotine-stained fingers, spoke with a strong cockney accent and scurried around so fast that we suspected him to be on either coke or speed.

A tall, beefy, Scot crewmember named Geordie took us in hand and we helped unload two lorries, hauling crates, assorted gear and reels of cables into the hall. While we emptied the trucks, the roadies strung a rat's nest of wires, hooked up the lights and set the sound and lighting control boards. With the grunt work done, we sat on empty crates stacked against a back wall and enjoyed the choreographed pandemonium. Rudy dropped by, asked us to hang around to help dismantle the set after the concert and gave us a fiver each. The band members arrived in a van and we helped them haul their gear.

The performance started late, apparently a normal occurrence, but was worth the delay. The lead singer, Freddy Mercury, was a slim, longhaired man who had a terrific voice with an amazing range and owned the stage from the moment he opened his mouth. Queen played *Liar, Keep Yourself Alive* and *The Night Comes Down* among other songs. The concert lasted until midnight, the audience was wild and got two encores after which the players packed their instruments, jumped in their van and drove off.

* * *

Two weeks passed; fourteen fun days busking, reading books, exchanging ideas with my new friends and meeting drifters passing through the city. The latter spoke of destinations like Amsterdam, Ibiza, the Greek islands or the south of France.

One afternoon, Gina at work and Ian at school, I said to Trev, "I'm becoming way too comfortable here."

"Getting itchy feet, then?"

"If I don't get back on the road, I'll never leave."

As much as I enjoyed partying in the West-End dives, at friends' places and making love to Gina, I couldn't help feeling a fidgety, nagging sensation that time was slipping by. I had left Israel, embarked on a journey to the east, and now realized I was in peril of giving it up for the joy of easy sex and the comforts of domesticity.

"I'm thinking of leaving for Amsterdam. Hitchhike through northern France, Belgium and Holland."

The scouser stared dreamingly into space. "Yeah, I'd like to travel there myself. Have you told Gina yet?"

"Er... No. That's the rub. I'm not sure how to go about it without hurting her feelings."

"Just tell her. She'll understand, man. You were clear about London being only a stop on your journey."

We lit up cigarettes and stared at the smoke spiraling up, glowing as it drifted through the beams of sunshine angling in from the windows. Mick Jagger was singing *Lady Jane* on the stereo, one of my favorite Stones tune.

"What about you, Trevor? Are you ready to hit the road?"

"Yeah. I may even have transportation for us. I'll let you know tonight."

The next day, to my cowardly relief, Gina said she had to go back to Liverpool to be one of the bridesmaids at her cousin's wedding. This gave me the opening I was hoping for and I told her about heading out. She gazed at me wistfully, her beautiful face sad. "You won't be here when I get back." We were lying in her bed after a bout of lazy sex. I propped my head on one hand and gazed fondly at her, fingers gently toying with one of her nipples.

I observed her body arching in response and replied, meaning every word, "No Ginny. I'm heading for Amsterdam. You know, I'll never forget you."

The last night we slept together our lovemaking had an urgent tenderness and we spent a lot of time holding each other. The morning of her departure, our mood gloomy and sad, Ginny and I rode the Tube to the train station. We were silent most of the way, sitting close in the subway and when we kissed goodbye at the terminal I, again, experienced the heartache, which is the price paid by drifters. Ginny, vainly holding back tears, hugged me, walked away and soon became lost in the crowd and in that simple way, forever disappeared from my life.

* * *

Shortly after Ginny left, Trev's uncle, a mechanic nicknamed Irish, swung by the apartment in a VW minibus. He was a tall, wide man in his late forties with a graying fringe of reddish hair surrounding a bald pate. His broken crooked nose dominated a flushed and veined round face and his slightly bulging, pale-blue eyes squinted in the brightness of the sunny morning. As we shook hands, he tried to grind my bones with his callused paw but the years in the kibbutz had equipped me with a strong grip and I just smiled at him as I squeezed right back.

Irish told us that a Dutch couple had left the van with him when the engine cratered and, now that it was repaired, needed it to be transported to Amsterdam. He led us around the bus, a 1964 Kombi, whose dark blue and white body seemed in good shape barring the odd scrape and dent. The van sported a roof rack, thirteen windows and double side-doors that swung outwards to give access to the camperized cargo area. It had a one-point-two liter engine that produced an anemic thirty horsepower. We had lawnmowers back home with more power!

Although familiar with the Volkswagen bug, I'd never driven a Kombi and I climbed in the driver seat with some trepidation. I wanted to instill confidence in Irish or he would not let us take the van to Amsterdam and I was relieved to see the minimalistic dashboard consisting of a single large speedometer, a couple of switches, knobs and a few colored indicator lights.

Irish handed me the keys and we took off. The camperized Kombi accommodated six people comfortably. Two sat in the front (a tiny third person could be shoehorned on the bench, if necessary) and four faced each other on the pair of padded benches in the cargo area. A Formica table on a stand between the seats could be detached and slotted to the benches to make a bed. Cupboards and a short counter along the van's right side aft of the double doors served as a mini kitchen. A padded ledge over the engine bay beneath the rear window offered convenient storage and a section of the van's roof, just above the table, cleverly popped up to provide added height when camping. Blue and white curtains, printed with a windmill motif, slid to screen all the windows giving the interior a private, homey atmosphere.

Following Irish's directions, I drove about half an hour west to his shop in Chiswick. I noted that the van's transmission shifted smoothly although the clutch slipped a bit; everything else seemed to work fine: brakes, steering, lights, wipers and a pathetic-sounding horn. It was an easy vehicle to drive and aside from my natural tendency to scoot to the right lane, I managed to get us there without incident.

The garage sat in a row of mechanical and auto parts shops, conveniently close to the Crown and Anchor pub. Irish unlocked and rolled up the corrugated steel door and invited us to follow him. Vehicle parts, stacked tires and racks of equipment covered the cracked and stained concrete floor. A long steel workbench littered with tools, oilcans and greasy mechanical bits ran along the brick wall. The garage smelled of solvents, gasoline, hot metal and burned rubber. An air compressor at the end of the bench started with a metallic clatter startling Trev and I.

A battered wooden desk and chair hunkered in the back corner next to a filing cabinet. A lamp with an incongruent tasseled yellow shade illuminated a stack of papers, bills, shop manuals, note pads, envelopes and a tea mug full of pencils and pens. Irish asked for my international driver's license and said, "So, you think you can do the job, yeah?"

I stared him in the eyes and replied, "Piece of piece, man. The tranny has some play between first and second gear and the clutch slips a bit but should hold for a while yet. I didn't notice any smoke in the exhaust even when downshifting, the engine doesn't ping or knock and the inside of the tail pipe is an even gray color."

Irish gave me a thoughtful look, while Trev beamed approval. "Paid attention, did you? That's good and you're right, the van is old and the motor will need rebuilding before too long, but it runs good enough for this trip."

He peered at us, pondered for a moment and then decided, "all right! You have the job. Mind, if you two jokers fuck me over, I'll rip your heads off and spit down your throats. Yes?" I looked at Trev who was smiling fondly at his uncle and nodded in agreement. Irish wrote down my driver's license and passport information in a notebook, riffled through a file folder and pulled out the van's paperwork from which he retrieved the address of its owners. We chatted for a while, debating the merits of various routes from Calais to Amsterdam. Irish gave us a creased road map of northern Europe, ferry fare and walked us to the front of the shop where he shook my hand, hugged Trev and waved us off.

While retracing our route to the apartment, my mood, subdued after parting with Ginny, began to lift and, as we drove through the busy city, I felt the enthusiasm and excitement of being on the move again fill my soul.

Ian took the news of our imminent departure poorly. He wanted to come with us but couldn't leave until school was out around mid-May. After assurances that we would keep in touch and that he could join us in Amsterdam in time for the Floyd concert, he helped us load the van. As we drove off, I saw him in the rear view mirror standing at the curb like a lost waif. He waved and stared at us until we were out of sight and for all I know, was still there when we boarded the ferry.

* * *

Chapter Four

Going Dutch

Amsterdam, April 1972

In Context:

- -In response to the invasion of South Vietnam four hundred American airplanes bomb North Vietnam in the heaviest attack since 1968.
- -Major league baseball players stage first ever strike and delay the start of the season.
- -Seventy-four nations including the U.S. and USSR agree to ban biological weapons but both superpowers continue nuclear weapons testing.
- -Bangladesh becomes a member of the Commonwealth
- -Sweden passed the world's first law officially recognizing change of gender.
- -*The French Connection* wins the Academy Award.
- -Thousands of people are killed by an earthquake in the Fars province of Iran.
- -As a gift from the People's Republic of China, the National Zoo in Washington, D.C. receives Ling-Ling and Hsing-Hsing, the first giant pandas in the United States.

* * *

We arrived at the Dover ferry docks as the sun set over the choppy waters of the Channel. Gulls, cawing raucously, flitted over the piers in small flocks in search of tidbits. After paying for our passage at a multilane drive-through, I parked amid a sea of lorries, buses and cars facing the loading ramps. The terminal was illuminated by banks of floodlights perched on tall poles and we could hear loud metallic bangs from the waiting vessel. Our line of vehicles crawled forward, up a ramp and, following the directions of crewmembers waving lighted wands, into the ferry's cavernous car deck.

We grabbed our coats, locked the VW and climbed a series of steep, narrow stairways to the passenger decks and the canteen where we ate a late dinner of double-sausage, eggs, beans, toast and chips. After the meal, we leaned on the railing of the highest open deck for a post-prandial smoke and watched the darkened coast of England shrinking behind us. The famous white cliffs of Dover appeared as an indistinct grayish blur bracketed by the lights of surrounding communities. The briny coastal air carried hints of diesel fumes mixed with the reek of high tide rotting seaweed.

The sounds of the ferry's hull crashing into the waves comingled with the throaty burble of the engines and formed a soothing background, interrupted at times, by the boat's deep horn as we sailed through one of the busiest sea-lanes in the world. In the distance, islands of bobbing lights indicated various ships sailing up and down the English Channel heading for exotic destinations across the globe.

Disembarking in Calais, I followed the line of vehicles, now driving on the familiar, normal, right side of the road, out of the terminals complex and on a four-lane highway heading south. We took the exit ramp and drove into the city's quiet, deserted downtown. It was very late and my plan to get gas money couldn't be implemented before morning. I parked the minibus near the train station along a small park, propped open the roof hatch and slid all the curtains closed including the divider that stretched over the front bench. Trev lifted the table and its stand from the floor, unscrewed the short aluminum pipe and slotted the Formica rectangle between the benches. He extracted a green foam pad from the storage box beneath the rear seat and spread it over the table so that together with the seat cushions it made a double bed. We unrolled our sleeping bags, turned the interior lights off and went to sleep.

We caught some Z's until a loud pounding on the side panel rudely awakened us. I opened the doors and squinted at the blinding flashlight held by a frowning French Gendarme. In the dawn's gray light the man loomed as big as an armoire and looked pissed off. "Mais, qu'est-ce vous foutez ici?" ("What are you doing here?"), he snarled.

I replied that we waited for the morning train and asked if there was a problem. The cop sputtered and informed us that it was illegal to camp within the city and that he would give us fucking hippies mere moments to pack up and get the hell away. I hurriedly threw on my shoes and drove the van into the warren of narrow, cobblestoned streets until I found a neighborhood bakery showing early signs of life. We parked nearby and, accompanied by the tinkle of a small bell attached to the door, entered the brightly lit shop.

I inhaled deeply, mouth salivating, as the scrumptious aroma of fresh croissants and baguettes filled my nostrils. If there is a heaven it must smell like a French bakery first thing in the morning. The baked goods were coming out of the ovens and batches of piping hot baguettes cooled on racks. I ordered half a dozen croissants and a baguette from the baker who was loading a cylindrical rattan basket for early delivery. Back in the van, we dismantled the bed, raised the table on its stand and sat on the benches to devour the delicious, flaky pastries and the bread.

Trevor swallowed a mouthful and said. "Good thing you speak French. I don't think that cop knew any English."

A short distance from the bakery, a café opened for business and we finished breakfast with hot and sweet cafés-au-lait served in large bowls suitable for dipping bread in the French fashion. Later, after taking turns washing ourselves in the café's washroom, we drove back to the railway station, where, just in case the flic still roamed nearby, I parked in a side street. We walked up the station's wide stairs and entered a vast, marbled-tiled, pillared lobby. I stood facing the entrance holding a piece of cardboard on which I had printed in large block letters: Bruges.

Most of the people entering the lobby peered curiously at us, noted the long hair, the army-surplus jackets and the placard, and gave us a wide berth as they hurried towards the ticket booths. Parents tightened their grip on their children's hands dragging them along studiously ignoring us but the kids stared at us in unabashed curiosity and waved shyly back when I flashed the peace symbol.

Trev nudged my elbow and pointed his chin towards a new arrival. An attractive young woman carrying a rucksack and wearing a knee-length sheepskin coat over bell-bottom jeans, stood just inside the terminal scanning the large information board hanging over the kiosks. I raised the cardboard and waved it at her smiling invitingly. She glanced at us tilted her head to read the sign and joined us.

"Bonjour," she said as she dropped the bulging rucksack on the floor.

Trev elbowed me aside and replied, "Bone jure to you too. Do you parlay English?"

"Mais, oui." She was a tallish brunette in her twenties with a long braid hanging down her back. Her large hazel eyes sparkled as she lifted her delicate eyebrows and slightly wrinkled her small freckled nose. "My name is Monique," she added with a pronounced French accent. "You are looking for passengers to Bruges?"

I nodded and said, "Er… We're going to Amsterdam but we're driving through Bruges so we're offering rides to both."

"Formidable! I'm also heading for Amsterdam. How much do you charge?"

I looked at Trev, shrugged my shoulders and asked for half of what the train fare would have been. Monique gladly accepted and handed over a couple of bills.

Trev, beaming, asked Monique to hold the sign as she'd have a better chance of attracting would-be customers in our new transportation venture. "Now if we can find a few more riders we'll be all set." Monique enticed two sixteen-year old boys travelling to Bruges to ride with us instead of taking the train. We boarded the Kombi after stowing everyone's luggage on the roof rack and hit the road.

The cloud deck broke up revealing a pale blue sky, presaging a cool, clear spring day. A light breeze blowing from the docks carried whiffs of briny water with hints of dried fish. I swung the van into the eastwards lanes of the E-forty highway and tucked in behind a German-made MAN truck. Our two young passengers, Andre and Marcel, impervious to social niceties, immersed themselves in their comic books and ignored the rest of us for the remainder of the trip.

Monique knelt on the bench behind us facing forward and glanced through the windshield bantering good-naturedly about the lush rolling Pas-de-Calais countryside. Her home was in Cherbourg, a Normand town in the north of the Cotentin Peninsula, and she was familiar with the area's turbulent history. She entertained us with stories of the Normans dating back to Roman days including the centuries-long occupation by the English and the decades-long wars fought over the region. The young woman confided she just turned twenty-five years old, worked at an art gallery and, despite her best efforts, couldn't fit-in with her contemporaries in the Cherbourg social set.

"They're too… Provincial." She made a moue with her lips. "Most of the 'fun' people I hung with in high school moved away after graduation. The ones who stayed in Cherbourg got married, started families and transformed into comfortably ensconced bourgeois."

"So what are you looking for?" I asked.

"There has to be more to life than being a baby factory! I'll travel for a while, visit art museums, see notorious ruins, enjoy other countries' cultures and meet interesting people. But I'm a bit worried, vous savez, travelling like a gypsy."

"I can dig it, man," Trev said. "It's a big decision, leaving everything and everyone you know behind."

I nodded in agreement. I understood Monique as I'd felt the same back in the kibbutz where my straight contemporaries believed that drugs, sex and rock'n'roll were the surest way to perdition.

* * *

We entered Bruges' outskirts at dinnertime after breezing through the Belgian border. As early as '72, if you were a citizen of the six founding European Community countries you could travel through them without immigration hassles or the need for visas and even Trev just showed his and passed with a casual wave probably because the UK was on the verge of joining the EEC

Andre and Marcel directed us to their destination and we dropped them off in the northern burbs. We then drove towards downtown and the train station. Bruges lived up to its historical reputation with beautiful old buildings crowding around the central town square dominated by Saint-Salvator, a huge church-cum-cathedral. As night fell, floodlights illuminated the churches' walls and spires highlighting the elaborate façade and casting interesting shadows on the jutting tower.

We stretched our legs by strolling through the main plaza until we found a large Brasserie, the Belgian equivalent of a pub. Supper consisted of typical Benelux fare — sausages, potatoes and sauerkraut - washed down with superb local beer, served ice-cold the way God had intended it to be. During the meal, we held a lively conversation about literature and discovered that Monique shared our favorite genres, fantasy and Sci-Fi. In school, she told us, she had written an essay on Tolkien's Lord of the Rings and frowned at me as I put a finger in my mouth and pretended to gag.

"Are we hoping to find passengers from here to Amsterdam?" Monique asked as she stole a chip from Trev's plate.

"Yeah, man. I'll make a placard." I rummaged around my things and grabbed the cardboard we'd used in Calais. I flipped it over, wrote "Amsterdam" and held it up to show my companions.

A young guy sitting nearby noticed the sign and said, "Hello, we couldn't help overhearing. We're also heading for Amsterdam." He indicated his female companion. A large backpack leaned against their table and they wore matching woolen sweaters with a colorful pattern of fall leaves.

I invited them over and explained, "we're looking for passengers to share the gas for our minibus."

"This is my wife Nicolle. I am Luc."

We introduced ourselves and shook hands all around. Luc was blond, tall and thin with a clean-shaved chin and wide, green eyes. Nicolle, in contrast, was petite, also blonde, with long fine hair framing an oval face, blue eyes and a pert nose perched over a smiling full-lipped mouth. We agreed on the fare to Amsterdam (again, half the train ticket), which included dropping them wherever they wanted. Trev and Luc settled the pub bills and we all walked back to the bus.

The distance from Bruges to Amsterdam was about a hundred eighty miles and I estimated a six-hour drive through the night, including the border crossing. I planned to skirt a number of big cities like Gent, Antwerp and Breda. At a large service center on the eastern outskirts of Bruges, I topped the gas tank while Trev checked the tires and cleaned the windshield. The night turned colder, a strong wind blew from the north and a solid blanket of clouds reflected the city lights in shades of yellow and orange.

On the highway, the conversations ebbed as our passengers succumbed to the drone of the engine and the steady road-noise. A petrol-burning heater in the back of the van hissed softly while providing a modicum of heat. We followed the E-forty to Gent and the traffic dwindled to occasional tractor-trailers trucks and the odd speeding car. Trev, in the passenger seat, turned to look at me. His face was a pale blur in the van's darkness. "Getting tired?" he asked.

"I'll be okay. I drank enough coffee to last until Antwerp."

He fished around in his vest pocket and withdrew a small pill bottle from which he shook out a couple of tablets. "I have bennies."

"Cool, man." I popped the little yellow Methadrine pills and saw him toss his head back to swallow two of his own. Another reason why we meshed so well, I reflected, Trev and I had an innate enthusiasm for self-abuse. If it got you high, we'd do it.

"You know, I wanted to get some speed back in London but with all the preparations for departure I forgot," I said.

"Well, Ian procured these for us. He gave them to me just before we left, sort of thing."

"Good old Ian. Always thinking." I maneuvered the van around a slow moving semi and returned to the right lane.

Trev lit a couple of smokes and passed one to me. "I meant to ask how you're doing for money."

I shook my head and admitted ruefully, "London was a bit expensive." All the partying, clubbing, drugs and drinks ate a big chunk of my original stake. "I was thinking about getting a job at the Munich Olympics. I hear they need all the workers they can get."

"What about a work permit?"

"Similar to your deal with Rudy and his roadies. We should be able to find work under the table. You?"

"All in, I managed to put together a hundred quid. I'd like to go to Munich with you and earn more."

"Right on. Let's spend a few days in Amsterdam and then head down to Munich."

* * *

We reached Amsterdam as the soon-to-rise sun painted the horizon in faint pastels. High altitude wind had shredded the clouds during the night leaving a pattern of pink herringbones spread across the sky. The temperature was near freezing this early in the morning but we expected a decent spring day once the sun quit procrastinating and hopped to it. Luc and Nicole, huddled together under a sleeping bag, gave me directions to Schiphol airport where they would meet friends arriving from the States. Monique, draped in our spare blanket and hunched sideways on the bench, peered owlishly through the windshield.

We drove towards Schiphol's arrival terminal where I double-parked in the taxi lane. Luc jumped out of the van with their backpack. Nicolle blew us a kiss and joined her husband on the sidewalk. Monique closed and latched the doors and we took off just as the first irate cab driver in the line-up started honking his horn.

Irish's instructions were to drop off the van at the home of the owners, Gerd and Ute. They lived in Heemstede, a burb west of the airport and a short way from Amsterdam. But first as per our agreement we offered to drive Monique anywhere in the city and, as it was too early to bother the van's owners, we decided to head for the notorious Vondel Park and find some breakfast.

The park spread out over a hundred and twenty acres in a roughly rectangular shape. It encompassed a collection of shaded grassy areas interspersed with tree-lined meandering, streams and small calm ponds. A network of paths and arched bridges crisscrossed the area, which featured a rose garden, the Blue Tearoom, statuary and even a bandstand in the center of a tiny, round, island. The shaded banks of the streams made a perfect, sheltered campground with access to water and were home to Amsterdam's large population of hippies, Freaks, stoners and drifters.

In 1970, the park achieved worldwide fame as it experienced its own Summer of Love with stoned longhairs fucking all over the place. During our stay in April of '72, we noticed scores of tents and haphazard shelters made of cardboard, tarps, sheets of plastic and various other materials strung beneath the stately trees along the western stream. In the spring, as the travelling season started in earnest and the weather moderated, transients from around the world arrived in Amsterdam and blankets, sleeping bags and backpacks littered the green swards.

We parked the van on a street bordering the northern edge of the park and found a café nestled among the residences and small hotels. We ordered breakfast and I noted with amusement that despite the flower child, free love, "we're-all-brothers" posters on the walls, the server wanted to eyeball cash before she put the order in.

A sign on the wall depicted a happy cartoon joint and pill encircled in green and a red circle with a diagonal line overlaying an angry syringe. The waitress explained the signs were displayed prominently in many establishments in the city and meant that only 'soft' drugs were permitted on the premises. Those Dutch, I thought, sure had their shit together. The bennies had worn off and I felt ravenous. We tore into a large breakfast of eggs, sausages and plate-sized pancakes.

Trev mopped some yolk with a piece of pancake and asked "Er… Monique, do you have a preference on where you want us to drop you off?"

The woman pushed back from the table and said, "I'm not sure. I guess the park is as good as anywhere else." She glanced at the newly leafed trees through the windows. "What are you guys doing next?"

"We'll drop off the van in Heemstede and come back to Vondel," Trev replied. "We'll probably stay in Amsterdam a week and then go to Munich." He gave her a shy look. "Er, if you don't have other plans we'd love to hang around with you, sort of thing."

She smiled back. "Wonderful! Let's meet here after you deliver the bus."

By the time we left the café, morning had broken - as Cat Stevens would say – and as we drove past the Vondelkerk, a cathedral-sized church, we spied a number of longhairs crossing a canal on the verge of the park and heading towards a large brick edifice. We parked nearby and joined the stream of people, nodding back amiably and flashed peace signs. From behind, I thought, it was almost impossible to determine if a Freak was male or female. Everyone had long, unkempt hair with varicolored beads in or on their tresses, hairbands or hats. Ponchos, jean or khaki jackets, tee shirts or brightly colored loose shirts and tunics covered by vests made from leather, cloth or wool conspired to add to the gender confusion. Bell-bottoms were de rigueur. In reply to my whispered observations regarding androgyny, Monique said, "You can tell by their derrière."

"I'm not comfortable staring at some guy's ass," I muttered back. She laughed and replied that she had no such compunctions. A young man intercepted us and bummed a smoke. I offered him my pouch of Drum tobacco and a pack of zigzags and, pointing at the stone building asked, "What is in there?"

"That's the infamous Paradiso." He expertly rolled a cigarette and added, "It used to be a church and now, officially, it's a youth center. Everyone uses it as a meeting point. My name is Lodewijk, Lode for short." He looked like the quintessential Dutch man: a red-headed, six-foot-three, wide-shouldered, two-hundred-forty pound big-boned, healthy man. His long, thick hair framed an elongated face dominated by a large nose, a bushy mustache and a shaggy beard. He had piercing blue eyes and an engaging smile. He spoke excellent English and told us he was from Antwerp but now lived in Amsterdam.

The building's front doors, set tight in a high-arched narthex, were made of tall, massive wooden panels with wrought-iron handles. They were open and as we entered the foyer, I noted that the doors were made of boards six inches thick and seemed fossilized with age. Inside the lobby, an entryway led to the main hall - closed this early in the day - and wide stairs descended to the basement. A corkboard covering most of one wall held an assortment of notes, envelopes, drawings, pictures and advertising posters for upcoming band concerts. The board served as a post office for transients, Lodewijk explained, as people camping in the park or drifting in the city could leave messages and information for whomever. Later, as we traveled through Europe and Asia we would encounter these bulletin boards wherever backpackers congregated, helping us to keep in touch with each other.

A hand-drawn wooden sign on the wall spelled "Café" in gothic lettering and pointed down the stairs. It was to be our meeting point after we dropped off the Kombi. The building's lobby filled up with people checking the board or heading for the basement so we exited the Paradiso and walked back to the van.

Lode offered to show Monique around Vondel until Trev and I returned from Heemstede and suggested that she drop off her gear at his campsite.

* * *

We retraced our route to the airport and took the A-nine heading north. An hour later, we arrived at a residence in a quiet neighborhood on the outskirts of Heemstede.

The van's owners lived in a row of narrow two-story houses, separated from the street by a water-filled ditch running parallel to the road. A short driveway bridged the ditch in front of each residence and I turned onto the one leading to Gerd's place.

Flowerbeds full of multi-colored tulips surrounded the house and a shiny, grey, recent-model Volvo sedan sat by the side door. I parked the van behind the car and rang the doorbell while Trev repacked our loose gear and policed the van's floor for garbage, butts and roaches.

A tall, thin, white-haired woman, wearing an apron dusted with flour stepped out and gave me a curious stare. She wiped her hands and asked something in Dutch.

I flashed the peace sign, smiled and said, "Good morning Ma'am. Sprachen zie English?" I hoped that Dutch and German were similar enough.

"Ya. A little bit, vat you vant?"

"Are you Ute?"

She shook her head. "Ute? Nein, no."

"Is this the house of Gerd and Ute?"

"Ya, but they are gone. They are in New Zealand for two, three years!"

Trev stood at my side and exclaimed in dismay, "Gone!"

"Ya. In New Zealand!" she said with a final headshake and started to close the door. I quickly explained the situation with the Volkswagen, pointing at the bus for emphasis but she would not let us abandon the vehicle in her driveway.

"Shit. Now what?" Trev asked as we climbed back in the Kombi.

I started the engine and shifted into reverse. "Let's get the fuck out of here before she calls the cops. We'll call Irish. He can decide how he wants to do this." We stopped at the first phone booth we found and placed a collect call to the UK.

"...Gone for two fucking years?" Irish shouted. I held the receiver away from my ear so we both heard him clearly. "What the bloody hell am I supposed to do now? Stupid fucking Krauts!" He ranted and, by the noise in the background, kicked his desk.

Trev glanced at me, a smile tugging his lips and shouted, "Dutch, uncle, they're Dutch."

"Dutch, Kraut, who fucking cares."

"Irish, do you have a different number for these wankers?" I asked before he launched another tirade.

"Let me check."

We heard the phone slam on the desk while he searched his filing cabinet. "The only contact they gave me is their fucking house number. I'll tell you what sunshine; I'll make a few calls. Call me back in an hour, yes?"

I hung up, shrugged at Trev and we retraced our steps to Amsterdam. The Paradiso café was a large rectangular room stuffed with an eclectic collection of furniture, including sofas and armchairs. Two youth worked behind a tall counter and were making and serving beverages from a bright red, two-spout espresso machine and an assortment of coffee grinders and flavoring syrup bottles. Trays of mugs, teacups, various canisters, a row of LPs and a component stereo system were on shelves on the wall over the cash register. An older woman stood behind a long, refrigerated display case containing pastries and sandwiches. Scattered light bulbs wreathed in roiling smoke dimly lit the room. The place smelled strongly of brewed coffee, hash, pot and tobacco. The stereo played the *Concert for Bangladesh*, Shankar's sitar wailing in atonal riffs. Children of various ages played with toys in a corner or ran, chasing each other, among the tables of longhaired Freaks and hippies. There was no sign of Monique.

We bellied up to the counter. "Peace man. A couple of coffees please and do you sell hash?"

The nearer of the two servers, a tall, lanky teenager replied in a thick accent, "You must be new in Amsterdam, ya? We don't supply narcotics. Raoul, over there, can help you." He pointed at a man sitting by himself in the center of the room. "I'll call you when the beverages are ready. Vat is your name?" I told him and we threaded our way to Raoul's table.

He was a short, stocky man in his forties with a bushy brown beard, a scraggly mustache and long, thinning hair streaked with gray. He wore a serape poncho over denims and sandals despite the coolish weather. An incongruous, battered, black briefcase stood by his knee.

"Hi, Raoul? I'm Dan, this is Trevor." We gripped hands. "The guy at the counter said we could score some hash?"

Raoul looked up at us and replied with a French accent, "Sit down, mes amis."

"Ah. Tu es Français?" I asked.

He nodded and added that he was from Brittany although he'd lived in Holland since '68. Laying the briefcase on the tabletop, he flipped the latches and opened the lid. Inside, a tray was divided into a score of compartments, each holding different types of drugs. There were tinfoil-wrapped lumps, baggies of pot, tiny vials, pill-bottles, small jars full of powders, desiccated mushrooms and even some small, circular pipe-screens and rolling papers. Trev and I, speechless, gaped at the contents. The Frenchman peered up at us with an amused expression and asked, "You like?"

Pointing at the vials, I stammered, "Uh... What are those?"

"Weed oil. These lumps are hash: red Leb, black Paki, green Turkish and Afghani. Here I have pot, Mexican, Columbian Gold and this new stuff, buds from California."

It was difficult to drag myself away from the mother lode when the young server called my name. Practically sprinting, I grabbed the two cups of Joe and hurried back.

Raoul listed the various drugs he carried or could get his hands on. The pill-bottles contained LSD, mescaline, bennies, Quaaludes and amyl nitrate poppers. He proudly showed us 'shrooms from the Canadian West Coast and, his most prized items, Peyote buttons from Mexico.

We purchased a foil-wrapped lump, called a finger, of Lebanese hash and I rolled a spliff. As we passed the small joint around, I chatted with Raoul and was amazed to find out that he knew my friend, Gerard, very well.

Monique and Lode entered the café, put in their orders and joined us at the table. Raoul conversed with Lode, as they were already acquainted, while we brought Monique up to speed about the bus.

"...And so we have to call my uncle back and find out what to do," Trev said.

I pointed at a public phone hanging on a wall. "Let's talk to him."

We called Irish collect. He answered on the first ring and accepted the charges.

"I managed to get hold of Gerd's dad," Irish said. "They're abroad for a couple of years and they no longer need the VW. They're turning it over to me in lieu of the repair bill. Fucking twits!"

"What do we do with it, Irish?" I asked

"You fairies aren't coming back here any time soon, are you?"

"Didn't plan on it. We'll be heading to Munich to work at the Olympics and get some cash."

Irish remained silent for a moment. "The thing is, those wankers owe me for the repairs but I don't really want the fucking van either."

"How much is it?"

"Two hundred and seventy-five quid. That's about all it's worth anyway."

Impulsively, I said, "I'll tell you what Irish. I'll give you two-fifty cash for the Kombi if you wait until we come back from Munich." Trev briskly nodded his head, gesturing that he'd participate in the purchase. Irish muttered into the mouthpiece as he worked out the angles, and, having little choice, reluctantly agreed. We returned to the table, smiling with excitement and told everyone the good news.

Raoul seemed interested that we had a vehicle and were planning to go to Munich. He stood up, gathered his gear, took his leave from the group and invited me to accompany him out of the café. I proudly showed him the minibus and the dealer asked in a serious tone, "What's Gerard's last name?"

I replied and, in that vein, he continued the grilling. "Holy shit," I thought. "This guy thinks I'm a narc." Tired of the questions, I proved my veracity by pulling out my notebook and extracting a photo of Gerard and me taken in the kibbutz.

"Sorry for the interrogation but I may have a business opportunity for you and your friends."

"I'm listening."

"Please come by my house later today." He gave me his address and suggested I ask Lode to guide me. Monique, Trev and Lode joined me by the bus. The sun shone warmly from a blue sky and dappled the sidewalk through trees lining the street.

Trev gazed at Monique and said, "Let's grab your stuff and lock it in the van for safekeeping." I tossed him the van's keys. "We'll meet you guys here at supper time," he added with a cheeky wink and they walked away.

I held Lode back as he started to follow them. "Lodewijk, old buddy, how about you show me around town? I'll buy the first beer." I waggled my eyebrows pointing at the retreating couple. The tall Dutchman tilted his head and gave me a resigned look. "Ya, she wasn't my type anyway."

* * *

Lodewijk led me along a network of streets and waterways, heading towards De Wallen near the center of Amsterdam. We walked on tree-lined, cobblestone lanes and crossed ancient arched bridges over still water canals where barges and fishing trawlers, cunningly converted into beautiful houseboats, were moored. The floating homes had a riot of colorful blooms cascading from flower boxes on railings and windows sills. Handkerchief-sized gardens, growing in planters and large ceramic pots were on every inch of free deck space. The shadow-dappled blossoms contrasted delightfully with the black hulls and teak decking.

As we walked, Lode and I discussed our favorite music, drugs, movies, chicks and underground magazines and we realized that despite our radically different backgrounds, we shared the same Furry Freak Brothers cultural values. As Freewheelin' Franklin said, "*Dope will get you through times of no money better than money will get you through times of no dope.*"

"De Wallen is over there." The Dutchman nodded toward the confluence of two canals. "The famous Amsterdam red-light district." He led us into a warren of narrow lanes and alleys at the heart of one of the oldest neighborhoods of the city. Looking like live lingerie mannequins, skimpily dressed women of all shapes, races and breast size lounged on sofas or beds in tiny rooms behind floor-to-ceiling display windows. They gestured provocatively to passersby in an attempt to encourage walk-in business. Faux-antique red carriage lanterns positioned above the doors gave the district its designation. When a client entered the salon, the prostitute simply slid brocaded curtains across the window to block the view.

Theaters showing live sex shows, small cinemas featuring porn movies and a sex museum were interspersed throughout the neighborhood. I grew up in a puritan, old-fashioned kibbutz and was immensely impressed with the Dutch nonchalance about sexuality.

As promised, I would stand the first beer so I followed Lode to a small establishment called The American Bar, located below street level in an ancient, brick building. We descended a set of worn stone stairs that could have been trodden by Van Gogh or even Rembrandt and entered a dim, narrow room. A long bar down one wall and a shoulder-width aisle separated a single row of high, round tables and stools along the other. A bead curtain screened a doorway leading to the kitchen at the back, allowing delicious smells of fried food to waft through. Fluorescent lights dangling from a vaulted brick ceiling cast a soft bluish light while a row of long and narrow, dusty windows set high up the wall allowed a modicum of daylight to illuminate the room. Movie posters featuring Casablanca, the African Queen and other Bogart classics, decorated the brick walls.

A very tall bartender named Gil dried and stacked beer mugs on shelves behind the counter. We sat at a table near the center of the bar and Lode ordered two pints of Heineken draft.

"Check out the slot machine," Lode said pointing at a chromed one-arm-bandit attached six feet up on the wall. Puzzled, I assumed it was just part of the décor until I looked more closely at Gil and realized the man was a giant who stood close to seven feet tall. He seemed to be in his late forties with a clean-shaven, lined face. His hairless, gleaming skull featured noticeable lumps. His ears stuck out like Mister Potato Head and bushy eyebrows, meeting in the middle, shadowed lively brown eyes. Everything about him was huge including his nose and mouth.

Gil grabbed two beer steins in one gigantic paw, filled them from one of the six taps lined in a row and reached over the counter to deposit them on our table; his arms were as long as a gorilla's.

"Danke," I said, handing him a ten-dollar bill. He checked the exchange rate on a card taped to the cash register and gave me back change in Dutch currency. I enjoined him to keep a guilder as a tip that, after nodding his thanks, he inserted into the slot machine and pulled the lever. The one-armed-bandit chimed and whirred loudly before three unmatched symbols appeared on the rollers.

"Damn!" Gil shrugged and turned to serve other customers.

"Do you know where Raoul lives? He invited me to stop by his place today," I asked Lode.

"Ya. Not too far from here. I'll show you later. Right now, I'm starving."

After an excellent and filling lunch of potato and leek soup with dark rye bread, we climbed back to street level. The balmy spring temperature, combined with a full stomach and lack of sleep the previous night, hit me like a hammer. A tiny park with a postage-stamp-sized lawn shaded by a few trees occupied the triangle formed by the convergence of a two streets. I pointed at the inviting patch of grass and said with a yawn, "I'm bagged. I need to catch some Z's for a couple of hours."

"Hokay. I have running around to do. I'll come get you after and take you to Raoul. Watch out for dog shit." Lode grinned as he walked down the street.

I sat on the lawn, after checking the grass, pulled out my notebook and updated my journal about the trip from London. My eyes were closing so I lay down, a folded jacket as a pillow, and fell into a deep, dreamless sleep.

* * *

The sun was sinking behind the buildings lining the streets as we headed towards Raoul's place in the Jordaan. Lode waved his arm encompassing shops, fashion boutiques and cafés. "This is one of the better neighborhoods. Anne Frank House is around here."

Raoul lived in a houseboat, a converted fifty-foot barge, moored in a row of similar floating homes to a bollard on a quay. The barge's black hull had a red and white strake running under the railings. The barge sat low in the murky water, its deck almost flush with the quay's flagstones and blossom-covered flowerpots shared the bow with planters while, aft of the main cabin, a rattan patio furniture set surrounded a charcoal grill. The superstructure, a long wooden rectangular cabin pierced with full-size windows, featured mundane-looking, pale yellow siding.

We boarded the boat and Lode knocked on a curtained, wood-slat door. The curtain twitched aside and a face I didn't recognize peered at us for a moment. Raoul's grinning mug appeared above the stranger's shoulder and the door opened.

We were ushered into a low ceilinged salon furnished with a couch, armchairs, a coffee table and shelving. A well-appointed modern kitchen with a dining table and chairs that could accommodate a dozen people filled the space beyond. Stairs along the waterside of the salon led down to the lower deck and, I assumed, the sleeping quarters.

Raoul introduced the stranger as a local stoner named Henk. The two men were stuffing fragrant weed into matchboxes that Henk sold around town. We shook hands and I rolled a hash spliff while Raoul retrieved four Amstel beers from the fridge. We chatted about the Pink Floyd concert in May, a much awaited event by the Dutch stoner and Freak communities, as we passed the toke around. Henk finished filling a score of matchboxes, stuffed them in a plastic bag, downed his drink and departed.

"When are you driving down to Munich?" Raoul asked.

I took a swig of the cold beer and replied, "In three or four days. What do you have in mind?"

"Munich is currently overrun with workers at the Olympic venues and short on dope. I'd like you to transport hash down there."

"You just met me for the first time this morning, Raoul."

He grinned and said, "I'm a good judge of character, but, to be safe, I called Gerard in Brittany."

"Great! How is he doing?"

"He got home a few days ago after skipping Tunisia and Algeria. He said hi and he'll meet us all at the end of May."

"Cool. How much dope are we talking about?"

"That will be determined by my associates. We'll take your bus to their shop and they'll determine the quantity you can safely carry."

"And our fee…?"

"We'll pay you fifty US dollars per kilo."

I whistled in surprise and nodded. "Of course, my partner will have to agree, but I'm pretty sure we can do business."

Raoul stood up and walked to a dresser where he grabbed a pill bottle and fished out four tiny orange barrel-shaped pills. "Take these hits of acid. Lovely Orange-Sunshine, three hundred fifty mikes of LSD, thanks to our good Californian friend Nick Sand," he said. "A gesture of goodwill. You and your friends have a trip on me and bring the van here day after tomorrow." We finished our beers and, headed outside.

The dark sky was cloudy as we stepped from the barge to the dock. Scattered streetlights emitted a yellowish glow, illuminating the canal and the quay with a soft, diffused light. Fractal reflections cast from the houseboats' illuminated windows danced on the black waters. A scrawny gray cat was taking a dump in one of the flower boxes. Raoul, standing in the doorway, spied the feline and swore loudly in French. He took two steps and kicked at the kitty, which easily avoided the swipe and darted off the deck. The sleek creature stopped ten feet from us, turned around and gave Raoul a condescending look before padding away.

Raoul, pissed, snarled, "That fucking cat! It always shits in my planters. I've complained to his owner time and again." He pointed to a houseboat moored further down the canal. "But they don't give a shit. One of these days…"

* * *

Still laughing about the spunky feline, Lode and I hoped on a tram and returned to the Paradiso. The old converted church was alive with people, the overflow spilling out onto the sidewalk and the surrounding areas. Loud music, heavy on the bass, emanated from the well-lit building and a mob filled the lobby. Longhairs milled in front of the message board, passing joints or just grooving to the vibe. Roiling smoke obscured the ceiling as if the foyer was on fire and a gentle fog hid peoples' faces.

We shoehorned ourselves into the crowd and made our way to the now open main hall. I poked my head through the wide-open doors and saw a five-man band on stage playing fast-paced, simple, two and three-chord songs. I recognized the tune they played as a Troggs oldie, followed by a number from Ziggy Stardust. Their rapid metallic style sounded new to me but had a raw energy reminiscent of the Velvet Underground and Iggy Pop. Scores of dancers bounced on the dance floor and hordes of longhairs sat around tables or squatted against the walls.

Searching for Trev and Monique in the basement café and the main hall was fruitless. We pushed our way back to the doors and out onto the sidewalk to wait. Half an hour and a spliff later they finally showed up.

"Well, well, surfaced for air, did you?" I chided. Trev only smiled sheepishly but Monique turned a charming pink hue.

I revealed the four orange pills. "Check this out." Trev immediately recognized the LSD and explained to Monique what I held.

She said, "We're going to the movies. Space Odyssey is playing here. I bet it's spectacular on acid!" We all agreed with enthusiasm. It was, by far, the best sci-fi movie ever made.

"Will it be in Dutch?" I asked.

Lode thought for a moment and shook his head. "No, it's in English with subtitles, you'll be all right."

We swallowed the tiny but potent orange pills and, following Lode, hopped on a tram going to the downtown district. The LSD spooled up as we disembarked from the tramcar. My vision sharpened as I started to hallucinate and colors transformed into dazzling psychedelic hues. The shine of lights from the restaurants, stores, clubs and cinemas lining the sidewalk shattered in my drug-affected vision so that it seemed as if we were floating through a burst of fireworks and I could feel each spark extinguish itself on my skin. Sounds were distorted and my hearing cycled between the Doppler Effect, slow motion and munchkin.

The acid trip progressed to the giggling stage, where everyone and everything is hilariously funny and you can't stop laughing. We snorted and chortled like a foursome of morons as we stood in line under a large cinema marquee advertising both the Space Odyssey and a brand new movie called Clockwork Orange.

The people in the queue studiously ignored us, probably used to weird, stoned longhair behavior. We shuffled with the line until Trev, at the head of our little group, approached the ticket booth and purchased four tickets by pointing at the poster of the movie. The Dutch kid in the kiosk asked him a question, to which the tripping fool replied with a shrug and giggled, his eyes attracted to the marquee's pretty, shiny lights.

We passed through a magnificent lobby dominated by a long, sinuous candy counter staffed by giant cartoon animals and into the darkened theatre and sat in the back row. The show was just starting.

I anticipated the delightful three hours of acid-trip-enhancing special effects of my favorite science fiction movie. However, instead of peaceful cosmic vistas and a mysterious, black monolith mentoring a band of apes in the finer points of organized warfare, I watched as a foursome of hooligans, dressed in white cod pieced clothes and dildo-nose masks beat the shit out of everyone they met.

Around the time the gang on screen was beating the rich guy and raping his wife, I heard distressed sounds coming from Monique and Trev followed closely by their panicked flight from theater. Later, as Malcolm McDowell, strapped in a dental chair with his eyelids clamped open by some kind of spidery metal device, was re-educated, Lode jumped out of his seat and, stomping on my toes in his haste, staggered out of the cinema.

I found myself alone at a bummer of a movie so I got up, walked out of the theater, and wandered off down the boulevard. I sat on a bench at a tram stop and rolled a smoke. Thank god for dope, I thought shaking my head, but honestly, Kubrick was just too much. I mean, fantasy aside, who would believe anyone owned furniture that ugly or be passionate about electronic Beethoven.

That first day in Amsterdam lived up to my wildest expectations. In the wee hours of the morning, I met three French Freaks and tagged along, smoking pot and drinking wine, to their campsite in the park. The acid trip evanesced and by dawn I crashed on someone's tent floor, curled up in my coat, sheltered from the dew.

* * *

I awoke late in the morning and after grabbing a bite to eat at the Paradiso, I bumped into Trev by the message board. I had pinned up a note with a suggested time and place for a rendezvous.

He broke into a wide grin, punched me on the shoulder and said, "Just the bloke I'm looking for."

"Where are Monique and Lode?" I asked.

"Monique is at the van. I haven't seen the Dutchman since we left the theatre."

"Yeah, speaking of which…Way to go, asshole! What a waste of a trip!"

The abashed Limey replied, "Yeah, I know. I kind of fucked up, sort of thing." As I couldn't hold my laughter, he broke into a grin and chuckled.

"You should have seen Lode stampeding out of the theater as if the Flying Dutchman was on his ass. Do you have time for a cuppa or is Monique waiting for you?"

"Nah, she'll come here when she's ready."

We descended to the café, lined up for mugs of tea with a couple of small vlaai pastries, and sat at an empty table. I sipped the fragrant brew loudly and said, "Raoul has a business proposition for us, man. He's looking for a dope transporter to Munich. It might pay for the van."

"As long as we're talking soft drugs, man. No smack or blow!" Trev drank his tea and finished the last of the vlaaien Dutch pastry.

"I agree. He means hash."

"Okay, I'm in." Trev smiled. "I like the idea of paying off the bus."

Monique descended the stairs and joined us. I glanced at her, noticing her possessiveness as she sat close to Trev and grabbed his hand. She looked great and glowed with contentment. We stayed in the café until everyone was replete then walked back to the Kombi.

"Did you guys find out if we can wash up around here?" I asked as I grabbed my gear.

Monique told me about the public washrooms strewn in the park and directed me to the nearest one with showers. When I was done with my personal grooming, we decided to spend the afternoon as tourists. We took the tram to Dam Square and spent the rest of the day walking around De Wallen, listening to buskers, checking out the varied sidewalk jewelry and hippies' crafts.

Monique dragged us into a macrobiotic restaurant and we ate overpriced, tasteless sprouts and seeds with lumpy multigrain bread. Everyone, including the staff, appeared starved, in a groovy sort of way. Darkness fell as we returned to Vondel and followed a stream of people heading towards a bandstand in the center of a tiny island in one of the park's ponds. Hundreds of longhairs sat or stretched out on the grassy banks surrounding the dimly illuminated, round stage. The ubiquitous smell of weed and hash wafted over the natural amphitheater and a constellation of reds and yellows flared, as joints and pipes lit up. The pond's edge seemed like a reflection of the starry sky above us.

Most evenings, our neighbors informed us, amateur and nearly famous musicians used the bandstand and these "happenings" drew a large enthusiastic audience. You never knew who would appear on the stage.

We listened and applauded as a succession of talented performers played pop tunes. A tall, angular, skinny man with curly hair and holding a guitar strode across the short bridge to the island, hopped on stage and launched into a flawless rendition of *Suzanne* followed by *Sisters of Mercy, Chelsea Hotel,* and *So Long, Marianne.*

Whispers of "Is that Cohen?" and "Hey man. He sounds like Cohen," swept through the crowd. The audience exploded in enthusiastic cheering, whistling and clapping and burning lighters held overhead imparted an ethereal quality to the swirling pot smoke. The mystery performer bowed once and disappeared into the darkness. The next day, we found out that

Leonard Cohen was in town performing at Concertgebouw. Go figure! That night, as Trev and Monique slept in the van, I crashed under a tarp in the park, sharing the shelter with two Freaks from the U.S.

* * *

Raoul was at the Paradiso café the next morning and I sat at his table, coffee in hand. "Comment ça va, mon vieux?" I sipped the steaming beverage. "We discussed your proposition. Count us in."

"Excellent. Why don't you pick me up this afternoon and we'll go visit my friends?"

"After lunch, then."

I strolled by the bus but the curtains were drawn. I slumped on a nearby bench and rolled a smoke, deciding I'd give the lazy bastards another thirty minutes before knocking on the doors.

Halfway through my cigarette, Lode emerged from the park. The tall Dutchman waved and sat beside me. I tossed the pouch of Drum tobacco to him and asked, "What happened to you? Where have you been hiding?"

He studiously avoided my gaze and started to roll a cigarette. "After the movie, Ya? It felt like a bad trip, so I went to the American Bar and hung around with Gil until closing time. I crashed at his place."

We smoked in silence for a while, watching the hippies wandering on the green swards across the boulevard.

"Anyway, Danny, can I join you guys when you go to Munich? I need to work for a bit."

"Sure! Do you have travel plans after Munich?"

"Ya. I've always wanted to visit Istanbul."

"Far out, man. That's where we're going!" We grinned like fools and I was pleased because Lode would make a wonderful travelling companion.

The van doors opened and Trev stepped down. Monique followed behind him, wished us a good morning and, towel in hand, walked towards the public bathrooms.

I asked Trev, "How much of this deal have you told Monique?"

"We talked about it."

"She's okay with our plans?" He waggled his hand in a 'so-so' gesture and said, "We'll talk some more but, either way, there will be no problems, yeah?"

He declined coming with us to meet Raoul's friends, as Monique wanted to visit a few art museums.

Early afternoon, Lode and I picked up Raoul and drove north to a three-bay shop in the center of a fenced junk yard in an industrial section of town. I parked in front of the garage doors, surrounded by mounds of rusting car parts and honked the horn. Two men wearing dark blue coveralls and ball caps rolled open a bay door and motioned me to drive into the shop and onto the ramps of a hydraulic lift. Raoul introduced us to Maarten and Pieter, brothers in their mid-thirties, who ran the business and were not averse to a bit of undeclared cash. The hoist raised the bus into the air and, holding work lights, they peered intently at the under-carriage and chassis, tapping with a wrench and muttering comments to each other. Having reached a consensus, they spoke with Raoul and Lode in Dutch.

The Frenchman turned to me and translated, "It will take them a couple of days to do the job. Leave the van here, grab what gear you need and we'll ride in a cab back to my place. Maarten will call me when the vehicle is ready and then you guys can head to Munich, yes?"

"How much stuff are we transporting?" I asked.

"About ten kilos of hash."

* * *

Chapter Five

Brat-worst and Holland-days

Munich/Amsterdam, April to May 1972

In Context:
- The North Vietnamese Army captures the South Vietnamese province and city of Quang Tri.
- J Edgar Hoover, who has the distinction of being the first Director of the Federal Bureau of Investigation and who held the office for forty-eight years, dies at age seventy-seven.
- The Grateful Dead play their first paying concert in Copenhagen, Denmark at the Tivolis Koncertsa.
- Paris Peace talks between the United States and North Vietnam are suspended due to lack of progress. Shortly thereafter, the United States begins the mining of harbors and continues bombing of North Vietnam.
- Edwin H. Land of the Polaroid Corporation demonstrates photographs that develop "right before your eyes."
- Israeli Special Forces storm a hijacked Belgian jet sitting at Lod Airport in Tel Aviv and free all 97 hostages on board, killing two of the three hijackers.

* * *

At the end of the week, we retrieved the minibus and prepared to leave Amsterdam. Our four backpacks and Lode's shelter bundle, a twelve-by-twelve-foot bright orange tarp wrapped around six-foot wooden poles, strapped to the roof rack made us resemble a safari expedition. Inside, the bus looked more like a rat's nest as towels hung to dry, clothing, sleeping bags and blankets were strewn on every surface. We were not a neat bunch.

The morning of our departure, we drove to Raoul's to say goodbye. He shook our hands and said, "We'll meet in a few weeks, oui?"

"You bet, mon vieux, we'll return in time for the Floyd concert," I replied as the rest of the crew settled in the van.

The Frenchman surreptitiously handed me a shoebox pierced with air holes. "Before I forget, here is what you requested." The lid of the box was secured with twine and the carton juddered as its occupant stirred. I peered through the openings, smiled at Raoul, raised a thumb and placed the container under the driver seat.

Monique and Trev snuggled on the rear bench and grinned in anticipation of our departure while Lode, sitting to my right, rolled a smoke. No one asked about the shoebox and so, with a last wave to Raoul we headed out of town.

The border crossing to Germany was a couple of hours south of Amsterdam on the A-one highway and Munich a further four hundred miles or a day and a half of travel. The weather was ideal for a road trip, sunny blue skies, a few cottony clouds marching eastwards and a light westerly breeze. The temperature, in the low teens, was perfect to prevent the underpowered engine from overheating.

Lode's gear included a portable Phillips cassette recorder and a stack of tapes. Trev shuffled through the pile, selected a tape and cranked the volume. The Stone's *Sympathy for the Devil* filled the van as the flat Dutch countryside unfurled before us. We reached West Germany around noon. The border-crossing complex, a collection of booths, sheds and hangar-sized inspection buildings, straddled the road splitting the lanes into six lines. Multilingual signs, attached to the drive-thru kiosks instructed us to have the vehicle papers and our passports ready. I stopped the Kombi behind a queue of cars and noticed a K9 unit van parked beyond the booths next to an inspection shed.

Turning to my friends, I said, "Here we go. If they use dogs, I have a deterrent. Just make sure you're clean."

When signaled to move ahead, I pulled up to the wicket and handed our passports and the van's papers to a beefy border guard. The large man wore a dark olive uniform and filled the booth the way a bear would fill a public phone box. His hairy hands were the size of dinner plates but with unexpected delicacy, he reached through the window and plucked our documents from my hand.

He rattled off some words in German but when I shrugged, he switched to English and said, "Villcome to Chermany. Und vere did you come from today?"

"Amsterdam."

"Und vere are you going?"

"Munich, Bavaria…"

"Ya gut. Vat are you doing in Munich?"

"Touristy stuff. Apparently the beer is fabulous."

"Ya! Best in country," he replied with noticeable pride. "I'm from Augsburg also in Bavaria." He flipped the pages of each passport, scanning the entries thoroughly, stamped Trev's, the only non-EEC documentation, confirmed the validity of the Kombi's insurance and registration, closed all four documents and returned them to me.

He pointed his finger beyond the booth and said, "Have a good visit." I realized that I'd been holding my breath and exhaled softly. I thought we were clear but another guard stepped in front of the van and directed us to a parking lane next to the K9 panel van. Lode was shaking his head and biting his lip while Monique was nervously clutching at Trev.

A customs officer approached as I parked and politely asked Trev and Monique to step out. The K9 vehicle's rear doors opened to disgorge a uniformed narc holding a gorgeous black German shepherd on a long leash.

The doggie cop pointed at Lode and me and said, "Please stay vere you are. Don't vorry about the hund. He hasn't eaten any hippies since yesterday." Snorting in amusement, he urged his charge into the bus. The big dog hopped in and effortlessly jumped onto the bench directly behind me. I felt his hot breath and wet nose brushing my skin as he sniffed down my collar. I reached under the driver's seat, hooked the twine holding the lid of the shoebox and with a quick yank, untied it.

A raspy tongue licked my finger and a furry head rubbed against my hand as the grey cat Raoul had so obligingly provided, wiggled out of the box. The feline crouched on the floor and I had to nudge it to the right to force it to hop onto the seat. Lode jumped in surprise.

The kitty saw the shepherd and arched its back, spitting and hissing. The hound snarled and lunged forward but the cat yowled and rocketed over the snapping jaws, through the open side doors, landing claws first on the dog handler's face. The blur of grey fur then leaped from the screaming man to the ground and tore off into a cavernous shed. The dog, baying at the top of its lungs, twisted around, knocked his handler backwards and ripped the leash free as it hurtled after the kitty.

Our original astonishment at the melodrama unfolding before us soon gave way to side splitting laughter. Cursing loudly and rubbing his bruised tailbone, the K9 handler rose to his feet and limped after his mutt. I glared at my companions in an attempt to convey, nonverbally, that I needed them to calm down. Lode, held his sides while tears rolled down his cheeks. Trev bit his lip trying not to laugh and Monique was a turning a fetching shade of crimson.

I turned toward the customs guard with a sad face and said, "Aw, man! Look what you did to my cat. Are you going to help me catch him?"

The man's cheeks reddened, his eyes bulged and, making odd gurgling sounds, his mouth opened and closed a couple of times. He stared at his colleague's retreating form chasing the barking dog loping after a small, dwindling, furry ball. Meanwhile, a dozen cars lined up behind us honking impatiently, some drivers leaning out their windows adding vocal imprecations to the general din.

The border guard, through clenched teeth, told Trev and Monique, "Get your arsch (ass) back on the bus." He slammed his fist on the roof on the VW, pointed at the exit lane and growled something indistinct that I took to mean get the fuck out of here! My German is poor but I'm certain I picked up references to cat stew as we drove away. Everyone in the van remained silent while I accelerated to cruising speed and the border was behind us.

Trev, unable to keep it in any longer, hooted and laughed, shouting, "Holy fuck!"

Monique gasped between giggles, "Why didn't you tell us you had a cat?"

"I was hoping for complete surprise. It worked!"

"Poor kitty. What's going to happen to it?"

Trev shrugged and said, "Well, nothing… As long as it stays ahead of the dog, it'll be fine. There were lots of high shelves in the shed."

We stopped for lunch at a roadside inn and hoisted pints of German beer, toasting the health of one small cat and wishing it a long and happy life.

* * *

The next afternoon we picked up Karl, a twenty-four year old German hitchhiker, thumbing his way back to the Olympic work site. He was five-feet-eight with powerful-looking shoulders on a stocky Teutonic body. Shaggy, shoulder-length, blond hair framed his tanned face, bright blue eyes and a scraggly moustache. Karl came from Einsbach, a small town northwest of Munich. In strongly accented English, he explained that he was returning to work after a two-day break.

He directed us to Olympiad Park, situated in the northern part of Munich, where a massive, unfinished, concrete stadium dominated the vast construction site. The partially completed venues, built on land still dotted with WWII bomb craters, occupied acres of dusty lay-down areas. Office trailers, tool sheds and wheeled air compressors congregated at the base of each structure and cars, vans and buses parked in clumps. Hundreds of workers bustled in and out of gaps in the towering walls, some carrying materials, others laden with tools or scaffolding sections. Large collections of equipment and materials were scattered everywhere and loaded flatbeds, tall yellow cranes and a fleet of tractors sat on the shoulders of dirt roads crisscrossing the site.

We slowly wended our way through the busy site feeling like ants in a disturbed hill, dwarfed by tall stacks of pipes, mountains of crates, giant cable spools and towering mounds of sand and gravel. West and south of the main venues, in what would become a landscaped park, lay an encampment on a field of scrub-grass and bushes.

"This is where we live," Karl said pointing at a shantytown of tents, shacks and caravans filling the area. A forlorn power pole, surrounded by temporary wooden electrical service panels, stood in the center of the field and a single drooping line connecting it to the construction site. A rat's nest of multi-colored extension cords twisted from the receptacles to the haphazard habitations.

We pulled up to a tumbled-down shack built from construction scraps, nestled between a tent and a canvas shelter. A tin pipe jutted crookedly from the shack's roof and a yellow extension cord snaked towards a service panel.

"You're welcome to set up your camp here," he said. "We have electricity and a latrine and there are functional public bathrooms by the venues. The ones by the main stadium have showers. Thanks for the ride." The young German disembarked and entered the shack. We studied the campsite in silence; a light breeze fluttered bits of plastic sheeting and drove empty paper bags against the shelters. I'd seen refugee camps that were more inviting.

I broke our contemplation by saying, "We can't all sleep in the Kombi for the next few weeks." I hopped off the bus, followed by my friends.

Lode paced the space between the van and Karl's shack. "There's enough room to set-up here. Two can sleep in the VW and two in the shelter."

"If you guys don't mind, we'll take the tent," Trev said.

We agreed, unloaded the roof rack and erected Lode's gear by stringing the tarp on the poles to create a tent, into which we tossed our belongings. Monique inspected her sparse new digs and looked dubious, but I reassured her that we would improve the austere accommodations as soon as we could start scrounging.

The Kombi had a pressing appointment with Raoul's connection so Lode and I drove into Munich. Our destination lay in an industrial section south of the city center amid a warren of warehouses and shops. The Izmir Construction Company was a two-story, four-bay long, grimy brick pre-war building surrounded by an unfenced yard full of piles of gravel, rocks, sand and stacks of lumber. A skeletal pipe stand along one edge of the property supported various lengths of iron pipes and sections of steel beams.

The left-most bay door clattered open and two men stepped out. The taller one, a swarthy man sporting a jet-black mustache and wearing gray coveralls, waved and beckoned us to join him. His companion flashed a friendly smile; climbed in the driver's seat and drove the van into the service bay where a third worker dragged a wheeled jack under the vehicle's chassis and rolled the door closed.

Our guide led us inside and up the stairs at the back. From the higher vantage point, I saw stacked lumber, wooden crates and steel drums strewn on the shop's floor. A yellow backhoe tractor sat beyond our van, its gaping engine bay empty, hoses and wires dangling from various access panels.

We went through a door on the upper landing and into a carpeted hallway the length of the building. A short pudgy man in a crumpled gray suit occupied the first office, a surprisingly large room. I assumed this was the boss. He waved us in and gestured at the two chairs facing his desk. He was speaking on the phone and as soon as we sat, abruptly handed me the receiver. Puzzled, I held it to my ear and said a tentative hello. Raoul's familiar voice replied, "Eh bien, Danny. Meet Mehmet. This call is to confirm that everything is okay. How was your trip?" I chatted briefly about our encounter with the K9 unit and Raoul asked to speak to Mehmet who, after a short conversation hung up.

"Welcome to Munich," Mehmet said as he stood up to shake our hands. He was a dark-skinned, thickset man, barely reaching my shoulder, built like a barrel with a broad chest and powerful arms. In his late forties, his hair had thinned enough to reveal a good portion of his tanned pate and he sported a bushy black moustache below a beak-shaped nose. "I'm pleased to meet you. Would you like coffee or tea?"

We both opted for java. Mehmet picked up the phone, jabbed a button on the base of the unit and spoke a few words in Turkish. Stacks of binders, bulging folders and notepads littered the surface of his desk and a framed picture of Mustafa Kemal Ataturk, the founder of modern Turkey, hung on the wall above Mehmet's chair.

"How was your trip?"

"No problems. Everything went according to plan."

"Jolly good!" A knock on the doorjamb interrupted him and a teenage boy entered the office bearing a tray holding three tiny cups on delicate saucers and a beautifully crafted bronze carafe. The youth, resembling a young, thin Mehmet, smiled at us, poured the coffee and left the room.

"Please excuse me for a moment," he walked to the steel door leading to the shop, opened it and bellowed back and forth with the guys below. "Mahmood and his men are retrieving the cargo. Then, they'll button up the vehicle. It will take about two hours. Raoul said you're looking for work?"

"Yeah, a few weeks at least."

"We provide workers to the Main Contractor at the Olympic park. My cousin Yusuf handles the business on site. I'll ask him to set you up."

"That will be great Mehmet, thanks."

"Don't mention it. We make good money providing cheap labor. Here's a note for Yusuf." He scribbled on a pad and tore off the page. "Look for him at the Izmir Construction trailer parked at the Schwimmhalle (Swimming Pool)."

Mehmet spoke of the thousands of Turkish workers spread throughout West Germany, so diligently instrumental in the country's economic success and the developing ties between the two countries. I told him of my desire to trek in the footsteps of Iskandar and how everything we were doing was to get us to India. Mehmet said he'd always admired the Macedonian warrior and listed towns and sites along the western Turkish coast renowned for their historical connections with Alexander and his armies.

Mahmood entered the office and babbled something in Turkish while pointing towards the shop. We all rose and followed him downstairs where five black plastic-wrapped, elongated bricks sat on a trestle table by the minibus. Mehmet pulled a wicked-looking switchblade knife from his pocket, sliced open one of the bundles and peeled away the plastic wrapping exposing black-green hash. He deftly shaved off a sliver of dope and lit it with his lighter.

The sweet aroma of hashish spread around us bringing a smile to everyone's face. Mehmet took a deep sniff of the smoke, nodded in satisfaction and hacked off a fat finger-sized lump of hash from the brick. He reached into his jacket, withdrew an envelope stuffed with bills into which he dropped the dope and handed it to me saying, "As per our deal, my good friend."

Not wishing to offend our hosts, I stashed it in my pocket without counting the cash, thanked the Turks and we left the shop. On the way back to the Olympic park, we stopped at an Aldi supermarket for groceries, a hardware store for extension cords and at a sports store to buy essentials for our campsite.

* * *

Night was falling and despite the powerful floodlights mounted on the park's power poles, a few stars were visible between thin clouds scudding across the dark sky. I poked my head into the canvas shelter, tossed Monique a shopping bag and said, "We got you a gift." She squeaked in delight as she pulled out two inflatable air mattresses and a compact foot pump.

Hitchhiker Karl wandered over and introduced us to his three roommates, Bruno, Ernst and Kurt, Bavarian lads all, jobbing for cash at the Olympics. It must have been crowded for them in the small wooden shack. We invited them to join us around a crackling bonfire and tell us about working on the venues.

Karl said, "These Olympics are special because they're the Happy Games!" In response to our looks of puzzlement, he added, "It's a German thing. The last Olympics held in this country were during the Nazi era. So this time they are called the Happy Games."

Once our guests went home, Trev followed me into the darkened van and I showed him the envelope from Mehmet. "The wages of sin," I said.

"Holy fuck! How much did we make?"

"Five hundred bucks, man. We can use that to pay off Irish if we decide to keep the bus. Also… check out the bonus." I tossed him the chunk of hash.

"All right! What do you mean if we keep the VW?" he asked sniffing the fragrant lump.

"Well, we need to decide whether or not to sell it after the Floyd concert in Amsterdam. If we're keeping the Kombi, we'll use this cash to pay Irish. Otherwise we'll split the dough four ways."

"We told Irish we'll buy the van."

"We will one way or another. If we decide to get rid of the bus, we'll just get rid of it in Amsterdam before we split south."

"I haven't really thought much about anything beyond the concert, sort of thing," he said sheepishly. "Only the van is so convenient…"

I marshaled my thoughts for a moment. "Consider this, we can only travel together as a group if we own the vehicle, otherwise we'll split up to hitchhike singly or in pairs. Also, owning wheels means we don't need to hump our packs." Trev nodded thoughtfully.

"On the other hand," I continued. "There's the extra cost of petrol, oil, maintenance and the ferries to consider. In fairness, we must each make that decision, right?"

"Yeah, but we have until Ian joins us in May to decide."

"True," I said and started rolling a spliff.

"I'll speak to Monique," Trev said. "We either spend a bit more but stay together or save money by traveling in ones and twos."

"And I'll ask Lode."

We shared a toke while we contemplated our respective missions. Trev left the van to speak to Monique while I stayed to finish smoking. Later, I spoke with Lode who, as I'd guessed, said he'd go with the majority. He liked the freedom the bus gave us but could just as easily hitchhike if that was the group's decision.

* * *

The morning dawned brightly with a cloudless blue sky that promised a comfortable, moderate spring day. Despite the early hour, the Olympic park was a hive of noisy activities. Vehicles of all sizes were maneuvering in and out of the massive concrete structures, engines roaring and emitting clouds of diesel fumes into the still morning air. Construction cranes swung heavy loads of material from a fleet of queuing flatbeds. Accompanied by a cacophony of announcements blaring from PA loudspeakers, an army of workers bustled purposefully throughout the complex, deftly weaving between moving vehicles and idle equipment.

We lined up in front of the Izmir Construction office trailer, one of a dozen parked in the lay-down area of the Olympic swimming venue. We stood amidst a crowd of Turks while Yusuf, clipboard in hand, dispensed work assignments. Yusuf was younger, taller and thinner than his cousin Mehmet was but the family resemblance was unmistakable. His tight mouth often pursed in a frown as he solved the daily challenges of his job. The laborers dispersed to their tasks and he turned to us asking if we spoke German. We shook our heads and he switched to broken although understandable English as I handed him Mehmet's note.

"Yis, yis." He nodded as he read the message. "Mehmet talked to me about you." The Turk spotted a man in blue coveralls walking down the road towards the stadium. He pointed at the worker and told us, "Go with Batur. Tell him you're on his crew and to set you up, yis?" We nodded and followed Batur inside the Schwimmhalle.

Batur, also Turkish, was in his late twenties and spoke good English. He stood a head shorter than me, was brown-haired and brown-eyed, broad-shouldered and powerfully built with a battered wrestler's face, which hinted of a youthful life as a brawler. I appraised his short, muscular neck and thick, strong-looking wrists while he studied us in silence, trying to decide where we would the most useful.

"Come with me," he invited, heading for a set of stairs leading to tiers rising vertiginously high from the empty rectangular, concrete pool. The skeletal frameworks of three diving platforms, including the ten-meter tower, loomed at the deep end, ready for the final cement pour.

"You will be bolting on the plastic seating. It is simple and easy work. Did Yusuf discuss pay with you?"

"No. You understand we have no work permits?" Lode asked in a low voice.

"Ah! Cash under the table, yes? Hokay, no problems. I'll give you a tally sheet to track your hours and we'll pay you every Friday. Here we are," he said indicating a flight of wide concrete stairs that appeared to go up forever. He showed us the crates of parts, mounting hardware and the tools we would use. We joined a group of laborers who demonstrated the simplistic, repetitive motions required to connect endless rows of seats. It wasn't hard to figure out and the time passed quickly.

After work while drinking Munich's excellent beer around a roaring fire, we shared stories about our work with our German companions.

"We're dismantling concrete forms in the main stadium," Karl said. "Labor-intensive but time goes fast."

Monique laughed and said, "We spent the day bolting plastic seats. Easy job except for the music."

"What music?" Bruno asked.

"They're testing the sound systems by playing *Popcorn* over and over." She was referring to Hot Butter's Moog synthesizer version of the Kingsley tune, which was a huge hit in many European countries.

"I will hear tut-too-tut-too-tut-tut-tut in my head forever," Lode said illustrating the invasiveness of the song. "How much longer are we to be punished?" he asked in mock despair.

"Until they're finished tweaking the PA systems. They should be done in about... oh, four weeks?" Monique smiled mischievously while everyone else groaned.

The party broke up early as we all had to get up at dawn. I was in the van updating my journal when Trev climbed aboard causing the gently hissing kerosene lamp swinging from the ceiling, to cast dancing shadows.

"Scribble, scribble Danny. What are you writing about?"

"Oh, anecdotes, descriptions of our surroundings and things I find interesting."

He turned the journal toward him. "What language is this?"

"Hebrew, so my notes stay private and I can say anything I want about you. This word here," I pointed at the Hebrew letters for Tuesday, "says Trev is a wanker."

He pivoted the notebook right and left scrutinizing my handwriting. "Fuck you too," he said amiably. "Shame you don't have a camera."

"I wish! But buying and developing film is too expensive and more hassle than I need. I'll buy postcards along the way."

"I talked with Monique about traveling in the van, sort of thing." He pushed the journal to the side and rolled a thin spliff. "She votes to keep the bus and pay Irish off with the five hundred bucks." I took the joint and lit the fragrant dope. The smoke rapidly filled the small space and Trev slid a window open. "She also said she definitely wants to go as far as Istanbul. Afterwards, we'll see, but I doubt she'll go much further."

"You don't think so?" I asked.

"Nah, she's not much for hardship travel, such as eating weird shit, sleeping on the ground and stuff like that."

"Yeah, man," I agreed chuckling. "She's not a Freak. I also vote to hold on to the bus and Lode said he'd go with the majority."

"Well then, all four of us are voting to keep the old beast."

The next day, Trev and I called Irish and told him we'd wire him five hundred bucks as soon as we reached the Munich Amex office. He was pleased, gave us transfer information and wished us a good trip while reminding us that the van's papers would expire in the fall. "Make the problem go away before the expiry date," he said. "You understand me Sunshine?"

"Consider it disappeared," we promised, confident we could dispose of the van one way or another.

Fuck me, I thought with exultation, I have wheels, me.

* * *

The week passed rapidly, Yusuf paid us in cash and we had Sunday off.

Saturday night, as we walked away from the office trailer, I asked Batur,

"Er, do you guys drink beer?" The Park's floodlights came on, dispelling the evening's darkness and casting sharp, black shadows on the ground.

"Of course, why not?" he replied, puzzled.

"Urm, uh, well, you're Muslims right?" I stammered.

"Ah! I understand. Let's just say that we're a lot stricter when we're back home in Turkey." He put a finger along his nose and winked at me. "Why don't you and your friends meet us later?"

"Sounds like a plan," I agreed. "Where?"

"We'll start at the Augustiner-Braustuben near the train station."

I showered, grabbed my friends and we headed out to meet the Turks. The Brautstuben, a brick building housing a pub in the brewery, smelled of hops and sausages. The beer hall was authentic and had a ton of atmosphere including a table reserved for the brewmeisters. We arrived earlier than the rest so we started with a round of Augustiner Edelstoff, a delicious tap pale lager and ordered platters of Schweinshaxe, which are roasted ham hocks served with fried potatoes and sauerkraut.

The taproom was moderately crowded, the noise level bearable and there were photos of past brewing dignitaries on the walls. We were drinking a second round, a darker lager called Dunkel, when Batur, Yusuf, and a couple of other Izmir workers joined us. One Turk peered, fascinated, at my plate and visibly shuddered at the sight of the hock.

They looked grim and drank their pints with serious intent. Batur told us that they'd just left the Bayerischer-Donisl, a beer hall nearby, where they ran into some loud-mouthed, obnoxious locals, who made rude remarks about the fucking Turkish workforce. Yusuf had averted the start of WW-three by controlling his hot-tempered employees, convincing them to walk away and ignore the assholes. We bought a round of draft and tried to lighten the mood by telling jokes.

The traditional enmity between Turks and Greeks is a well-documented fact and although they have many cultural characteristics in common, such as their cuisine and their booze - the Hellenics' Ouzo and the Turks' Arrack as an example- one must never forget their national competitiveness. "How do the Greeks separate the men from the boys?" Yusuf shouted over the surrounding din. Trev shrugged and raised his hands in a very Gallic gesture.

"With a crowbar!" Yusuf chortled, snorting beer from his nose. I guess because we were all a little soused, that seemed hilarious.

Batur, we learned, was a competitive professional arm-wrestler who won regional awards and almost made it to national ranking. He offered to teach us the proper method of arm-wrestling, including all the dirty tricks the professionals used.

Another trait both Turks and Greeks share is their single-minded obsession when trying to impress women and poor Monique became the center of attention throughout the evening. So, we boys left Monique to the tender mercies of Yusuf and his buddies while Batur demonstrated the various techniques such as rolling the hand to loosen an opponent's grip, using the torso and shoulders to add strength and other tricks. By the end of the evening, we were all in good spirits and promised to do it again sometime.

* * *

Monique endured a dozen days of work before announcing that, as she didn't need the money as much as we did, she would take a side trip to Vienna to explore the numerous museums. We drove her to the train station and consoled a forlorn Trev with copious amounts of beer and hash.

Between working hard all day and socializing at night, time passed quickly. Monique returned the second week of May, four days before our planned return to Amsterdam. To celebrate our reunion, our German friends suggested an outing to Ammersee, a popular resort lake about an hour southwest of Munich.

The sun shone brightly and a few high clouds marred the otherwise perfect blue dome above us. The air was fragrant with blooms and the fields rolling past the van windows were a deep emerald green from emerging sprouts. The lake appeared to our left and we got off the autobahn just before Greifenberg. We followed a busy, rural two-lane road southwards to a secluded spot along the lakeshore. Lode and I were suffering from epic hangovers, thanks to the previous night's drinking binge. After unloading blankets, towels and a carton of foodstuff we tossed our clothes in a pile and all of us dove into the inviting waters.

The clear blue water was only a hair above freezing and the shock almost stopped my heart. I jumped out of the lake howling and ran to grab a towel, followed by the entire group with the exception of Lode who continued swimming, calling us a bunch of pussies and wimps. We spent a lovely afternoon relaxing on the grassy banks under a sprawling canopy of willows sprouting green fuzz.

We searched for dinner in Utting, a resort town on the lakeshore, strolling through the old city following a snaking, cobble-stoned street, which debouched into a small Platzl lined with tourist stores and an ancient bierstube. At the center of the plaza a verdigris lion's head fountain spewed water into a murky basin enclosed by worn and weathered grey blocks of stone.

Two longhaired drifters sitting on the basin's wide rim displayed street jewelry arrayed on a bright red velvet mat spread at their feet: Necklaces, bracelets, anklets and earrings made of beads strung on lengths of nylon fishing line. A couple of huge backpacks leaned against the stones.

We approached the display, flashed the peace sign and checked out the merchandise. The white and brown beads turned out to be tiny, round organic-looking discs the size of dimes. Monique wrapped a bracelet around her wrist and examined the bauble closely. "What are these?"

"They're Puka shells, man," one of the drifter replied.

"I've never seen anything like these before. Where do they come from?"

"Well, mostly from Hawaii, but they can also be found in some Central American countries." He reached into one of the backpacks, fished out a plastic baggie full of the tiny shells and handed us a sampling. "They already have a hole in the center so it makes them easy to string."

We passed them around and noted that, indeed, every small disc was unevenly pierced. The delicate pieces, we learned, were the remnants of cone snail shells after decades of abrasion by the pounding of ocean's waves on the beaches.

"They're quite pretty," Monique said, returning the bracelet to the mat.

"And they sell like hot cakes in the States. Here, not so much."

We introduced ourselves and learned that Eric and Bill, twentyish Americans from California, were drifting through Europe. A commotion at the square's entrance interrupted our conversation. A group of about thirty tourists wearing loud, colorful clothes and draped with cameras, entered the small plaza following a tour guide. A harassed-looking man climbed on a park bench, urged his flock to gather around and instructed them, in English, to take a break, shop in the platzl stores and, for God's sakes, be ready to leave in an hour. The gaggle of well-fed Americans dispersed in all directions.

"Oh, look Henry!" A portly, middle-aged woman wearing a bright yellow shirt and a hairdo in the shape of a beehive pointed at us. "German hippie jewelry," she enthused and dragged her reluctant husband to the display. Her shrillness enticed others to gather in front of the Californians, pawing through the various items and commenting about the price. They seemed interested but hesitated, much as wildebeests do before crossing a crocodile-infested river; no one wanted to be the first to jump in.

"Wow! Is that really all you're charging?" Monique exclaimed loudly and pointed at a mid-sized necklace selling for ten bucks. "It's only half as much as what the other guys asked. They're real Pukas, right?" She made a show of pulling bills from her purse and proffered the money to Bill who handed her the strand.

The American woman had followed the exchange. She squinted at Monique and us suspiciously, as if we planned to snatch her purse and run. She whispered to her husband who sighed loudly, shrugged and reached for his wallet. The woman bought a choker and a bracelet, chortling in satisfaction when Eric mentioned their value in the States. The remainder of the group following the herd instinct and unwilling to be left out, clamored to buy.

We retreated to the bierstube at the edge of the square and observed, bemused, as the two American Freaks emptied their bags and sold most of their stock. When the tour group finally departed on the heels of their refreshed guide, Bill and Eric packed their backpacks and joined us in the tavern.

Eric seemed stunned. "Holy shit, man! They completely cleaned us out." "Yeah, that was a stroke of genius, buying the choker when you did," Rick said to Monique.

"I can't take the credit," she replied. "I saw that trick used by hippie street peddlers in Paris. It never fails."

Eric reached into his pocket, pulled out a necklace and ten bucks and gave them to Monique. "We want you to have this." We spent a couple of hours chatting and drinking excellent lager then returned to Munich.

* * *

The last evening before we were to leave Munich for Amsterdam, we invited our friends for drinks. We met at the Ayingers Speis und Trank beer hall in the

Munich platzl and sat outside at a long trestle table. Night had fallen, the temperature was balmy and streetlights, wall-mounted carriage lamps and strings of colored bulbs illuminated the cobble-stoned square. Strains of oompah music emanated from the open doors of the bar. Big-bosomed frauleins, hauling multiple trays of beer and heaping platters of food, bustled in and out of the bierstube.

Despite its door-like thickness, our table groaned under the weight of the plates, heavy steins and the pounding of arm wrestling bouts. We yakked and laughed, reminiscing about the previous six weeks, until five boisterous, loud, drunk Germans staggered into the small square.

Mehmet, unaware of the drunks behind him, stood up, stein in hand and proposed a toast. This attracted the attention of the newcomers and one of them insulted our Turkish pals in German. His companions attempted to drag him away as he ranted and gestured at the Turks. I didn't need to understand his tirade. One glance at our friends' irate faces was enough. Silence spread over the crowded patio as the patrons stared at the commotion. A server ran into the hall and returned with a large man in tow. The big bartender approached the drunken lout, made shushing motions with his hands and urged him to move along.

Batur rolled his neck, vertebrae popping as he tilted his head from side to side. He said, "That's the same guy we ran into a while back."

Yusuf laid his hand on Batur's shoulder and whispered hoarsely, "Just sit quietly, Batur. We don't need any trouble."

The bartender and the interlopers raised their voices in an intense argument. I recognized the word 'Polizei' and one of the drunks, exasperated, shoved the barkeep who lurched backwards a couple of steps and crashed into Mehmet who, still standing mug in hand, lost his footing and fell to the ground. Beer and shards of pottery flew in all directions. The bartender and the waiter scurried back inside.

Batur jumped to his feet and sprang at the German drunk growling, "That's enough!" The two men grappled, pushing and shoving, as each one tried to throw a punch. Batur, a head shorter and forty pounds lighter than his opponent, managed to avoid the heavier man's wild punches. One of the other drunkards sidled over to the combatants and swung his fist at Batur, barely missing the target.

"Fuck that!" I snarled and leaped, shoving the cowardly backstabber away from the brawlers. Lode and Trev, equally outraged, rose without hesitation and stood at my side.

The German stared at us with surprise and slurred, "Zis is nothing to do with you." He stepped back towards his companions.

"Let keep this a fair fight," I said doing my best Clint Eastwood impression.

The Teutonic twats, sobered fast by the sudden escalation, studied us, glanced at Yusuf and Mehmet and decided to stay out of the brawl. The scuffle ended as quickly as it had started. Batur, demonstrating an elegant economy of effort, grabbed his opponent by the collar and coat lapel, levered his right leg between the German's knees and effortlessly tipped the German backward, slamming him to the ground. The racist drunk landed hard on the cobblestones and lay on his back in a daze.

Batur straddled the sprawled German, cocked his fist for the coup de grace but paused when Yusuf shouted sharply in Turkish. Batur gave his boss a sullen sideways look, lowered his arm and reluctantly returned to the table.

The defeated loudmouth shook his head and scampered back towards his friends. "Zis is not over," he said. Wobbling, he spat in our direction and left the square, angrily shaking off his friend's helping hands.

"Holy fuck, man. You'd better watch your back at the site," I said looking at Batur.

The Turk shrugged and wiped the sweat from his face, "Life's a bitch, Danny."

"Yeah, and then you die." Trev added, "Hell of a move there, Batur."

Yusuf gave us a grateful look and said, "Thanks for the help,"

We nodded and shrugged. People at the other tables turned back to their dining and drinking and the ambient din returned to normal.

Lode smirked and chided us, "And here I thought you guys were peaceful hippies."

I gave him the finger and exclaimed, "Hey! There's no need to insult us. I'm all for making love not war but if you have to make war, do it fast and do it hard, right?"

"Fuckin' A!" Trev replied clinking his mug against Lode's and mine.

We were feeling no pain by closing time and it's a miracle we all found our way home.

* * *

The next morning, painfully hangover, we drove away from Munich and the Olympic park and headed northwest toward Holland. Karl bummed a ride as far as Saarbrucken and we arrived in Amsterdam late on the second day after leaving Munich.

Vondel Park resembled a faerie scene from a fantasy book, a first quarter moon's light diffracting through a thin mist hugging the grassy grounds. That night, it seemed as if tents and shelters filled every inch of the green areas while hundreds of sleeping bags lay on the banks of the streams under the stately trees. A galaxy of sparks, ejected from joints and pipes, flickered throughout the tent city and gently extinguished themselves in the damp night air or on the long hair of the milling crowds. The temperature was mild and the extensive rose gardens and blossoming flowerbeds released an intoxicating perfume mixed with whiffs of pot and hash.

"Wow! Check out at all those people," I said as we drove along the Van Baerlestraat Boulevard. Monique, Trev and Lode's noses pressed against the van's windows.

"School's out and many of these campers are probably here for the concert," Lode said.

"I thought the 'British Rock Meeting' in Germersheim would attract most of the rockers, sort of thing." Trev was referring to a three-day, outdoor music festival rocking Germany at the same time as the Amsterdam concert. The Rock Circus in Amsterdam was just a one-day event, highlighting Pink Floyd and other musicians including Donovan, Buddy Miles and Tom Paxton. Floyd was headlining both events.

"Oh, I'm sure a lot of people will be there as well. But where would you prefer to experience Floyd; in Germany or Amsterdam?"

"Without a doubt, here. Most stoners will surely choose Amsterdam. It's way easier to get dope."

We dropped Lode at the Overtoom tram stop. "I'll meet you guys in a couple of days at the concert." He disembarked, hoisted his towering backpack, pecked Monique's cheek, punched our shoulders and joined the queue. He wanted to visit his relatives one more time before we left Amsterdam at the conclusion of the Rock Circus.

We drove back to the Paradiso to check the message board. We'd instructed Ian to leave us a note and I hoped that my buddy Gerard was in town, too, at Raoul's. I planned to visit them later in the evening. Trev handed me a slip of paper plucked from the board. "From Ian. He got a ride here with Rudy, the stage manager. He's working the concert and Rudy's gang is at the Olympic park setting up."

We headed to the nearby stadium and cruised through a congested parking area full of truck-trailers and caravans sporting license plates from all over Europe and quite a few from the UK. We walked along the line of lorries, craning our necks, looking for Ian. Emerging from a loading bay in the back of the venue, he found us first, grinned and waved.

"Trev! Danny!" He flung himself at Trev and gave him a big hug before turning to me and doing the same. I had forgotten how slim and light he was, barely heavier than a child and still looking like an elf with long, ash-blond hair tucked behind pointy ears. Trev introduced Monique who gave Ian a peck on the cheek and he led us through labyrinthine corridors in the administrative area of the stadium.

As Ian babbled happily to Trev bringing him up to speed about common friends in London, Monique and I smiled at his exuberance. He gave me a glance over his shoulder and said, "Gina sends her love, Danny." I felt an unexpected tug in my chest when he mentioned her name. Monique must have noticed as she gave me a thoughtful look and seemed on the verge of asking a question but kept silent.

We made our way to the main building where Rudy, surrounded by a group of roadies, sat at a plain steel desk in one of the stadium's offices. They were poring over a stage-set blueprint, making notes in the margins and in spiral-wound notebooks. Clipboards, schedules, inventory sheets and empty cardboard coffee cups littered the desktop. We waited until the group dispersed and approached the desk.

With a big smile on his face, Rudy exclaimed, "Look what the cat dragged in! Hi Trevor, who are your friends, then?" He glanced at Monique and me. Trev introduced the Frenchwoman and reminded him of my name.

"Right, Danny. Good to see you all. You blokes want to work, yes?" He grabbed a clipboard from beneath a pile of forms, flipped a couple of pages and scribbled on the paper. "Let me think…We need all the strong backs we can get to unload the lorries and move gear and…" He studied Monique pensively. "I could use a runner, interested?" She nodded and grinned enthusiastically.

Rudy reached into a box beside the desk and retrieved three black tee shirts. The Tees had the Rock Circus emblem printed on the front and "CREW" emblazoned in big white letters across the shoulders.

"Go find Geordie by the transports and tell him you're his for the next couple of days. Monique, be here tomorrow morning at seven." He waved us off and picked up the phone.

"Ian, when did you arrive in Amsterdam?" I asked as he guided us back to the parking lot.

"We got in last night. I rode down in one of Rudy's truck." He gestured at the line of trucks.

"Is Rudy managing this concert?"

"Oh no, he's just one of half a dozen outfits working the event. How was Munich?"

We related the highlights of our stay in Germany and explained the deal we had with Irish concerning the bus. Delighted, he blinked at us. "We own the van?"

Trev waved his hand in a maybe gesture and replied, "For now. We have it until the papers expire in the fall. Before that, Irish wants us to get rid of it."

"Ian, do you have a driver's license?" I asked.

He shook his head and shrugged, "Sorry, never learned."

Trev didn't have a permit either and although Monique did, she disliked handling a big vehicle like the Kombi. Lode and I then, would do all the driving with Monique available in a pinch.

Ian led us to a group of men sitting in folding chairs and on cable reels by the caravans. He introduced us to Geordie, one of Rudy's foremen, a tall, blond Scot in his thirties. We shook hands all around, found seats and joined the group. Geordie spoke with a heavy Scottish burr and explained that we'd meet by the loading docks early next morning to unload the trucks. Ian suggested that we camp out amidst the roadies' caravans rather than at the park and I sensed some awkwardness between him and Trev, probably because of Monique's presence.

I was due to meet Raoul so I grabbed my jacket, threw the van's keys to Trev and headed toward the nearest tram stop.

* * *

Raoul welcomed me with a smile and steered me to the dining table where Gerard, my old friend and mentor, sat in front of a small mound of weed, a scale and a bunch of dime bags. Grinning widely, Gerard stood up and gave me a crushing bear hug.

"Danny, let me look at you." He eyed me up and down up, shook his head and said, "Still growing! Just like a big puppy. You seem well."

We talked, smoked pot and drank Heineken while weighting and loading baggies with weed the two Frenchmen would sell at the concert. It took us most of the night so, I crashed on Raoul's couch and managed to catch a few Z's before the alarm clock woke me up. Feeling tired and fuzzyheaded, I dragged my ass out of the dark silent houseboat and caught a tram to the Olympic Park.

I found Ian sleeping sprawled on the front seats, the VW parked between the roadies' caravans. I banged on the doors and laughed as Ian, Trev and Monique poured out of the van looking bedraggled and smelling of stale beer. I hoped they'd worked out whatever had been bothering them.

We joined Geordie and his crew queued in front of a catering truck and had a breakfast of egg and bacon sandwiches, washed down with mugs of hot, sweet coffee. Lorrie engines fired up and the parking lot soon filled with the smell of diesel fumes, streamers of bluish smoke hanging in the cool air before dissipating slowly. Trev, Ian and I spent the morning unloading and hauling a seemingly infinite assortment of crates, equipment, cable spools, gantries and scaffolding for the stage and sound towers. Later, we unloaded the gear for Joe's Light's outfit. They'd provide the concert's liquid light show and kaleidoscopic effects.

We helped erect an arching gantry, spanning the entire platform, festooned with a rainbow of lights and spotlights. A complex bundle of cables and wires snaked along the ground connecting various devices to their control boards. By evening the sound and light systems were being tested, adding to the general racket and chaotic confusion. Rudy released us as night set in and we retreated to the caravans parked behind the trucks.

Monique, eyes shining with excitement and her face flushed, had spent the day as a gofer for Rudy. Trev, Ian and I, nursing sore backs and legs, gratefully sprawled on improvised seats made of wooden crates, empty reels and up-ended buckets while Geordie charred sausages on a propane grill.

"What ever happened to that Scottish girl you were dating, Ian?" I asked.

"Wha' Scottish lass?" Geordie inquired, overhearing our conversation.

Ian turned to face the burly foreman and muttered, "She's an Academy student I was seeing."

"Ye didnae abandon the puir wee lass tae come here?"

"We only dated a few times, Geordie."

"Ye cannae just go oot and leave 'em pinin'. That's verrae cruel." The tall Scott was frowning at Ian and then broke into a big smile.

"Ach, don't fash yourself. Ah'm sure she'll be fine. Noo, who wants bangers?"

Rudy arrived in time for the impromptu dinner and joined us around a small fire burning in the bottom of a rusty half-barrel.

"Good job, lads!" He beamed at the group. "Have fun tomorrow, rest, relax, get drunk, sort of thing. Only be ready immediately after the concert to dismantle and pack the works, yeah?" He handed a bulging envelope to Geordie. "Here are the passes for you blokes. Hand them around." Rudy stayed long enough to down a bottle of beer, wolf down a banger on a bun and then he ran off.

Ian fetched his flute and Trev's guitar from the minibus. A few roadies and I joined them as an impromptu band, playing and singing popular tunes. Later that night, I retrieved my sleeping bag and crashed on the ground by the dying fire.

Concert day dawned with a cloudless sky, orange and pink hues painted the horizon matching the Rock Circus posters plastered everywhere in the park. The catering trucks returned and provided us with a profoundly welcome breakfast of hot coffee and egg sandwiches.

The vanguard of the sixty-thousand expected fans, who had camped all about the venue, lined up by the stadium's entrances and soon, as if on cue, joints and wine skins appeared and passed around. We joined the swelling lines and, when the gates finally opened, moved with the crowd. While slowly shuffling towards the entrance, I asked Ian how he'd made out during his term at the conservatory.

"Well, I finished it and requested a year off to study music abroad."

"Abroad, where?"

"Asia, man!" He gave me a beaming smile. "I'm going to India with you guys."

* * *

I have but a blurred recollection of the actual concert. I remember supremely loud music (sensed rather than heard), bright colors and a sea of people always on the move within the huge stadium. Having never been to an event of this size, the vibe generated by the performers and tens of thousands of stoned and drunk fans was a wonderful new experience. The day passed in a hazy succession of tokes, drinks, dancing, shouting and more smoking. By sunset, I collapsed, exhausted, in a seat halfway up the stadium. I had a good view of the stage when Pink Floyd started their set, accompanied by a mind-blowing kaleidoscopic light show centered on a flame-enshrouded giant gong. The crowd settled and the band played *Atom Heart Mother* (for the last time publically) followed by *One of those days, Careful with that Axe Eugene* and *Echoes*. The band played on and, when the crowd was sure there was no chance of encores, the venue emptied. I stumbled back to my sleeping bag and passed out.

The next morning, feeling horrible, practically voiceless and generally hurting like the victim of a hit-and-run, I donned my stained, filthy, smelly 'CREW' Tee shirt and joined Rudy's mob by a catering truck. The aroma of fried food almost undid me but I forced down a cup of scalding coffee and managed to eat a small bun.

The roadies formed a louche, surly group, as we dismantled and packed the stage. The stadium was littered and overflowing with detritus. It looked as if a garbage tornado had blown through leaving behind drifts of refuse. Empty bottles, discarded cardboard cups, food wrappers, cigarette butts and plastic bags that fluttered in the light breeze, covered the entire stadium. The cleaners working the tiers hooted in delight whenever they found underpants and bras, holding them up and waving them like flags at a parade.

Ian showed up around mid-morning looking and smelling as if he'd spent the night in a sewer. He grunted at me, I replied with a snarl, and we loaded a gazillion boxes and crates on the waiting trucks. He slept, he said, on Rudy's desk in the office and felt like shit.

"And you stink like it," I said with little sympathy and a moue of disgust.

By lunchtime, somewhat restored thanks to youth, gallons of water and a handful of aspirins, Ian and I searched for our missing friends. We found Monique standing by the van while Trev was rooting around the mess inside looking for his Tee shirt.

"Oy, the love-birds!" Ian shouted.

"Fuck off," Trev snarled, wiggling his torso into the rumpled shirt. Monique, her eyes bloodshot red, waved anemically at us.

"What we all need is a restorative toke," I declared, fishing in my pocket for my small brass pipe.

"Anyone saw Lodewijk?" I asked as I passed the toker to Monique.

"Nah. I never," Trev answered and Monique shrugged.

The hash took off the edge and, much mellower, the four of us ate ham and cheese sandwiches from the catering trucks and strolled over to the group of roadies relaxing at the back of a truck. Geordie nodded amiably and informed us that we were done. We had to check with Rudy for payment. We found Rudy in his office, slouching in his chair, looking tired but contented.

"Hullo, chaps," he said. "Good concert, yeah?" We all agreed. It had been one of best.

"Are you four heading back to the UK?"

"No," Ian replied. "We're off eastwards. Greece, Turkey..."

Rudy's payment was enough to make up for what we spent on drugs and booze the past three days, so we broke even and had tee shirts to boot.

Back at the Paradiso, where we hoped to meet Lode, I bumped into Gerard. We went to the café downstairs for a chat.

"Great concert," Gerard said. "Profitable too."

"Where are you off to next?"

"I'm taking a charter to New York. Then, I'll hitch across the U.S. to San Francisco."

"No shit? Cool, man."

"Last time I was there, in '68, a few French Freaks started a commune in the Napa valley. They wanted to start a vineyard, the crazy bastards. I'll check it out. What about you?"

"Five of us are heading for Greece. Do the islands, Istanbul and – India," I replied.

Gerard reached into his pocket, fished out a small spiral-bound notebook and said, "When you get to Corfu, go visit Guy, an old friend who lives in Ipsos. They have a beautiful property where they make hippie jewelry to sell to tourists." He jotted directions, tore the page and handed it to me.

I inserted the slip of paper in my journal and wrote down the location and names of his California hippies friends. The gang, including Lode, joined us at the table and I introduced everyone to Gerard who, after a short while, finished his coffee, gave me a goodbye hug and left the café.

And so, at the end of May, under a cloudless cerulean sky, we departed Amsterdam - that unforgettable city - heading south to the German border and the countries beyond.

* * *

Chapter Six

A Corfu-sing Situation

Corfu, June 1972

In Context:
-David Bowie releases "Rise & Fall of Ziggy Stardust"
-A U.S. patent is granted to IBM for the first "floppy disk".
-The botched break in of the Democratic National Committee offices at the Watergate Complex in Washington, D.C. is the beginning of the Watergate scandal that eventually leads to Nixon's resignation as President of the United States.
-*Grease* makes its Broadway debut.
-*Deep Throat*, one of the most famous porn films of all time makes its debut.
-Gold hits record $60 an ounce.
-Thousands die when the US bombs Haiphong, North Vietnam.

* * *

It took us two and a half weeks to cover the twelve hundred miles from Amsterdam to Brindisi, Italy and the ferry to Corfu. We drove short days, stopping often to admire the sights and to explore noteworthy local attractions including an ancient German monastery famous for its potent beer. The van ran well on flat ground but as soon as we started climbing through the German and Swiss Alps, the burden of carrying five adults and all our gear, taxed the underpowered engine, which now used almost as much oil as gas. Lode and I shared the driving and checked the dipstick at every stop.

We discovered that most automotive garages stored old oil, drained from serviced vehicles, in drums and the local mechanics were quite happy to sell us a few liters of the murky, stinky, black, viscous liquid. An engine rebuild was out of the question, so we carried a five-liter plastic gas can filled with "previously used" lubricant. I scrounged a scrap of fine-mesh steel screen to strain the black oil in an effort to keep bigger particles out of the motor.

In this manner, we crossed the Alps and entered into northern Italy. We drove by Como, Milan and Bologna before reaching the Adriatic coast at Rimini. The weather remained pleasant and we camped out wherever seemed most inviting at the end of the day. Occasionally, a friendly local farmer allowed us to sleep in his barn, snuggly ensconced on dry, fragrant bales of hay.

We earned food and gas money by busking in the scenic, tourist-rich towns on the way south. Monique, an accomplished artist, drew large chalk pictures on the sidewalks as Trev, Ian and I played our instruments. Lode, our shill, mingled with passersby and encouraged their generosity by nodding and making comments about the superior quality of our talents while tossing coins and bills in Trev's guitar case.

If it rained, instead of busking, we sat in cafés challenging the locals to arm-wrestling competitions and shamelessly used Monique, in a skimpy dress, as a distraction. This worked particularly well in Italy. We thus financed a comfortable journey through the Po Valley and made enough to afford a youth hostel and its amenities every few nights.

At Guilianova, a town on the Adriatic coast within a day's travel from Brindisi, Trev and Monique left to take a side trip to Rome. They planned to hitchhike west on highway A-twenty-four, explore Rome's museums and monuments and meet us in Corfu later in the month. Monique, always eager for local educational experiences, felt it would be a shame to miss the Italian capital with its plethora of cultural treasures.

Ian's mood, temperamental at best, turned gloomy at this sudden change of plans but he bit his tongue and remained silent. The next morning, as we drove away after dropping Trev and Monique off at a busy intersection, I tried to distract the downcast scouser.

"Look at the bright side, man," I said cheerfully. "With only three of us we can all sleep in the van."

Lode pushed the Kombi to a breathtaking fifty miles an hour and added, "Ya, and without their weight the bus runs better now. We'll arrive by nightfall if we don't stop too often." Ian's spirits elevated a little.

The afternoon found us outside Bari on the shores of the Adriatic when

Lode said, "Hey guys, do you hear the knocking from the motor?"

I concentrated on the clattering racket from the rear of the van and sighed, "Oh shit, man." I peered intently in the side mirror and asked Ian if he could spot any smoke from the engine. He climbed over the sleeping bags and assorted junk strewn on the back ledge and glanced behind us. "I can see faint, white exhaust."

Lode gave me a meaningful glance. "Do you think we'll make Corfu?" I could only shrug in reply as I thought through our route.

"Yeah, the road's pretty flat from here to Brindisi and as long as we keep the oil level topped up, we'll reach the island."

"And then what?" Ian returned from the nether regions of the bus and perched on the bench, peering between our shoulders at the bug-splattered windshield

"If we can get away with just replacing the piston rings and gaskets, the motor will last until we make Turkey."

Lode nodded slowly, "Ya, I agree. We'll need to borrow tools."

"Gerard gave me a contact in Corfu. He might be able to help."

We nursed the van the rest of the way to Brindisi stopping often to top up the oil level. South of Bari, I relieved Lode and took the wheel keeping below the speed limit, which in Italy, gets you curses, rude gestures and constant honking by every driver behind you. We limped into Brindisi well after midnight, *Little G.T.O* by Ronny & the Daytonas was on the cassette player and I wished I was driving one. With the music blasting to hide the worrying engine noises, we drove through deserted streets to the ferry terminal.

It had rained earlier but the sky had cleared and the air smelled wet and fresh. Puddles, in low spots on the road, reflected streetlights. I parked the van by the dark closed ticket booths. We'd be the first in line when they opened in the morning. We played rock, scissors and paper, Ian wisely declining to arm wrestle, to determine who got the choicest resting spots. I lost, curled up in my bag on the front seats and immediately fell into a dreamless sleep.

* * *

A brisk banging on the van's door startled us into waking. I wiped the condensation from the window and blinked at a uniformed man peering back at me. He grinned, gestured at the dazzling, illuminated ticket booth, now open for business and walked to the next car behind us.

The sky was still dark, an hour before dawn, but the ship sailed at six a.m. and loading commenced at four-thirty so we paid the fare and drove to the vehicle ramps. Following the directions of gesticulating crewmembers, we boarded the ferry through a gaping side hatch, parked, grabbed some gear and ascended to the restaurant on the main deck. We ate a hot breakfast, washed down with espresso shots, after which, buzzing from the caffeine, we leaned on the promenade deck's railing and watched the awakening port as our vessel slowly navigated out of the congested harbor. The sun rose from the sea straight in front of us, painting the sky in lavenders, pinks and bright orange. Soon after the glorious sunrise, Lode re-entered the salon leaving Ian and I alone.

We sat, in companionable silence on long life-jacket lockers lining the deck, watching the eternal march of the waves. A breeze blew from the ship's bow dispersing the smoke of our cigarettes. A small flock of noisy seagulls glided effortlessly over the wide, creamy wake, dipping down to inspect the frothy surface for edible floaters. Apropos of nothing, Ian gave me a searching look and asked, "What do you think of Monique?"

"She's cool, you know?"

"Is Trev serious about her?"

Now we're getting somewhere, I thought. "Seriously in lust, yes." I chuckled.

"Nah, you don't know Trev like I do. He isn't good at casual relationships, sort of thing. If Monique…No, when Monique splits, he'll take it hard." Ian shrugged with a forlorn sigh and stared at the heaving horizon.

"We talked about that Ian. Trev understands that drifting means you meet people, you hang out for a while and then you move on."

He shook his head and turned to face me, "He may know that, here," he pointed at his skull. "But he'll still hurt. A lot…"

His platinum hair whipped across his eyes as the breeze teased the strands. "Thing is, when Trev hurts, he self-destructs. He turns to drink, drugs. Back in London, it wasn't a big deal. He always came around, eventually. But here…" He opened his arms in a gesture indicating the entire world.

"Don't worry, Ian. If and when that happens, we'll keep an eye on him."

He smiled for the first time since Trev and Monique had left. The breeze strengthened and the temperature dropped as the ferry picked up speed. It would take eight hours to reach Corfu so we repaired to one of the ferry's salon to play cards. The large room, filled with tables, chairs and padded benches, was illuminated by tall windows offering an unimpeded panoramic view of the ship's bow and the Adriatic. I produced a well-used, dog-eared pack of cards and a unfolded a plastic crib board. We played rapid hands, inching our pegs to the finish line.

"Fifteen-two, fifteen-four, fifteen-six, a pair is eight and a run for eleven." Ian advanced his peg twelve holes farther towards the end.

"Hey cheater!" I moved his marker back a space while, unnoticed, positioned mine two extra spaces ahead. Later, I caught Ian cheating again, gave him shit and chuckled, as the small, unrepentant bastard missed me adding a few unearned points to my pegging.

By mid-afternoon, the Albanian coast loomed over the distant horizon. The mainland's craggy Ceraunian Mountains filled the skyline and the island of Corfu rose to starboard. The ferry, threading its way through the North Channel, dodged tiny, barren islands, little more than large rocks jutting from the water, and a flotilla of fishing boats before aiming straight at Kerkyra and the terminal. The Tanoy speakers requested that we return to our vehicles. Ian and I climbed down to the car deck and found Lode prostrate in the bus, passed out and snoring.

After an interminable time of the ferry lurching sideways like a drunken mule and loud bangs reverberating from the steel walls, the bay doors opened revealing a sun-drenched quay lined with cranes and warehouses.

I started the engine and, to my embarrassment, a vast, expanding cloud of white smoke exhausted from the back of the van, obscuring the cars in line behind us. A crewman, obviously familiar with hippie vans, reached for a fire extinguisher but with little finesse and lots of brute strength, I rammed the shifter into gear and drove off the boat. Red-faced, I accelerated away from the dock area and promptly got lost in a warren of narrow streets. Lode and

Ian recovered from their hysterical fits of laughter and, acting like eager dogs on a Sunday drive, stuck their heads out of the windows to enjoy the scenery.

Kerkyra was a beautiful, hilly, sunny town. Many of its buildings, painted blinding white with red tile roofs, glowed, shaded by eucalyptuses, palm, fig and lemon trees amid esplanades and small plazas. The streets down by the harbor were narrow and crowded with pedestrians who spilled from the sidewalks and crisscrossed through the choked traffic. A congestion of cars, trucks, buses and the odd donkey-cart crawled at a snail's pace while diesel smoke and vigorously honking horns added to the chaos. Kerkyra felt like home.

Lode and Ian behaved like kids, pointing out palm trees, cacti and skimpily dressed young females. I had to keep my eyes on the traffic, as the locals seemed to switch lanes or just stop their vehicles on a whim and without signaling.

I spotted a gas station a block away and maneuvered the van into the lot. I purchased a roadmap of Greece with an inset of Corfu and, as the attendant spoke a bit of English, I showed him the address of Gerard's friend so he could indicate, on the map, the best route. It turned out that Guy's place, north of a resort called Ipsos, was a mere twelve miles from Kerkyra. After topping up the oil reservoir, we travelled a narrow two-lane blacktop on the edge of turquoise waters fringed by yellow sand beaches.

At Ipsos, the road dipped toward the sea and ran along a kilometer-long stretch of sandy beach lined with a row of hotels, resorts, restaurants and tavernas. At the southern edge of the strip, a small harbor shaped like a fishhook jutted out into the bay. West of the line of buildings craggy, tree-covered mountains rose abruptly and, in spots, villas perched on the cliffs like Martin' nests. We drove past the beach and the highway continued along the coast. As instructed, I found and followed a gravel lane snaking up the side of a mountain.

* * *

Guy's commune was the first farm at the base of the towering heights. The farmhouse, a two-story, white building was flanked on either side by single storied additions, all roofed with the omnipresent Mediterranean red-tiles.

The left wing was a rundown, doorless, covered garage, sheltering a couple of vehicles and benches; the right was more substantial and appeared to be a shop. The juxtaposition of the structures created a central, shaded, graveled courtyard with half a dozen scrawny chickens strutting, clucking and pecking at the gravel. At the edge of the property, a large black dog slept under a majestic palm tree.

As we climbed down from the VW, a short, burly man with a wide smile splitting his craggy face came out of the house. Guy was five-feet-five tall, had a strong Gallic nose, bright blue eyes and a bushy nicotine-stained moustache.

"You must be Gerard's friend, Danny. He described you perfectly," he said in French. As he enfolded me in a tight embrace, I noticed his longish, sand-colored ponytail was graying. His overly large, powerful hands reached up to grip my shoulders so he could pull me down to bestow the traditional continental two-cheek kiss. I gently disentangled myself and introduced my buddies. More hugging and kissing accompanied Guy's greeting of, "Welcome to Ipsos commune. Come meet some of the others."

He led us to the building on the right of the house and pulled open a double-door. It was a large artisanal shop containing wooden workbenches, wall-mounted shelves, and pegboards holding an assortment of hand tools. Tall, dusty windows allowed sunlight to fill the workshop, dust motes sparkling and settling onto twig and string dream-catchers and fragile-looking mobiles dangling from the roof's open beams. Lengths of driftwood, large pieces of timber and assorted planks rested in the rafters above a wide round table in the center of the shop. Hand tools, spools of copper wire, jars full of Venetian glass beads and lengths of leather thong cluttered the tabletop amid boxes of odd-looking nails and bits of wood. Cat Steven's *Miles from Nowhere* issued from a cassette player on a nearby shelf while three people sat around the table working.

"Say hi to my wife Suzanne and to Brian and Mark." We shook hands and learned that all three came from the States.

Suzanne was a tall, willowy woman in her late twenties. Her beatific smile made her emerald-green eyes glitter and her freckled nose crinkle. A loose reddish-brown braid cascaded down her back, almost reaching the swell of her firm ass. Her wholesomeness reminded me of beach bunnies from the surfer movies. The two guys in their early twenties were college dropouts hiding in Corfu to escape the U.S. draft. They could have passed for brothers, six-feet-tall with slim but fit builds, long brown hair and hazel eyes. Brian and Mark were bending odd-looking nails with round-nosed pliers, curving the metal slivers into 'S' shapes.

"How do you know Gerard?" Suzanne asked.

"We worked in the same kibbutz." I sat next to Brian, reached over, grabbed a spike and scrutinized its odd shape.

"Horseshoe nails," Guy explained, giving us each a sample. The three-inch steel nails had a flat body tapering to a point at one end and flared to a square head at the other.

"We make jewelry with these and sell them to the tourists." He reached for a pendant consisting of six, multi-sized spikes bent so their pointy ends curved into loops. The nails, grouped together, were tied with a thin, shiny copper wire and resembled an inverted, six-pointed fleur-de-lis. A leather thong and a few colorful Venetian beads completed the necklace.

"We craft chokers, pendants, earrings..." Suzanne added pointing at the items strewn on the tabletop. Each piece was unique and striking; the combination of leather, steel, glass and copper giving it an organic look. We had never seen it's like in London or Amsterdam.

"Where do you get the nails from?" Ian asked, studying the pendant.

"We buy boxes of different sizes from a blacksmith store in Kerkyra," Guy said pointing at a dozen heavy-duty card-boxes on a nearby shelf. "The earring mounting hardware comes from a craft shop."

I held a shiny, chromed spike up to the light and asked, "What about these?"

"I send them to Italy to get dipped but I don't think we'll do it again because it's too expensive."

I watched Ian and Lode, who seemed as entranced as I was by the glittering baubles. "Would you teach us?" My companions nodded fervently and added 'please'.

Guy studied us for a moment and glanced at his wife who smiled and nodded her approval.

"You have to understand, there is more to this than just bending and tying nails together." He made an all-encompassing gesture and we understood he meant the whole commune. I didn't know where this was leading but nodded anyway. Ian gave me a discreet side-glance and I slightly hiked my shoulders in response.

"We'll teach you to make jewelry in exchange for your labor around the property. We all do chores."

Relieved that the conditions weren't going to be onerous, we loudly agreed and assured our new hosts that we'd gladly work for room, board and knowledge. We stepped out of the shop and unloaded the van. "I was afraid they were going to get religious on us," Lode said. "I have a cousin in a commune led by some kid Guru. It's not at all my cup of tea."

"Aw, I don't believe my friend would recommend a place like that," I assured them although, inwardly, I knew that with Gerard's wicked sense of humor anything was possible. "Anyway, the bus is grounded until it we can fix it. We need to rebuild the top-end and repair the clutch."

"Um… Do we want to spend that kind of money?" Lode asked.

I pondered his question. The van's international insurance and license plates expired in the fall at which time we had to get rid of the vehicle. Did it make sense to throw money into repairs or should we ditch the VW here and now?

I shrugged and offered, "How about this, we price the parts and then decide what to do. Fixing the clutch will cost very little, just gaskets and seals. I know a trick to refurbish it enough to last until fall." Lode and Ian agreed.

We emptied the minibus, shouldered our packs and entered the farmhouse. The Dutch-style double doors opened onto a tiled hallway that extended to the back of the house. On the right, a flight of stairs led to the second floor, the railing made of ornamental wrought iron. To our left, a bricked, archway opened into a roomy kitchen adjoining a dining and living room. Paintings and rustic weavings adorned the walls, interspersed with large windows. Dark wooden rafters accented the white-plastered ceilings and wide flagstones paved the floors.

The kitchen was redolent with the fragrance of herbs and spices. Onions, garlic and dark-red dried chili peppers hung in braids from the ceiling beams. A mixed collection of copper pots and pans dangled from hooks over a central island and an assortment of cans, spice canisters and jars ranged along the back of a U-shaped counter.

We followed Suzanne to the rear of the building and onto a wooden patio deck, which led to a one-story addition. The dormitory housed half a dozen double-bunk beds; a door at the far end led to the communal bathroom.

"This property belonged to the owners of a taverna," Suzanne said inviting us to enter. "Guy and the boys built this dormitory when we started the commune."

I threw my backpack on a bare mattress. "How many people live here?"

"Let's see… We have eight permanent members and we can put up ten guests. Brian and Mark, for example, stay in this dorm."

Ian sat on a bed and bounced lightly. "There are actually five of us. The other two, Trev and Monique, detoured to Rome but will meet us here in a couple of weeks, if you don't mind."

Suzanne tilted her head and gave him a calculating look. "That's cool. There's a ton of work needs doing."

Guy, Suzanne, and two other couples had started the commune in the mid-sixties. Suzanne's kid sister, Mary, Brian and Mark typified the transients who stayed for a while before drifting off. The farm offered shelter and sustenance to a variety of hippies, drifters and Freaks passing through Corfu in exchange for labor, stories and songs. The yard behind the farmhouse spread over a sloping acre of land enclosed by a five-foot tall boscage hedge of spiny bushes. A couple of goats grazed on weeds while ducks and three geese pecked at the ground around a bleached-wood rickety coop. A lush vegetable garden, surrounded by a chicken-wire fence, grew in the sun-drenched yard. I recognized the fern-like tops of carrots and saw Cannabis-looking plants, which Suzanne said were tomatoes.

To help finance the commune, its members made jewelry and other artisanal crafts sold on consignment at the Ipsos' tourist stores. The artisans would drive to Kerkyra or even as far as Athens, to sell at open-air markets and fairs during the summer.

The sun was setting behind the mountains, its last rays gilding the craggy peaks of the Albanian range across the bay. Other communards had returned and we ate a late supper of chicken, rice and veg, all grown mere feet from where we sat.

Mary, Suzanne's kid sister, was a cute, vivacious, nineteen-year old, who laughed a lot and immediately started flirting with Lode. The feelings were quite obviously mutual. Stan and Shirley, a couple of older Australian hippies nodded a welcome and focused on their food, following a macrobiotic regimen of chewing each mouthful fifty-two times. The other permanent residents were on the Mainland, Guy said, attending the first Artisanal fair in Sparta. They would return in a few days after their stock of jewelry and leather goods sold out. We drank wine and smoked pot until late. My last thought preceding sleep was, "What a great place to be stuck."

* * *

The next day, I walked over to the Kombi and joined Guy, who squatted on his heels and scratched the black dog's belly.

"Say hi to Ouzo," he said in French, nodding at the dog. I crouched and petted the mutt who licked my hand.

Guy grinned. "Ah, to be able to speak French again! Everyone else here is Anglo or German. I rescued Ouzo a couple of years ago. Some fucks on the resort strip fed him alcohol until he was" - he lifted his hand, thumb and forefinger almost touching and shook his head in disgust - "this far from dying. Now he knows better, he stays on the property."

"Guy, the bus needs some work. Do you have mechanic's tools I could use?"

"In here." I followed him into the doorless garage. An older-model, grey Ford van and a tiny, faded red Fiat 500 stood next to each other and a long wooden workbench supporting a vise and a toolbox leaned against the back wall. Guy slid open the toolbox's drawers, revealing an assortment of wrenches and screwdrivers. "What's wrong with your van?"

I explained the repairs I wanted to do, depending on availability and the cost of parts.

"Hmm," he said. "There's a German cars dealership in Kerkyra. They'll be able to get whatever you need. We're going to town later today. Come with us and check them out"

I pointed at the parked vehicles. "So what's the deal with these wheels?" Ouzo followed us into the shed, ambled to my side and nudged my hand.

Guy looked at the mutt with genuine fondness. "You made a new friend. He doesn't come near most people." He patted the hood of the van saying, "The Ford is our main transport. It runs but needs maintenance. The Fiat was abandoned by an American who stayed here for a while last year. I couldn't start the car and I'm not sure what's wrong."

"I'll gladly take a gander and I'll also check out the Ford."

"I was hoping you would. None of us are really good with cars," he admitted ruefully.

* * *

I started on the Ford by changing its oil, cleaning the spark plugs and performing some basic maintenance. After I finished, Brian, Guy and I hopped into it and drove to Kerkyra. As we passed by the kilometer-long strip of businesses along the Ipsos beach, Guy differentiated, for me, the tourist traps from the genuine Greek tavernas. "They serve the best octopus at Bouzouki's." He pointed at a sprawling restaurant fronted by a luxuriant vine-covered pergola. "And next door in the taverna they have a wonderful retsina wine."

We climbed above the tiny Ipsos harbor and soon reached the outskirts of Kerkyra. Guy dropped me off at the German Auto dealership, a single-story building surrounded by new and used vehicles, near the city center. I entered the showroom and walked towards the parts counter where a middle-aged Greek wearing khaki pants and a golf shirt perched on a tall stool in front of a fiche reader.

The parts man was efficient, helpful and spoke excellent English. From a three-ring binder, he extracted a clear, plastic page containing what looked like large strips of negatives, positioned the sheet so that the imbedded microfilm fit the reader's carriage and turned on the ultra-modern microfiche reader. Those Germans; always on the forefront of technology!

He swiveled the monitor to show me an exploded view of a VW engine. "It sounds like the piston rings are worn off so you'll need a top-end gasket set and you also want a clutch housing seal." The lot came to just under twenty bucks, a price I thought quite reasonable, so I nodded my agreement and handed him a twenty-dollar bill. He disappeared amid the floor-to-ceiling shelves occupying the back of the shop and filled the order.

From there I strolled down the narrow, quaint streets to the sun-drenched quays of the harbor, enjoying the open-air markets with fragrant stalls selling an interesting variety of freshly caught fish and crustaceans.

Kerkyra was a picturesque, busy town that reminded me a lot of Haifa. Near the waterfront, I spied the Ford van parked in front of a tall building housing a chandlery and hardware store. I entered the shop and found Guy and Brian wandering among the aisles, filling a shopping basket with crafting supplies.

"We use a special kind of tool to bend nails," Guy said. He led me to a wall-mounted pegboard displaying numerous kinds of implements. He grabbed smallish, round-nosed pliers and pointed out the smoothness of the cone-shaped nose.

"Always use smooth-nose. The regular types have grooves for better grip but they'll mark the nails and ruin the finish." I tried different-sized pliers some with rubber-coated handles, others just plain steel and chose a set that fit comfortably in my big paws. I also picked out a couple for Lode and Ian.

After shopping, we returned to Ipsos in time for lunch. As we drove along the sandy strip, the sheer number of people on the beach surprised me. It seemed that glistening sunbathers and equally well-oiled ball game players covered every inch of the golden beach. Frisbees soared gracefully over the sun worshippers while gaily-painted kites rose and fell chased by curious seagulls. Just offshore, a flotilla of ski boats zoomed between paddleboats and small, single-mast dinghies.

Guy explained that Ipsos was one of the most popular resort areas on Corfu, offering not only a mile of sandy beach and a protected bay for water sports, but also a frenetic nightlife with clubs, bars and discos. The resort's popularity supported the surrounding farms, including the commune, by ensuring brisk sales of their wares and providing steady employment in the hospitality industry.

Back at the house, I found Lode and Ian in the shop bending nails under Mark's guidance. I gave them the new pliers and they in turn showed me how to mark and bend the tough metal spikes. Although the work was simple, creating eye-catching pendants required skilled planning. The nails needed two bends of the sharp point to make a complete loop. I was surprised at how much brute force it took to bend the little buggers. No wonder Guy had arms and hands like a gorilla.

"Do you also shape the nails?" I asked Suzanne.

"Nope," she said, her cheeks dimpling adorably. "That's the men's job. I'm the Artiste. I bind them with copper wire and attach the leather thongs." I continued bending nails but also noted what Suzanne was doing. Any brute could bend nails but, if I wanted to succeed at jewelry making, I needed to master composition and artistry. We carried on with our tasks until supper and I don't think my hands had ever been that sore. After the simple meal, Guy took pity on Ian and me and had us wash dishes while the rest of the group worked in the yard and garden.

"This is a peaceful place," Ian said. "Do you think Trev and Monique will be able to find us?"

"No worries, man. Trev has the address and there's a bus from Kerkyra about ten times a day."

"The jewelry we're making is fantastic. I bet we sell as much as we can make."

"I'm sure you're right, Ian. I've never seen anything like it on the streets. We'll stockpile a bunch to take with us when we move on."

"How long do we stay here, then?"

I shrugged with a deep sigh, "Well, I don't know about you but I'm almost broke... again. We need to earn at least couple of hundred bucks each to make it to India."

He nodded. "I think we're all in the same boat."

"So, between repairing the van's engine and waiting for Trev, we'll be here till the end of the month?"

He calculated for a moment while stacking the squeaky-clean plates in a cupboard and agreed with my assessment.

With a plan solidly in place, Lode and I started dismantling the VW's engine after completing our chores. We worked late into the night and fell into bed exhausted.

* * *

The next week passed quickly as we settled into a pleasant routine. We did chores in the mornings; taking turns tending the garden and the coops and, in the afternoons bent nails. Evenings, we worked on the vehicles.

After dismantling the Volkswagen motor and inspecting the oily cylinders, I said, "We're lucky the walls aren't scored too deep." The piston rings were loose and allowed an excessive amount of oil to pass through and burn. We replaced the worn parts installed new gaskets and buttoned up the motor. We then removed and dismantled the clutch assembly and I showed Lode how to refurbish the friction plates using a trick I learned in the kibbutz. I ignited the discs' oily surface with a torch and burned off the imbedded, glazed deposits thus restoring their rough surfaces.

"It is only a stop-gap measure that will do for two, maybe three thousand miles at the most. After that we'll dump the bus," I said as we re-assembled the unit.

After our careful ministrations, we drove the van to Kerkyra and the VW felt like a new vehicle. The engine ran clean and strong without smoking, the Kombi climbing hills as deftly as a goat on bennies and the clutch never slipped once. To celebrate we invited the commune gang for drinks at a taverna. As the sun set over the glittering bay, nine of us strolled down the lane and along the row of hotels.

An exuberant crowd of people loitered on the strip before heading to the various tavernas and clubs. The evening was warm and the fragrance of blossoming flowers mingled with the heady, charged energy of the revelers.

We entered the taverna Guy suggested and drank excellent (once you got past the after-burn taste of paint stripper) retsina accompanied by platters of delicious fried calamari and salad. A raucous crowd filled the club; Greek music blared from speakers vying with the loud racket of voices and clattering crockery and glassware.

A group of people clustered in a back corner, cheered lustily as two red-faced men struggled in an arm-wrestling match. I glanced at Lode who smiled and with a nod, indicated he was game. We sauntered over and joined the spectators gathered around the table. Lode, Trev and I had often successfully challenged local he-men as we traversed Germany, Switzerland and Italy because it was a fast way for us to earn gas money.

We studied the two men and noted that neither seemed to use any technique other than plain muscle power. The burly man on the left snorted and, with a sudden show of strength, flattened his opponent's arm to the table. The crowd cheered while the winner scooped the money and the loser stood up and departed.

I slid into the vacant chair and gave the fellow across the table my best innocent weakling look. My opponent was in his early thirties, had a powerful, muscled neck and big upper arms. He smirked as he noted my long hair, hirsute face and skinny, ropey arms.

He slapped a C-note on the tabletop. "One hundred Drachmas, hippie."

I nodded amiably, fished out a bill that I placed atop his and extended my right arm with my elbow firmly planted on the wooden surface. My opponent made a show of rolling his neck, rotating his shoulders and flexing his fingers. He reached for my hand, grasped it firmly and counted aloud to three. He applied all his strength in an attempt to shove my arm down and, with his powerful grip, forced my arm to within an inch of the tabletop. I countered by swiveling my palm, forcing his fingers to loosen their grip. I levered his arm back to vertical never looking away from his blood-shot eyes and using my shoulders for added strength, crushed his fist onto the table. I thanked him and collected the two C-notes.

With my newfound wealth and in the spirit of communal living, I bought and shared too many bottles of retsina.

* * *

I awoke the next morning lying on the beach, gritty sand in my mouth and ears and the rising sun painfully piercing my eyelids. From behind boulders marking the end of the sandy strip and the harbor's breakwater, a rhythmic wet slapping noise was loud enough to keep me from passing out again. I had a pounding headache and my tongue tasted like turpentine mixed with chicken shit. Fucking retsina! I crawled to the water's edge, rinsed my face and mouth with seawater and rolled a smoke of Drum tobacco. Somewhat refreshed my curiosity peaked: What the hell was that peculiar noise?

I managed to navigate the boulders and on the other side, I saw a short, middle-aged Greek, wearing an apron over a striped shirt and dirty, white pants. He was bashing a grey-brown, rubbery something against a rock. Upon closer inspection, I recognized tentacles and realized it was an octopus. Two buckets, brimming with limp octopuses, sat on the sand by the rocks.

The man grinned toothily and dropped the boneless creature into one of the pails. He greeted me in Greek and fired a few sentences, which sounded like, well, Greek to me. I shrugged my shoulders and held my hands palm up in the universal sign, "I have no idea what you are saying. I am an idiot," I tried

English and French, neither of which he spoke, but he mimed smoking so I tossed him the pouch of tobacco and the lighter. He rolled himself a cigarette and lobbed my gear (now slimy and smelling of fish) back.

I pointed at the buckets, lifted my eyebrows asking what he was doing to the poor things and he replied by making exaggerated chewing motions and grimacing as if eating rubber. I gathered he was tenderizing the cephalopods by repeatedly smashing them against the boulder. Live and learn, I thought as I waved and turned to go.

This early in the morning, only a few eager tourists swam in the cool sea and the resorts' workers were in the process of laying rows of chaises longue and green umbrellas on the beach. I walked at the very edge of the lapping wavelets where the wet sand offered solid footing and began the trip back to the commune.

A welcome light breeze from the sea cooled me as the fierce sun rose above the Albanian mountains across the strait. I trudged up the road and Ouzo met me at the commune's boundary. He poked my hand with his snout, I scratched behind his ears and we entered the house.

Suzanne smirked as I stepped into the kitchen and shook her head at my bedraggled appearance. A delicious aroma of sautéed onions rose from a sizzling frying pan. "Well, well. Tied one on last night?"

"Argh…" I grunted too parched to speak.

She pointed at a tall coffee maker burbling away on the counter. I filled a mug and swallowed half in one burning gulp. Eyes tearing, I gestured at Suzanne with an empty cup, she nodded and I filled it, topped mine and carried both to the counter. My stomach rumbled. I searched for quick edibles and picked up a glass jar full of a light brown, smooth paste. "What is this?" I asked.

"You mean you've never had peanut butter? Try some." She handed me a spoon. It had the texture of thick Tahini, a sesame seed paste that we used at home to make sauces, but was slightly sweet, salty and peanutty. My tongue was stuck to the roof of my mouth but I tried to convey my enjoyment.

Suzanne laughed, delighted at my reaction. "Usually we make peanut butter and jam sandwiches, most people don't just eat it straight like that. It's a particularly American delicacy. Guy says you speak French fluently. Are you from France?"

"No, I'm from Israel where I lived in a kibbutz in the Galilee. My parents are French and we lived in Paris when I was younger."

"Oh, I read a lot about the kibbutz. What was it like?"

I took a swig of coffee while marshaling my thoughts. "It's similar to your commune, only on a much bigger scale and many of the settlements are located along the borders. For instance, my kibbutz, Tel Galil, abuts the old Syrian border, at the foot of the Golan Heights. After the Six-Day War, we, like our neighbors, used some of the no-man's-land as a pasture for our cattle. Unfortunately, not all the land mines planted by both countries over the years have been dug out and, occasionally, we'd hear the distinct crack of an explosion reverberate from the surrounding hills. It usually meant that one of our cows stepped on an old mine and the next day we'd see vultures gliding on thermals above the carcass."

Suzanne, her eyes wide in disbelief said, "Oh, you're making this up,"

I assured her I wasn't. In fact I had played down some of the hazards we experienced living on the border, such as having to armor our tractors because of Fedayeen sniper fire and spending successive nights in bomb shelters when rockets peppered the settlements.

"Your kibbutz sounds so, frontier-like."

Our serious conversation ended as Lode, Mary and Ian, who looked worse than I felt, staggered in from the bunkhouse and slumped on the chairs around the dining room table. "How did I end up on the beach last night?" I asked; they had the decency to look guilty.

"Man, we were so loaded. You wandered off and we thought that maybe you found yourself a chick. We came back here and crashed hard. Sorry," Ian answered. Lucky for him the other residents took their places and the conversation turned to the day's schedule of chores.

We ate a hearty breakfast and I was rejuvenated enough to tackle the inert engine of the diminutive Fiat 500. I connected jumper cables from the Ford and tried to jumpstart the car but the only response was a repeated clicking from the starter solenoid indicating it was fucked. I killed the rest of the day doing routine tasks in a zombielike, brain-on-automatic manner.

After supper, Ian was sitting on the back porch of the house puffing away on a hand-rolled cigarette. I joined him gazing at the myriad of twinkling stars above the darkened bay. The evening was calm and peaceful; the sweet aroma of freshly cut grass mixed with subtle fragrances from the garden while the cloudless sky formed a black velvet showcase for the entire galaxy. Faint snatches of music and laughter drifted up from the resort strip while around us, frogs croaked and cicadas clicked. "You know, a guy could get used to living here. A corner of paradise on Earth; perhaps this is as far as we need to go. What do you think Danny?"

"Tempting, man. Make jewelry and work part-time in one of the tavernas," I replied, but I knew that ultimately, even this Eden would pale over time and I'd want to move on.

* * *

Another two weeks in these pleasant surroundings passed rapidly. The weather remained idyllic, every day was sunny and warm with a clear blue sky; I was losing track of the days.

I finished repairing the Fiat; it now started every time and ran well. The Ford Transit seemed to have a new lease on life and our VW drove without burning oil. When not busy with the vehicles or other chores, I spent hours bending horseshoe nails and amassed a diverse collection of necklaces, pendants and earrings. Suzanne gave us a three-by-three-foot mat made of shiny, deep-blue silk on which to display the jewelry.

On a Sunday, we climbed in the Ford and drove to Kerkyra. Guy took us to the esplanade leading to the Old Fort where tour buses dropped groups of tourists throughout the day. A score of stalls selling souvenirs, crafts, ice cream and beverages lined the edge of the wide-open plaza and a small colony of artists painted scenic pictures of the fort. We strolled by the row of vendors, looking at the wares the artisans had to offer, everything from leather belts, hand woven scarves and ponchos, to wood-and-seashells wind chimes. Ian, Lode, Mary and I pooled our jewelry and spread the lot on the bright blue cloth. Guy thankfully left us a couple of beach umbrellas to ward off the merciless sun before driving away.

Lode sat under an umbrella to one side of the mat and unpacked his tools, loose nails, leather thongs and a spool of copper wire. Ian and I, sitting cross-legged under the second umbrella, played our instruments to attract potential buyers. Big air-conditioned buses pulled up to the plaza and disgorged clots of passengers. The tourists, herded by slick guides wearing dark sunglasses, meandered through the Old Fort with its unique architecture and then returned to the esplanade for a shopping break before continuing on their tours.

A group of thirty Americans, by their accents, strolled down the line of vendors pawing at and commenting on the merchandise. A dozen people arrived at our display and formed a semi-circle around the glittering jewelry as Lode, trying to impress, renewed his efforts bending nails, grunting with the strain. The shoppers seemed interested in the shiny baubles but no one was buying.

Mary, wearing white shorts and a bright yellow halter-top, nimbly inserted herself among the tour group moving forward until her sandals touched the edge of the blue mat. She meticulously examined the baubles and squeaked breathlessly, "Oh my God! Those are perfect for Aunt Lisa." She held a necklace and peered at the tiny price tag. "I can't believe how cheap it is here! I think I'll get a couple."

"Excuse me," one of the women interrupted her. "We were first, young lady."

"Er... I'm so sorry, of course. Please, you go." Mary relinquished the necklace, backed away through the crowd, winked at us and walked towards a stall selling cold drinks.

The dam broke and the tourists, paying in American dollars, jostled each other in order to buy the "best" pieces, virtually cleaning us out. When they left to board the waiting buses, we sat in stunned silence. Paradise indeed!

Guy came to collect us and laughed when we told him of our success. He said, "We call it seagull sales. The tour groups, like a flock of seagulls, land, make a lot of noise, flap their arms, shit all over everything and everyone and then fuck off."

Back at the commune, no one wanted to cook and, as we had done so well selling our jewelry, Suzanne suggested we celebrate by going out for supper. With high spirits, we walked down to the restaurant strip in and followed Guy to Bouzoukis, a sprawling white building surrounded by a veranda and vine-covered pergolas.

He ordered a classic island meal: Greek salad, a large appetizer platter with meatballs, spanakopita and calamari and a main course consisting of braised octopus with vegetables. The food was delicious, the retsina delicately turpentined and the octopus melted in the mouth. As we demolished the meal, the chef came out of the kitchen, greeted Guy and Suzanne and winked at me. Delighted, I recognized the octopus-basher from the beach.

* * *

Trev and Monique arrived the following week grinning like fools and sporting dark tans. We introduced them to the commune's inhabitants and helped them settle their gear in the bunkhouse. They'd had a wonderful time in Rome and took turns regaling us with their adventures. I glanced at Ian from the corner of my eyes and was relieved to see him relaxed, raptly listening to Trev's stories.

Later I dragged Trev to the van and told him about the work we'd done on the engine and clutch.

"Wow! Good job. Hitchhiking is fun but doesn't come close to having our own wheels."

"For sure. After we dump the bus we'll still be facing a lot of miles before we get to India."

"I'm guessing you're not thinking on settling here, then?"

"Obviously you talked to Ian. He loves this place. As tempting as this place is, I still want to follow Iskandar's journey and he started from the east side of Greece. What about you?"

"I'm with you. Monique wants to visit Istanbul. Have you asked Lode? He seems comfortable here, wink-wink, nudge-nudge, know what I mean?"

"Mary is a nice girl and I'm not sure what he'll decide but knowing him he'll make up his mind at the last minute."

"So, when do you want to head out?"

"How about the end of the month? It gives us enough time to stockpile a bunch of jewelry to sell in Athens. We should be there at the beginning of July."

We told Guy and Suzanne that we'd be leaving soon so they offered us a tour around the island and a picnic on a beach located on the west side of Corfu. The next morning, we piled into both vans and followed twisty, scenic byways up and down the central mountains. Groves of olive trees covered the hills abutting the roads. Guy said that when the olives ripened, October to November, so many fell on the pavement and were squished by passing vehicles that an oil slick developed and driving became a major hazard.

We drove through Paleokastritsa, a renowned village and resort area; a famous beauty spot consisting of six stunning beaches, numerous hotels, and countless tavernas. From there we travelled south following the coast stopping at points of interest. We swam in the sea and had our picnic in a sheltered cove, a satisfying end to a day of sightseeing.

The rest of our time in the commune, we bent nails and made enough jewelry to ensure rich pickings. During the day, we did our chores and spruced up the commune's buildings and in the evenings we'd either sit around a bonfire playing music, goof off in the backyard or pub-crawl along the strip. Trev and Monique would often disappear returning with sand in their hair, I guessed they'd found a secluded spot, hidden amid the boulders on the beach.

The day of our departure, we loaded the van, strapped all five backpacks on the roof rack, Ian and Lode deciding to continue the journey with us, and profusely thanked our hosts.

"You know you're always welcome here," Guy told me as we hugged. "I'll write Gerard and tell him you were here."

"Thanks for everything Guy," I said, truly grateful for all he and his family had done. "And thanks especially for showing us how to make horse-shoe nail jewelry." Suzanne kissed each of us in turn and assured me that Mary, after moping for a few days, would get over Lode's departure.

We drove away from the Ipsos commune, waving madly through the open windows, and returned to the ferry terminal in Kerkyra. The crossing from Corfu to Igoumenitsa on the mainland was a short hop and by afternoon we were in the Peloponnese and stopped at Patras. The next day we pushed on, crossed the Corinth canal and reached Athens by late afternoon.

* * *

Chapter Seven

Ode to a Grecian Earn

Athens and Ios: July 1972

In Context:

-Prime Minister of India Indira Gandhi and President of Pakistan Zulfikar Ali Bhutto sign the Simla Agreement. They resolve to peacefully negotiate future disputes, release prisoners of war and withdraw their military forces behind their own sides of the four-hundred-sixty-mile long border.

-The Watergate burglars receive the first payment of "hush money" to keep them from implicating the White House in the break-in of DNC headquarters.

-Palestinian author and spokesman Ghassan Kanafani is assassinated in Beirut, by a bomb in his car. It is believed to have been arranged by Israeli forces in retaliation for the Lod Airport massacre.

-Paul McCartney & Wings tour for the first time.

-The British House of Commons narrowly approves the United Kingdom's entry into the European Economic Community.

-A herd of stampeding elephants kills twenty-four people in Chandka Forest India.

-The Soviet space probe Venera 8 lands on the planet Venus. The satellite transmits data for fifty minutes before shutting down due to extreme temperature and atmospheric pressure.

-Actress Jane Fonda posed for photographs at a North Vietnamese anti-aircraft gun at Hanoi. Pictures of the actress, gazing through the gun sight of a weapon used to shoot down American planes during the ongoing Vietnam War, ran worldwide.

* * *

We reached the outskirts of Athens during the late afternoon rush hour and inched our way across the teeming city. A brown haze hovered over the metropolis magnifying the sun's stifling heat. The air was a pungent mixture of car exhaust, hot pavement and fried food; horns vied with loud, smoky mufflers to create pandemonium.

We parked the van at the Plaka, the old Turkish Quarter, nestled below the Acropolis and stretched our cramped legs by strolling through the crowded neighborhood. Monique, drawn to the street artists lining the sidewalk, tilted her head to better contemplate a painting of the Parthenon. Ian said, "We should find a youth hostel for the night."

Lode pulled out his dog-eared Michelin guide, a faded yellow, tattered paperback and found a listing located in the Omonia quarter. "There's a warning about Omonia: A seedy neighborhood full of druggies, prostitutes and thieves."

Trev quipped, "Groovy, man. Our kind of place." We chuckled in agreement.

The hostel was located on Athinas Street, off Omonia square and had enough vacancies to accommodate us. The hotel, three-storied and narrow, was sandwiched between a bric-a-brac shop and a run-down taverna fronted by a tattered, sun-faded, green awning shading the sidewalk frontage. A dozen low round tables and short rattan stools squatted on the impromptu patio under the canopy.

After checking in and dropping our gear in the dorm, we repaired to the taverna and sat with our backs leaning against the warm brick wall. We ordered meze, which consisted of small dishes of grilled octopus, chopped salads, sliced hard-boiled eggs, bowls of assorted olives and a variety of cheeses. Served with warm garlic-bread pitas and a glazed ceramic jug of retsina wine, meze was the perfect meal for the stifling Mediterranean evening. The relentless sun finally sank below the surrounding hills, the traffic noise calmed to a susurrus and a warm breeze wafted through the hot dusty streets carrying hints of brine from the sea.

Trev and Ian fetched their instruments and we started playing a few Dylan tunes, enticing travelers returning after a day of sightseeing and Greek passersby, to sit and order jugs of wine. The taverna's lights, bare, colored bulbs strung at the edge of the awning, came on. Looking up, I noticed a mass of spiders, from tiny to palm-size, feeding on each other and on flying insects attracted by the lights, thriving on the underside of the canopy. I wisely didn't comment on the arachnids above our heads to keep my friends from possibly, freaking out but I did move my chair farther out.

Backpackers staying at the hostel wandered down to the bar and regaled us with stories about the different Greek Islands: the over-exploited ones to avoid, the tourist traps and the few remaining drifter-friendly oases. Most Freaks agreed that Ios was one of the nicest locations to visit; it was the least developed, had beautiful beaches and offered little attraction for tourists due to lack of amenities and a small village reachable only on foot or by donkey.

The following day we planned to take in the sights, check for mail and choose locations for our sales operation. Just a tad inebriated, we loudly said our goodnights and went into the hostel and bed.

* * *

We headed for Syntagma Square and the American Express office to check for mail. Between Syntagma and the Greek Parliament building, we watched the Changing of the Guard ceremony at the Tomb of the Unknown Soldier. The Presidential Guards marched with solemn precision, the spectacle marred only by the uniforms worn by the fierce-looking armed soldiers: black-tasseled red beanies, bright white full-sleeved dresses with short gathered skirts, beige tights and black pompoms on red shoes.

At Amex, the clerk handed Lode and I letters from home and Monique a care package from her mom. At a café near the King George Hotel, we read our mail. Monique examined the battered box, peeled the brown paper wrapping and lifted the lid to reveal clothes and two dozen, mostly intact, homemade cookies.

Lode grabbed a cookie from Monique's parcel and ate it with undisguised relish. With a full mouth he mumbled, "Where should we sell our jewelry?"

Monique finished reading the letter from home and suggested, "The Parthenon? We'll hit most of the tour buses." We debated setting up at the Theater of Dionysus, the Areopagus and the Tower of the Winds in the Roman Agora. We also contemplated the Arch of Hadrian and the Temple of

Olympian Zeus, all notorious tourist destinations. In the end, we chose the Acropolis.

Following a tour group through the magnificent ruins eavesdropping on the guide's narration, we reached a vantage point on the towering hill with a spectacular view of the city sprawling below us. Trev and Monique wandered among the street vendors lining the esplanade to evaluate their merchandise; meanwhile Ian, Lode and I spread out our colorful display mat and covered it with jewelry. Rubbing his hands and chortling, like Fagin in Oliver Twist, Trev returned and said, "No one sells horse-shoe nails, we'll make a killing."

Monique wore her 'best' clothes and acted as our shill, mingling with potential buyers. Trev, Ian and I sat to one side of the jewelry mat and sang popular tunes, starting with the Beatles' version of *The Hippy Hippy Shake*, drawing people to our display.

Lode, on the other side of the mat, had a handful of nails, tools and spools of copper wire on a leather apron draped over his knees and he bent spikes to make more pendants. The pitiless sun, pounding on the ancient bricks of the esplanade, reflected rays of light from our metal jewelry adding glitter and glitz to the display.

To lure an approaching group of German tourists, we switched to Geoff Stephens' *Winchester Cathedral,* a tune very popular in Germany that summer, while Lode answered questions about making our unique product. Monique performed admirably nudging hesitant buyers and loudly praising our artisanship and low prices. With most of our merchandise sold, we returned to the Hostel. Our faces and arms sunburned red, suffering from dehydration and heat exhaustion, we invaded the taverna's inviting patio.

Trev inhaled the first cold beer, burped loudly and said, "I was chatting with the Swede Freaks, sort of thing. You know the couple selling leather goods? Only they're on the way back from Turkey and told me that in Istanbul they were almost thrown in jail when they tried to sell their stuff."

"Holy shit! Were they trying to flog their wares in a mosque?"

"Not at all. They set up among the regulars, but in Turkey you have to be permitted."

"Did they try to get one?"

"Yeah, but they couldn't because they entered Turkey as tourists. The only other option is to let a permitted vendor in the bazaar take your stuff on consignment."

We paused to digest the disconcerting news. We'd hoped to make and sell our baubles as far along our journey as possible. Leaving our jewelry with a local merchant was out of the question. Monique summed it up. "We'll just have to sell everything before we cross the border."

I finished my beer, gestured at the waiter for another round and said, "The problem is that staying in Athens is too expensive." Everyone nodded. "Why don't we go to one of the islands where we can camp on the beach and use up the rest of our nails to make as many pieces as possible? Then we'll return here and sell everything in two or three days and carry on to Istanbul?"

The gang liked the idea and we fell into friendly bickering about which island we should visit. Ian, Lode and I voted for Ios while Monique and Trev preferred the rich history and numerous ruins of Crete. In the end Trev and Monique decided to detour through Crete before joining us in Ios. Trev didn't seem too enthusiastic at the prospect of gallivanting all over Crete to see Daedalus' famed labyrinth, home of the Minotaur and the myriad of other ruins, several of which were just piles of old rocks. Served him right I thought bemused; speaking of bulls led by the nose...

We could not take the van to Ios but luckily, Panayiotis, the taverna's owner, offered to let us park the Kombi behind the restaurant, between a rusted dumpster and a sagging brick wall, where it would be safe until our return.

The five of us left on a bright sunny morning and took a bus to Piraeus where we caught our separate ferries to the islands. Trev and Monique boarded a large, modern ferry heading straight to Heraklion, Crete, while Lode, Ian and I climbed aboard a much smaller ship doing the milk run between the mainland, Serifos and Ios.

* * *

We lounged on wooden lockers lining the upper deck of the ferry. Ian looked around and commented, "You notice there are no fucking flies for a change?" Lode nodded and said, "Hey, you're right. What a relief." They were alluding to the curse of the Mediterranean: the ubiquitous houseflies, which seemed to appear magically out of thin air as soon as we sat still for more than a few minutes. The persistent bugs had bedeviled us since we hit Greece.

The ferry's passengers mostly consisted of islander merchants standing guard over boxes or bales of goods so a quartet of blond, twenty something females sitting by their backpacks drew us inexorably. They could have passed for sisters, sharing the same alabaster skin, ash-blond hair and striking blue or green eyes.

Tall, svelte Kirsten explained, in excellent English, that most Scandinavians preferred to spend their summer vacations soaking up the rays in the Cyclades islands and taking advantage of the ultra-low cost of living. Co-workers in a Copenhagen bank, she and her three companions Annika, Dagmar and Maja travelled like a flock of delicate exotic birds to Ios in an annual migration to spend the summer months basking on the sunny beaches.

The trip passed pleasantly with the girls for company and by mid-afternoon after a stop at Serifos, one of the many small islets scattered over the Aegean Sea, the ship sailed into a bay on the northwestern side of a barren-seeming, hilly island. We lined the rails eagerly as we approached our destination. The village of Chora, perched in a saddle between two low summits overlooking the sea, glistened and sparkled as whitewashed houses and windows reflected the bright afternoon sun. Blue painted domes added a cool splash of color to the brilliance.

Kirsten pointed at and expounded about landmarks as the ferry made its slow approach before finally docking at the only pier long enough to accommodate its modest size. The port of Ios, at the head of Ormos harbor, consisted of a handful of short piers jutting from a curving road lined by sheds, warehouses, stores and a sleepy taverna. The buildings followed the curve of the bay before running out of flat ground at the foot of the hills that rose from the sea and loomed stark brown against the pure blue sky. Black birds, gliding on thermals, circled high above the island. A spotted, emaciated dog sniffed the base of a bollard before lifting his leg and pissing on it.

Half a dozen unshaven men wearing once-white clothes loitered on the dock ready to catch the mooring lines. Somnolent donkeys, flicking their long ears and rhythmically swishing their tails like hairy metronomes, had two-wheeled cargo carts hitched to their swaybacks and waited at the end of the pier.

We disembarked onto the pier's flagstones, shouldered our backpacks and, with Kirsten and her mates leading the way, climbed the steep rocky trail up the hill. After twenty minutes of steady ascent, we reached Chora; a picturesque settlement of bright whitewashed, two-story houses with flat roofs or blue domes connected by sculptured streets, covered alleys and flagstone-paved courtyards.

Kirsten, hardly winded, smiled and said, "You'll soon learn to appreciate flat ground. In Ios, you're always either climbing up or down."

Ian wiped his sweaty brow and asked, "Are there any other sizeable villages on the island?"

"No, the Chora is the only one. There are a few tiny hamlets - four houses and a church - like Theodoti and Kalamos. We camp on the beach in Mylopotas, where all the regulars hang out."

"Sounds cool. Is there somewhere we can leave a message for a couple of friends?"

"Yes, at Theo's place." Kirsten led us through the village to a long, low building overlooking the sea. The taverna and general store stood between the village's blacksmith and a shaded courtyard strewn with half a dozen wooden picnic tables and benches. The sharp fragrance of pines mixed with the scent of flowers, coffee and hints of pot. Two young men, seated among a group, played guitars and sang a Cat Stevens tune.

We dropped our backpacks against the wall by the store's open brightly painted blue doors and followed the girls through a bead curtain. Theo's was refreshingly cool and dark after the bright, hot, sunny streets. A serving counter ran the length of the left wall, two tables set end to end occupied the uneven flagstone floor in the center of the room and shelves loaded with a bewildering assortment of goods lined the right side. Ropes of garlic, dried herbs, sausages and hard cheeses hung from the ceiling rafters and an ancient Coke machine anchored one end of the counter.

Kirsten pointed at a large corkboard covered in messages, envelopes and pictures hanging on the wall between two windows. I ripped half a page from my notebook, wrote, "Trev/Monique we're at Mylopotas Beach" and pinned it on the board.

The girls bellied up to the counter and introduced us to Theo, a stocky middle-aged Greek with longish brown, curly hair and fading, Mediterranean good looks. He smiled revealing bright white teeth, shook hands with us and leaned over to kiss the four girls on the cheeks. "Kirsten, my love. Welcome back to Ios. Will you work for me again this summer?"

"Down at the Mylopotas store?"

"Yes. I'll come down in a couple of days and we'll get you started?"

We purchased and drank well-chilled soft drinks and headed down a steep path snaking downhill from the village to the hamlet of Mylopotas. A dozen stone houses, a small church and Theo's beach store nestled around a square at the bottom of the trail. To our left, the beautiful sandy beach arced south, terminating at the foot of a tall escarpment.

Inland, a valley, cleaved by a meandering, stony wadi and dotted with farms, ran eastwards before fading out in the far hills. Low stones fences enclosed sparse pastures in which goats sheltered under olive trees. A donkey nearby started braying and distant dogs barked in response. Our steps crunched on the crushed rock as we walked through the square toward the beach. Annika pointed at a small concrete basin at the foot of a rusty hand-pump and said, "Drinking water's in the square and there are showers behind Theo's."

Mylopotas was a breathtaking, kilometer-long, sandy arc curving inland between two hilly promontories. We followed a narrow trail at the edge of the beach past tents and makeshift shelters huddling in the lee of scrawny, twisted pine trees. Kirsten pointed at the far end of the bay where a steep hill, covered with boulders and crisscrossed by a network of white dusty paths, rose from the sea. "Drifters live in caves and shelters on the slope. I stayed in one for a while a couple of years ago but they're cramped and dirty and you risk life and limb climbing in the dark."

We walked past the last group of tents and picked a spot to pitch our camp. After the trek down from the Chora, the warm soft sand leant welcome relief to our aching feet. The girls deftly erected one-person, nylon tents while Lode, Ian and I foraged for driftwood. With the necessities taken care of, we sat on the beach admiring the vivid bands of orange, yellow and purple painting the sky as the sun set over the northern promontory. Without looking away from the show Lode said, "Tomorrow I'll scrounge for tarps and lumber. We'll build a decent shelter so we can work in the shade."

Ian looked wistfully at his stash pouch, empty of drugs and containing only a pack of zigzags. "I'd like to scrounge something to smoke."

"You mean kief, yes? The guys in the caves usually have pot or hash but for now, catch." Annika smiled, reached into her shoulder bag and tossed Ian a flat tin.

"Right on, man!" He rolled a joint, lit it and passed it around the circle. He unpacked his flute, I grabbed my harp and we launched into Long John Baldry's *Boogie Woogie*. The clear beautiful voices of Kirsten and Dagmar provided an appealing counterpoint to Lode's braying. Our singing, and the smell of kief drifting in the air, attracted two couples from Germany, who brought wineskins of retsina as admission.

As evening turned to night, we lit a bonfire that beckoned most of the Freaks camping on the beach. They joined us, in ones and twos, bringing food, booze, firewood and drugs. At the height of the impromptu party, twenty or more sat around the crackling fire and our band had grown to include two guitars, a mandolin and a number of real or improvised percussion instruments.

Our first day on Ios ended with us pleasantly stoned and buzzing on wine. I vaguely remember stretching my bare feet towards the fire pit stones, falling into a deep sleep to the sound of waves kissing the sand.

* * *

I woke up in the morning with sand in my hair and reeking of wood smoke and old wine, so I stripped and waded into the calm sea until I could no longer feel the bottom. The water temperature was perfect, cool enough to clear the cobwebs and just right to enjoy drifting on my back like a log. Splashing nearby startled me and I rolled as I spied a pale form gliding under me. Kirsten surfaced blowing bubbles and shook her long platinum hair from her eyes. She too was naked. Her small, pert tits bobbing with the waves and I was able to confirm she was a true blonde. She giggled at my sudden intake of breath and quick hiding of my hard-on and we swam back to the beach.

She skipped to her towel and she briskly dried her hair saying, "Chora has a wonderful bakery. If we get there early enough we can buy fresh raisin bread."

We both dressed, me trying to hide my visible sign of attraction and her trying hard not to look. Once in the village Kirsten led us through narrow twisting lanes and up sets of stairs to a small esplanade bordered by a church and a couple of stores. A dozen people stood in line in front of the bakery and we managed to score one of the last loaves of piping hot white bread peppered with sweet raisins.

"The tradition on the beach is not to share with lazybones," Kirsten said tearing a crusty end from the loaf. "Anyone who wants raisin bread has to get off their ass and score in person." I would have granted my approval of this sensible tradition but I was too busy stuffing my face.

We meandered through the village, sat under a café's vine-covered pergola and ate our loaf with tiny cups of strong Greek coffee. The early morning was still pleasantly cool and the shade trees towering over us hosted small twittering birds flitting between the branches and our feet, picking crumbs we threw on the ground.

Kirsten talked about her work at the bank in Copenhagen and living with her parents while attending marine biology night classes. The job paid for her university education and for these once-a-year trips to the Greek islands. I told her about my background and my desire to follow Iskandar's journey, which indirectly brought me to Ios.

"I considered spending a summer in a kibbutz," Kristen said. Since the Cyclades are getting increasingly crowded, working in Israel sounds attractive. In a couple or three years, even Ios will be spoiled." She raised her arms encompassing our surroundings. "This is happening all over the Aegean… Hotels, resorts, bars and souvenir shops popping up like mushrooms after a rain. Can you imagine Mylopotas covered with acres of sun-bathers, the beach crowded with volleyball players, Frisbees flying everywhere, the bay buzzing with ski-boats and every islander working in the tourist trade?"

"Yeah, we spent time in Ipsos on Corfu and I witnessed what over-crowding did to a beautiful spot. There are three and a half billion people on this planet and I want to see the good parts before it all goes for shit."

"Where would you like to go after India?"

I tore into a piece of bread and chewed thoughtfully. "The Americas, North and South. I'll get a work visa for either Canada or the U.S. and have a home base in one of those countries, a place I can travel to and from for the next few years."

Kirsten asked, "Why the Americas? I mean, why not south-east Asia or

Africa?"

"I've been to West Africa when I visited my dad who works in the Ivory Coast. I would like to visit Thailand and Bali someday; however, the Americas have a special attraction. Have you ever been obsessed by a particular tune or a melody?"

She thought for a moment and nodded, "Yes. If a song is evocative or fits the mood, I'm in."

"Uh huh, evocative is the right word. When I first listened to Ravi Shankar's music, the sounds of sitar and tambalas stuck in my head and I knew I had to go to India. The same thing happened when I heard the Zampona pan flute in Simon and Garfunkel's *El Condor Pasa*. Those two pieces of music gave me direction. In my head the songs are playing, pulling me towards them and the cultures that spawned them."

I softly whistled the opening bars of *El Condor Pasa* and Kristen sang the opening lyrics. We finished the song and without a word headed down the hill.

* * *

On the way back to the beach, I spotted a pile of planks and wooden poles lying at the bottom of a ravine below the Chora. When I pointed at the lumber, Kirsten explained, "Garbage from a construction site. I've seen workers use these for scaffolding. What a mess, those assholes!"

At our camp, I told Lode and Ian about the discarded poles and we clambered up the stony ravine to fetch a dozen, three-inch thick, ten-foot lengths and a few faded grey planks.

"I'll go scrounge for stuff to cover the walls," Ian said and walked towards the hamlet.

We dumped our haul in the sand, Lode fished out a roll of twine from his pack and I helped him erect a sturdy lean-to frame that we covered with planks. Ian returned with empty cardboard boxes and bits of plastic sheeting, which we dismantled and attached to the sides of the shelter.

Lode circled the lean-to and examined it with a critical eye. "Not a bad start but nobody sneeze."

A bronzed, bare-chested guy with a pronounced Spanish accent said, "I know where there's a big tarp nearby." He grinned and offered his hand. "I'm Carlos, I live in those caves." He pointed halfway up the path-riddled hill at the end of the beach.

Ian shook his hand and said, "Yeah, I remember you. You're the chap from Venezuela and you played the guitar last night." Carlos nodded and they fell into a discussion about the finer points of Jethro Tull tune as they headed inland to retrieve the tarp.

Kirsten and I hiked up to Theo's beach store. The single-story, white stone building was narrow, dark and cool and resembled his shop up in the Chora. An antique cash register sat on a counter flanked by baskets of bread and pastries. An open wooden cask held black Kalamata olives floating in wine vinegar and chunks of assorted feta cheeses swam in a white pail below hanging sausages and dried herbs. The feta, skotiri and Niotiko kefalotyri cheeses smelled and tasted of the diverse aromatic herbs and flowers dotting Ios' hills.

Greek music blared from a transistor radio by the register. An opened door led to the backyard where tables and chairs sat under shade trees; a plywood shack housed showers and a couple of toilets. A water tap poked out of the shack's wall, above a concrete trough that drained into a ditch behind the property.

Kirsten waved at the store and said, "This is where I'll work for Theo, make a few drachmas and score leftovers."

"Lots of people camp down here during the season?"

"Oh yes! Hundreds, more and more every year."

When I returned to our campsite Lode and I unpacked our jewelry-making paraphernalia, cleared a spot under the lean-to and spent a few hours bending horseshoe nails. He bent over his workings and said, "I'm looking forward to Istanbul. All this…" He waved at the beach, the campsites and the surrounding hills. "It's great and a lot of fun but still, sort of familiar. You know what I mean?"

"I think I do, man. Even though Ios is radically different from France and Holland, it's… civilized, yes?"

"Exactly! Not very exotic. I'm hopping Istanbul will be more, um, eastern?"

We were bending nails at a good clip as we chatted about our expectations and I reflected on how adept we'd become at creating the unique jewelry.

I glanced at my companion. "Did you decide where you're going after Istanbul?"

"Ya, I'd like to continue east with you guys but I'm a bit worried about money." I held up a cross-shaped pendant I'd just finished binding with copper wire. "This jewelry should help."

"For sure, if we keep an eye on our spending."

"True. We spend money like drunken sailors in a whorehouse."

He nodded and we continued in companionable silence for a while.

"A propos of nothing, have you ever done mescaline? One of the Germans we met yesterday has mesc for sale. I've never dropped mescaline, what's the trip like?" I asked.

Excited at the prospect, Lode replied, "Ya! Mesc is like acid's big brother, way better trip. Let's buy some." I guessed that despite his concerns, spending money on drugs was okay.

By early evening, Ian and Carlos returned carrying a long, cylindrical, orange bundle on their shoulders, which unfolded into a twelve-by-twelve-foot heavy plastic tarp with brass eyelets spaced evenly along the edges. Delighted at the find I said, "God I hope you didn't steal this! People will see it all the way from the mainland."

Carlos laughed and replied, "Don't worry. The tarp is a loan from a farmer I know. We'll return it when you guys leave." Lode circled the large orange sheet muttering in Dutch and directed us to plant another four poles in front of the lean-to. We spread the tarp, secured it with twine and staked the bottom edges in the sand. It formed a remarkably spacious pavilion with an enclosed section at the back that could easily accommodate half a dozen sleepers and their gear.

The Danish girls returned from swimming, their skin a shade of medium rare pink and admired the carrot-hued shelter. They said they were starving. When they invited us to go to the village for lamb kebabs, we packed our tools, donned sandals and followed their luscious bikini-clad behinds up the incline. We sat outside, ate our fill and drank enough retsina to make going home in the dark a precarious endeavor.

By the time we got back to the beach, someone had already started the fire and there were a few beachniks lolling nearby. The bonfire was fully stoked and burning when Kirsten grabbed my hand and said, "C'mon Danny, let's go for a walk."To the sounds of hoots and catcalls, we ran down the beach to a secluded spot.

Her pale body shimmered like an alabaster statue in the silvery light from the half moon. I untied her bikini top and bottom, slowly lowering her to the soft sand, still warm from the day. My own clothing disappeared in an instant. I kissed her working my way down from her welcoming lips, to her hard tight nipples to her belly. She was moaning quietly, her breath quickening while I licked and nibbled the inside of her thighs and she gasped loudly when my questing tongue finally found her sweet spot.

Suddenly, she grabb ed my hair and yanked my head up. Thrusting her hips forward and using her legs, she levered me onto my back. Wow, I was fucking a Valkyrie. As she mounted me, her face tilted toward the sky, the moonlight bathing her with eerie light. I was so entranced with Kirsten's ethereal visage that I kept watching her until, forced by our mutual orgasms, I closed my eyes and grunted. We screwed, barely resting between bouts, until dawn painted the sky and our sweat-moistened bodies with orange and pink highlights. We fell into a stupor, cuddled like spoons.

When we were dressing before heading uphill to score a loaf of raisin bread, she admitted she'd had her eye on me since we met on the ferry. When I asked why, she said that I looked Mediterranean and mysterious, a surprise box she needed to open.

The next few days were idyllically repetitious: A refreshing swim early in the morning followed by fresh raisin bread and cups of strong Greek coffee. Kirsten worked at the store from mid-day until dark and fed us well on unsold leftover kebabs and day-old pitas. Lode, Ian and I bent nails and strung jewelry and napped during the hottest hours of the afternoon We met the girls for supper and spent the evenings at our campsite or at our neighbors' campfires; smoking, drinking and playing music. Kristen and I held hands, casting longing glances at each other until the sexual tension was unbearable. We'd leave the group, run to *our* spot, fuck like bunnies and return to the party.

Ian was conspicuous by his absence at night. He would typically show up after breakfast in time to help with the jewelry making, and reply, when asked where he was, that he crashed with the cave dwellers, refusing to risk his life negotiating the steep goat trails in the dark.

On one of those evening, Lode, Annika, Kirsten and I slipped away from the communal fire and walked to the south end of Mylopotas. The western sky showed the last wisps of sunset reds. A gibbous moon was rising over the island casting shadows among the rocks at the edge of the beach and short pine trees growing on the littoral edge, leaned away from the sea, spindly branches resembling tortured limbs.

We found a sheltered spot at the foot of the craggy hill and sat on the warm sand amid bleached driftwood logs. I passed the mescaline around and we chased the little white pills with swigs of retsina from Lode's wineskin.

The trip started much like acid with a gradual ramping up of feel-good-everything-is-hilarious phase, soon followed by enhanced hallucinatory visions. Every object I scrutinized took on a shimmery, faceted appearance and glittered in wonderful vivid colors. I was able to examine things and see the smallest details. I remember playing with a washed-out, white shell, amazed at the wealth of details on its corrugated surface. I stared at the shell until my vision narrowed like a microscope; I could see the shell down to its atoms.

At the peak of our trips, we drifted away from each other. Alone, I watched the moon and the stars wheeling over me. As I lay down at the edge of the sea, I sensed hissing wavelets traveling along my legs, whispering to me in an alien language. I followed a small crab scuttling among the wrack looking for food, its eyestalks waving and winking at me as if we shared illicit knowledge. I sat and stared at crooked pine trees, seemingly alive when brushed by the offshore winds.

Dawn lighting the eastern hills, I trudged toward our campsite but the sand was sucking at my feet slowing me and trying to pull me down. I finally made it to the lean-to and collapsed on my sleeping bag. I closed my eyes and tried to sleep but I was still too fucked up from the psychedelics so, I just lay there humming and hallucinating until Morpheus (really, the actual God) claimed me.

* * *

Trev and Monique arrived mid-morning a week later. They admired our camp and shelter, which by then had sprouted primitive looking decorations made of interesting driftwood, twisted pine branches and seashells of various shapes and colors. We proudly showed them the hundreds of bent nails we'd stockpiled, awaiting final assembly to become marketable necklaces, earrings and pendants. Ian greeted them both warmly but was subdued and not really listening as they babbled about Crete and the ruins they'd visited, the large Freak community living in caves at Matala, the warm hospitality of the local Greeks and the friendly tavernas where native musicians diverted them with Greek folk music.

We spent four days working together, binding the nails with coils of fine copper wire and stringing them on leather thongs and earring clips until we used up all of raw material. I made an elaborate Maltese cross pendant and gave it to Kirsten as a memento of our friendship.

The night before we left Ios, we invited everyone living in and around Mylopotas to our campsite and had a farewell party. We gathered driftwood all afternoon and built a huge fire on the beach. There were over a hundred people, even Ian and his cave buddies, cavorting around the bonfire which burnt so brightly, I'm sure seafarers, as far away as Mykonos, mistook it for the Naxos lighthouse.

I spent the last night on Ios with my little Danish mermaid and will forever cherish the memories of her wonderful vivacity, intelligence and generosity. I gave her my parent's phone number and urged her to call if she decided to try kibbutz life.

We packed and dismantled our camp early the next morning. Those of our friends who were awake wished us luck and staggered away. Kristen and Annika hugged us all and made us promise to call them if we were ever in Denmark. With monumental hangovers and a touch of sadness, we boarded the ferry and sailed across the sea back to Athens.

* * *

We had traded the pristine, quiet, uncomplicated pace of the islands for Athens' bustling crowds, incessant traffic noise, smog and the stench of car exhausts. Athenians and tourists dashed everywhere, pushing, shoving, shouting and spitting. The chaos kept us tense until we reached the hostel in Omonia. We found our Kombi covered in a thick sheen of grey dust speckled with black smog particles, sitting askew because of two flat tires but still safe behind the taverna.

We checked into the hostel, stashed our gear and headed out to wash the van and pump the tires. For the next three days, we worked the crowds at Athens' most famous ruins, moving from one temple to another, selling jewelry to tourists. Carefully husbanding our money, we only ate from street vendors in the Plaka, Monastiraki, the market district in Psiri, and Kolonaki. We sold practically our entire stock of horseshoe nails jewelry and presented the last few pieces to our friends at the taverna.

At last, we could leave Europe. We loaded our gear, secured the backpacks on the roof and drove out of Athens on the E-seventy-five heading northeast to Turkey and into the sunrise.

The distance to Istanbul was about seven hundred miles of mountainous, twisty, narrow two-lane roads with unceasing traffic. We saw heart-wrenchingly beautiful scenic landscapes, our enjoyment occasionally interrupted by terrifying encounters with buses, trucks or livestock materializing around blind, hairpin turns. We slept in a grove outside Thessalonica and the next day crossed the border near Ipsala.

The crossing into Turkey was a slow and excruciating ordeal as the van's papers were in English and Dutch, which, of course, none of the guards could read. We found an English-speaking Turk and thus started a three-way Abbot and Costello routine as we explained how a Dutch-owned vehicle had a temporary UK registration, international insurance, an EEC yellow transit license plate and was driven by French and Dutch nationals.

Gesturing, shouting and waving papers, the guards allowed us across the border only to stop us ten feet further, steering us to a customs shed in which dour-faced, fiercely mustachioed, uniformed officials searched every inch of the bus. They tossed all our belongings, including the benches' cushions, onto the oil-stained concrete floor and had us empty our backpacks on long steel-clad tables where an inspector pawed through our possessions.

Monique's skimpy underwear was quite popular, passing from one set of official hands to the next. Two other guards, wearing vests with NARKOTIK written large on the back and leading a big, drug-sniffing Doberman, swarmed over the van. They even used mirrors on extended stalks to investigate under the chassis. I fervently prayed that we hadn't left any roaches on the floor or that when Trev rolled the last of our pot back in Thessalonica, none had fallen between the cushions. The Turkish narks did not find illegal substances and reluctantly gave up tossing our belongings. They pointed to the crap from the van still sitting on the floor and using exaggerated gestures mimed, "Pick up that shit and get the hell out." So we did.

* * *

Chapter Eight

We Earn our Hash Marks

Turkey, August to September 1972

In Context:

- Sixty-five people are killed in Pakistan when a passenger train from Karachi to Rawalpindi crashes into the back of a parked freight train at the Liaquatpur railway station.
- The last American ground combat units are pulled out of South Vietnam.
- The 1972 Summer Olympics open in Munich, West Germany. During the second week of the games, members of the Palestinian terrorist group, Black September, kill two Israeli athletes during the kidnapping of nine others of the Israeli team from the Olympic village. The next day, following a botched rescue attempt by the German police, Black September murders all nine of their captives. The police kill five of the terrorists.
- Bobby Fischer of the United States wins the World Chess Championship defeating defending champion Boris Spassky of the Soviet Union. It ends twenty-four years of Russian domination.
- Prime Minister Indira Gandhi instructs scientists at the Bhabha Atomic Research Centre to manufacture India's first nuclear bomb.
- Moody Blues release "Nights in White Satin".
- M*A*S*H premieres on NBC television network.
- In retaliation for the killing of Israeli Olympic athletes, Israel's air force bombs Palestinian strongholds in Syria and Lebanon.

* * *

We followed the highway along the Sea of Marmara and reached the western outskirts of Istanbul as the sun set behind us. Istanbul, famed gateway to Asia, was everything we had hoped for and imagined. A multitude of tall, spiky minarets, spires and squat domes jutted out above a sea of disparate structures interspersed with palaces, museums, churches and mosques. The narrow, crowded streets, hemmed in by ancient four and five-story buildings adorned with ancient stone arches and carvings, had constricted worn sidewalks in front of the businesses, restaurants and apartments.

Garishly colored billboards, posters and business signs, written in a familiar alphabet, displayed incomprehensible words containing umlauts and other strange diacritical marks. Laundry hung from balconies like multicolored, fluttering pennants and pigeons flitted between spindly TV antennas that leaned at random above the roofs. Pedestrians weaved through the slow traffic as overburdened trucks, buses and cars honked their horns at an endless stream of nimble two-wheeled vehicles, scooters and bicycles.

I stifled a shout as I observed a toddler, wearing nothing more than a frayed tee shirt, totter between two carts at the edge of the curb and take a hesitant step into the busy street in front of an oncoming bus. A brown arm, bangles dangling at the wrist, casually reached over from behind a cart and pulled the infant back to safety just as the juggernaut blew by. A man on a bicycle, one hand balancing a large, woven-reed tray of bread on his head, pedaled past us with a manic grin on his face. Merchants stood in front of their stores keeping a watchful eye on a bewildering assortment of goods that overflowed onto the sidewalk. Burqa-wearing women sailed through the crowd like black galleons parting the waves while men with jet-black moustaches, wearing shabby suit jackets over baggy pants with enormous inseams, stared at us impassively as our vehicle crawled in the traffic.

Istanbul sprawls on both sides of the Bosphorous, a strait linking the Sea of Marmara to the Black Sea, and bridges Europe and Asia. Every Freak we'd met had mentioned the Lale Restaurant, better known as the Pudding Shop, a legendary meeting place located in the Sultanahmet neighborhood in an area called the Golden Horn in the European side of the city; the start of the Hippie Trail,

Divan Yolu, a broad boulevard lined with parks, mosques and ancient buildings, led into the ancient quarter of Sultanahmet, home of the Blue Mosque, Hagia Sophia, Topkapi and other historical sites. Crooked cobblestone alleys branched off the street offering tantalizing glimpses of courtyards, workshops and modest stores tucked away from the commotion of the main thoroughfare. As in Italy and Greece, it seemed that drivers indiscriminately used their horns. Like symphonic conductors, cops whistled shrilly and gestured with an elegant simplicity of motion as they moved traffic through congested intersections.

We drove passed a large bazaar and an intoxicating olfactory mixture of spices, fruits and fried foods with acrid hints of manure and piss, assaulted our noses. As night fell, peddlers packed their goods on carts and shop owners moved their wares from the sidewalk back into the stores, preparing to close for the day. Strings of lit bulbs outlined the spires and minarets of the larger monuments.

The Pudding Shop was an unimposing single-story building with an attached garden. Longhaired Freaks loitering in front of the doors disturbed the busy flow of pedestrians and confirmed we'd arrived at the right spot. We parked at the Hippodrome among a score of brightly painted VW, Ford and Bedford vans from all over Europe. Two incongruous London double-decker buses with "Katmandu" placards, loomed over the smaller vehicles.

Ian pointed at the double-deckers and said, "Magic Bus tours! London to Katmandu via Teheran, Kabul and New Delhi. I know a guy who traveled that way in 1968."

We crossed Divan Yolu, shouldered our way through the loafers and entered the Pudding Shop. The small place, packed with drifters, was fragrant with the delicious aroma of chicken and cinnamon, an entrée called Tavuk göğsü that was one of the puddings that gave the restaurant its nickname. Layers of messages, envelopes, bus schedules and photos of smiling people (singly and in groups) buried a notice board on the wall. The adjoining garden offered a view of Hagia Sophia and the Blue Mosque, their domes illuminated by spotlights. We squeezed around a table close to a foursome playing *House of the Rising Sun* on guitars and tambourines. Ian assembled his flute and joined the band while Trev, sounding just like Eric Burdon, sang the lyrics.

I met Alain, a Frenchman wearing an ornately decorated sleeveless vest over a cotton-embroidered shirt, baggy pants and an abundance of beads, attire we'd see often as we travelled eastwards. We chatted in French and he recommended the nearby Hotel Güngör saying it was affordable and relatively clean.

After the meal, replete and tired, we mulled over our options for the night. Ian and I volunteered to guard the VW by sleeping in it while the other three would check into the hotel. We would alternate every few days to allow everyone access to the hotel's showers. Mindful of Istanbul's notorious thieves, we removed all our possessions from the roof rack and stowed most of the gear inside the bus. Ian and I accompanied our friends to the Güngör hotel where they sprung for dorm rooms. The third-floor dormitory held a score of two-tiered bunk beds and reeked of garlic, dirty socks and unwashed bodies. A dim naked bulb dangled from the ceiling, providing enough illumination to reveal a room crammed with sleepers and their baggage.

* * *

The next morning I awoke rested and eager to explore Istanbul. My heart skipped as the full realization sunk in that I was poised on the edge of Asia. From here on, I would follow Alexander's route along the western Turkish shores, which Herodotus called the 'Persian Royal Road', to Iran, Afghanistan, Balochistan and, finally, India. I strolled to the hotel carrying a towel and soap and ran up the stairs to the third floor. The shitter, of the alaturka or squat type, was the first challenge we faced and this particular example was nothing more than a two-foot long, oval ceramic plate with two raised footprints on either side of a hole. These squat shitters were the norm from Istanbul to India, ranging from luxury models with a built-in flush system to disgusting common public toilets which were little more than covered cesspits.

Washed, dressed and ready for a day of sightseeing, I repaired to the Pudding Shop for breakfast where I found Lode and Ian sitting in the garden.

I joined the pair. "Trev and Monique still in bed?"

Lode, flipping the pages of an old Time magazine answered, "They were getting up when I came down."

They'd ordered breakfast and one of the Çolpan brothers, the restaurant owners, set down two heaping plates and gave me an inquisitive glance. I asked for eggs, caught myself in time before saying "bacon" and called for bread instead.

Lode smirked and said, "You almost asked for bacon, didn't you? Ian wanted ham!"

Ian shrugged. "It never occurred to me…"

"Welcome to Islam, man. From here on, forget about pork."

Trevor joined us as I was mopping up the last of the eggs with a chunk of delicious, fresh white bread. "Monique will come down in a few minutes. Be warned, she's in a mood, sort of thing."

Ian smiled at him. "Not delighted with the amenities?"

Trev glared at him in annoyance. "That and some other things…" He waved at İdris Çolpan who came over and took his order for breakfast.

I sat back from the table and told my friends, "I learned something interesting from Alain last night. First, he warned me about getting visas for Pakistan and India. We'd best get them here because the Indian embassy in Teheran won't issue them." I searched their faces and they nodded in understanding. "Second, and more disturbing," I continued, "apparently Iran, Pakistan and India implemented a new policy about backpackers traveling overland. We have to show we carry sufficient funds before they'll let us in the country or they'll refuse us entry."

Lode slammed his palm on the tabletop, rattling the glasses and the cutlery. "Fuck! How much do we need? What bullshit. Did he say how they're getting around these new rules?"

I hesitated for a moment, nodded and answering in a quieter voice, I said, "Alain said you just have to demonstrate that you have money. He had a hundred bucks. Some of the Freaks run a scam on Amex. It works like this…" I glanced up as Monique approached our booth. Trev squeezed against Ian and made room for her.

"What about Amex?" She asked with a frown.

I repeated my news and continued, "What we do is go to the Amex office and report the loss of our Travelers Cheques or claim they were stolen. They will replace them after which we only use the new cheques. We stash the old ones and produce both sets at border crossings. That way, we'll always have money to show. Voila!"

Lode seemed dubious. "And this works?"

"Alain said the guards only want to ensure we're not broke. They don't actually check serial numbers."

Ian shook his head in admiration. "Smart! We should do this while we still have a goodly amount in Traveler Cheques."

Back at the kibbutz, Gerard explained how unscrupulous moneychangers throughout Asia would buy un-endorsed Amex Cheques for half their face value. I chose not to relate this bit of info to my friends until, and only if, we found ourselves desperate.

* * *

The next few days were leisurely and we saw little of each other. One afternoon, I encountered a forlorn looking Trevor hanging about outside the hotel. The tall Scouser's head hung down, his shoulders drooping as if under burden. "Monique won't go any further east. She wants to go home."

I invited him to join me for a snack and we walked through a twisting, narrow alley to a tiny Muhallebi (desserts) shop. I ordered two helpings of their delicious Asure pudding and, sitting at a low table, we ate the delectable treats. Istanbul was a stoner's paradise. Small shops selling various delicacies ranging from pastries to Loukoums (Turkish delights) were everywhere, ideal for satisfying dope-induced munchies.

I smiled sympathetically at Trev and said, "You knew this day would come. She said she didn't want to go to India. That's life on the road, man; People come and go."

He thought about what I'd said for a moment and nodded. "Yeah, you're right."

I glanced at him and asked, "So, what are you going to do?"

"I'm not sure. On the one hand, India seems so far from here, like the other side of the world. On the other hand, at the bazaar, I touched carpets from Kurdistan and Persia and I could smell the fragrance of exotic spices and incense from Pakistan and India. There were even horse saddles from Afghanistan."

"So now India seems closer, more real?"

In London, Amsterdam or even as recently as Athens, whenever we talked about India, the long journey had seemed more like an ephemeral concept than an actual destination. Here, on the other hand, we could feel, touch and taste Asia and India had become more real and reachable. Trev squared his shoulders and grinned. "I'm going all the way. Someone's got to keep an eye on you wankers!"

I punched his arm lightly and returned the smile. "Is Monique taking one of the Magic Buses?" I asked, referring to the Hippie transports that deadheaded back to London or Amsterdam and offered reduced rates to travelers heading west.

"Yeah, I'll help her choose the right one, you know, someone reliable."

Trev returned to the hotel and I ambled to the Lale restaurant where I found Lode just back from visiting the Topkapi palace and museum complex, a wonderful hilly site on Seraglio Point overlooking the Golden Horn. I'd explored Topkapi soon after arriving in Istanbul and loved the museum and its treasures. It was everything I'd imagined after seeing Peter Ustinov and Melina Mercouri in the wonderful heist movie of the same name. I told Lode about Monique's plans to return to France. He shook his head. "Aw, poor Trev." His sunburned, ruddy face creased in concern causing his bushy red moustache to droop towards his beard.

"Where's Ian?" I asked. Neither of us had seen him since breakfast.

"He said he was going to the Turkish bath." Many of the westerners we'd met had recommended that we try the hamam (Turkish bath) while we're in Istanbul.

* * *

We spent the next week traipsing throughout the Golden Horn, visiting mosques, palaces, museums and beautiful gardens. We also drove to the Iranian, Indian and Pakistani embassies to get visas. One hot, sunny afternoon, sweaty from hiking through the Gülhane Park, Lode and I accompanied Ian to the Çemberlitas hamam. Some of Istanbul's greatest monuments surrounded the hamam including the Atik Pasha Mosque and, to my great amusement, the tomb of Ali Baba. The bath's entrance was at the bottom of a flight of well-worn stone steps. The entryway was cool, dark and reeked strongly of mildew overlaid by chlorine and industrial soap. A corridor, lined with marble and smooth flagstones, led to the domed dressing room areas in the men's section. Elegantly decorated arches supported finely carved columns holding the domes; a patina of antiquity imbued the whole complex.

Ian strode with an assured pace, waved at the attendants and acted with a familiarity denoting frequent visits. So this is where he'd been hanging out, I thought. I knew that Ian prized cleanliness, a fact that we mercilessly teased him about.

We relaxed in a large, vaulted bath section, letting the hot water turn our muscles to jelly and used the adjoining washing stalls to scrub the embedded dirt from our pores. Ian suggested we take massages pointing at a bevy of muscled, young Turks idling at one end of the chamber. Lode and I declined and returned to the locker room while Ian and a massager disappeared down a side corridor. We left the baths and, cleaner than ever before, headed back to the hotel.

* * *

I found Monique seated in the Pudding Shop's yard staring at minarets jutting above neighboring rooflines. The setting sun adorned the mosque's many domes in fiery shades of orange and pink. I sat across the picnic table from her and said, "Hello, Mademoiselle. Any luck finding transportation?" Since announcing that she was returning to France, the winsome woman had seemed somewhat distant.

She looked fondly at me and replied, "Oui. One of the buses is leaving for London the day after tomorrow. I'll catch a ride until Calais. You know, I envy you. The sights and the experiences you will have."

"Come with us Monique. Think of all the art, monuments and ruins you'll be missing."

"You're sweet to ask Danny, but this is as far as I want to go. I'm homesick and miss France. The months I've spent with you guys have been quite the experience and I learned much about myself. Remember when I joined you in Calais? I was conflicted and uncertain about my future. Now I feel more centered and ready to settle down."

"I can't really blame you, I said. "I suspect our journey will be a lot rougher after we lose the van. We're gonna have to hitchhike, walk and ride buses or trains.

"Can I ask for a favor? Since you're always writing in your diary, send me a postcard once in a while. I'll give you an address." She jotted the information in my notebook and I promised to keep in touch.

The morning of Monique's departure, the five of us had a last breakfast together and helped stow her backpack in a mostly empty, twenty-passenger bus parked at the nearby Hippodrome. Trev strove to act casual but I noticed him glancing sadly at his girlfriend and he seemed to have a lump in his throat. Monique hugged and kissed each of us leaving Trev for last. Finally, with moist eyes, she climbed aboard and the maroon bus disappeared down the boulevard. Trev said, "I'm going to get shit-faced. Who's with me?"

We bought two bottles of Arrack and a chunk of hash. The rest of the day was spent smoking and drinking on the ancient, mostly deserted, crenellated battlements below Topkapi while looking at the hectic marine traffic on the Sea of Marmara and trying not to fall off the wall.

The next morning, bleary-eyed and painfully hung-over, we planned the next stage of our trip. I ticked off visas and replacement Amex Cheques on my mental list and spread the van's papers on the table. Ian pointed at the bundle of documents and asked, "How much longer can we use the van, man?"

"A month and a half. Insurance and registration expire October tenth. We have to… um, dispose of the bus by that date."

Lode studied a map of Asia Minor, measuring distances with his fingers. "We could easily reach Iran or maybe even Afghanistan."

Trev cleared his throat. "Best we dump the VW in Turkey. I bet if we call Yusuf and Mehmet they can help us make it disappear."

I nodded and said, "Good plan, man. If we just abandon the vehicle somewhere, it might be traced back and bite Irish in the ass." I glanced at Trev who acquiesced. "Also, the bus is on its last legs and if it breaks down in the deserts east of Teheran we'd be seriously fucked."

Ian pointed at the map. "Well then, let's drive as far as Izmir. Shall we head out first thing tomorrow?" There were no objections and we dispersed to nurse our headaches and pack our gear. I drove the Kombi to a nearby gas station and checked fluids, tire pressures and topped up the tank. I haggled with the attendant for a road map of Turkey and we settled for half of the original price plus my tattered European road atlas. We spent our last evening in Istanbul in the Pudding Shop's garden amid a throng of travelers; surrounded by minarets, domes and the affecting skyline of the Golden Horn glimmering in the setting sun.

* * *

Izmir, (once called Smyrna), dating back almost nine thousand years is one of the oldest settlements in the Mediterranean. Located on the western coast of the Anatolia peninsula, Izmir is about four hundred miles from Istanbul but you could shave sixty miles from that distance by taking a ferry from Yenikapi on the south shore of the Golden Horn to Yalova on the Asian mainland across the Sea of Marmara.

The boat ferried a ragtag collection of trucks, buses, cars, bikes, scooters, bicycles, donkeys, mules and the characteristic dolmuş (pronounced "dohl-moosh"), which are shared taxis traveling between cities. The word dolmuş literally meant "stuffed to the brim" in Turkish and aptly described them. We saw an astonishing volume of livestock, cargo and people aboard each van. Many westerners told hair-raising tales of riding in these conveyances, commonly used from Turkey to India, and I believed those stories after narrowly avoiding several head-on collisions on the Turkish coastal roads as fully loaded dolmuşlar came around blind corners, unashamedly ignoring every rule of the road.

The road we followed, unlike the coastal highway, twisted across mountainous ranges and was technically challenging as it followed narrow valleys through a succession of small villages. We skirted the western shores of Lake Iznik; a vast body of water dotted with modest sailboats net fishing and passed patchworks of cultivated fields and small orchards that had changed little in centuries. Farmers used oxen, horses, donkeys and mules, working the land in the same manner as their ancestors. The Turkish backcountry looked medieval and the infrequent times we spotted another car – old and battered usually parked by the single village store – it seemed out of place. What traffic we encountered on the largely empty roads consisted, most often, of extravagantly decorated six-wheeled lorries, buses and, of course, speeding dolmuşlar.

To pass the time and to cheer Trev up, we played Name That Tune; someone would whistle or hum the opening bars of a number and we'd guess the title of the song and the artist. Trev, a veritable walking rock 'n roll encyclopedia, often showed off by also reciting the tune's release date and top-forty ranking.

We worked our way south and west, spending nights in pullouts amid orchards or fields and eating at local inns. The locals were friendly, curious and happily jabbered at us in Turkish. Despite the language barrier, we managed to converse using a lot of gesturing, pointing and sometimes, resorting to sketches.

We reached Izmir, a large city of half a million inhabitants sprawled at the edge of a deep bay on the Anatolian coast, the afternoon of the third day. The lower township was dominated by the Kadifekale fort (called the Velvet Castle in Turkish), which sat on a hill overlooking the harbor. The Persian Emperor, Cyrus the Great, destroyed Old Smyrna in 545 BC following his conquest of the Aegean coastal cities. Iskandar (Alexander the Great) re-founded the city around 340 BC after defeating the Emperor Darius III at Issus in 333 BC.

Using the contact numbers given to us by Mehmet, our friend from Munich, I tried to reach him from the first payphone we found. A German-speaking man answered and I handed the receiver to Lode, who learnt that Mehmet was still in Germany. Yusuf, however, was in a town called Silifke further down the southern coast of the country. Back in the Kombi, we huddled around the Formica table, studying the roadmap.

Ian said, "I make it six-hundred miles along the seashore. Seems like a pleasant drive."

Lode pointed at an alternate road cutting through a mountainous region. "It would be shorter driving inland."

Trev lit a cigarette, drew in a puff and passed it as if it was a joint. "If we take the coastal way, we'll go through Antalya. That Brit couple we met at the Pudding Shop said it was worth the trip."

I nodded and added, "We should camp on beaches as long as we can before we start heading for the interior. Once we head east, we won't be near the sea until we reach India."

"Good point, all these decisions are making my guts knot," said Lode.

"Speaking of knots, did I ever tell you about Alexander and the Gordian knot?" I ignored my audience's exaggerated groans and continued, "No? Well, the story goes that when he was in Gordium, not far north of here, he undid the famed knot tied by King Midas' father who prophesized that the person who untied it would rule all of Asia. Our wonder boy, according to the historians, took one look and slashed through the knot with his sword." The end of my tale was met by a blizzard of flying objects hitting me in the head and cries of, "Enough! Jesus H Christ!" and "I wish that stupid Greek was alive so I could kill him again!" Some people have no appreciation of history.

We drove the short distance to the harbor, parked the van and stretched our legs by walking along the piers. We admired the clock tower, an ornate sculpture of white stone, visited the Kemeralti bazaar and the ancient Kizlarağasi caravanserai. We wandered in the old city exploring the shops, small bistros and found a café with a patio, on the Pasaport Quay. While the sun set over a forest of boat masts and hanging fishing nets, we ate some of the Izmiri specialties: vegetables prepared in a variety of ways, tarhana soup and a local mutton dish called keşkek.

As we enjoyed our food, I noticed a tanned young man with long brown, curly hair repeatedly glancing in our direction from the edge of the café's patio. He appeared to be in his late teens, wore a fringed black leather jacket over a black tee, jeans and had cowboy-style leather boots. I waved him over and invited him to sit.

"Hi, man, do you speak English?" Lode asked.

Our new friend replied with a slight American accent, "Yup, sure do." Close up he looked more like a local: He had a dark, olive complexion, deep brown eyes, a strong nose, thin fuzz for a moustache and a wispy Vandyke beard. He was a slim five-feet-eight and I lowered my estimate of his age to sixteen or seventeen.

"I'm Kemal." He shook hands all around but couldn't seem to drag his gaze from the food on the table. The poor kid seemed starving.

"Have some grub, man." I slid the basket and a couple of the vegetable dishes towards him. He hesitated for a moment but hunger won over and he devoured the food. Lode and Trev watched smiling while Ian waved the waiter over and ordered more tea and another serving of the meat dish.

As our guest mopped the last crumbs with a crust of bread, Trev asked, "You from around here Kemal? Your English is excellent."

"No, Ankara. Just drifting, you know. My dad works for the government. We spent years in the Sates before I was forced to come back to Ankara last spring." Kemal's reply was surprising bitter but I thought I understood his frustration. He'd grown up in a free, exciting western culture only to be uprooted and relocated to a repressive, old-fashioned Turkish lifestyle.

Ian said, "You've been around for a while. Do you know where the drifters hang out in Izmir?"

"There's a beach west of town where backpackers and the local stoners camp. To thank you for the meal, I'll show you," Kamal said.

We returned to the Kombi and Kemal directed us westward along the bay, through slums and industrial sections, before arriving at Özürlüler Park. The grounds spread over a sandy promontory jutting into the Aegean. Short wind-twisted pines and scrub grass sloped to the rock strewn water's edge. There were a dozen tents and makeshift shelters scattered amongst stubby bushes and we spotted the flickers of campfires.

Kemal opened his arms, encompassing the park. "Backpackers, drifters, stoners, as requested. I'm staying over that way." He pointed at a spot further down the beach.

"Are you by yourself?" Lode asked.

Kemal hesitated and stared at his feet. "Um, you know, I travel alone but we all share the campfires."

Trev pounded the slight Turk on the back and said, "Well, you're welcome to join our camp, sort of thing." Kemal's nodded enthusiastically and ran to get his gear.

"Poor kid," Ian shook his head in commiseration.

Lode muttered, "I bet he ran away from home. I can dig it."

I said, "We sure could use a translator, if he's interested."

And so Kemal, a conflicted, fifteen-year old, run-away from Ankara, joined us on the trip to Silifke. Following the coastal road we came to Bodrum, called Halicarnassus in ancient times, famous for housing the tomb of Mausolus from which the word mausoleum is derived (one of the classical world's seven wonders) and Bodrum Castle, a Crusader fort overlooking the harbor.

August turned to September and the weather remained hot during the day, turning cool after sunset. We drove short jaunts along the coast and camped on the beaches most nights. Every third or fourth day, after supper, we'd drop Kemal in front of a cheap inn and parked the van nearby. The kid would haggle for the lowest rates and rent a single-occupancy room on the ground floor. After dark, we stealthily climbed into the hotel room through an open window to use the shower, wash our clothes and crash on the floor.

One day Kemal phoned his sister in Ankara and sweet-talked her into wiring him some cash. He came out of the local post office grinning and with a money order worth a hundred liras (about ten US bucks). "It's from my big sister. She said she talked Dad out of calling the police... Oops." He hung his head but when he finally looked up and saw us smiling he stammered, "Uh, um... you guessed I ran away from home, huh?"

Lode ruffled Kemal's hair and replied, "Yeah, we did. It's good to know we won't be arrested for aiding and abetting."

We followed the road to Fethiye, a medium-sized city on the shores of the Aegean, renowned for its rich history. We picked up two Italian hitchhikers on the outskirts of the town and strapped their backpacks atop the gear on the overburdened roof rack. In return for passage, they offered tokes of Turkish hash, which helped us to better tolerate the overcrowded van.

Fethiye, named Telmessos during Alexander's invasion of Anatolia, had an amusing legend. When the young Macedonian entered the Telmessos harbor with his fleet, he encountered deep suspicion, hostility and a wall of sharp-pointed weapons aimed at his boat. He asked permission to allow his musicians and slaves to enter the city to rest from the hardships of a long sailing. King Antipatrides, the local monarch, granted his approval and that night, Alexander's warriors, disguised as slaves and musicians, captured the town. We visited the Hellenistic theater and for supper bought kebabs from food stalls on the quay. Kemal got directions to a beach about ten miles from town called Öludeniz, frequented by Freaks and backpackers. In Fethiye, we restocked our supplies, organized the van then drove a narrow, twisting road to a small resort area half an hour south.

Öludeniz was a spectacular scenic paradise that unfolded as we climbed down from the surrounding hills. The road turned right and opened onto a breathtaking, blue-water lagoon with a picture-perfect beach.

Lode, riding shotgun, craned his neck taking in the breath-taking view. "Reminds me a bit of Ipsos." The sandy shore was crowded with tanned, skimpily clad tourists sunbathing on chaises-longue, playing volleyball, throwing Frisbees and strolling along the water's edge on the golden sands. Offshore the waters frothed as ski boats zoomed, barely avoiding fleets of sailboats and catamarans.

We camped a few miles south of the resort area at a neighboring beach and partied with the Freaks living there. Öludeniz was similar to Ios with

Brits, instead of Scandinavians, taking advantage of the weather and the low cost of life. Our two Italian hitchhikers decided to stay so, we gave a lift to a Brit and a Frenchman when we drove away the next morning. The road took us inland in a wide semi-circle before returning to the coast and the city of Anatalya, where we dropped our passengers and checked into a hotel.

We decided to do some sightseeing, clambering over the ruins of Hadrian's Gate, the fluted minaret and the Hidirlik Tower, remnants of some kind of fortification. Strolling along the harbor area that evening, we bumped into two German travelers named Bernhard and Friedrich; we last saw them at the Pudding Shop in Istanbul. We compared notes and were impressed with their guidebook, called the German BIT guide, which listed hostels, inns, restaurants and the various transports available.

They asked to ride with us and, when we departed the next morning, the extra weight in the Kombi was noticeable, particularly during the long climbs through the coastal mountains. The underpowered minibus slowed to a walking-pace as we crawled up the sloped roads and this prompted Bernhard to tell us anecdotes about older series VW vans, with even weaker engines that could only climb steep grades in reverse gear.

The serpentine, mountain highway was scenic and traffic was sparse. It was harvest time and entire families worked the fields. We passed donkeys, prodded by children wearing dirty-white robes, plodding on the pavement and loaded with huge loads of golden hay. Halfway to Silifke we stopped in Anamur for the night. The town was the southern-most point in Turkey, jutting out into the Mediterranean, and was home to the remnants of an impressive Crusader castle called Mamure. We camped east of Anamur on a deserted beach bordered by a lush a banana grove.

By noon the next day we reached Silifke, a city of about twenty thousand inhabitants. The town surrounded by low, barren, rocky hills, had a large regional market in which coastal farmers sold a cornucopia of produce, fruits, olives and tobacco and sprawled inland on the banks of the Göksu River.

We parked by the town's Otogar (bus terminal) and Kemal called Yusuf's number from a public phone. He spoke in rapid Turkish and turned to us saying, "The receptionist says he's out of the office. He's gone to Ankara. She doesn't know what day he's returning. Apparently, while Yusuf is out, Batur is in charge. Do you want to talk to him?" I could hear the woman's strident voice blaring from the phone and winced as Kemal handed me the receiver.

"Merhaba (hello)." I heard a familiar-sounding voice rumble in my ear.

"Batur? It's Danny... We met in Munich?"

"Danny? Yis, of course, I remember. Where are you?"

"I'm calling from the Otogar in Silifke. Can we meet?"

"Yis. There's a restaurant called Naz Dürüm a block from the Otogar. I'll meet you there in ten minutes."

Lode climbed to the van's roof rack and lowered Bernhard and Friedrich's backpacks; the German pair waved goodbye and headed out. The rest of us walked to the restaurant and sat at a table, on the sidewalk shaded by a red canvas awning, to wait.

Silifke's streets and sidewalks were thronged with merchants and peddlers selling all sorts of goods. Dray animals pulling carts laden with burlap sacks overflowing with produce, hay and fruits snaked amid garishly decorated six-wheeled trucks, buses, mopeds, cars and dolmuşlar. Traffic moved at a snail's pace as vehicles maneuvered around pedestrians, delivery boys on bicycles, braying donkeys and mangy, stray dogs. The air smelled of exhaust, manure with occasional whiffs of fruit and grilling meats. Batur joined us with a wide smile on his face. We shook hands and introduced him to Ian and Kemal. Our Turkish friend had not changed much since we'd last seen him in Munich.

"Where is Monique, the beautiful French woman?" he asked raising one of his bushy black eyebrows.

Trev shrugged and replied, "She returned to France."

Batur gave Trev a pitying look but recovered quickly and ordered lunch for all of us. We yakked about our adventures since we met. He was working for Yusuf, doing odd jobs around Silifke, waiting for a new project in Germany.

"Where do the hippies stay in Silifke?" I asked as we set to a hearty lunch of beef stew and vegetables.

"There's a place half an hour from here called Kizkalesi. It has a beautiful castle and there are a couple of resorts and restaurants along the beach."

After the filling meal, Trev and I took Batur aside and explained our need to discreetly dump the van. The Turk ran a finger along his luxuriant jet-black moustache as he pondered the matter. "Let me ask around. I'm pretty sure I can find a buyer," he said.

We separated, Batur returned to work and we promised to contact him later in the week. Before leaving for the beach, we shopped for supplies at the bazaar and then followed the coastal road east for ten miles, reaching the resort village of Kizkalesi in the late afternoon.

The hamlet, hemmed between the Taurus Mountains and the sea, featured two forts. One was the romantically named Maiden Castle, a fortress on a tiny island offshore, which reminded me of Dumas' Chateau D'If in *The Count of Monte-Cristo* and the ruins of the second, smaller Korykos fort, lay on the eastern side of town. Small plots of produce and orchards surrounded Kizkalesi adding pleasant verdure to the tawny hills surrounding the village.

A man at the local store directed us to a camping area just past the last houses east of the hamlet. As in Öludeniz, the majority of the resident Freaks were Brits who seemed to have adopted Turkey as their second home. We spent the next few days lazing on the beach and exploring the fortresses' ruins. After being cooped together in the van for so long, I was happy to beachcomb by myself, collecting interesting shells and stones.

A few days later, Lode awoke with crippling pain radiating from his lower abdominal area and a high fever. We suspected appendicitis and drove him into Silifke, where Kemal guided us to the nearest hospital. The Doctor confirmed our suspicions: Lode's appendix required immediate surgery. Lode, on a gurney pushed by a brawny attendant, waved forlornly at us while as was propelled down the hall to the operating room. The Doctor explained to Kemal that, although Lode should be well enough for release in a couple of days, he would require a fortnight of rest to recuperate properly.

With Kemal translating, Ian asked, "When can we visit him?"

"Come back tomorrow afternoon."

Spotting a payphone in the lobby, I called Batur who invited us to his nearby office. Our friend's business was on the second floor of a three-story brick building in the business district along the Göksu River and lorries departed, laden with crates, from the large warehouse occupying the street level. A narrow red wooden door at the side opened into a stairway leading to the upper floors.

We entered a small reception area staffed by a matronly Turkish woman who pointed down a hallway. Batur sat behind a large wooden desk in a large, brightly lit, square office full of boxes, filing cabinets and small crates. Binders, folders and stacks of forms tottered in piles on every flat surface. A framed picture of Ataturk, the Father of Modern Turkey, dominated the wall behind the desk while colorful posters of Munich and Bavaria adorned the other walls.

Without a word, he passed me the front page of a Turkish newspaper on which I recognized the words 'Munich Olympics' in bold black letters. Kemal leaned over my shoulder and gasped as he read the headlines aloud "Eleven Israeli Olympians Massacred at Munich Olympics. Five Palestine Terrorists are Killed by Police."

Batur said mournfully, "I'm very sorry. That was a shitty thing for the Arabs to do."

I absorbed the news and silently, reflected on how isolated Israel must be feeling. I also knew, with certainty, the bloodshed had just started. Golda Meir would not rest until every single culprit involved in the massacre was found and put down like the rabid dogs they were.

I told Batur about Lode's hospitalization. "…So we'll need a place in town. Can you help us find something cheap?"

Batur nodded, rifled through the piles of papers covering his desk and pulled out a black address book. He dialed a number, spoke for a few moments, hung up and said, "Hokay, I found a house in the old town that's available for a couple of weeks. You'll like the price but it's primitive."

"Right on, man, no worries. It can't be any more basic than sleeping on the beach," Trev assured him.

"Well, let's go take a look."

We jumped into our van and Batur directed us to the western edge of Silifke. The neighborhoods crowded at the bottom of the ancient castle hill looked like nothing more than shantytowns. The only buildings with electricity were a tiny restaurant and small stores servicing the neighborhood. The houses, one or two-stories tall, built of weatherworn, never painted wood, sat on cinder-block foundations and had rusted, corrugated metal roofs. The homes had no running water — there was a hand-pump located at the four-way intersection in the center of the quarter - and stinking open sewers snaked down the lanes. Scrawny, mangy dogs, feral cats and the odd goat, rooted in garbage piled in around the buildings. Half-naked, grimy toddlers splashed in puddles while their older siblings chased a semi-inflated soccer ball.

The few stores on the street sold a variety of household goods that cascaded onto the packed dirt in front of their doors. The shopkeepers stood leaning in doorways chatting with their neighbors while radios blared Turkish music. We loved it! This part of Silifke seemed timeless and as close to the original Seleucia of antiquity as we could get.

"Man, we're a long way from Carnaby Street," I said as I slowly maneuvered the bus in the congested lanes.

Trev peered at a beggar slumped against a wall and exclaimed, "Did you see that guy? He's missing a nose and most of his fingers!"

"Leprosy," Kemal said, "It's fairly common in the slums." He smirked and shook his head at our shocked reaction. The further we drove into the quarter the less pleased he seemed and his nose twitched at the stink of the sewer.

A number of people seemed afflicted with eye diseases; partial blindness to aggravated squints and Batur told us that malnutrition during infancy often caused this common affliction among the poorer Turks.

When we reached the upper part of the quarter, Batur pointed at a two-story claptrap house built against the ochre-colored slope. The structure's lower level was a six-foot high, three-sided enclosure made of cinder blocks, its open side facing the lane like a doorless garage. The hard-packed dirt floor held stacks of dusty firewood, two barrels of water, a small pile of gravel and some indistinct trash. A shitter, partitioned with plywood, occupied the far corner.

Wooden stairs, attached to the side led to a gallery that ran the length of the upper floor and we gingerly mounted the creaking steps. Batur opened the door and we trooped into a twenty-by-twenty-foot room lit by a window on each of the four walls. Along the left wall ran a counter with a sink and uneven cupboards. The chipped-enamel sink didn't have any faucets and its drain emptied into a rusty, battered bucket. In the center of the room, a black, pot-bellied, cast-iron wood-stove sat on a brick platform, a rickety table and five chairs to one side and half a dozen thin pallets to the other. A thin, faded-orange, frayed area rug covered part of the grey floorboards, adding a bit of color to the otherwise monochrome weather-beaten look.

A small stack of firewood and kindling lay, strewn on the floor, near the stove and a battered aluminum kettle perched on top. Tin canisters and glass jars aligned on a shelf above the sink, shared space with a few soot-blackened pots and pans. A set of mismatched chipped plates and cups were haphazardly stacked on a shelf above the counter. Two dusty Kerosene lamps hung from the open-rafter ceiling and candle stubs, like off kilter toadstools, dotted the windowsills.

Ian looked around and asked, "How do we wash, you know? Ourselves, dishes and so on?"

"You use these two buckets." Batur indicated a couple of blue plastic pails under the kitchen counter. "You noticed the barrels downstairs? You fill them from the nearest public pump. Alternatively, you can buy water and firewood from a peddler who does the rounds with his donkey cart."

"How much is the rent?" I asked.

"Twenty liras a week. Cheap, yes?"

"It's perfect. Please tell your friend we'll take it and thank-you both. C'mon, I'll give you a ride back to the office."

"I'll come with you," Trev said, "We can grab supplies on the way back."

Trev, Batur and I got into the van and started back into town.

"Hey, Batur, any progress selling the van?" Trev asked as we drove down the hill.

"I have a buyer. He'll pay two hundred US dollars, cash. He will need a bill of sale for appearances but you can use any name you want."

* * *

We decided to keep our faithful minibus until Lode was out of care. When the hospital released him, we used the van to transport him to our new home and the next day, Batur and two middle-aged Turks he introduced as Ali and Mustafa came to the house. We chatted amiably, accepted tailor-made cigarettes and sipped fragrant, sweet mint tea mad by Kemal. Trev wrote a bill of sale using a fictional name, handed it and the VW's keys to Mustafa, receiving a roll of bills in exchange. We shook hands, Trev slipped Batur twenty bucks as finder's fee and we trooped downstairs to see off the three Turks and say goodbye to the Kombi.

I was absurdly sad as I watched our van disappear around a corner. The blue and white van was the first vehicle I (sort of) owned and, despite its mechanical quirks and challenges, the old bus had served us well. I considered it as much a member of our small group as any of the guys and I would greatly miss it.

Ian broke our brooding silence. "Fuck me! We're really backpacking from here on."

I thought about my bulging, heavy backpack and all the extra crap I'd accumulated since London, sighed and said, "I'm going to sort through my shit."

Everyone except Kemal nodded in resignation. Until now the luxury of having our own transport meant we could disregard weight and storage space. From here on we'd be humping our belongings on our backs. Trev split the cash into four parts, changed a twenty into fives and handed Ian, Lode and I forty-five bucks each; a quarter share of the van.

Lode recuperated rapidly and a week after his operation we accompanied him to the clinic where the Doctor checked the stitches and grunted in satisfaction at the sight of the healing scar. The Turk re-iterated the need to rest for another week, charged him twenty bucks for the surgery and sent us away.

With the prospect of spending seven more days in Silifke, we settled into a daily domestic routine consisting of hauling water and firewood, fetching groceries from the market and drinking endless cups of tea or strong coffee. Kemal arranged for a nearby eatery to deliver hot meals every evening and although the fare was monotonous (mutton stew with okra and bread), the food was filling and, more importantly, inexpensive.

The neighbors were fascinated by our group and came to visit (males only, of course) bringing gifts of sweet Turkish pastries covered with nuts and dripping with honey or small bags of oranges. They evinced an inquiring curiosity at our outlandishness and were fascinated by our backpacks, clothing and musical instruments. With Kemal translating, we satisfied our own inquisitiveness and asked many questions in turn.

One of the things that really piqued my interest was the odd-looking trousers - baggy crotches reaching to the knees - that almost every Turk male wore and the fact that all their shoes had broken backs and were worn like slippers.

I asked Kemal, "Why do their pants have huge inseams and what's up with the flattened shoes?"

He rolled his eyes. "Oh, that. There's a myth that the Prophet will be born from a man. The big crotch is to catch the infant before he falls to the ground." He shrugged. "In reality, the bagginess acts as an insulator against cold temperatures and is cooler when it's hot, and they flatten the backs of their shoes to make it easier to get them on and off five times a day when they pray."

A couple of days later, Batur and Yusuf came to visit bringing gifts of fruits and Loukoums. Yusuf had just returned from the capital and we shared the treats while we reminisced about Munich. In an attempt to be a good host, I checked the stash jar.

"I'd offer you a spliff, but we're out of dope and don't know where to get more," I apologized.

Batur shook his head in sympathy and replied, "The whole town is dry. All I can find is crappy dried-up Syrian weed."

Yusuf snorted in distain. "That old shit? You can't get stoned even when you roll giant joints."

"Have you considered making hash?" I said. The room went silent and six pairs of eyes goggled at me.

"You know how to make hashish?" Yusuf asked.

I nodded and explained the simple process. Yusuf and Batur conversed in rapid-fire Turkish, gesturing emphatically. I wasn't sure if they were arguing or excited.

The latter turned to me and asked, "What kind of supplies do you need, how much will you charge to do about a kilo and can the hashish be flat and no thicker than a quarter inch?"

I smiled broadly and assured them, "I can shape it into any desired size and I'll make you a list of supplies." I glanced at my companions who eagerly nodded their heads. "And it will only cost you a few grams." Batur was a true friend and I saw this as a way of paying back his kindness both here and in Munich.

* * *

To celebrate Trev's twentieth birthday and Lode's recovery, we sprung for a meal at a restaurant downtown, along the river walk. The meal cost ten times what we usually paid at our neighborhood eatery but we were flush with cash, cast parsimoniousness to the winds and enjoyed the dinner. After, we climbed the ruins of the ancient Byzantine castle overshadowing the town, and drank arrack until well after dark.

Batur drove up to the house early the next day and the boys hauled boxes and bags from his car while I unpacked the items I'd requested. We dumped the weed out of two, bulging burlap sacks into a dusty mound on the floor of the room. The stack of desiccated, greenish-brown cannabis was a tangled mass of stems, twigs, seeds and small, curled leaves. I grabbed a handful and rubbed it between my palms briskly, crushing the pot while allowing the dross to fall out. To my relief, a bit of brown, sticky residue collected on my skin. Ian took some of the grass and filled a pipe. He hacked and coughed, frowned and said the weed tasted terrible, was harsh and irritated the throat. We all grimaced as a smell reminiscent of burnt, moldy hay filled the small room.

I searched through the gear in the boxes and extracted a large plastic bowl and a pair of pantyhose. I cut the legs from the panty and pushed the bowl inside one of them until it was taut over the opening. I positioned the stocking covered drum-like implement between my knees, picked up some weed, discarded the larger pieces of stalk and rubbed the leaves and buds into the stocking. I ground the pot until only seeds, twigs and bits of stem remained atop the drum. I dumped the detritus into a bucket and repeated the process a few times, watched intently by everyone in the room. I carefully pulled the bowl out of the nylon and nodded as I saw a thin, fine brown powder stuck to the curved plastic wall. I knocked the powdery substance loose by gently tapping the bowl until a tiny mound gathered in the bottom.

I passed the bowl around and explained, "This is kief. After we extract all of it, we'll press the dust into cakes of hash."

Lode stuffed some of the powder into a pipe, lit it and inhaled deeply. His eyes crinkled in satisfaction and he exhaled a fragrant cloud of smoke and passed the pipe to me for reloading. I offered the next hit to Batur who, after tasting the sample, grinned, nodded in appreciation and asked us to press the hashish into quarter-inch thick slabs for smuggling to Europe.

"A quarter inch it will be. How do you smuggle the shit?" I asked.

"Turkey exports hand-made backgammon sets. You must have seen the folding marquetry boxes with the beautiful ivory inlays?" We all nodded; the game was almost a national obsession here and every café had several sets for the use of their customers. Batur continued, "The slabs are inserted between the wood and the veneer."

He left shortly thereafter and we proceeded to make hash. The supply boxes contained enough bowls and stockings for everyone. We processed the weed by first removing the larger stems and twigs and then, by cutting the remainder into small pieces, the pile reduced to two bucketsful of finely diced pot. Our kief production line caused a brown haze, comprised of marijuana dust mixed with smoke from continuously refilled pipes and burned down cigarettes, to coalesce against the ceiling.

By dawn we had extracted all the kief and had a quarter-pail full of brown powder weighing a little over a kilo. Tired and wasted we decided to stop and crash for the rest of the day.

We resumed work as the sun set behind the castle. Mid-September in Silifke meant warm days and cool nights; a gentle reminder that fall wasn't far away. The evening breeze carried the fragrance of braziers grilling meat as every household in the neighborhood cooked supper.

I asked Kemal to fire up the wood stove and Trev and Ian hauled up and stacked another load of firewood. From a bundle of old newspapers, I pulled out a double page and cut it into five long, narrow strips. Following my example, everyone grabbed scissors and newspapers and we soon had enough in the stack. Kemal and I fetched buckets of water and placed them by the stove.

I rummaged through the supplies and found a foot-wide roll of thick, transparent cellophane, a wooden ruler, adhesive tape and a small brass scale. I cut a ten-inch long length of the crinkly material and folded it to make an envelope. Ian and I experimentally stuffed and weighed the cellophane envelope with kief and concluded that a packet could hold about a hundred grams. As we had about a kilo of kief, Ian grabbed the ruler, unfolded the cellophane roll and cut ten pieces, which we folded into packets and stuffed with the remaining kief. I asked Kemal, "How's the fire?"

The young man lifted the firebox's latch with a stick, opened the door and peered at the flames. "There's a thick bed of coals. Ready when you are."

I grabbed a set of iron tongs and a pair of short two-by-ten-inch planks that I lay on the floor by the stove. We stopped for a smoke break while I explained how we were going to make hash cakes. "I'll do the first one slow and easy. Then we'll do the remainder assembly-line like."

I dunked one of the long newspaper strips into a bucket of water and wrapped it around the first cellophane packet. I repeated this with five additional strips of paper, alternating from side to side, until the package was completely encased in soaked paper strips. Once inserted into the coals, the intense heat would soften the kief making it readily compressible while the steam from the wet paper would protect the cellophane from burning.

I carried the soaked bundle to the stove and nodded at Kemal who unlatched and opened the small door. I clamped the packet with the iron thongs and thrust it into the heart of the firebox. The outer layer of paper steamed fiercely for a few seconds before bursting into flame. The second layer lasted a few moments longer and then it too burnt. I kept the bundle in the flames until four successive layers of paper were consumed at which point, I pulled the package out of the fire and laid the steaming, charred mess onto one of the planks on the floor. I quickly placed the second plank on top of the packet, stepped on it and rocked back and forth to distribute my weight evenly on the impromptu press.

After a minute, I lifted the flat package and stripped away the last remaining layers of paper, revealing a shiny, dark black-green, quarter-inch-thick, rectangular slab. Ian snatched it from my fingers, sliced a corner of the cellophane and inhaled deeply. His eyes lit up and, with a big grin, he passed the hash around. We each fondled and sniffed the little treasure we had worked so hard to produce.

It was morning again and our labors were complete. Kemal hiked out to a pay phone and told Batur that his goods were ready for pick-up. Our friend arrived, shortly, and his face lit up at the sight of the ten pieces of hash. He gave us a fat finger (a dozen grams) of the fresh dope and bundled the rest into a bag. Before leaving he offered to fetch us in the morning and take us to the Otogar.

We spent our last evening in Silifke sorting through our belongings and mercilessly discarded unessential items to lighten our packs. We invited Kemal and the neighbors to help themselves to whatever they fancied and they made short shrift of the pile.

* * *

Chapter Nine

Life's a Pisser but Not on Opium

Iran - Afghanistan: October 1972

In Context:

- -Thirty-one people are killed in a fire at a restaurant on the Greek island of Rhodes, after a short circuit sets fire to bamboo paneling. Most of the dead are Scandinavian tourists.
- -Kung Fu premieres on the ABC network.
- -In Rome, two agents of Israel's Mossad shoot Abdel Wael Zwaiter eleven times. Zwaiter is suspected by the Mossad to have been part of the Black September planning for the Munich massacre.
- -At the Paris Peace Talks, North Vietnam's negotiator, Le Duc Tho reaches an agreement with Henry Kissinger of the United States on ending the Vietnam War.
- -Elton John's single "Crocodile Rock" is released.
- -In France, The Airbus A300, the first airliner built by the Airbus company flies for the first time.

* * *

Batur drove us to the Otogar, shook our hands, pounded our backs and left us amid a throng of Turkish passengers. Kemal, on his way home to Ankara, would travel with us as far as Tarsus where he would catch a northbound train. We shouldered our backpacks and followed Kemal through the terminal, purchased tickets and boarded the bus. We had debated whether we should hitchhike but decided to take a bus until Tarsus, a major transportation hub, near where two main highways joined and headed east.

The venerable thirty-passenger Mercedes bus drove at a moderate but steady speed and Silifke receded behind us as we followed the coastal highway. I sat by a window captivated by the rolling countryside. Until now, as one of only two drivers, I'd rarely had the opportunity to truly appreciate the scenery; driving on the narrow Turkish roads required concentration and alertness.

We arrived in Mersin at lunchtime. The bus parked in a dusty square and everyone, following the driver and his spotter, disembarked for the break. We lined up in front of a food stall where we ate meat kebabs and skewers of roasted vegetables. Ian fastidiously licked his greasy fingers and remarked, "I worried about bus fares but so far they seem quite reasonable."

Lode said, "I hear it only costs fifty bucks from Istanbul to India."

I remembered Gerard back in the kibbutz delighting us with stories about riding the rails in Pakistan and India. "After Afghanistan we'll travel by train and they're even cheaper than the buses."

The town of Tarsus, although smaller than Mersin, was home to a vast Otogar fitting its location as a major crossroad and transportation hub. Lode read from his travel guide. "Listen to this. Tarsus is famous for being the place where Mark Antony first met Cleopatra. It is also the birthplace of Paul the Apostle."

We gathered our belongings and threaded through the milling crowd of passengers to the ticket kiosks. Kemal, choked with emotion, said his goodbyes and walked out of the bus terminal heading to the nearby train station. We would miss him. He was a good friend and an invaluable guide and translator.

I hoped the time he spent with us had helped center him and speed up his acceptance that, for better or worse, he now lived in Turkey and must adapt to his country's culture. I understood the dichotomy as I too, had grown up with a contradictory, bewildering mix of old-fashioned values and modern desires. My development was disrupted by the Freak's counterculture of sex, drugs and rock 'n roll. (Although, as far as the stoner's culture went, there was very little of the first and lots of the other two).

I consulted our tattered roadmap, folded it and said, "Gaziantep is about a hundred-and-sixty miles from here. Who's for hitchhiking?"

We divided into pairs, Lode with me, Ian with Trev and aimed to reunite at Gaziantep's bus terminal. Our three-hour long hitchhiking attempt failed miserably as we immediately attracted an inquisitive crowd of gawking passersby who pestered us with questions and advice on bus schedules. Every vehicle that stopped for us demanded a fare before allowing us transport. For some reason, the concept of a free ride did not sit well with the Turks and I learned interesting curse words when we refused to pay. I wondered if Trev and Ian were having better luck. We finally gave up and hopped on a dolmuş to Adana's Otogar to catch a bus.

Gaziantep (or Antep in days of yore) was a substantial agricultural and industrial center on the southern coast and was nestled amid vast olive, pistachio and fruit groves. Trev and Ian, who'd arrived by bus before us, left a message at the ticket booth and we met at an inn by the Otogar. We checked into a room and then enjoyed a distinctively unique, local meal of rice, soup, kebabs and meatballs. For dessert we had a sweet baklava pastry accompanied by tiny cups of strong Turkish coffee.

The server spoke a little English and translated questions and comments from the other patrons, Turkish merchants and businessmen, who were puzzled by our clothing and long hair. They had a good laugh at our expense when we told them about our attempts to hitchhike and they explained that Turkish drivers would expect rich foreigners to pay for a ride.

At breakfast the next morning, the same server introduced us to a truck driver who was deadheading to Dyarbakir (halfway to Tatvan) and would give us a lift for a very reasonable fare. We rode, in the lorry's open bed, perched on a heap of empty jute sacs printed with the word PEANUTS in Turkish and English and arrived as the sun set. The driver dropped us off at an inexpensive inn where we crammed into a tiny room for the night.

The next morning we awoke to gray skies and a cold drizzle, which convinced us to continue our journey by bus. The road, often following the sinuous banks of raging streams, twisted through narrow valleys edged by rugged, snow-capped mountains. Farmers prepared their small fields for winter while their children shepherded flocks of sheep and goats to the lower pastures.

The bus stopped at every village, allowing us precious glimpses of rural Turkish life. Women, dressed in black, balanced large reed baskets on their heads. A ragtag group of children chased a soccer ball while younger kids ran behind a freewheeling bicycle rim that they propelled and steered with a stick. Dogs, cats, goats and poultry rooted in trash piles while donkeys, mules and oxen, bearing towering loads, ambled slowly through the hamlets. Adolescent boys toiled in small, hole-in-the-wall shops, squatting on their heels as they wielded hammers and tongs or pumped hand-bellows in front of forges while others walked briskly carrying shiny brass trays loaded with tiny coffee cups and pastries.

During a stop in a village perched in the lower reaches of the Taurus Mountains, a slim, lanky youth with vivid green eyes and a wide basket of bread balanced on his head, rode a bicycle toward the bus. I whistled, beckoning him over and we bought two delicious, fresh, still-warm loaves.

East of Dyarbakir, we entered Kurdish country and noticed a marked difference in the clothing and architecture. The women wore colorful vests or long-sleeved jackets over gowns with underskirts and puffy pants. The men wore dark coats over regular pants with no sign of the oversized crotches so prevalent in the western provinces. My nose glued to the window I said, "The chicks are prettier here. They have finer features and are slimmer."

Lode snorted and shook his shaggy head. "How can you compare? All the ones we saw before wore veils and burkas."

* * *

At Tatvan the weather cleared and the sun peeked from dispersing clouds. Trev and Ian opted to continue by dolmuş while Lode and I walked to a truck service station, the modern equivalent of the caravanserai and asked around for a ride to Van. A young Kurd named Kezeban offered us a lift in his lorry for a modest fee. He ordered his spotters, two teen-aged Kurd boys, to hop in the back and with a flourish invited us into the cab.

Kezeban spoke in a mixture of pidgin English-Turkish and we spent the entire trip talking about rock'n'roll and debating whether the Rolling Stones were a 'manlier' band than the Beatles. As he negotiated hairpin turns that seemed too narrow for two-way traffic, I desperately wished for him to shut the fuck up and pay attention to the precipices lining the abrupt, shoulder-less road. He had the terrifying habit of turning to look at us when he talked.

Iskandar had conquered the city of Van and surrounding country in 331BC and numerous ruins from that era dotted the shores of the lake. Kurds formed the majority of the population and we saw several groups of men on horseback, leading mule-trains, laden with huge stacks of firewood, down from the hills. The D-300 highway followed the southern lakeshore and when the road dipped down to the water's edge, the far snowy mountain peaks reflected perfectly in the calm waters. An icy breeze blew from these slopes; for protection, the locals wore sheepskin coats, Karakul hats and gloves.

In Van, Kezeban dropped us off in front of the Iskelesi train station and his two helpers scampered back into the cab giving us the finger and looks of hatred. I couldn't blame the kids. They must have frozen their asses off and had a nasty, bumpy trip in the back of the truck.

Lode and I squatted along the wall inside of the long terminal, taking turns at guarding our belongings and snoozing the afternoon away. I pulled out and updated my journal adding a sketch of a Kurdish fur hat. Peddlers serviced the station carrying trays of strong, sweet tea, pastries and skewers of grilled goat meat. Throughout the concourse, Kurds huddled in family groups around their belongings that often included chicken coops and a lamb or two. Small children burned excess energy by chasing each other between clumps of people. The late afternoon sun kissed the surrounding peaks and the fluorescent lights on the ceiling flickered to life as the train from Iran pulled along the platform and disgorged a flood of travelers heading west. For a while, total pandemonium reigned in the terminal as scores of arriving passengers with their baggage attempted to reach the building's exits through the crowd waiting to board.

Two longhaired backpackers disembarked from the train, stumbled into the milling crowd and drifted towards our little bivouac just as Trev and Ian entered the station from the other end. Roger and Craig, Canadians from Toronto, had traveled as far as Kabul where they fell ill and decided to return home. In their mid-twenties, they were deeply tanned and cadaver-thin. We quizzed them about Teheran: where the Freaks and drifters stayed, eateries and the best way to get to Herat.

Craig, his eyes fever-bright, warned us that the Iranian cops had started all-out war on drugs. "In Turkey they lock smugglers in jails but in Iran they execute them!" he said.

Roger nodded. "Man, Turkey feels like the free world compared to those assholes. Be careful. The guy trying to sell you dope in Teheran is most likely a Savak agent; you know, the secret police. They can do pretty much anything they want in Iran including executions." Luckily, I reflected, we had smoked all of our stash.

I asked about Afghanistan and they painted a picture of a medieval paradise: Hash and opium openly sold in the markets and you could live comfortably on less than a buck a day. Rural Afghanistan had changed little in the millennia since the days when Iskandar and his army passed through on their way to conquer India.

The Canadians left to find transportation west and we joined the mob of people waiting to board the train. The train left Van as night fell and we settled for the long ride to Teheran only to stop, two hours later, at the border. Everyone was obliged to disembark and queue up to get their passports stamped. A border guards glommed onto Ian, searching his backpack thoroughly and asking him to show his money. He nervously produced the 'lost' Amex cheques, as well as his current ones, and resumed breathing when the satisfied guard waved him through.

On the way back to the train we walked under harsh halogen lights casting sharp black shadows and saw a group of Iranian soldiers holding on to straining dogs. Once all the passengers re-boarded, the train's cars lurched with a loud bang, the locomotive blew its horn and we finally rolled towards Tabriz. Using our fake student IDs, we had purchased the cheapest tickets available and now occupied wooden benches facing each other. Luggage racks on both sides of the aisle overflowed with baggage and sleeping children while vendors lurched along the crowded cars flogging food and beverages. The car soon acquired a unique reek of tobacco smoke, spicy food, live chickens and sour BO.

A peddler sold packs of cigarettes, matches and lighters from a tray suspended from his neck. Up to now, we usually bought shag tobacco and rolled our own smokes (much cheaper than buying tailor-made) but the Iranian brands were as cheap as hand-rolled and came in packs of fifty cigarettes. Although the vendor spoke no English, he managed to impart with hand gestures that he would also exchange our Turkish liras for Iranian rials and since he offered a decent rate of exchange, we dumped all our liras. In 1972, a US dollar was worth sixty-five rials or six and half tomans. For example, a plate of mutton stew cost about ten rials and a hotel room forty rials.

We had popped all of our remaining bennies before crossing the border so we didn't sleep most of the night. As the sun cleared the distant hills, painting the wispy clouds in rose and purple streaks, the train followed the northern shores of Lake Urmia where huge flocks of flamingos waded in the shallows.

In Tabriz, new peddlers boarded the train and sold local delicacies such as Chelow Kabab and Kofta, a large meatball stuffed with rice, leeks and other mystery ingredients. In the afternoon, they offered assorted confections, biscuits and cookies, chased with small cups of sweet, mint tea.

* * *

Near midnight, twenty-six hours after leaving Van, the train pulled into Teheran. We climbed down from the railcar, shouldered our packs and, dragged out of the terminal by the pull of the exodus, stepped into the surprisingly hushed, night.

Every drifter familiar with Teheran recommended we stay at the Amir Kabir hotel, which was within walking distance of the Grand Bazaar. We piled into a dolmuş and left the train station driving through deserted streets and along a large park, which the driver called 'Shahr', although it sounded more as if he'd hawked up. The hotel, located on a street of the same name, was an odd-looking three-story building above an automotive shop. A yawning clerk checked us into a room on the third floor of the outer wing and, exhausted from our bennie-fueled sleepless train ride, we collapsed on our pallets.

I arose earlier than my companions and slipped out of the room, down the stairs, through the bustling business on the ground floor and onto the sidewalk. A tall, lean, ponytailed man in his mid-twenties stepped out of the hotel and came over to chat. His name was Jim and he came from the States. He'd been in Teheran almost a week and was also heading to India. When Trev, Ian and Lode finally appeared, we all headed for breakfast.

During the day, Amir Kabir Street was alive with a gridlock of honking vehicles and pedestrians crisscrossing through the slow moving traffic. Stalls and carts on the sidewalks sold everything from beverages and food, to watches and sunglasses.

Jim led us a couple of blocks south of the hotel to a restaurant in a quiet side alley. We sat at a crumb covered, cup-ring-stained table. The eggs, cheese and bread special was only twenty-five rials (about thirty-five cents) so Jim waved at a man behind the counter and flashed five fingers. A server brought tea, utensils and a basket of delicious, hot sangak, an oval Iranian flatbread with a dimpled surface. Around mouthfuls of food, we quizzed Jim about the city.

"You have to see the Grand Bazaar. There's also a bevy of ancient mosques, palaces and so on," he said.

Lode dropped his voice and asked, "What's the deal with dope?"

Jim waited until the waiter finished placing steaming plates in front of us before saying, "I've been doing opium, man. It's easier and cheaper to buy than pot or hash. Teheran is a major stop for Afghan opium on its way to the Turkish heroin labs."

"What about the cops? We heard they shoot people here," Ian said.

"Well, you have to be discrete. Know who you're dealing with."

I said, "I swore I'd try everything at least once. Can we score?"

"After breakfast we'll go to the bazaar and I'll introduce you to Farrokh."

When we were done, we walked along the Golestan Palace complex, which our guide said we should visit later and followed a street lined with shade trees. Teheran had a mixture of ancient monuments, old mosques, and modern buildings interspersed with well-tended parks. Jim led us into the renowned Grand Bazaar through the Sabzeh Maidan (Green Square) and we strolled along the covered, central alleyway from which narrow lanes branched out in a maze of shops and stalls. The market spread over six miles, encompassing small, cozy courtyards where fountains and pools offered a cool, restful break from the crowded lanes. The air was heady with the fragrances of spices, flower blossoms, fruits, incense and tobacco smoke.

We followed Jim to the bakeries section. Each store displayed reed baskets groaning under heaps of pastries, loaves of bread, sangak flats, pitas or syrupy confections dripping with honey. At one such shop, Jim introduced us to a young man, who spoke passable English, named Farrokh. Jim asked for bread. Farrokh scanned both sides of the alley, took a loaf from a basket, walked through a beaded curtain and into the back of the shop. Re-appearing after a moment, he bagged the bread and handed it to Jim who paid and then, walking away, motioned us to follow. He led us into a small, enclosed, empty courtyard where we sat on benches encircling a central, gently splashing, fountain.

Jim removed the loaf from the bag and pointed at a small hole in the crusty end. He tore the end of the loaf revealing two amber-yellow, six-inch long, pencil-sized rods embedded inside. He extracted one and gave it to Trev, who sniffed the dope and passed it around.

The American beamed and said, "Pure opium, man, worth three hundred rials (about five bucks)." We dug in our pockets, counted bills and reimbursed him.

Ian whistled in appreciation, examining the opium. "Do you smoke it?"

"I prefer to eat opium, it lasts longer that way." Jim pulled a penknife from his pocket, deftly sliced the rod into five small pills and handed them to us. I picked up a pill and popped it in my mouth.

Jim tried to stop me. "No! Don't… Aw, shit!"

I jerked back, coughed, retched and spewed the slug into the fountain. Opium was the bitterest thing I had ever swallowed. The horrible flavor made me salivate profusely and retch until my throat ached. I gasped, tears streaming, rinsing my palate in a vain attempt to wash away the pungent taste. Once I was able to speak again, I said, "That's the grossest shit I ever ate."

Jim shook his head. "Yeah, usually we wrap it first."

He demonstrated by wrapping a Zigzag cigarette paper around an opium slug and swallowed the whole thing with a swig of water. He passed the pack of papers and we followed his example. I retrieved the dope from the fountain, wrapped it and swallowed it, fast.

We left the Bazaar and walked back to our hotel, uncertain about the effects of the drug but eager for the experience. Eating opium, I exulted to myself, one more tick on the list of self-abuse substances. I had read books by notorious opium-eaters like Thomas De Quincey, Francis Thompson and Branwell Brontë (the Brontë sisters' less well-known brother) and, according to some theorists, opium (ingested and marketed as laudanum) boosted the creativity of the Romantic Era poets. Damn, I hoped there were no puffy shirts, lace hankies and couplets in my future.

By the time we reached the hotel, we were truly stoned, floating up the stairs and into our room where we sprawled on our pallets. The drug gave us a mellow feel-good buzz for almost four hours and elicited vivid daydreaming. I experienced an unexpected side effect when I had an urgent need to urinate: to my utter consternation, I could not eject as much as a drop, despite the growing pressure. I stood in front of the urinal for what seemed an eternity trying to piss by using every trick in the book: I ran water in the adjoining sink, imagined a big waterfall, a deluge of rain, a raging river. I tried to relax my agonizing bladder. I talked to myself, I begged and swore until finally, in pure ecstasy, I produced a tiny, thin dribble.

Too bad that's what I remember the most about eating opium: the drug's disgusting taste and the inability to piss. Since then, I read that the Chinese, notorious abusers of the drug, attributed enhanced sexual prowess to opium because of its ability to 'arrest seminal emission'. I understood exactly what they meant.

Jim left the following day headed for Herat. The four of us ate more opium and, wasted, walked west along Amir Kabir to Shahr Park where we spent a delightful afternoon idling in the shaded glades and blooming flower gardens. We played music that attracted a small crowd of Iranians teens, who, after initial shyness, requested popular tunes. We did *Whiter Shade of Pale*, by Procol Harem, Led Zeppelin's hit *Stairway to Heaven* and, of course, *House of the Rising Sun* at least half a dozen times. Ian, inspired by the drug, handled his flute so well he brought tears to our eyes.

The next day we returned to the Bazaar to get more opium and to shop. I purchased a saffron colored shirt, Lode scored a cotton tunic and Ian bought pajama pants. We roamed the busy lanes in search of Farrokh but quickly realized we were hopelessly lost. We walked from one end of the souk to the other without finding the Bakers' quarter. To no avail, Trev accosted passing shoppers seeking anyone who spoke English.

A short, slight, young man loitering by a luggage shop approached us and, in accented English, offered to help. He said his name was Mahmood and his oily, slicked back hair, one-eyed squint and a gold tooth that flashed when he opened his mouth, made him look like an Iranian version of archetypical silent movie villains. Trev asked how to find the bakery section and Mahmood offered to guide us. Insisting we only needed directions, Trev thanked him. The Iranian, feigning concern, stated he would feel guilty if we got lost again. Lode gave me a meaningful look and I wondered how to lose Mahmood short of knocking him on the head. Adding insult to injury, the smarmy Iranian asked us if we would be interested in buying some dope.

Trev, keeping his voice low, replied, "Nah, man. We don't do drugs."

Mahmood, speaking loudly and waving his arms, said, "No, no, it's okay. I have first class stuff! How about opium? You want some opium? Morphine? Hashish? You hippies like drugs. Come on."

"No thanks! We're good, man. And please keep your voice down," Trev shushed him, nervously glancing at the shoppers walking by.

Mahmood, ignoring Trev's frantic quieting motions, said, "I sell you opium. Good stuff, good price, look…" To our mounting horror, he pulled out a couple of the amber rods from his pocket and stabbed them toward us.

With thoughts of Savak hauling us to jail via the torture chambers prior to having our heads cut off, we turned and ran. The persistent maniac followed with his hand extended, holding up the opium sticks while bellowing, "One hundred and fifty rials! Come on, cheap price! Slow down hippies. One twenty-five, my last offer. No need to run."

People stared as we jogged passed chased by the loud Iranian. Trev, in the lead, turned his head and told us to split up. Lode and I spun into a side-alley and put on speed while Ian and Trev disappeared in the crowded main street. Having confirmed we'd lost the obnoxious dealer, we slowed to a rapid walk, looked at each other and laughed nervously.

As we headed towards the bazaar's exit, I thought I recognized a stall selling leather goods at an intersection of two alleys. The aroma of baked goods guided us to the start of the baker's quarter. Something useful would come from our bazaar antics; we scored dope from Farrokh. The next three days passed in a stoned stupor as we ate opium every day and lounged in our room or in the park.

Even under the influence of opium (and its induced apathy and indolence) I was feeling the old familiar itch to get on the road. This urge intensified each time we encountered drifters on Amir Bakir Street, travelers going to or returning from India. Finally, on a warm, sunny morning, we piled into a taxi and rode to the northern bus terminal. We purchased tickets for Mashhad, mindful of the warnings about hitchhiking from Teheran. Being marooned in the Dasht-e-Kavir desert, a horrible, inhospitable place, could literally be the death of us.

* * *

The road to Mashhad was about six-hundred miles long and skirted south of the Alborz mountain range following the edge of the Dasht-e-Kavir (also known as the Great Salt Desert). The forty-passenger bus stopped at the larger villages dotting the rim of the vast desolation. We disembarked at each stop to stretch our legs while the driver and his helpers tossed down bales of goods and baggage from the roof racks.

We spotted more camels than donkeys, mules or horses in these villages. Both the houses, made invariably of thick, sun-dried mud bricks, and the animals shared a similar spare, dusty appearance and blended into the landscape. The people dressed in brightly colored and patterned loose cotton tunics and pants, as if rebelling against their austere surroundings. A spindly minaret jutting above the houses would sit atop the mosque; the only building decorated with color and built of brick and mortar or stone. The general (and only) store in each hamlet served as the bus stop, post office and bank; grandiose names for little more than a small counter in a corner of the shop. We purchased food and beverages there, where I learned to appreciate the universally available hot, sweet, minty tea served in a curvaceous glass, which despite the walloping desert heat was extremely refreshing.

We reached Mashhad the next morning, after a fitful sleep in the oven-like, noisy, swaying bus. Sometime during the night, we left the arid, barren desert and climbed onto a hilly plateau lush with green fields and pistachios groves. Mashhad is the second largest city in Iran and the site of spectacular mosques including the elaborately decorated and multi-domed Imam Reza's shrine. Mashhad is to the Shia Muslims what Jerusalem is to the Sunni: a revered and deeply holy destination.

Hefting our backpacks, we walked away from the teeming bus terminal. The temperature, about sixty degrees Fahrenheit, felt cool and refreshing after spending time in the Dasht-e-Kavir. The sun shone from a cloudless, aquamarine sky and the air was fragrant the aroma of citrus fruit and of freshly baked bread. We wandered until we found a small restaurant serving breakfast.

Lode stretched and twisted his torso causing his vertebrae to crack loudly. He said, "What a trip."

I shuddered remembering the long, desolate road and said, "God, can you imagine if we'd driven the Kombi on this stretch? We'd be stranded in the desert, nothing more than bleached skeletons sitting in a husk of a VW! We did that van a favor leaving it in Turkey."

Trev snorted. "And that was the easy part. From here the road gets fucking tough."

"Speaking of which, what's next?" Ian asked.

We discussed our options while finishing our meal and decided to stay in Mashad until the next morning. We found an inexpensive hotel near the bus terminal and were lucky that Naser, the front desk clerk, spoke a modicum of English.

Lode unfolded a map on the counter and asked, "Naser, we want to go to Herat. What's the best way in your opinion?"

The Iranian thought about it for a few moments and replied, "You can take a bus but they only drive as far as Taybad. It is just as cheap to go *darbast;* you hire a cab exclusively for yourselves and the driver will not try to get more passengers. It will take you the one hundred-fifty miles to Islam Qala at the Afghani border and there you can catch a transport to Herat. The trip takes half a day." Naser fished out a creased business card from a drawer beneath the counter and offered, "If you wish, I can arrange for a taxi to come here tomorrow and pick you up."

We agreed, thanked him for his help, booked a room with four charpoys (knotted rope bed frames) and went upstairs to drop off our packs. From this city, Iskandar led his army to Herat using the same route we would be taking tomorrow morning but there were things I had to do first. I wanted to see Mashhad's world-renowned mosque, considered a jewel of Islamic architecture and we had to procure Afghani visas.

We'd heard stories about Afghani officials giving longhaired Freaks a hard time so we cleaned up thoroughly and wore our best clothes. I slicked down my long curly hair and asked Lode to pull it into a tight ponytail that I tucked inside the collar of my shirt. The other three followed suit and, by either luck or design, we encountered no hassles at the legation and returned to the hotel, our passports stamped with the appropriate visas.

Trev and Lode, the lazy bastards, opted for an afternoon of sloth. Ian and I hopped on a city bus and headed to the Imam Reza Shrine, a magnificent tomb and museum complex. The bus stopped at the immense crowded esplanade fronting the Shrine. The compound sprawled as far as the eye could see and encompassed the mausoleum of Imam Ali Reza (the seventh descendant of the Islamic prophet Muhammad), a library, seminaries, prayer halls and even a cemetery.

Gilded domes and minarets rose above intricately decorated buildings. Pilgrims from all over the Islamic world filled the main plaza leading to the shrine and, according to the pamphlet, tens of millions of pilgrims visited Mashhad every year, a pilgrimage second only to the holy Hajj in Mecca. We noticed that women here wore a black chador - a full-body-length tent with a veil in front of the face.

We spent the afternoon touring the magnificent collection of beautiful buildings and marveled at the exquisite artisanship: The handcrafted blue, orange and white ceramic tiles covering the walls, the acres of priceless Persian carpets and the golden fittings adorning the Imam's tomb.

We met back at the hotel, had a quiet evening and crashed early, the echoing cries of the muezzins calling the faithful to the evening prayer.

* * *

Early the next morning, a battered taxi-van pulled up in front of the hotel. The driver, a thin, dark Iranian named Hafez, spoke enough German to converse with Lode. Naser, haggling furiously in Persian, negotiated the fare on our behalf, told us the price and said, "You get a good deal. Hafez is my cousin by marriage."

We thanked Naser, slipped him a few rials, loaded our packs onto the van's roof rack and piled into the taxi. Hafez drove through Mashhad with one hand on the steering wheel and the other on the horn while babbling non-stop in pidgin German. I sat on the backbench of the old van, not seeing the modern city on the other side of the dust-streaked window but imagining a young, seasoned Alexander at the head of his vast army, elephants, horses and the immense logistics train advancing along this same path.

Leaving Mashhad the road meandered along a wide valley heading southeast. We drove past a patchwork of fields and pastures; Hafez said "Zaffron" and pointed at the south-facing slopes of the surrounding hills covered by purple flowers with tall green leaves. Apparently Iran, and Mashhad in particular, produced most of the world's saffron and October was the height of the flowering season. We threaded our way through a succession of farming villages and stopped at Torbat-e Jam, a smallish town two hours from Mashhad, to stretch our legs.

Hafez ushered us to a general store selling, among other goods, a variety of nuts including hundred-pound sacks of the native specialty. He pointed at an open jute sack brimming with shiny roasted Fandoghi pistachios and explained that these were in great demand throughout Iran and the Middle East. He spoke with the storeowner and handed us a handful of nuts to taste. They were delicious with a tangy aftertaste of lime and saffron. Hafez said that the pistachios were coated during the roasting process. We bought a kilo bag and drove the rest of the way to Afghanistan spitting empty shells from every window.

The Afghan border crossing, a few miles from Islam Qala, consisted of two scruffy guards wearing mismatched uniforms who stood beside a wooden pole serving as a barrier. They raised the barricade and waved Hafez through. We drove along the road to Islam Qala - a walled compound containing various low mud-brick structures, some with domed roofs - housing a police detachment, customs and a medical office. Dozens of trucks, buses and taxis sat in a dusty lot beyond the complex. Hafez made a U-turn in front of the compound's gate and helped us unload our packs. We settled the fare, shook hands and entered the buildings.

We spent the rest of the afternoon going from one building to the next as various Afghan officials laboriously recorded information in large ledgers, checked and stamped our documents. The sun was sinking behind tawny, distant hills by the time we finished with the formalities and a border guard waved us over into Afghanistan. We sauntered towards the parking lot and smiled as the sweet aroma of hash wafted from a group of drivers squatting on their heels by a bus. They were puffing on Afghan water pipes, which are different than the nargiles commonly seen in the Middle East. The Afghan pipe's body, fabricated of clay or brass, had a rigid length of bamboo for a tube. Later we learned that these pipes, unlike the tobacco-smoking Hookahs, were specifically for smoking hash.

A tall, thin Pashtun, wearing a brown pakol (a soft, round-topped cap) on his head, a sleeveless gray vest over a red sweater and baggy white pants, rose from the group of squatters and approached us. He had a tanned face, dark-brown eyes and a bushy black mustache and beard.

"Taxi?" he asked.

We nodded and he prompted us to board a battered red ford van parked among the motley collection of vehicles. I discreetly studied our driver looking for any Semitic traits. There was a theory floating around the University of Jerusalem postulating that the Pashtun were descended from the lost tribes of Israel, a thought gaining ground as their history matched critical markers. I admit that their fierce, dark countenance, beaked noses and hirsute faces would not have been out of place amid the orthodox Jews in Jerusalem.

The drive to Herat, on a paved road that ran through a barren, ochre-colored valley south of the Harirud River, lasted almost two hours. Goats grazed forlornly on the leaves of thorny bushes and neglected, low buildings made of dried mud and weathered lumber, blended with the arid hills showing no lights or signs of life. Despite the bleakness of our surroundings, a warm glow spread through my chest. The Silk Route appeared little changed and I could easily imagine long caravans carrying trade goods in both directions. Soon, night claimed all details beyond our vehicle's headlights.

Our first glimpse of Herat was the looming citadel –a big rectangular darkness blocking the stars on the skyline - called the Old Fort. Squatting on a rocky hill at the edge of town, the fortress stood on the foundations of a fortification built by Iskandar in late 330 BC when he captured Artacoana, the Arian capital.

Herat was a vast collection of mud-colored houses, domed minarets and mosques bordering narrow streets and twisting alleys radiating from the walled Old City. Motor vehicles, unable to drive in the ancient part of town, parked at the foot of the remains of a fortified wall. Our taxi dropped us off among buses and trucks parked for the night. A piercing cold wind blew from the western hills stirring the trash lying about and we entered the warren of poorly lit streets. A gang of half a dozen kids, all boys and none older than ten, materialized around us; hands out, shrieking in Pashtu and laughing.

Ian asked the oldest for a hotel repeating the word and pointing at the surrounding buildings. One of the kids replied volubly and beckoned us to follow. He led us along a twisty, narrow street to a three-story stone building. The diminutive Afghan held his palm up and chanted, "Otel… Otel!" Ian dropped a coin in his hand and the pack scampered off.

The hotel's door opened into a narrow hallway with a desk standing against the back wall and a steep stairway that led to the upper floors. Kerosene lamps cast a soft yellow glow on the orange walls. An Afghan, seated behind the desk and below one of the hissing lamps, was reading a newspaper. He peered at us and reluctantly welcomed us in strongly accented English. We took a room on the second floor and paid ten rials each for a charpoy (rope-bed).

We were starved for food and hash so we walked down the street looking for a restaurant. Lode found a large chai-khana (teashop) near the hotel where we sat cross-legged on a raised dais covered with woven rope mats and faded carpets and waited for our food. A murmur filled the cozy, lamp-lit room as Afghan patrons sharing the platform ate from common platters and others sucked on water pipes. The place smelled of stewing meat, spices and hashish and we relaxed as we absorbed the atmosphere. A server gave us chai and a basket of flat bread followed by large bowls of mutton stew with rice and assorted vegetables.

As the waiter cleared the trays he asked if we wanted sheet. Bemused, we looked at each other to see if any of us understood what he was asking. The waiter repeated the word sheet, pointing at a group of locals who waved, smiled and waggled their water pipes. Comprehension finally dawned, we nodded eagerly and the Afghan patrons who had followed our exchange laughed and shouted encouraging comments, pointing at their pipes and repeating, "Sheet, sheet!"

The waiter returned carrying four pipes. In each pipe's bowl sat a goolie of hash: a ball of black dope the size of a chickpea. Before lighting mine I rolled the small sphere between my fingers noting how soft and fragrant it was. Well-fed and reasonably buzzed, we made our way back to our room.

* * *

After breakfast at a chai shop, we strolled into the medieval Old City to the Chahar Su bazaar - the name means "the four directions" - in search of a moneychanger. We found a slim, bearded Tajik with startling green eyes sitting cross-legged on a worn bit of carpet with a hand-held balance scale, brass weights and stacks of bills and coins on a low table. Trev showed him a fistful of rials and pointed at a stack of afghan bills. The Man spoke a few words of English and invited us to sit on low wooden stools at one side of the carpet. He shouted at a kid who tore off into the market and returned moments later balancing a copper tray on which wobbled five cups of chai. I loved the hospitality in the east. Nothing is so urgent that you can't take the time to chat amiably and sip a cup of tea. We exchanged all our rials (they were more or less at par with afghanis), some American dollars and five British pounds.

Afterwards we meandered through the souk looking at the enormous variety of merchandise displayed. For a pittance, I bought a chillum carved out of dark red stone and a silk bandana but I will forever remember one particular store as the defining, quintessential Afghanistan.

This general-goods emporium occupied the ground floor of a building at the edge of the bazaar. Among the merchandise on display, we saw a forty-five-gallon drum filled to the rim with loose small-arms ammunition. Stubby nine mil bullets, long seven-sixty-two NATO rounds, three-oh-three and three-fifty-seven ammo jumbled together like assorted nuts. The shop owner watched us rummaging in the barrel and, smiling invitingly, pointed at the wall behind him on which hung a collection of guns. These ranged from homemade-seeming wire-wound flintlocks to scarred WWII-era Belgian FNs, twelve-gauge shotguns, hunting rifles and army-surplus carbines. Astounded, I stared in awe at an antique nine-mil Mauser that must have dated back to the Boer war. We politely declined the shopkeeper's offer and left.

It occurred to us later that such shops were necessary for the rural trade. You could always recognize the out-of-town Afghans because they invariably strode through the bazaar with a belted wickedly curved knife and a shouldered rifle.

* * *

Gerard had given me the address of an old friend of his named Jacques. A few days after our arrival I set out to find the Frenchy and followed one of the wider thoroughfares north of the Old City until it dwindled into a labyrinth of dirt-packed lanes. Compounds surrounded by tall mud walls and rusted steel gates hid the houses and made finding Jacques' address almost impossible. Luckily, I soon attracted an entourage of small children and by repeating the word "Ferengee" (foreigner) they led me to a once-red metal gate. I gave the kids a coin and knocked on the steel panel. A turbaned Pashtun opened the gate, looked me up and down and rattled off a few sentences.

"Ferengee Fransosy Jacques?" I asked uncertainly.

To my surprise, he understood and invited me in, closing and locking the door as soon as I cleared the threshold. A two-story cinder block house overshadowed a small paved courtyard; a plain, wooden stairway ran up the side of the building. The Afghan pointed at a door at the top of the stairs and said, "Jacques."

I climbed up and knocked. "Allo? Jacques?" I asked in French.

A chair scraped on the floor and the door creaked open revealing a medium tall, thin man with long grayish hair drooping from a balding pate.

"Oui?" he said blinking bloodshot, pale blue eyes.

I introduced myself and when I mentioned Gerard, Jacques smiled and invited me in. His digs, a single large room lit by a pair of narrow windows, was sparsely furnished with little more than a rope-bed, a small table and two chairs. A hurricane lamp hung from the ceiling above a squat, compact cast-iron stove that huddled on a brick platform in one of the room's corner.

Jacques was quite a character. When I asked how he ended up in Herat, he explained that one day in 1968, he stepped out of his apartment in Paris to get a pack of smokes and just kept on going. He rambled around the Mediterranean, spent a summer in the Greek islands, lived in Turkey for half a year and ended up in Herat where he made an adequate living selling drugs to western backpackers.

While we sat at the table and chatted, Jacques chose one of a dozen glass jars aligned on a shelf and fished out a chunk of black and amber marbled hash. He shaved off a few shreds, stuffed them into a small brass pipe, torched it with a scuffed zippo and took a single, long toke. He tapped the bowl in an ashtray, refilled the pipe and passed it to me. I fired the hash and inhaled a single, long toke savoring a surprisingly complex flavor.

"Opium/hashish from Pamir. The best shit comes from the north of the country," Jacques said.

I believed him. That one puff practically paralyzed me. I was as stoned as if I'd dropped acid though thankfully, the initial effects diminished rapidly and leveled into a steady, strong buzz. Jacques, less blitzed than me, threw some sticks in the wood stove and stoked the fire. He filled a blackened, battered kettle with water from a plastic jug and positioned it on the stovetop.

His droopy eyes swiveled toward me and he said, "I collect...Mmm, exceptionally rare dope. Friends bring me shit from all over." He waved his hand at the glass jars on the shelf and I rose to study the containers: they held a variety of diversely colored and shaped lumps of hashish.

"Go ahead, take a sniff."

I opened a jar labeled "Bhutan" and inhaled deeply. The reddish lump was redolent of hashish, mushrooms and green grass. Another contained a fist-sized, black and brown chunk emitting a spicy fragrance with undertones of honey, a label on the lid said Nepal. I scrutinized and sniffed bewildering varietals rarely seen in the west. White-streaked black lumps from Kashmir, brown lumps from places like Kyrgyzstan, Balochistan and Sikkim.

"The Pamir dope is certainly strong enough. Can I buy some?" I asked. The kettle started whistling and Jacques filled a ceramic teapot with the boiling water.

He shrugged. "Oh, that stuff is not very rare. I'll sell you a few grams."

He poured tea into two enameled mugs and set them on the table. While I stirred sugar in mine, Jacques broke off a small chunk of the marbled hash and handed me the lump. "About six or seven grams cost you sixty afghanis (about a buck). This country is a stoner paradise. Besides hash, you can buy opium, morphine or heroin. The down side is too many junkies."

"You must have seen some pretty strange shit, living here," I said.

"Yes. Don't get fooled by the trappings of civilization. Herat is still medieval. Most of the time things are quiet, people go about their business." He refilled our cups. "But, during religious holidays... Well, then you have to be careful."

* * *

We drank and smoked as Jacques told of one particular Ramadan in 1970: two French Freaks, eighteen and nineteen years old, arrived in Herat at the tail-end of Ramadan. They walked through the bazaar, hungry, thirsty and frustrated because all the chai-khanas closed until sunset. Ramadan requires thirty days of fasting from dawn to dusk. As the two Freaks meandered between the stalls, one of them surreptitiously grabbed a handful of pistachios from an open bag and stuffed the nuts in his pocket. As luck would have it, the stall owner spotted the theft and raised an outcry. An infuriated mob seized the Frenchmen, roughed them up and shoved them at a Mullah's feet for good, old-fashioned Sharia justice.

"Are you familiar with Sharia?" Jacques asked.

I nodded. The Arabs in Israel also used the Islamic law.

The Mullah and the victim of the crime - Jacques continued his story, - both notorious fundamentalists renowned for their dislike of everything western, held a Jirga, an assembly of elders to determine punishment. The hapless French youth was condemned to a traditional Islamic chastisement for theft: Amputation of the appendage used to commit the offense, in this case, his right hand.

Jacques raised an eyebrow and asked, "You understand the meaning of the right and left hand in this culture?"

"Eh, pardis!" I replied. We'd been wiping our asses without paper since leaving Istanbul. In the east, touching someone or eating with the left hand was worse than an insult. Cutting off the right hand condemned a man to virtual banishment from society.

Jacques who had observed the Jirga was appalled. He was sure the local civil authorities would not dare interfere (Afghanistan in those days had a sketchy civil legal system) lest they caused a riot and he knew the Mullah could use this God-given opportunity to make an example of the hated Ferengee hippies.

Jacques, thinking fast, approached the Cleric's court and offered his services as a French translator. The Mullah agreed and allowed Jacques to visit the two terrified backpackers imprisoned in the backroom of a store, guarded by a fierce-looking, riffle-totting Uzbek.

The naive youths had not understood a word of the charges brought against them or of the verdict delivered by the Mullah. Jacques explained the situation and the near certainty that Islamic justice would exact the penalty soon. The poor thief burst into tears while his partner begged Jacques to contact the French embassy in Kabul. So he contacted the consulate and relayed an urgent request for assistance.

A consular aide asked Jacques to try and delay the execution of the sentence until the consulate could send someone to Herat. Jacques returned to the Cleric's court and petitioned the Mullah to wait until the French official's arrival before proceeding any further. The Mullah magnanimously deferred the proceedings until the following day. Jacques spent the night with the two drifters, sprawled on a pile of stinking sheep hides, listening to their heart-breaking sobs and whimpers in the darkness of the windowless storeroom.

A black Peugeot covered in dust and splattered with bugs, flying the French flag on its front fender, arrived in the pre-dawn gloom and pulled up in front of the Old City. Marcel, a consular aide, jumped out and ushered a white-bearded robed and turbaned Afghan out of the vehicle.

The Uzbek guard holding a kerosene lantern in one hand opened the door of the makeshift cell, flooding the room with light and waved Marcel and his Afghan companion inside. The guard hung the lamp from a ceiling beam and closed the door. Marcel introduced himself and the elderly gentleman, His Eminence the Mujtahid Omar Obaidullah, revered scholar of the Qur'an and sometime consultant to the international legations in Kabul. After listening to the accused and to Jacques, the two officials called for the guard and departed.

Later that morning, the Mujtahid and the Mullah started an intense, public, three-day-marathon of debates, arguments and counter-arguments about the finer points of the Shari'a and Islamic law, The devout Herat male population reveled in this rare meeting and treated it as if it was a sports event. The scholars lounged comfortably on sofas in a shaded courtyard while spectators, sitting, squatting or standing in every nook and cranny of the yard, nodded their heads and stroked their beards.

For the duration of the debate, the Mullah released the two youths into Jacques' custody and he kept them stoned, fed and watered in his room for three days. Marcel had returned to Kabul having promised to return, if needed, after the scholarly debate.

"So, what happened?" I asked as Jacques trailed off.

"Well, the Mujtahid managed to prolong the deliberations and delay the verdict for three days until the end of Ramadan, which is followed by Eid ul-Fitr..." He peered at me, his eyebrows raised like a teacher prompting for a response. I shrugged in ignorance and he said, "Eid is a holiday during which devout Muslims are encouraged to be charitable and forgiving."

The Mullah, delighted by the attendance of his flock and the notoriety the dispute garnered, graciously commuted the sentence to banishment and the two drifters immediately left for Mashhad. Everyone agreed that the scholarly debate was the best they'd seen in a long time. We looked at each other, shook our heads in wonderment and laughed. It was getting late so I thanked Jacques for the story and refreshment, took my hash and returned to the hotel.

Days passed in a stoned blur. Time slowed, its passage marked only by the calls to prayer repeating from every minaret in town. We indulged in a haze of hash and opium, lived comfortably on pennies per day and ate if we remembered. The hotel had few amenities; no showers and no electricity. We used kerosene lamps and candles in the room and the fly-infested, malodourous shitters were medieval-filthy.

Despite the lack of modern comforts – in fact, because of that - I loved Herat. Climbing the creaky wooden stairs to our floor, lighting the candles on the room's bureau and sleeping on a charpoy, imparted a sense of enchanting, peaceful timelessness. It was easy to imagine living here centuries ago when caravans traversed this region on their way to trade in Samarkand and beyond.

We ventured out and wandered through the city and every day backpackers passing through would treat us to their stories about Pakistan, India and Nepal. We were now tantalizingly close to our destination but our tight little group, which had travelled together since Amsterdam was on the verge of splitting up.

Ian and Trev considered going to Kabul while Lode and I intended to head for Kandahar, then to Quetta in Balochistan (Pakistan) from where we'd take the train to Karachi. We argued back and forth but in the end, the two Scousers decided to go as far as Kandahar with us then choose whether to carry on to Kabul or to come east to Pakistan.

* * *

Chapter Ten

It's Been Quetta Trip, Man

Quetta/ Karachi, November 1972

In Context:
- The Soviet Union's fourth and final attempt at launching a rocket powerful enough to carry a manned lunar orbiter fails. The rocket explodes twenty-five miles up.
- Atari Games releases the arcade version of Pong. It's the first commercially successful video game.
- Dow Jones Index closes over 1,000 for the first time.
- Richard M. Nixon wins re-election by a landslide.
- Dr. Solomon H. Snyder and his assistant, Candace Pert, make the critical discovery that receptors for opiates are in each brain cell and the search begins for opiate substances within the body.

* * *

We decided to travel by bus rather than hitchhike. The fares were cheap and other backpackers said that Afghan and Pakistani car drivers always demanded cash for fuel. So, on a bright cool morning the four of us boarded an ancient bus for Kandahar. The old vehicle had seen better days (the benches' padding had long worn off) and the passengers included chickens in a cage and a goat tethered in the aisle. We followed a pot-holed two-lane road through an arid desolation reminiscent of the Dasht-e-Kavir desert and stopped for lunch in a small village. At prayer times, everyone disembarked and the men spread their prayer mats on the verge by the road and as a result the trip was longer than it should have been.

After Gereshk, we crossed the Helmand River over a rusted Bailey bridge and drove eastwards along a range of hills skirting parched-looking fields and sparse, rocky pastures. The district suffered from a crippling drought that year and the few dusty trees we saw offered little shade. We reached Kandahar (named after Iskandar) well after dark and found rooms at a tourist hotel near the town center. The stores and restaurants were closed at this late hour but the hotel clerk gave us a dozen pieces of stale naan we devoured appreciatively.

Next morning after breakfast in a nearby chai-khana, we set out for the post office to check for mail. Kandahar was larger than Herat with a corresponding increase of traffic and crowds. Minarets and domes towered over the roofs and the Muezzins' calls to prayer echoed from loudspeakers perched at the top of the spires.

We met a tall, young Danish drifter named Axel, on the way to the post office. He wore a bulky sheepskin thrown over his broad shoulders and, thanks to his six-foot-four frame and to his long, shaggy red hair and luxuriant beard, he resembled a barbarian warrior from the mountains.

There was no mail for any of us at the poste restante so we loitered downtown, taking in the sights. Later, Axel led us to a chai-khana frequented by Freaks and travelers near the central bus terminal. The ancient-looking restaurant, once a renowned caravanserai was a sprawling single-story building in which patrons, eating from bowls on trays, sat cross-legged on floor mats. We ordered food and beverages and the servers brought tea and platters of the day's fare.

Lode asked how far it was to Quetta. Axel swallowed a mouthful of mutton stew and replied, "About a hundred-and-fifty miles. Counting the time to cross the border it takes pretty much the whole day. There are mountains on the Pakistan side but they're not as tall as the Pamirs."

Ian pushed a chunk of boiled potato to the edge of his plate and asked, "How far to Kabul?"

"Cobble?" Axel pronounced Kabul in the local manner. "Twice as far as Quetta and you have to cross the Khyber Pass. This time of year, what with the snow and the cold, the trip can be miserable. You gonna finish this?" He speared a big greasy lump of mutton congealing on Ian's plate.

Lode and I left them and walked to the bus terminal to inquire about transportation to Quetta. We had a choice of four departure times throughout the day; the earliest leaving at seven in the morning and arriving at the Chaman border crossing by noon. From there we'd hop on a Pakistani bus to

Quetta.

I sighed and said, "Decision time."

Lode gave me a pensive look. "Danny, I'm for heading south. It's going to be full winter soon and I'd rather not hang around in Kabul."

I nodded in agreement. "Yeah, I know. Better head for a tropical setting like Karachi and then push on to India."

We returned to the hotel weaving through a crowd of merchants, peddlers, laden donkeys, camels and pushcarts. Small children threw stones at scrawny dogs nosing in piles of garbage.

Lode cleared his throat and asked, "Have you thought about how you'll be getting home, you know, after India?"

"Get a job as a deckhand on a freighter in Bombay or Goa," I said.

"Good idea, there's a lot of traffic from Bombay to Europe. What about documents?" He was referring to Seamen's qualification certificates and the like.

"Gerard gave me a contact in Bombay who can get us fake papers. Apparently if you're willing to work for passage rather than pay you'll have no problems getting a berth."

Lode's mood lifted as he mulled over the idea of working on a ship.

We found Trev and Axel smoking hash in the hotel's backyard. We joined them on the weathered benches, basking in the weak sun's warmth.

"Where's Ian?" I asked Trev as he passed the pipe.

"He discovered there's a hamam in town…"

I shook my head. Ian's fastidiousness bordered on obsession. Although to be fair, I thought, we all smelled ripe, as there had been few opportunities to wash up in the last couple of weeks. In Herat, taking a bath required heating water on the hotel kitchen stove and hauling a number of buckets to a tin tub.

I glanced at Trev and reflected about all the miles and adventures we'd had since leaving London, how we'd become like brothers during the journey. It was depressing to think that from here we would go our separate ways with little likelihood of meeting again.

He must have had similar thoughts because he looked at his feet and said, "Aw, fuck it! We decided to carry on to Quetta with you wankers. You'd probably get lost if we didn't hold your hands, sort of thing." He glanced up at us with a widening grin matching my own.

That evening Axel steered us to a chai shop near the blue-domed Friday Mosque. After the meal, as the staff lit kerosene lamps, we settled to smoke hash in the amiable company of the locals. Some of the patrons played odd-looking stringed instruments and soon everyone in the restaurant was singing along. I since learned that the bizarre-looking instruments were a Dutar, the pear-shaped, bouzouki-like lute and the Rahab which is partially covered in goatskin and has a number of different strings, some made of nylon and others of steel.

* * *

The bus to Spin Buldak, the Pakistani port of entry at the Chaman border crossing, left Kandahar on schedule and by mid-morning, we were bumping our way along the northern edge of a vast expanse of reddish sand dunes called unimaginatively the Red Desert. The russet and ocher wavy mounds abutted a desolate, arid mountain range sparsely populated by Noorzai Pashtuns; most were armed to the teeth.

Smartly turned-out, armed Pakistani soldiers staffed the crossing at Chaman, which seemed much busier than Islam Qala. Scores of people, livestock and vehicles jammed the road waiting to cross into Pakistan. Drovers leading grumbling camels, mules and braying donkeys weaved in and out of the stalled traffic, adding to the overall sense of total chaos. The bus dropped us off and after retrieving our backpacks, we followed the other pedestrians past one last Afghan outpost. We paid an exit fee and had our passports stamped. We had been advised to change all our afghanis here at the Chaman crossing. They were worthless outside the country so we converted them into rupees and took a beating on the exchange.

A couple of hours later, we finally boarded a Pakistani bus for Quetta and started the laborious climb through the Black Mountains to the Khojak Pass. The road twisted back and forth in tight, hairpin curves bordered on one side by steep, rocky cliffs and a sheer drop on the other. From this high vantage point, I had an excellent appreciation of the route Iskandar and his army had traversed on their way to conquer India. His engineers had built bridges to span gorges and widened goat trails to allow the elephants and the immense supply train to keep up.

We reached the outskirts of Quetta in the early evening after descending from the surrounding hills and were surprised at how spread-out the city was. Quetta's lights sprawled for miles along the bottom and sides of an elongated valley. The bus drove through crowded streets to the northern terminal and I felt a jolt of elation as we arrived in the capital of Balochistan. We gathered our gear, shook the dust off our packs and walked out of the bus terminal. I noticed with consternation that the nylon webbing around the frame of my backpack was badly frayed and holding on by a few threads. Too many miles on the roofs of various vehicles, I thought, I'd have to fix the pack or get a replacement.

Trev asked an English-speaking passerby for directions to the Lahore Hotel, near the railroad station and we trudged down a wide boulevard drinking in the sights and sounds. The Balochi men sporting beards and thick black mustaches had darker skin and finer features than the Afghans did. They wore turbans and shalwar pants (legs wide at the top and narrow at the ankles) and kameez (long white tunics worn over the baggy pants). The stalls and shops prepared to close for the night. Merchants and their helpers moved displayed goods, from the sidewalk back into the stores, before rolling down gaudily painted, corrugated steel doors.

The Quetta train station occupied an entire block of a wide boulevard and its lights glittered like a small city. Clouds of fluttering insects dive-bombed the light fixtures, some occasionally falling down on the people milling in front of the terminal. We found the Lahore Hotel nearby and paid for four manjaas (charpoys) in a room on the third floor.

Lode asked, "How are we doing for rupees?"

"We have almost forty. That should be enough until we find a moneychanger in the morning," I said.

After ditching my backpack, I followed a familiar scent down the hall to a room and saw, through the open door, a pair of Freaks sitting on a manjaa passing around a chillum of hash. I introduced myself, took a deep toke of the proffered fragrant dope and sat on other bed with my back against the wall. A few moments later Lode and Trev poked their heads through the opening and joined us.

I made introductions. "Lode, Trev. Meet Don and Greg from the States."

The Americans were going to India and had been on the road for two months. The other four chatted while I prepared a toke with hash I had inadvertently carried across the border. By now, preparing the chillum was routine. I tore a piece of the silvery, inner wrapper from a pack of smokes and burned off the paper layer leaving pure foil, which I rolled into a tight little ball the size of a pea and dropped into the bottom of the pipe to block any coals from being sucked through the mouthpiece. Next, I thoroughly mixed tobacco with crumbled hash and tamped the dope mixture into the deep bowl.

We preferred to use a wet cloth to cool the smoke and, after soaking and wringing a red bandana, I wrapped it around the chillum's stem covering the mouthpiece. I leaned towards Trev, who lit a match and applied the flame to the tobacco mixture. I inhaled deeply drawing in a large amount of smoke, held it and exhaled. As the chillum moved from person to person, hashish smoke shrouded the room's ceiling.

Greg ran his fingers through his long blond hair, expelled an astounding amount of smoke and exclaimed, "Holy shit! This is great stuff. Can I take a gander?" He sniffed and squeezed the black lump I'd tossed him and passed it on to Don who copied his friend.

"That's Nepalese and when it's fresh, just holding it in your hand is enough to soften it," I explained.

Lode asked, "Did you guys come from Kandahar or Kabul?"

Greg reached for his backpack, extracted a tattered road map from a pocket and laid it on the floor. He traced the route with his finger and he said, "Neither. We bypassed Afghanistan altogether and came from Teheran via Qom, Isfahan, Zahedan and across the Kavir-e Loot desert."

"Right through the wasteland." Don, his tanned face split by a maniacal shit-eating grin, pointed at a point where the borders of Iran, Afghanistan and Pakistan joined.

* * *

The next morning we met the Americans in front of the hotel and repaired to a restaurant nearby for breakfast. We ordered eggs and naan and sipped on the hot, sweet chai that had appeared as soon as we sat down.

Greg asked, "Where are you guys going from here?"

"We'll take the train to Karachi. We've had enough deserts. Just think, palm trees, coconuts, the Indian Ocean…" Ian replied with a dreamy look in his eyes.

"The Arabian Sea," Lode corrected and got two fingers in reply.

"Tramp freighters sailing up and down the coast offer inexpensive passenger service as long as you don't mind camping on the deck like the natives, sort of thing," Trev said.

Don and Greg nodded thoughtfully: most backpackers chose the route from Kabul to Peshawar to Lahore, through the Punjab and arrived in New Delhi (located in the north of India), which was relatively close to Nepal. Alternatively, our route would take us south to the Pakistani coast and then to Bombay on the west coast of India.

I mopped the runny eggs with a piece of naan and added, "From Bombay you can reach Nepal by train through Kanpur and Lucknow, avoiding Delhi completely, or go south to Goa and Ceylon."

After breakfast, the Americans went their way and the four of us strolled to the railroad station in search of a moneychanger. We found three Balochis competing to sell rupees for U.S. dollars — the official rate was seven-and-a-half rupees per dollar - and dealt with a short, swarthy man who offered twelve rupees. I changed a U.S. tenner and returned to the hotel to inspect my backpack. I hoped it was repairable but discovered that the nylon fabric wrapped around the aluminum tubes was disintegrating. The faded, threadbare material gave out easily and the outer pockets either had holes or were torn and dangling. I fondly remembered buying it in Haifa with Gerard.

I emptied the pack on the bed and contemplated my pitiful few remaining possessions. I had little worth keeping: a worn pair of jeans that would make cutoffs, a couple of frayed, oft-repaired shirts, three mismatched socks, a mangy sheepskin coat and two tee shirts so thin they were almost transparent. The soles of my Pataugas boots were separating from the canvas body and what was left of the sleeping bag stank worse than a decomposing goat. It was doubtful, I thought, that I'd need a sleeping bag, boots or the sheepskin coat any time soon as we were heading south towards tropical climes.

I grabbed the empty backpack, left the hotel and asked a passerby for directions to the bazaar. He pointed me towards Shahrah-e-Liaqat, relatively close to the hotel. Walking to the market, the morning's harsh light made me notice how monochromatic Quetta appeared: the barren hills, the streets and the houses were a colorless mud-brown as if God had spilled a giant cup of chai all over the city.

The sprawling market held a multitude of carts and booths laden with bolts of silk and cotton, bushels of fruits and pistachio nuts, barrels of olives, pickles and coffee beans, swaths of fresh-cut flowers, flats of bread, pitas and slabs of dried meats. The air reeked of wood-burning stoves sizzling with spiced kebab skewers of goat meat and other non-descript bits of mutton.

Poultry in wood-latticed crates sat by tethered goats and sheep adding their voices to the raucous din of vendors hawking their wares. Hobbled donkeys and camels brayed as they swished their tails in rhythmic motions to keep away swarms of flies. One section of the bazaar offered fur coats, jackets, vests, sandals and various satchels. I fingered a large bag made of hand-woven, orange-red dyed cotton and embellished with a small inset panel of Balochi embroidery. The satchel's strap was wide and reinforced with leather while the stitching was heavy gauge white twill.

The stall's owner spoke Pidgin English and we haggled over the price of the bag. I offered to trade the backpack, which he carefully inspected with a knowing eye. He discounted the frayed fabric but his eyes lit up as he tested the light aluminum frame that could haul much heavier loads than I had. In the end we settled for half the satchel's asking price plus my old pack.

Back at the hotel, I discarded everything except the best of the two shirts and the thickest tee shirt. I hacked my old jeans into shorts and threw out the socks and boots. From here on, I would wear only sandals. I packed all these items in the shoulder bag, added my journal, knife, chillum, harmonica and other knick-knacks collected along the way and slipped my head and arm through the strap. The satchel was light and fit comfortably.

I felt an absurd sense of freedom without the bulky backpack that had so often acted as a burden and an anchor. Now unburdened, I no longer had to worry about theft or the pack's safety as it bounced on roof racks. Everything I owned was snuggly by my side, highly portable and always available. When Ian spied the new satchel, he just had to have one and pestered me until I took him to the bazaar where he purchased a similar bag although he chose one with quite a bit more Balochi embroidery.

Don and Greg, looking wan and tired, returned to the hotel at sunset. They'd heard that they could sell their blood for five bucks and had walked half the length of Quetta in search of the right clinic. We four could always use money so the next morning after breakfast, we took a bus to the Mission hospital on Suraj Ganj road and sold our blood. The attending doctor and nurses seemed pleased to get westerners' blood – probably because it wasn't tainted with the myriad of diseases endemic to the region – and treated us very nicely. Thus started a pattern that, unbeknownst to me, would cost me dearly in the end.

The two Americans decided to join us on the trip south to Karachi and the next day we walked to the Quetta railroad station. Using our fake students IDs, we purchased discounted economy class (the cheapest) tickets and joined the dense crowd of Pakistanis, with their livestock and piles of luggage, on the concrete platform. We waited for the "Express-four Bolan Mail" train (Rawalpindi-Lahore-Karachi) and I was happy to continue following in the footsteps of Alexander; he'd used the same route south to conquer India.

* * *

The train pulled into the station at noon and the sea of waiting passengers stood up and surged toward the cars' doors. The antique locomotive was badly in need of a paint job but as soon as it stopped moving, half a dozen railroad wallahs (workers) jumped down, opened access hatches along the length of the venerable engine, lubricated and tightened everything that moved.

We lined up to climb aboard a battered third-class car passing by a gorgeous, dark-green, first-class coach. The passengers crowding the platform shook their heads, shouted in Urdu and Pashto and tried to shoo us towards the green car. We smiled and, taking advantage of the confusion, elbowed our way to the steps and climbed aboard the more modest coach. Wooden benches facing each other in pairs lined both sides of a central aisle the length of the wagon. Luggage racks extended from the wall above the seats and there was a toilet stall at the end of the car.

Trev found an empty pair of benches about halfway down the aisle, shoved his backpack on the storage shelf above and sat by the window. Ian, Lode and I followed suit while Don and Greg shared the adjacent set of benches. Apparently, each pair could accommodate six smallish people (jammed together) but we four, Ian's slenderness notwithstanding, with our broad shoulders and long limbs, left no room to spare.

The car smelled of tobacco, old curry and chicken shit; an endless stream of passengers shoehorning themselves and their belongings into every inch of space. A slim, turbaned Balochi carrying live chickens in a crate made of thin wooden slats remonstrated us in Urdu and gestured for Lode and I (we sat across from each other on the aisle end) to scoot over and free up a spot. We ignored him until he tried to park his scrawny butt on the sliver of available seating beside Lode and attempted to shove the Dutchman sideways. Lode smiled sweetly and thrust his hips towards the aisle propelling the hapless man and his poultry to the floor. The crate's hatch flew open and squawking chickens took off chased by their owner and a number of small enthusiastic children. Passengers standing around us witnessed the bit of drama and lost interest in the space.

The train pulled out of the station and soon after leaving town, a succession of peddlers carrying wicker trays or tall chai urns pushed their way through the crowded wagons, offering everything from hot beverages to naan and pastries. We followed the valley southeast of town then the train climbed and crossed the Bolan Pass.

An elderly, turbaned man sitting across the aisle from me spoke English and we struck up a conversation. Mohammad wore a luxuriant white beard and bushy, long mustache, which complemented his teak-colored face. He was traveling with his two sons, their wives and a bunch of kids, who spent the entire voyage running up and down the rail car slipping between, under and over obstructions like eels in a stream.

Mohammad was curious about us and strove to understand why rich westerners would travel in these appalling conditions. Lode and I explained the whole "going to India" experience and although the old gentleman asked many questions and often nodded, he clearly didn't or maybe couldn't, understand mystical India's appeal to Freaks like us.

The train meandered through successive valleys quilted with fields and villages. South of the Bolan River and the long lake of the same name, we entered an arid desert lined with towering red colored mesas. Tunnels pierced the hills allowing effortless transit through the ridges.

A strong aroma of curry and fresh naan flooded the air, soon followed by a number of men carrying stacked aluminum dishes. Mohammad called them dabbahwallahs and suggested that we buy supper before all the food was gone. We waved at a wallah and he detached tin dishes (Indian-style tiffin) held in a carrying cradle. Each container held a generous portion of curry chicken with veggies, potatoes, lentils and a folded piece of naan bread. A single meal cost fifty paise (half a rupee) or about five U.S. cents. Chaiwallas carrying ornate bronze urns with long spouts, followed the dabbahwallahs and poured mud-colored, sweetened tea-and-milk into enameled mugs.After the meal, I stood up and stretched, swaying with the moving railcar. At six-feet-two, I towered over the people crowding the wagon and I could only stand upright without banging my head, in the very center of the car. I slowly walked down the aisle through packed humanity, nodding and smiling at the curious passengers who greeted me in Urdu. People and their belongings filled the car while kids slept on the luggage racks, boneless limbs draped over suitcases, bales and boxes. I reached the far end and used the opportunity to take a piss. The toilet was an abomination and stank to high heaven. I had to breathe through my mouth and noted that the shitter consisted of nothing more than a shit-spattered hole in the floor of the car through which I could see the rail ties zipping by.

By the time I returned to our little enclave, the setting sun hovered over the western mountains. Orange-colored waves of heated air glimmered around the rocky pinnacles and painted the horizon in reds and yellows. High above the hills a few wispy clouds glowed with a pinkish hue. A skinny cow, its legs distorted by the heat waves, stood on a rise and appeared as a dark undulating silhouette backlit by the gigantic incandescent orb of the sun.

Darkness spread over the countryside and the train's windows showed only our dimly lit reflections. The overhead lights dimmed signaling quiet time. Parents corralled their boisterous kids and the noisy Urdu babble quieted as, lulled by the clickety-clack of the iron wheels, people settled to sleep.

* * *

The next day, the terrain changed from the arid, yellow-brown hills of Balochistan to the Hindus river-delta's vivid greens. Luxuriant fields, fruit orchards and tall, majestic palms rolled by as the tracks ran through hamlets, villages and small towns, separated by lush farmland.

Karachi was the largest city in Pakistan and had been the country's capital until the late 1950s. The metropolis sprawled astride the vast river delta and was home to more than five million people, most of whom it seemed to me, chose this day to congregate at the railroad terminal. We disembarked from the train, pushed our way through the crowd in the station and headed towards the Saddar (town center) where we would find cheap accommodations and the Freak community.

After the slow pace of Afghanistan, Karachi's colorful, smelly, loud and hectic streets came as a shock. Overwhelmed by the multitudes and as a preventative measure against trampling, we backed against a building's wall and stared in awe at the frenzy surrounding us. Brightly garbed people rushing in all directions, attempted to avoid squatting peddlers whose wares lay displayed on the sidewalk in front of them. Carts and stalls lined the curbs selling goods, services or a huge variety of foods and beverages such as lassi and crushed-on-the-spot, iced sugarcane juice.

I watched with fascination an ear cleaning stall where a client, head tilted sideway, sat on a stool while the practitioner delicately twirled oddly shaped bamboo implements inside his ear. Another cart sold wristwatches and sunglasses while the one next to it offered instant tailoring services, clients standing in skivvies while the tailor pedaled an antique sewing machine. Dogs and small children rooted through the detritus collecting between the stalls and in the gutters.

The streets were packed with a dense clot of bicycles, mopeds, bikes and motorized, three-wheeled rickshaws (called chinchis) that vied with cars, buses, trams and lorries. A cacophony of horns, bells and engine roars assaulted our ears as the incessant traffic jockeyed around stalled vehicles, slow-moving livestock and pedestrians balancing large loads on their heads. A variety of dray animals ranging from oxen to horses, pulled gaudily decorated carts heaped with produce, firewood or sacks of grain. The air reeked of diesel exhaust, dung, burning wood and kebabs with occasional hints of incense and perfumed flower blossoms. Passengers crammed buses and tramcars hanging precariously from any handhold in and outside. I saw riders dangling from roof racks while others balanced on the bumpers or bulged out of overcrowded doors.

Squatting near us an old crone wearing a saffron-colored sari, safeguarded a tray of Paan , a betel leaf wrapped around an areca nut. The cheap, chewable tidbit was popular (like chewing gum in the Western world) but Paan caused profuse salivation along with a light narcotic buzz and its millions of users, stained the city's sidewalks with red spit.

I ventured over to a cart selling lassi and, scrutinized with morbid curiosity by my friends, took a sip. The iced beverage consisting of yoghurt and fruit was delicious and refreshing. Sugarcane juice served on ice and the fruity lassis would become our favorite beverages. Feeling braver, we walked towards the Saddar. The colorfully garbed multi-cultural throngs made up of Muhajirs, Sindhis, Punjabis, Kashmiris and Balochis and others I couldn't identify, enthralled me. Although Karachi was predominantly Muslim it was also home to Christians, Hindus, Parsis, Ahmadis and a bevy of other religions, we saw a wide diversity of garishly decorated churches, mosques and temples liberally adorned with gaudy statuary and elaborate carvings.

We found the Katmandu hotel in a quiet, shaded alley off the main street and entered the cool, dark lobby. The hotel, a four-story building, sat in a walled compound surrounded by a yard choked with riotous growth.

A friendly, busty American brunette named May greeted us from behind the front desk. She was thirtyish, tanned and her bright yellow silk sari complimented her green eyes. A number of thin, hammered metal bracelets on both her wrists tinkled when she gestured. Beside her an oscillating fan on the counter moved the humid air and fluttered notices and photos pinned to the walls. A bead curtain behind her led to the Manager's suite, from which emanated the fragrance of spices and freshly baked bread. To the right of the lobby a stairway climbed to the upper floors.

Correctly assessing our financial means, May suggested that we rent one of two empty dorms on the top floor as they each accommodated eight people and cost less than paying for six individual beds. It made sense so we registered and climbed to the fourth floor noting the strong smell of hash at every landing. Our dorm consisted of a room brightly lit by wide windows overlooking an inner courtyard. Eight charpoys, four against each of two walls, left enough space in the center for a wooden table and mismatched chairs. Beyond our room the hallway led to the floor's shared washroom;

merely a concrete sink and faucet and the shitter.

Ian dropped his gear on one of the rope-strung, wood-framed charpoys and in falsetto sang, "Be it ever so humble, there's no place like home."

Trev leaned over the windowsill and surveyed the courtyard below. "'S not bad…"

A young man with a frizzy blond afro poked his head through the door and greeted us in a strong cockney accent, "Hullo neighbors. I'm Clyde from the Big Smoke. Welcome to Karachi!"

We shook hands with the young Brit who, like Ian, was short and slim. He wore an orange cotton tunic over white, baggy pantaloons and walked barefoot. Clyde invited us for a toke in his dorm, which was a twin of ours except it had posters on the walls. Seated around the table, Clyde's roommates, two American drifters and a pair of French women, smoked hash from a bamboo bong. Old food leftovers, crumpled greasy wrappers, empty bottles and dirty glasses littered the room. The place smelled rancid despite the masking cloud of hash smoke.

When I tired of the small talk and eager to explore, I descended to the lobby where May was writing in a ledger.

She looked up and asked, "Are you guys happy with your room?"

"Yeah, it's perfect, thanks for the suggestion, man."

"I'm curious, how did you hear of the Kat?"

I told her about the Freaks we encountered on our travels and segued into a condensed version of our journey from London, finishing with our hopes of catching passage on a ship to Bombay.

"That won't be a problem. Freighters from Karachi are plentiful. It's faster and way cheaper than taking a train back up to Hyderabad then getting to Ahmedabad and Surat." she said.

I wondered how she ended up in Karachi and she explained that she had drifted along the hippie trail and her karma had deposited her in Karachi; a city so engaging that she decided to go no further.

May looked up at me with an intent gaze. "This town has everything: drugs, booze, exotic foods, temples, great beaches and if you're seeking spiritual salvation, Karachi has more holy men than any other city. With so many religions rubbing elbows you can find Gurus, Sufis, Sadhus, Rishis, Swamis and their attendant pantheons. There are more ashrams than whorehouses." She had a distinct and contagious burbling laugh.

"Really, I thought that being Islamic, you know, life would be somewhat more restrictive."

"Nah, Karachi is not at all like Teheran or Kandahar. You can buy alcohol in stores, non-Islamic restaurants serve beer and wine and any kind of food you want."

I nodded and said, "I understand why you love it. Speaking of drugs, how do I score hash?"

"My old man Rajesh will get you some. He's the manager and we're shacked up in here. She pointed her thumb over her shoulder at the bead curtain behind her. "He'll be back in a couple of hours. Until then, here's a chunk." She handed me a gooli-sized lump of black hash.

I thanked her, stepped from the lobby into the shaded courtyard enclosed by tall concrete walls and stretched my limbs as I explored the garden. Date palms and mango trees growing along the perimeter, projected over riotous flowerbeds. A light breeze rustled the palms and carried fruity scents. A verdigris-covered, bronze elephant fountain with its trunk curved in a frozen salute dribbled a thin stream of water into a round brick pool. Wrought iron, benches, chairs and tables coated in flaking white paint were scattered in a rough circle around the fountain. The city din was muted and hardly noticeable. Lode and Trev emerged from the hotel and joined me by the fountain.

Trev admired the yard and exclaimed, "Man! I think we're in paradise." I nodded in agreement while I prepared a chillum.

Lode picked up and sniffed the gooli of hash. "No wonder so many Freaks never go beyond Karachi."

I passed him the loaded pipe and with satisfaction, said, "Karachi is the furthest that Iskandar reached. This area was named Krokola when he camped in the vicinity to prepare a fleet to sail to Babylonia after completing his campaign in the Indus valley."

Trev punched me lightly on the shoulder and said, "Why, Doctor

Livingstone, I give you joy for reaching your goal! You followed in the footsteps of Iskandar all the way from Greece."

I smiled fondly at my friend and replied. ''Aw...Thank you, Watson."

"That's Stanley you idiot."

* * *

We wallowed in Karachi's easy life. The famous Zainab Market was close to our hotel and we strolled through a labyrinthine mall of small shops and stalls selling handicrafts - both Indian and Pakistani - shoes, pashmina shawls, leather goods, and garments. We bought cotton shirts and pantaloons and dressed like the locals in a modestly successful effort to beat the oppressive heat. The merchants were friendly and truly believed every foreign traveler to be filthy rich. They would chase us through the crowded aisles shouting ever-decreasing prices before giving up and returning to their stalls.

In Europe and North America, an early and unseasonably cold winter drove a multitude of travelers east and we saw an increasing influx of backpackers arriving in Karachi. We routinely checked for mail at both the Amex and the Poste Restante at the central post office and one day to my astonished delight, I received a letter from my father. The airmail envelope was tattered and extensively covered with rubber-stamps and annotations in Urdu. I turned it over and examined the various marks as I sat cross-legged on the sidewalk leaning against the hot, sunbaked wall.

My dad's illegible scribbling crowded both sides of a single sheet of thin, pale blue paper folded around a U.S. fifty dollar bill. I fondly deciphered his crabbed writing. The news from home was reassuring, everyone was fine and the cash made me feel like I had won the national lottery. I celebrated by buying an ice-cold mango lassi.

With Clyde's French roommates, Don and Greg left Karachi on a train bound for Hyderabad. From there, they would find transportation to New Delhi. We spent a succession of idle days at the long, beautiful sandy beaches of Sandspit and Hawkesbay on Karachi's seaside. Newly arrived tourists with their blindingly white limbs shining like milky fish bellies, rode the length of the beach on horses or camels led by young kids. The sea was calm at this time of year and we snorkeled, usually quite stoned, for hours watching a remarkable variety of colorful marine life swimming below. Sandspit housed unusual rock formations and was a popular spot with both locals and Freaks.

About two weeks into our stay, Trev and I rode the tram back from Hawkesbay our wind-snarled hair crusty with salt and sand. The hotel's shower consisted of a rubber garden hose dangling from a hook on a wall in the courtyard. I showered under the tepid stream of water vigorously soaping my hair when I noticed a wriggling bug on the concrete beneath me. Thinking nothing of it, I continued rubbing my scalp but I could discern a subtle plopping click of something hitting the pad. Upon closer examination, I realized with revulsion that lice were falling out of my hair and writhing at my feet. I swore loudly, grabbed the hose and started rinsing them away.

Trev, waiting by the fountain for his turn at the shower, was laughing so hard he nearly fell in. Between gasping breaths he said, "Stop freaking out, man. Only, we all have them. The fucking place is crawling with bugs. I can't believe you're only noticing now."

Lode joined us as I was toweling off and Trev was under the hose. "I spent the afternoon at the harbor," he said as he fired up a beedie (sometimes spelled: bidis, they were inexpensive local cigarettes, little more than tobacco flakes rolled inside a tobacco leaf tied with a string). "I met an Engineer's mate from The Hague and we had a couple of beers. He confirmed that if we can get the right papers we'll be able to work for passage back to Europe." Lode unfolded a scrap of paper. "We need to have a Certificate of competency and a Level two NVQ (National Vocational Qualifications)."

Surprising us, Trev snarled, "Where the fuck are we supposed to get those kind of documents and how do we pay for them?"

"We'll find them in Bombay, man. You remember the travelers' cheques we 'lost'. We can sell them." I said.

"Ah yes. Well, right then."

He dunked his head under the stream of water and mumbled an apology. Lode went up to the room but I stayed on the bench waiting for Trev to finish his shower.

"Hey Trev, is there a problem I'm not aware of?"

He finished toweling his hair and stared at me. "It's Ian, sort of thing. You haven't seen the little wanker much the last couple of weeks, yes?"

"Now that you mention it, no I haven't but we've all been out every day.

What's the problem?"

"He's been hanging out with a Brit he met at the baths." Trev gave me a look loaded with meaning, which unfortunately passed right over my head.

I gestured for him to go on. "Yes, and…"

"Aw, fuck! You moron. His friend is a guy. Get it yet?"

I mulled it over for a moment and asked, "You think Ian is a homo?"

He put his hands on his hips, stared at me with a hard look and remarked snidely, "Maybe you should ease off on the dope, Danny. God, but you're thick!" He shook his head in irritation and kicked a small rock with his bare toe. "Ow! Yes. That's what I mean."

"But…, but, like, when did that happen?" I sputtered and then realized that Ian had been broadcasting signals since Ios in Greece where he often slept in the caves with his friend Carlos and he had spent a lot of time in the baths in Istanbul. I shook my head and conceded. "Ok, I'm an idiot, but so what? We don't judge, right? Go with the flow, man."

"The guy he's involved with is a junkie. I'm pretty sure he's got Ian shooting smack."

"Oh shit!" I lit a beedie and took a couple of deep drags to keep the crude cigarette going. "What do you want to do?"

"I think we should get the hell out of here and carry on to Bombay before Ian's way over his head."

We found Lode, brought him up to speed, decided to check the sailing schedules and rode the tram to the harbor where we walked along a dock lined with shipping offices and ship chandlers. The Scindia Steam Navigation Company offered the cheapest fares on their Bombay-bound freighters so we purchased four tickets, deck space only, on the Jaladhanya scheduled to sail to Bombay the next afternoon.

We returned to the hotel and Lode asked, "What do we tell Ian?"

Trev gnawed on a fingernail as he pondered the question. "Yeah, it will be tricky. Ian is very stubborn, sort of thing, and if we mention anything about his shooting up he'll just dig in his heels and be a total berk."

"Here's something." I showed them the front page of the Dawn, Karachi's English daily newspaper that Rajesh left in the lobby for the convenience of his lodgers. Karachi was plagued by major labor unrest in the industrial areas of Korangi-Landhi, the paper reported, and the police had killed and injured several protesters. Workers had briefly occupied some factories and the newspaper predicted further clashes as the situation worsened.

"This could affect the dockyards if the stevedores' union goes on a sympathy strike and shuts down all travel by sea," I continued, "We need to leave now while we still can or we'll be stuck here until they sort their problems."

Trev nodded his head and said, "That will do it! And we have the tickets." Later that evening when Ian returned to the hotel, I unobtrusively studied his pale, drawn face and his hooded eyes. His pupils appeared normal and I couldn't spot any needle tracks on his arms. Trev spoke with his compatriot, produced the newspaper and waved the boarding passes. Surprisingly Ian didn't object much and I wondered if Trev had misjudged the situation.

Ian shrugged, licked his lips and said, "'S kind of a rushed decision. I have people to say goodbye to, sort of thing."

"We're not boarding until noon. That gives you enough time?" Trev offered, "I'll come with you, if you'd like, and we could go straight to the harbor from your friends' place."

Ian nodded and rooted among the bags of left-over take-away strewn on the table.

* * *

Chapter Eleven

India's Awesome But It Still Bugs Me

India, December 1972 to March 1973

In Context:

- India and Pakistan exchange prisoners of war taken during the 1971 war. Five hundred fifty two Pakistanis and six hundred Indians are repatriated.
- Apollo 17, the last manned trip to the moon launches from Cape Kennedy after a delay of nearly three hours.
- Pink Floyd's The Dark Side of the Moon is released in the U.S.
- Denmark, the United Kingdom and the Republic of Ireland join the European Economic Community.
- Hussein Al Bashir, the Fatah representative in Cyprus is killed by a bomb planted under his bed. Israel believed him to be the head of Black September in Cyprus.
- The United States and Vietnam sign the Paris Peace Accords and end the longest war and military draft in American history.
- The Concert for Bangladesh wins an Emmy for Album of the Year.

* * *

We boarded the Jaladhanya amidst a group of forty passengers bound for Bombay, Goa and ports further down the Indian coast. The freighter's hull was black with a stained, once-white strip running just below the scuppers; scabrous patches covered the aft superstructure towering over the long deck and, like the entire ship, could have used fresh paint. Rust streaks oozed down the hull from various openings and to my surprise, a large cast iron swastika adorned the bow of the ship. Until then, I was unaware that the Nazis had stolen their cherished symbol from India, where swastikas often embellished buildings, temples and even wedding cakes.

Dark-complected, turbaned deckhands directed us forward of the superstructure to where a dozen cargo hatches (massive, rectangular steel lids) ran all the way to the ship's bow. We dropped our gear onto the rust-red iron deck, between a pair of three-foot high hatch coamings that offered protection from the wind as well as a modicum of privacy. Acknowledging our fellow travelers, squatting on their heels with their backs against the coaming, we prepared to camp out during the passage.

In late afternoon, the ten-thousand-ton freighter reeled in its mooring lines, blew its horn and ponderously made its way out of Karachi harbor. We sailed toward the setting sun over the Arabian Sea and the lively chops made me sway and lurch as I walked toward the stern. Karachi turned into an indistinct brown smudge on the horizon; the Manora Lighthouse at Cape Monze flashed every few moments and soon was the only sign of the distant shore. In less than forty-eight hours, my nine-month journey would culminate with our arrival in India.

That evening loudspeakers shrieked an announcement in Urdu prompting the passengers to head aft. Our neighbors mimed eating gestures and motioned us to join them in the growing line queuing in front of a serving hatch at the side of the superstructure. A galley-wallah handed out beat-up aluminum trays holding a plate of mystery-meat curry with rice and soggy vegetables, a cup of chai and a ragged sheet of naan bread folded in a triangle. The galley's floor must have been particularly wet and greasy because as the ship pitched, the nimble man slid from side to side and deftly thrust the tray through the opening before sliding out of reach again.

We returned to our spot and scarfed our meals, all but Ian. He gave his food to Lode then laid down curled in a fetal position, his head pillowed on his satchel. I squatted facing him and asked with concern, "Not feeling good, man?"

He shrugged and replied in a small voice, "I'm just not hungry."

"I've got fruit and some snacks if you prefer." He gave me a baleful look and turned away.

After supper, Trev and I walked to the starboard edge, lit beedies and stood at the railing. He had changed a great deal since we left England, I reflected. His face was rawboned and when illuminated by the harsh deck lights, his cheekbones like blades beneath his skin, gave him a hard look.

"What's wrong with Ian?" I asked while gazing at the hissing, phosphorescent turbulence created by the ship's hull.

"He's probably going through withdrawal symptoms. Do you have any opium left you can give him?"

I nodded and returned to our camp where I filled a small brass pipe with the last of our stash and handed it to Ian. He sucked on the stem like a drowning man on an air hose then laid back on the deck looking more relaxed as he fell asleep.

* * *

A breeze from the east, heralding the end of our two-day voyage from Karachi, brought a great earthy stench of rotting vegetation with overlays of excrement. The passengers shouted excitedly, pointing at a brown smudge on the horizon that soon resolved into Front Bay, Bombay's port on the western shore of the looming Indian landmass. An English-speaking passenger named Anurag informed us Bombay was the capital of Maharashtra and the largest city in India.

The diminutive, tanned Hindu looked to be in his mid-thirties and was returning from the Arab Emirates where he'd worked for the past year. Eager to re-unite with his family, he gazed wistfully at the horizon and said in a singsong accent, "We can't bring our families with us to the Emirates. Only workers can stay and only for the duration of their employment."

"Are there many Indians working in the Gulf?" Lode asked.

Anurag said, "Oh yes, tens of thousands of Indians and Pakistanis. Everyone sends money back to support our relatives and we try to come home to visit once a year."

Trev shook his head in sympathy. "Must be tough being away for so long, man."

The Hindu shrugged his shoulders and replied, "Karma! We're lucky to have those jobs and after a few years of work abroad I'll have enough money to buy a living: a small business in my home town."

As we slowly sailed into the congested bay, our Indian guide pointed at a hilly, wooded island and said, "Elephanta Island, also called Gharapuri. It is a big tourist destination because of the caves full of ancient religious carvings."

The Jaladhanya took on a harbor pilot who guided the ship to a pier lined with gigantic steel gantries that towered over us like enormous skeletal insects. Hundreds of vessels of every type filled the busy approaches and a cacophony of ship horns, screeching winches and metallic clatter blanketed the frenetic port. Dhows, dinghies, coracles and motor boats, playing a dangerous game of dodge'em, crisscrossed the waters ferrying people and goods.

Anurag pointed at the crowded shore and said, "The city has about six million inhabitants and the slums add another three million. Bombay is the commercial and entertainment capital of India and it makes New Delhi look like a village."

Lode, studying the bustling maritime traffic asked, "Speaking of slums is that where the hippies are staying?"

"I don't know where they live but I doubt it is in Dharavi, the bigger of two slums in Bombay."

A shabby tugboat, frayed rope fenders drooping from its bow and sides, pushed the Jaladhanya against the dock. Deckhands threw mooring lines to waiting stevedores while a crane lowered a gangway to the ship's deck and we lined up to disembark.

India, at last!

* * *

Following Ian's and my example, Lode and Trev had jettisoned their worn-out backpacks before leaving Karachi. Cold-weather clothing, boots, sheepskin coats and sleeping bags, were exchanged for light cotton tunics, pajama pants and sandals. It was with light steps that we alit on India's soil and headed out of the port area towards the Leopold café where, according to my notebook, Freaks and drifters congregated.

Bombay was vibrantly crowded, colorful, noisy, fragrant and bustling with sidewalk businesses. Vehicles, people and livestock packed the streets from edge to edge: rickshaws (pedaled and motorized) vied for space with, motorcycles, mopeds, bicycles, taxis, cars, buses, trucks, oxen, donkeys, horses and to my delight, we spotted elephants, pulling two or four-wheeled carts hauling produce, construction materials and firewood. Dogs and cows wandered through traffic, blithely ignoring the blasting of horns and shouting and forcing drivers to brake hard or swerve urgently to avoid collisions. The streets were redolent with complex aromas of wood smoke from braziers, grilling meat, freshly baked breads and incense intermingling with whiffs of rotting produce, urine and manure.

We wandered through the streets of Bombay captivated by the colors, smells and sounds, in time arriving at the Leopold, a mid-sized restaurant, on the Colaba causeway where we stepped in to grab a bite to eat.

Inside, we happened on Paul and Scott: Two Americans draft dodgers now living in Bombay. They'd dropped out of a Los Angeles college in 1970, drifted through Europe and Asia and washed up in Bombay where the inexpensive cost of living, the salubrious climate and the easy availability of drugs made the city a perfect place to hang out. The pair of Californians rented a flat with two bedrooms and, as their previous roommates had recently continued on the road to Nepal, they offered us one of the bedrooms to share rent and expenses. We gladly accepted the offer and followed them back to their flat.

The apartment was within walking distance of the world-renowned Taj Mahal Hotel, famous for hosting the Beatles, the Stones, Led Zeppelin and other rock legends. The flat was well lit by wide, unglazed windows and consisted of two bedrooms, a privy and a large common room that served as kitchen, dining and living room. We took over one of the bedrooms furnished with four manjaas beds and a large armoire.

Only three days after we moved in with the Americans, Trev and Ian met Charlie and Neville, also Brits, who enticed them to share even cheaper digs at the Colaba hotel and, to my dismay, my two friends grabbed their few belongings and left with their compatriots. Lode and I were surprised at the suddenness of their desertion but knew we would see them often.

* * *

A few days before Christmas, a fortnight after our arrival in Bombay, I awoke with an agonizing toothache. A neglected cavity in an upper molar, which I'd ignored for too long flared into a steady pulsing pain and a red swelling of my gum. Minding Gerard's advice about medical help, I looked up the location of the French Consulate and asked our building wallah Vijay, for directions.

I flagged down a motorized rickshaw (called 'auto' in Bombay) and haggled for the fare in Urdu. Thanks to my aptitude for learning new languages, I'd acquired the skill in Pakistan and now spoke with relative fluency. I squeezed into the back of the three-wheeled Vespa-like contraption and the driver took off, merging into the dense traffic. He dropped me off in front of the consulate's medical clinic, a single-story building on the edge of a fenced compound in a quiet neighborhood near other foreign legations. I followed the signs to the admission desk where a nurse took my passport and invited me to sit in a hallway near the examination room.

I heard the high-pitched whine of a dental drill and almost walked out but the constant pain and the fear of runaway infection in this tropical climate convinced me to wait my turn. The door opened and a middle-aged woman looking pale, sweaty and faint tottered out of the room. A short, stocky young man in his late twenties with longish hair, sideburns, brown eyes and an easy smile, waved me to the dentist's chair.

We shook hands and chatted while a nurse pulled out a tray of stainless steel instruments from the autoclave and positioned them by the chair. In French, laced with a pronounced Provencal accent, the dentist said his name was Philippe and although born and raised in Marseille he'd recently graduated from the Sorbonne in Paris. After a yearlong internship in France, he was serving his mandatory army enlistment by working for the Consulate in Bombay.

Philippe, fascinated by the tales of my trek to India, dragged a stool closer to the chair and said, "I always wanted to travel like you but I have to pay back the government for my education so, I'm committed for the next few years."

I eyed, with apprehension, the gleaming steel picks and pliers. Hoping to delay the inevitable I asked, "Are you staying in Bombay the whole time?"

"I doubt it. I'll rotate between different legations but I'll be in India at least a couple of years." He selected a probe and a tiny round mirror and poked at my molar shooting pain all the way to my toes. Then after shaking his head dolefully he said, "I'm afraid it's much too late to save your tooth. You should have seen a dentist when you first developed the cavity. Now I have to extract it."

Philippe was a compassionate man who empathized with his patients and abhorred pain. He injected enough anesthetic into my gums to cause the loss of all sensations from the neck up. He confirmed that I was numb and extracted the rotten tooth with repeated twists of the pliers, after which he liberally applied antiseptic and packed gauze in the hole.

I gurgled my thanks and staggered from the chair. As we stepped out of the examination room, we saw a short, plump, sari-clad Indian woman and a teen-aged boy standing at the reception desk. The agitated woman, using a mixture of English and Urdu, was talking loudly and gesturing angrily at the despairing receptionist. Philippe gave me a bewildered look and asked if I understood what was going on. I nodded and tried to help despite my numb tongue and lips. Grateful for the intervention, the receptionist handed me a notepad and pen. I scribbled that the woman was an Indian national and her son, although born in Bombay, had dual citizenship by way of his French dad and needed dental care. Philippe agreed to help the boy, thought for a moment and asked me to return when the freezing wore off

I walked to the nearby central post office and I purchased a pre-stamped international airmail letter blank (a flimsy, pale-blue, single-sheet of paper), which also folded into an envelope. I wrote to my mom apprising her of my whereabouts and my general wellbeing. When the anesthetic finally wore off, I returned to the consulate where Philippe offered me a chair in the office adjoining the examination room.

"Would you be interested in a job?" he asked.

"Depends on the work. What's the offer?"

He twirled a pen with his fingers and explained, "Once a week I hold a free clinic in the slums; it's a consular charity thing. I really need a translator, someone who works cheap and preferably a French national, as that would save me a lot of paperwork."

"Well, I get by in Urdu; I understand Hindi and am fluent in English."

He said. "I barely speak English and I'm trying to learn Hindi and Urdu but for now I could use all the help I can get. What do you say? I'll pay you a daily wage."

I jumped on the offer as he offered twenty francs per day (about five U.S. dollars or seventy rupees on the black market) and the opportunity to observe, first hand, how India's most destitute lived. With the prospect of a steady source of revenue thus secured, I splurged on a black and yellow cab (called a Padmini) and spent most of the trip home haggling amiably with the driver.

When I arrived home, Paul, the sole occupant in the apartment, was sitting at the long dining room table crumbling a gooli of charas (hashish in Bombay). He waved as I entered and loaded a small brass pipe, lit it up, took a long drag and passed it to me. Vijay our building wallah, procured ganja (weed) also called sukha and Punjabi charas. Both drugs were inexpensive and plentiful in Bombay, a fact we routinely witnessed when we watched the religious Sadhus puffing on chair-leg sized joints of sukha rolled in strips of newspaper or consuming bhang, a cheap cannabis intoxicant.

I drew deeply on the pipe and sighed as I exhaled the pungent smoke. "Much better. It should help with the pain. Hey, I read a recent Time magazine at the consulate. Seems as if Nixon is willing to stop the war with Vietnam. Good news for you and Scott."

"Yeah, my sister wrote the same thing in her last letter but who knows how long it'll take to sort it out." Paul's already bleary hazel eyes teared up and he dropped his head so that his long brown hair covered his face. "I hope it's soon, I sure miss the States," he said under his breath.

To save him further embarrassment, I grabbed a towel and a bar of soap and climbed the stairs to the roof where a makeshift shower serviced the entire building. The contraption consisted of a couple of steel drums lashed in a wooden frame about seven feet above the flat roof. A plastic showerhead at the end of a short length of rubber hose and a shutoff valve completed the jerry-rigged amenity. Bombay's climate ensured that the water was always tepid and a water-wallah charged a tiny fee to top up the barrels every couple of days, hauling buckets of water by hand. The run-off simply drained through a hole in the parapet and spouted into the narrow back alley behind the building.

As I rinsed my soapy hair, watching lice wiggling in the suds and a large rat foraging in the corner, I heard angry voices shouting in Bambaiya (a Bombay slang composed of a blend of Marathi, Hindi, Urdu, and Indian English) drifting up from the alley. I leaned over the balustrade and looked down at four people squabbling over the pool of dirty water collecting in the lane's gutter. The street sweepers were fighting over the right to pan for gold in the open sewer. We learned about the gold miners when Vijay explained that the tenants on the second and fourth floors were Bengali goldsmiths. Gold dust, which accumulated in their hair and clothes at work, sluiced off as they showered and the sweepers panned the gutters for the precious metal, fighting viciously to preserve their privilege.

Lode had hooted in delight, exclaiming, "You're shitting us!"

The Punjabi concierge had put a hand to his breast, wobbled his head from side to side and said, "I'm most assuredly not shitting you, hippie. In this town the poor will do absolutely anything to make a rupee."

During our stay in the city, we often saw other examples of the innovative salvaging industry that the poorest inhabitants of Bombay perfected while mining the town's gigantic trash heaps for anything of value.

* * *

In January, Philippe held five free clinics in the Dharavi and Kurla-Ghatkopar slums. On those days I met him for breakfast at the Taj coffee house where we dined while watching the construction of an adjacent new tower to replace the defunct old Greens Hotel. Fascinated by my bohemian way of life, the Frenchman asked, "What do you do when you're not working with me?"

"I hang out at the beach or explore the city. It seems like there's a religious festival of one type or another almost every day in Bombay."

"What do your friends do for money?"

"Well, let's see: Lode helps at the Netherlands-Belgium Club, Trev and Ian do occasional work at the Slip Disc (a notorious club in Colaba) and we all sell blood. Once in a blue moon, we get a bit of cash in the mail from relatives."

He shook his head in wistful admiration. "Amazing! I envy you, free to come and go. Here one day, gone the next."

Afterwards, we'd hop in the consulate's minibus and head to the slums driven by a uniformed Hindu driver named Danvir. He was in his mid-thirties, tall, fit looking and immaculately dressed in khaki pants and shirt. Danvir wore dark sunglasses, seldom spoke and, I suspected, he also acted as consulate security keeping an eye on the young Frenchman.

Clinic days in the slums opened my eyes to the courage and ingenuity the desperately poor inhabitants demonstrated in the face of pitiable destitution. From Istanbul to Karachi, we'd seen countless examples of deprived, poverty-stricken people, some horribly disfigured or crippled such as the lepers of Silifke and the beggars of Quetta. Bombay's slums on the other hand, although home to some of the most impoverished people in the third world, bustled with frantic activity and had a noisy, smelly liveliness that belied and ignored the stigmata of dire poverty. It seemed that every slum resident, be it a small child or an old crone, toiled incessantly to earn a few coins.

We set up the clinic on the second floor of a two-story cinder-block building above a garment shop on the edge of the slum. The large rectangular room contained a score of child-sized desks and chairs. Drawings and educational posters papered the walls and a faded blackboard hung behind a wobbly wooden desk. Philippe explained that a Christian charity organization ran the schoolroom, one of the very few schools in the entire slum.

The day passed rapidly as Danvir and I herded a never-ending stream of patients to a makeshift dental chair (the teacher's wooden chair tilted back against a desk) where I translated the patients' complaints as well as Philippe's replies and instructions.

"Twenty-two extractions and I don't know how many cavities," Philippe sighed as Danvir drove us back to the Apollo Bandar neighborhood where I was staying.

"Is that unusual?" I asked.

"Not really. All that betel chewing is rotting their teeth. " He reached into his pocket and withdrew a small roll of bills. " Before I forget, here is your pay." He handed me a few limp, damp notes. I thanked him feeling as rich as Shah Jahan, the ancient Indian mogul, who built the Taj Mahal in the 1600s for his main squeeze, the Empress Mumtaz.

* * *

January twenty-ninth, my nineteenth birthday, Trev, Ian, Lode and I, reunited for the occasion and took the ferry from the Gateway to India Monument (at the edge of the city's harbor) to Elephanta Island. The small islet in the center of the bay was a popular attraction because of the cave temples carved out of the island's rock, the hundreds of indigenous monkeys, the fortress and its

canons left since the heydays of the British Raj and the plethora of peddlers'
stalls selling souvenirs, food and beverages.

Just like old times I thought looking fondly at the two Brits as we chatted
and joked during the hour-long crossing. Ian looked emaciated: he'd lost the
last of his baby fat but he seemed excited and acted almost giddy as he leaned
over the ferry's rusted railing pointing at the various small boats heading to
and from the island. Trev's face was gaunt and the corners of his eyes crinkled
with worry lines but he smiled a lot as we swapped stories about the past
month.

Later that evening back in town, I invited everyone to a birthday dinner
at a restaurant nearby. We stuffed ourselves with Punjabi delicacies and
reminisced about our adventures on the road to India. How much we'd
changed in the last ten months, I reflected: gone were the naïve Freaks from
the Galilee, London and Amsterdam; we were now a seasoned bunch of
drifters able to survive and thrive anywhere.

After supper, the two Brits invited us to accompany them back to their
digs at the Colaba hotel. The Colaba was a narrow four-story building that sat
between two office buildings in the heart of a busy commercial quarter.
Dating to the early part of the century, the hotel occupied the three upper
floors reached by climbing a set of narrow steps that led to an elongated,
rectangular lobby. Trev and Ian led us up to the third floor on stairs that
reeked of stale tobacco and piss.

We entered a spacious room containing four manjaas against one wall, a
long, scuffed, wooden table and chairs in the middle and a dilapidated sofa,
two sagging armchairs and a coffee table abutted the other wall. Open
windows and a light breeze couldn't dispel the stench of body odor, old food
and cigarette smoke. Flies crawled in and out of the trash strewn around the
room and buzzed around our heads. Unmindful of the dirty dishes, greasy
wrappers, old newspapers, overflowing ashtrays and empty bottles of beer
covering it, Charlie and Nev sat at the table.

Charlie, an emaciated, sallow-faced man with stringy long blond hair was
holding a bent spoon over a lit candle while stirring the contents with a
wooden toothpick. The tablespoon held a small mound of grayish-white
powder and a few droplets of water. As the mixture heated up the powder
dissolved in the liquid forming an amber-colored slurry.

Nev pulled his curly black hair into a ponytail and then handed Charlie a pinch of yellow, fluffy material, which I recognized as a decorticated cigarette filter. Charlie carefully positioned the filter in the concoction and, using a graduated glass syringe and needle, sucked up the liquid. Nev then tied a tourniquet around his sinewy left bicep, made a fist and flexed his hand until a vein rose in the crook of his elbow. Charlie leaned over his arm, poked in the needle and injected the content of the syringe. Nev untied the rubber tourniquet, tossed it on the table and reclined back in his chair. He closed his eyes and rode the rush.

Lode asked, "What is he shooting?"

Without lifting his hungry gaze away from Nev, Trev replied, "Speedballs."

Ian, aquiver with anticipation added, "Morphine and speed. Your birthday gift, Danny! Lode, want some?"

Lode visibly recoiled in revulsion and shook his head. I on the other hand, believed that I should try, within reason, everything at least once and although I loathed needles, (I spent a year as a teen getting weekly allergy shots) I was very curious. To this point, I had happily self-abused with opium, psychedelics, uppers, downers and all manner of cannabis derivatives but had never shot or tried any "hard" drugs. I nodded and said, "I'll try anything once."

Charlie waved me to a seat to wait my turn after Trev. He repeated the ritual by dissolving a measure of powder he spooned out of a small cellophane packet. Trev tied the rubber tube and Charlie injected him. Trev screamed in pain and shot out of his chair holding out his extended arm with the tourniquet dangling from his bicep. Tears in his eyes, hoping from foot to foot, he showed us his forearm, which had swollen with a huge blister.

Charlie shook his head in dismay and said, "Oh fuck, man. I missed the vein. Sorry. Here gimme."

He grabbed Trev's limb, held the syringe almost parallel to the skin, poked in the needle and sucked fluid into the rig. The blister shrunk and Trev stepped away swearing and kicking at the wall. Ian doubled over in laughter and even Charlie had a hard time keeping from laughing, Lode smirked with an "It serves you right" expression. Trev calmed down and shot up again, the drug easing any remaining pain. Then it was my turn.

I sat by Charlie, tied the tourniquet around my left bicep, made a fist and flexed it repeatedly as a vein rose and bulged beneath my grimy, tanned skin. Charlie rinsed the rig with water he extracted from a mug and squirted the last few drops into the spoon. He repeated the performance with spoon, candle and match, after which he sucked up the brownish concoction. He grasped and rotated my arm stabbing at the vein with the needle but wasn't able to penetrate. He poked harder cursing under his breath muttering about fucking blunt points. A burning pain in my elbow indicated that he succeeded and a swirl of blood flowed back into the syringe. Charlie slowly pushed the plunger emptying the speedball into me.

I barely had time to pull on the dangling end of the rubber tie to undo the tourniquet before the dope hit me. At first, it seemed as if warm liquid spread throughout my body immediately followed by intense rising euphoria. I closed my eyes and leaned back as the rush ratcheted up, notch-by-notch. A tiny conscious part of me, along for the ride, was wondering if it was possible to feel so good without my heart exploding and, as that thought flashed through my mind, like an accelerating rocket, I succumbed to an ever-increasing ecstasy.

I passed out for a while and woke up more stoned than I'd believed possible. I vaguely remembered staggering out of the room and down the stairs in need of fresh air. Thankfully, Lode, carrying my shoulder bag, accompanied me back to our apartment and I recall being so fucked up that I actually walked smack into the side of a slow-moving bus. The astonished look of the driver and the passengers as I rebounded from the vehicle was priceless and gave me a fit of giggles. My embarrassed friend jerked me off the street and steered me to safety.

That was my only experiment with the needle. I knew the high wasn't worth the risks. The next day I felt a bit depressed, partly because of coming down from the speedball, but also because I realized that Trev and Ian had become full-blown junkies with all the misery that entailed. I blamed myself somewhat because we rarely saw each other since their relocation to the Colaba and I had a gnawing suspicion that had we remained together, Lode and I could have counteracted their tendencies to self-destruct.

* * *

In the days following my birthday, Lode and I wandered through various parts of the sprawling metropolis and along the beaches lining both sides of the peninsula. There was so much to experience: the captivating, noisy festivals, ritual processions and naked Sadhus or Yogis performing amazing contortions and deeds. We watched in awe as religious adepts sporting numerous body piercings attached harnesses to huge steel hooks poking from the skin of their backs and pulled four-wheeled carts. Everywhere, colorfully garbed people mingled amid the performers handing out coins, gifts of food and flowers. We explored the endless markets, souks and bazaars sprawled throughout the neighborhoods while improving our grasp of Urdu and Hindi.

Every few days we stopped by the Amex and post office to check for mail and to rap with backpackers passing through. In front of the American Express office, we met Dagmar and Kerstin, a pair of beautiful Swedish girls dressed in light cotton saris with embroidered Balochi tops that complimented their pale yellow hair and freckled sunburnt faces. They invited us to share their refreshing mango lassis and in exchange, I rolled a cigar-sized joint of bhang that we smoked on the sunbaked sidewalk. They came back to our apartment where they crashed for the night. They were only in town until the next day and would then board a train to Ganeshpuri where they were booked to stay at the Shree Gurudev Ashram to learn transcendental meditation from Swami Karnataka. Lode covertly rolled his eyes when Dagmar primly explained their plans.

"You should come with us," Kirsten said, "Everyone is welcome at the ashram."

"Especially their money," Lode muttered under his breath.

I elbowed his side and replied, "You know, I always wanted to find out what the deal was with gurus and ashrams. We could detour to Ganeshpuri on the way to Nashik."

Lode reluctantly agreed as we'd planned to visit Nashik, further inland in Maharashtra, one of India's holiest sites and home to hundreds of temples and shrines and highly recommended by everyone we'd met.

The next morning, with the Swedes in tow, we purchased second-class train tickets and joined the masses waiting on the platform. Despite the overcrowding that forced passengers to perch on the cars' roofs, we plowed our way through and secured four seats on a pair of facing benches. There was ungodly screeching and shouting coming from above us as a troop of macaque monkeys swept down from the overhanging trees and raided the passengers' bundles and luggage in search of edible goodies. Although the distance from Bombay to Ganeshpuri is relatively short, the train ride lasted four hours because of numerous delays due to rail switching (our train would sit on a siding while a higher-priority train went by) and breakdowns. At every scheduled and unscheduled stop, a steady procession of vendors proffered trays, baskets and buckets of everything from beverages and snacks to jewelry and lighters.

From Ganeshpuri depot, a modest train station consisting of a small, single-story cinder-block building covered by a corrugated steel roof, we walked two miles to the ashram. It consisted of a temple and halls surrounded by well-tended fields and orchards. Despite the stifling heat, there was a bunch of hippies working in the fields, weeding between rows of green produce or hauling baskets. The pastoral scene reminded me of my kibbutz and, uncharacteristically, I felt a sharp pang of homesickness.

"How much does the guru charge you for joining the ashram?" Lode asked.

Dagmar named a number and his eyebrows shot up in surprise. The steep fee could support a guy, living in the city, for three months including all the dope he could smoke.

"You pay that much and you have to work in the fields?"

She replied with a goofy smile of delight on her face and said, "Of course! It's part of the whole experience. Working the land makes you one with the universe."

It was my turn to roll my eyes but I swallowed my retort as a slight, very brown, incredibly wrinkled old man wearing a saffron-colored sari came to meet us.

"Welcome. Welcome," he intoned in a high, singsong voice. "I am Balvindra, please follow me to reception."

"Are you the guru?" Lode asked.

"Oh, no! The Swami is much too busy to welcome all newcomers. Come, come, you will meet Him this evening after the chores are finished."

The two Swedes shouldered their packs and followed the short man into one of the halls lining the driveway. I held Lode back and pointed at the figures toiling in the insane heat. "You believe this?"

"I talked with a German hippie passing through Bombay a while back. He spent a couple of weeks here and said that the whole operation is a rip-off. I thought, maybe it was just him being cynical. Now I'm not so sure," Lode said.

"What did he say about the Swami?"

"Apparently the Swami likes his girls young and blonde. Everyone else works their asses off, chants, meditates and starves until they get all transcendental."

"Well, shall we continue to Nashik then?"

We hightailed out of the ashram and back to the train depot. So much for seeking Siddhartha or emulating the Beatles and other notorious rockers, I thought. It seemed that without money, tits or laboring like a slave, I would have to pass up the search for existential wisdom and the attainment of transcendental enlightenment. Om, mani, fucking padme, humbug!

* * *

We arrived at the Nashik Road Railway Station the following day after sleeping on the benches of Ganeshpuri's station and took an auto for the six-mile trip to the city center. The rickshaw dropped us in front of the Vaishali Hotel in the Gole Colony, two blocks south of the river, where we paid a couple of rupees to secure manjaas in a dorm and then went sightseeing in the ancient town. We wandered through the magnificent Shree Sunder Narayan temple, dedicated to Vishnu, Laxmi and Saraswati. The Naryan, built with black rocks, dated back to the eighteenth century and had a large round dome. Bright blooms and colorful banners covered the walls, the altars and every statue in the complex.

We tagged along with processions of priests, brightly garbed pilgrims carrying statues of Gods and intricately decorated elephants meandering among the milling crowds. The air was fragrant with incense, dung, brazier smoke and grilled food while drums, cymbals and odd brass or wood instruments vied with the traffic noise. Nashik was alive with tens of thousands of pilgrims, priests, acolytes, holy men, yogis and the usual collection of peddlers and merchants selling flower blossom chains, incense and religious offerings. A large crowd of devotees congregated at the banks of the river as bathers of all ages dipped in the muddy brown water with fervent purpose.

Danvir, Philippe's driver, told me about a revered pilgrimage in Nashik every twelve years called Kumbh Mela, the largest religious festival in the world. In 1967, Nashik set a record when twenty million pilgrims arrived for the festivities. Although this was no Kumbh Mela, I could well imagine standing amid millions of believers and felt a part of the India of my dreams: the country I'd been lured to by Ravi Shankar's music and the counterculture literature.

The next three days we visited the Kalaram, the Naroshankar and the Sundernarayan temples that brimmed with pilgrims burning incense and giving gifts of food, money and hair. We stood by an altar and witnessed a ceremony called Chadakarana, a young boy's first haircut, one of twelve mandated sanskaras or rituals. I admired the helpless fortitude displayed by the tiny three-year old as priests and family members fussed over his head. The smell of bhang intermingled with the fragrant incenses where skeletal, ash-covered Sadhus smoked huge joints and engaged in an array of religious body contortions.

At the end of the week, sated with religious architecture and tired of the constant frenetic activities we returned to Bombay.

* * *

A few days after our return, as we finished a dinner of chapattis and dhal (lentils) at our apartment, Lode sighed and said in a low tone, "Guys, I'm broke… again and I don't want to sell any more blood. I want to return home to Holland."

I was not surprised. My friend had become increasingly intolerant of the lice, the fleas, the flies and the oppressive heat. Lately, he'd often complained about the filth, and the ubiquitous beggars who inhabited every nook and cranny of the city.

He shook his head and added, "It's been fun. The elephants, the wild monkeys and the cows everywhere, but I'm homesick."

I studied his long face, noticing the sunken eyes, the cracked lips and the pronounced facial bones and realized that, like all of us, he'd lost weight and seemed tired all the time. I nodded in agreement and said, "Considering you were only going as far as Istanbul to begin with, you've done pretty well! What are you gonna do?"

"Back in Kandahar you mentioned fake maritime papers."

The next morning we took the train to Mahim Junction and rode a bus to the edge of the Dharavi slum. I asked a young boy loitering near the transit stop if he would guide us to the Mishra electronic shop. He nodded, put his hand out and boldly requested ten rupees. I laughed, offered fifty paise and we settled for one rupee up front and a second when we arrived at our destination. Following the kid, we entered a dark, dank world where the streets were little more than crowded, narrow dirt lanes, flanked by flimsy one and two-story shanties, assembled using an assortment of disparate construction materials: cinder blocks, corrugated steel, pieces of lumber and plastic tarps. Stagnant, reeking sewers ran through the centers of the alleys occasionally bridged by wobbly planks.

Sari-clad women toted tall plastic or brass water urns or woven baskets on their heads. Peddlers pushed bicycles, mopeds and three-wheeled barrows. Small, naked children rooted in the refuse, competing against skinny dogs and huge rats scavenging for edible garbage. Despite the apparent destitution and poverty, Dharavi was a hive of mercantile activity. The ground floor of most of the buildings housed workshops and stores selling everything from refurbished automotive horns to repaired radiators, cash registers with missing keys and flaking paint, gold jewelry, food and beverages. It seemed as if every other workshop recycled used materials and housed young children and adolescents squatting on their heels as they labored in the dark depths. Gaudily decorated wheeled carts parked tightly against building walls, sold watches, rings, flowers and a huge variety of delicacies.

The slum reeked of unwashed humanity, rotting vegetables, stagnant sewers, damp earth and the acrid smell of piss. As we walked past the food stalls, the aroma of curry or brazier-grilled meats, fleetingly overpowered the slum's native stench. Dharavi's muddy lanes reverberated with the shriek of kids, the crowing of confused roosters, the yipping and barking of scrawny dogs, the blare of transistor radios and the sounds of scooters, mopeds, and motorcycles (the only motorized vehicles able to negotiate the narrow twisting alleys) carrying loads taller by half than the riders.

As soon as we entered the labyrinth, we lost all sense of direction. The lanes snaked deviously and the shanties leaning towards each other blocked the light from above us. We kept an anxious eye on our diminutive guide, whose unerring familiarity with the bewildering maze, lead us through and stopped in front of a dim, hole-in-the-wall shop on the ground floor of a two-story gray cinder-block building. The grimy tyke held his hand out to me, pointed with his head at the business and said, "Mishra." I gave him a rupee. His grubby face broke into a wide smile revealing surprisingly white teeth and he ran off as we stepped into Mishra's electronic salvage shop.

The crammed store overflowed with crates, baskets, boxes and loose piles of disassembled electronic components. Old phones, switchboards, radios and broken appliances in various stages of dismantling, were stacked against the walls while wire harnesses, cables and diverse cords dangled from the ceiling. A slim, bearded, swarthy man wearing a beige turban squatted on his heels behind a knee-high table surrounded by tools, bins and jars of electronic parts. Two scrawny adolescents sat cross-legged in the back of the shop. The man peered up from the radio he was taking apart, docked a smoking soldering iron in a holder and rose to greet us.

Lode salaamed and said, "We're looking for Mandeep."

"I am Mandeep, how can I help you?" the man replied in fluent English.

I explained our connection to Gerard hoping it would prove our bona fides enough for him to supply the fake documents we sought. Mandeep held up his hand to interrupt me, told his helpers to mind the store and motioned us to follow him. We squeezed through a gap between two buildings and up an open, wooden stairway to the second floor. He led us into a dwelling consisting of a single room serving as living, cooking and sleeping quarters. We sat on a carpeted square of flooring strewn with colorful and ornately decorated cushions. A large, gilded, framed picture of the Golden Temple of Amritsar surrounded by smaller pictures of Sikh holy men hung on the plywood walls. A small, plastic-covered window over the kitchen counter allowed a diffused sunbeam to highlight dust motes swirling in the air.

"What kind of documents are you looking for?" Mandeep asked.

Lode pulled out a piece of paper and read, "Maritime Certificate of

Competency and a level two National Vocational Qualifications for a General Hand or Oiler/Wiper."

Mandeep reached for the scrap, studied the writing and tucked the paper into his shirt pocket. A very young girl entered the room balancing a brass tray with three cups of chai, shyly handing them to us while studiously avoiding eye contact. She scampered out after giving her father the last cup. Mandeep sipped his tea and avowed that he could obtain the documents for the right price.

Lode put his teacup on the floor and asked, "How real will they look? Will they be good enough to pass muster?"

Mandeep replied, "Oh, they'll be genuine. There is no shortage of foreign seamen getting drunk and rolled in whorehouses all over Bombay, or foolishly losing more money than they have in the gambling joints."

The price was one hundred U.S. dollars for a set of certificates. Lode pulled out our old 'lost' travelers' cheques (two hundred bucks worth) and proffered them to Mandeep who counted them, rubbed a note between his fingers, nodded in satisfaction and inquired if they were stolen or misplaced. We assured him they were reported lost. Satisfied, the slim Indian stashed the cheques in a pocket, slurped the last dregs of his tea and led us back down the stairs. We shook hands and Mandeep invited Lode to return in a couple of days. He then instructed the kid in the store to guide us out of the slum and back to the bus stop.

* * *

Later that week with his fake documentation in hand, Lode searched for a berth amid the shipping offices in the harbor and it wasn't long before Vijay handed Lode a reply from a maritime firm.

Lode read the note and exclaimed, "I've got a job! Wiper on the Unigoolar. She sails from Bombay to Barcelona via the Suez Canal."

"When do you leave?" I asked with growing feelings of sadness.

"In three days. I must get down to the harbor and sign on." He ran out of the building after scrounging ten rupees from me for an auto.

Paul and Scott entered the apartment herding two backpackers that they introduced as David and Malcolm. The two Australian drifters were tanned, fit and wore their long sun-bleached blond hair in ponytails. They were on their way home via Bombay, Goa, Sri Lanka and Indonesia and would crash with us for a few days.

I asked Scott, "Have you seen Trev or Ian?" With Lode leaving for home I felt the need to contact our two friends.

He replied, "We spotted Trev at the Leopold a while ago but he was leaving when we got there, so we just waved at each other."

I grabbed my satchel and said, "I'll see if they're home."

I hailed a rickshaw and headed towards the Colaba. The driver prattled on about India's national sport and proudly told me that the national cricket team beat England two to one in five matches. The losing English team and their entourage were guests of honor at a glitzy party at the Taj Mahal Hotel, which was shining like an island of lights in the early evening. As we rolled by the front of the majestic old hotel, I saw that its wide sidewalk overflowed with formally attired partygoers.

The Colaba Hotel, in sharp contrast, was shrouded in darkness with only a few bulbs dimly illuminating the stairs and the scrofulous hallways, which stank of backed-up toilets. Trev's door was slightly ajar and after knocking a couple of time without a response, I walked into the dim room. The stale air was oppressively hot so I pushed open the windows' wooden shutters and switched on the lights. Trev, passed out, slumped in one of the armchairs with his leg dangling lifelessly over the frayed arm. The low, scratched coffee table held a few tattered magazines, an ashtray full of butts, empty cups, bottles and junkie paraphernalia. Feeling apprehensive, I examined the Brit and noticed he'd lost even more weight and his face was pinched and sallow. I shook his shoulder until he opened bloodshot eyes.

"S'up?" he mumbled.

"Wake up, Trev."

I surveyed the mess on the small table looking closely at the dirty syringe with spots of clotted blood staining the glass and at the bent spoon with its bottom blackened by innumerable flames. Trev staggered up and padded to the loo down the hallway. On his return, he grabbed a bottle of water from the dining table, dropped into the armchair, upended the bottle and drank deeply.

He offered me the bottle and said, "Danny boy! How was your trip?"

I waved off the drink and replied, "Great, man. What are you shooting?" I pointed at the rig on the coffee table.

"Straight morphine. Talk about a rush!"

"Where are Ian and your roomies?"

"Ian should be back soon. Charlie and Nev split to Delhi. There's just the two of us now. Where's Lode?"

I explained that Lode had scored a berth on a ship and I regaled him with tales of the trip to Ganeshpuri and Nashik. Trev's eyes lit up as I described the ashram and the temples and for a while, it was just like old times: chatting with my friend, the smart-ass scouser Freak, the walking rock 'n' roll encyclopedia.

The door opened and Ian walked in. At first glance, I hardly recognized him. He wore a green sari and a sleeveless, embroidered vest revealing his sunken chest. A shell necklace adorned his neck and bangles on his bonny wrists clinked and clattered as he dropped his shoulder bag on the table. His face was drawn, his ash-blond hair lusterless and I noted his mouth had taken a new hard cast.

"What the hell..." I started but swallowed the rest as Trev gave me a cautionary look and shook his head.

Ian looked up and said, "Hey Danny! Good to see you."

We chatted about inconsequential things while inside I was screaming, "Who the fuck are you and what have you done with my friend?" To my relief, Ian sauntered to the washroom and I noticed that he favored his right side and had a slight limp.

I stared hard at Trev and asked, "So, what's going on?"

He averted his eyes and muttered, "He's doing what he likes, sort of thing, getting paid to go out with, you know... friends."

"You mean like a whore?"

"Yeah, I need a fix." Trev scratched his arm absently and rooted around the trash on the coffee table.

I rose and said, "I'm leaving. Let's get together tomorrow morning to send off Lode, okay?"

I didn't wait for an answer and turned away lest he saw the revulsion on my face. I returned to the apartment as the warm tropical night settled over Bombay and despite the warmth, goose bumps emerged on my arms and a shiver ran down my spine when I thought about my two lost friends. Ian looked grotesque and Trev had become a hardcore junky.

* * *

It was hard for me to watch Lode's reaction to the diminished state of our friends when they met us at the Leopold the next morning. The Dutchman dropped into his chair as if poleaxed and his dazed expression gave way to palpable grief. It was indicative of how far gone Trev and Ian had become that they didn't even notice. I spent the last of my cash on breakfast but no one had much of an appetite. Between uncomfortable attempts at conversation, we simply pushed the food around our plates.

Outside on the sidewalk we looked awkwardly at each other until Lode broke the silence and said he had to report to his ship. After all the miles and months of traveling together since Amsterdam, we had little to say. He hugged each of us, promised to keep in touch, squeezed into the back of an auto and rode out of our lives. I was demoralized. Trev and Ian were lost to me, living in an alien world of grasping need, filth, syringes and smack. I left them in front of the hotel and strolled on Marine drive oblivious to the beautiful promenade alongside the crescent-shaped bay. I drifted along the palm trees-lined walkway until the sun set over the Arabian Sea and, as night fell, I slept on the beach.

Lode's departure presaged the end. A few days later, I contracted a debilitating stomach ailment that caused painful, crippling cramps and the runs. I couldn't keep any food down and rapidly lost weight. My worried roommates urged me to seek medical help and I queued up at a nearby clinic where a young Indian Intern handed me two aspirins and shooed me away.

David and Malcolm, the Aussies crashing at the apartment, took the train to Goa while Paul and Scott talked about joining them in the beautiful coastal town. It seemed I would shortly add homelessness to my other problems as I could hardly afford the rent by myself. I could always share a room with Trev and Ian I thought dismally. The following dental clinic day, as I helped Philippe and Danvir set up in the slum, the burly dentist studied me and shook his head. "You're in bad shape mon vieux and you're losing weight too fast."

"Yeah, I can't keep any food down because of killer runs, man," I replied. We stacked plastic crates against a wall in one of the slum's schoolrooms.

"You need medical attention. This place is crawling with tropical diseases and parasites. Some are fatal."

"An Indian doctor at the clinic checked me out…" I started but Philippe stopped me with his raised hand and a very Gallic shrug. I knew what he thought of the local free medical help. "A French Doctor cycles between here and Delhi. I'll book you an appointment."

That evening on my way up to the apartment, Vijay handed me a message from Trev. The brief note said, "Ian missing. Come to the Colaba." The sun dipped over the Arabian Sea as I set out. A light breeze carried Bombay's unique blend of aromas: diesel fumes, brazier charcoal smoke, grilling meat and the omnipresent whiff of shit.

At the Colaba, I found Trev, the room's only occupant, flipping through a tatty magazine while sprawled on the sofa. He glanced up as I entered the room and his eyes widened noticeably as he took in my wasted body, pallid face and sunken eyes.

"What's wrong with you?" he asked, "Are you using?"

I sat in one of the armchairs and replied, "Not dope, man, stomach bug. How long has Ian been missing?"

"Since the day before yesterday. Normally I wouldn't be worried but lately he's been coming back looking pretty rough."

I straightened up and gave him a searching glance. "How rough?"

"Bruises, limping and sores, sort of thing." He avoided my eyes and peered at his feet. "Let's give him a couple more hours. Maybe he'll come back. I don't want to embarrass him."

I wasn't sure about the advisability of that but my illness exhausted me and I didn't relish the thought of running around the streets of Bombay.

"What are you reading?" I asked to fill the ensuing awkward silence.

Holding the Rolling Stone magazine forward he pointed out an article about the latest Stones' album *Exile on Main Street*. I pulled my Blues harp from my satchel and said, "Hey, grab your guitar and let's play some tunes while we're waiting for Ian."

He glanced away. "Can't, man. I sold it." I was speechless; Trev loved the guitar he'd lugged and coddled all the way from London. "Ian had to sell his flute and we cashed our 'lost' Amex cheques."

The situation was worse than I could have imagined. Trev was getting antsy, absently scratching at his arms and rocking back and forth. Looking covertly at him, I realized that the poor fucker was truly hooked. I offered him a toke of hash hoping to alleviate his craving and we reminisced about London wondering how our friends were fairing.

The door crashed open making us jump in our seats and Ian, looking like shit, staggered in. His once-beautiful face was a mess: the bruised left eye turning color and his split upper lip dripped bright red blood on his clothes. He took two steps into the room and sank to the floor. I rushed over and picked him up while Trev cleared the sofa. It was alarming how light Ian was, like carrying a child. I stretched him on the couch noticing the ugly contusions and scabbed needle tracks running from wrist to elbow on his bare arms. His face was made up with kohl and lipstick, earrings dangled from both ears and he wore a thin, embroidered sleeveless vest over a cotton tunic and a long sari.

"What happened to him?" I asked Trev.

He used a wet towel to swab the blood from Ian's chin and lip. "Sometimes his... clients get violent and he gets beat up, but I've never seen him this battered before."

Ian opened his good eye revealing a bloodshot sclera and he whispered, "Give us a shot Trev. Take the pain away." He fumbled in his vest pocket and fished out a small white cardboard box the size of a pack of cards.

Trev eagerly grasped the packet, tore open the lid and tipped the contents into his palm. Half a dozen slim, thin glass ampoules clattered out, each almost full of a clear liquid. He held up one of the morphine vials by the base, scored the neck with a nail file and flicked off the tapered tip. His tongue sticking out in concentration, Trev sucked up the drug into the syringe, tied a tourniquet around Ian's skeletal arm and injected the liquid into a small vein on his friend's inner wrist. Ian exhaled noisily, closed his eyes and passed out.

Trev rinsed the syringe with bottled water and he squirted it towards the wall. He raised the rig in my direction in mute questioning. Nauseous, I shook my head and offered to call the cops.

"No, man, don't. They'll just throw him in a cell."

"What about the British Consulate?"

"I went there once looking for rehab information," Trev admitted bitterly as he prepared to give himself a shot. "They couldn't give a crap about a hippie-faggot-junkie."

Deeply disturbed I walked to the door and said over my shoulder, "I'll come by tomorrow morning." However, Trev was beyond response as he reclined in the armchair, eyes fluttering closed in drugged ecstasy.

* * *

That night I spent more time squatting over the foul shitter-hole than in bed and I woke up to find my arms and legs covered in maddeningly itchy red spots. I suspected bedbugs and scratched furiously as I swore at my streak of bad luck. Paul, Scott and I had planned to sell blood that morning so we headed towards the clinic, which occupied the corner of a block-long, brick building. After a short wait, it was our turn and we rolled our sleeves for the admittance examination. Paul and Scott were led to a pair of cots but the nurse took one look at my inflamed, red-spotted skin and shook her head.

"I'm sorry but we can't take your blood. Those spots could be chickenpox!" she said.

Bewildered, I replied, "These? They're just bug bites."

She pointed at the exit. "Come back when they're gone."

The Americans smirked and shouted that they'd meet me back at the apartment unless the plague claimed me first. I walked to the French consular compound and asked if Philippe was free. The Frenchman took one look at me and ushered me into the examination room.

"Mon Dieu, you're getting worse and our Doctor is not due in Bombay for another week." He told me to stay put while he left to make a phone call. I looked at my reflection in a wall-mounted mirror and was startled at how sick I appeared.

Philippe returned and said, "The U.S. Consulate has a physician in town this week and he agreed to check you out right away. I'll ask Danvir to take you there."

We drove through Bombay's busy streets to Nariman Point where most of the foreign legations were located. At the U.S. Consulate, a greying middle-aged man introduced himself as Doctor Johnson. His nurse took blood samples and the American doctor gave me a thorough examination.

Afterwards he washed his hands and said, "I'll tell you what I suspect. You most likely have dysentery, which explains the stomach cramps and the severe diarrhea. You're dehydrated, malnourished and show signs of both bed bugs and lice. I also suspect that you're having an allergic reaction."

When clinically recited like that, it occurred to me that my illnesses were in part self-inflicted. I must have been an idiot for ignoring my health and I think the doctor thought so too.

"The Indian nurse suspected chickenpox." I was vainly trying to regain an iota of dignity.

"Nonsense! You have no oral or nasal sores. I think you're either reacting to an allergen or got bit by bugs." He scribbled on a prescription pad, tore off the page and handed it to me. "These pills are antibiotics for the dysentery. Take them with lots of fluids." I thanked him and rejoined Danvir by the minibus.

Back at the French consulate Philippe met us in the lobby and said, "I talked to Doc Johnson. I also spoke with the Deputy Consul and recommended that you be repatriated to France immediately." I was speechless and shook my head. I had not even considered leaving India but could not marshal any convincing counter-arguments. "Listen Danny," Philippe pressed on earnestly, "The Doc figures you won't last more than two weeks if we don't do something immediately. The Consulate will contact your next-of-kin." He took the prescription from my hand and gave it to his nurse who walked towards the dispensary. "Whom should we call? Preferably someone in France to help expedite the repatriation process."

I wrote Cousin David's address and phone number on a prescription pad and gave it to Philippe. The nurse returned and handed me a pill bottle and a tube of lotion. "The pills are antibiotics and the salve contains anti-histamines. Rub it on your skin and the spots should disappear." She smiled and left.

Philippe shooed me towards the exit. "Now, Danvir will drop you off at the apartment. Come back tomorrow morning, we'll have your plane ticket ready."

"Ok, man. Thanks. I'll talk to you before I leave?" He assured me that he would say goodbye before I left.

Danvir drove out of the compound and headed towards my apartment but I asked him to take me to the Colaba instead. The tall Indian shrugged and changed direction. As we approached our destination, the traffic came to a standstill. Peering through the van's windshield, I saw groups of bystanders in front of the hotel while an ambulance, lights flashing, stood by the building's doors. Two cops kept the curious crowd back from the entrance. Suddenly apprehensive I jumped out of the minibus, shoving and pushing through the mob until I reached one of the police officers.

"Excuse me, sir. What's happening?" I said.

The man studied me, replied that there had been an incident and asked, "Do you live here?"

"No, but I have two friends staying on the third floor."

He nodded and let me into the lobby, which was crowded with agitated hotel staff and curious guests. I climbed the stairs wondering what the fuck was going on but in my heart, feared the worst. On the third-floor landing, two ambulance attendants and a gurney stood against the wall. Inside the room, three plainclothes cops argued in fast-paced Urdu interspersed with English words. I stepped in and cleared my throat.

The senior of the trio crooked his finger and ordered, "Come here."

I advanced into the room and saw Ian lying on the sofa, his waxen face harshly highlighted by the midday sun pouring in from the open window. Trev, in the comparative darkness of the room's corner, sprawled limply in an armchair, his head flung back and his feet propped on the coffee table. The scene assumed a surrealistic quality almost as if I was tripping on acid. Trev's cloudy eyes stared at the ceiling. Flies buzzed around us and a length of faded, yellow rubber hose dangled flaccidly from Trev's arm like a limp, deflated snake. A syringe lay on the floor where it had fallen below his lifeless fingers. I felt wetness on my cheeks and tears stung my eyes. My chest constricted as reality sucker-punched me: Trev and Ian were dead.

The older cop motioned me to the table and pointed at a chair. I gingerly lowered myself and numbly answered a whole lot of questions. Sometime during the interrogation while the cop assiduously recorded my answers in a spiral-bound notebook, the medics bagged the bodies and removed them from the room.

"How… how did they die?" I asked.

The policeman answered, "We won't be sure until the autopsy but we suspect an overdose of drugs. Morphine, yes?" I nodded and he continued, "There's been a rash of deaths among the city's junkies recently."

"Bad dope?"

"On the contrary! The stuff coming from Afghanistan and Pakistan is almost pure. Too pure. Users overdose and die."

He asked to see my arms. A flash of irrational anger consumed me but I suppressed it and, with a shrug, obeyed. He commented about my skin rash and I was tempted to tell him I had the pox but instead told the truth. The detective closed his notebook and slipped it into a pocket.

He studied me for a moment and said, "We'll contact the British Embassy. Do you have any belongings here before we bag everything?"

I thought about it and looked around. Trev and Ian's pitiful few possessions strewn around the room were mute testimony to how destitute they'd become. I picked up the well-used, small, brass hash pipe Trev had carried since London and placed it in my shoulder bag. Night had fallen when the cops let me go. The lobby was empty, the ambulance and all the curious bystanders had departed.

I wandered westwards, sometimes walking, oft times staggering, alone among a crowd of noisy, boisterous, short brown people and ignored the cries of peddlers hawking food, beverages and betel leaf paan. I mourned my friends. Even though we'd drifted apart these last few months, we had been as tight as brothers, sharing all that we owned and surmounting all obstacles. Their absence left a painful void. Wrapped in these sorrowful thoughts I'd unwittingly walked clear across the peninsula to Mahim Bay on the western shore of Bombay. I waded into the lukewarm waters of the Arabian Sea, contemplating the vast watery expanse bordered by far Arabia and aware that somewhere out there, Lode was sailing home

At dawn the rising sun, an enormous fiery orange ball, ascended from the ochre-colored, dusty horizon and found me at the foot of the ancient ruins of Fort Worli. I stood facing east as the immense orb rose across the bay painting the massive stones in a palette of delicate pink, orange and purple pastels.

For a moment, I sensed a tenuous link to the old deserted fortress bathed in the light of the new day. How many deaths had these impassive boulders witnessed; how much misery and pain had lapped these ancient rocks like waves crashing against a breakwater. Then the sun rose above the horizon washing out the delicate colors and replaced them with an unforgiving tropical glare.

> *And thou art dead, as young and fair*
> *As aught of mortal birth;*
> *And form so soft, and charms so rare,*
> *Too soon return'd to Earth*

- Lord Byron (1788 - 1824)

* * *

Epilogue

Paris, April 1973

I tucked the scraps of paper, train ticket stubs and postcards between the pages of my notebook and slipped the rubber band around the covers. I sat there staring blankly at the library wall and pondered whether I should write Gina in London and explain what had happened. Ian and Trev's families would arrange to bring their boys home and I wanted Gina and Irish to know about the good times we had shared.

By now, Lode would be making his way across Europe and I should write him as well, care of his parents in Antwerp. Monique too, I thought; so many letters to write and in the end so little to say. Someone once said: dying is easy, living is hard.

David entered the wood-paneled room and stared at me. "Well, look at you! Shaved, a haircut, you're almost human."

I smiled and the burdensome weirdness I felt, receded. I realized that in time, I would get over these gloomy feelings and put to rest my Bombay ghosts. I showed David my journal and said, "I was reminiscing about my trip."

"Will you ever go back?"

"I'd like to. See New Delhi, Nepal, Ceylon. But, first I want to travel to the Americas."

My cousin's eyes lit up. "Ah, the States! California, beach bunnies and cruising the boulevards."

Startled I glanced at my cousin and asked, "Did you travel to the US?"

"Oh, yeah. In the 50s I rambled from New York to San Francisco. Fun times." We chatted about his travels until Asunción announced dinner was ready.

A week after my arrival in Paris with the dysentery under control and all the parasites dead, I boarded an El-Al flight to Tel-Aviv where my poor mother almost fainted at the sight of my ravaged body. She hugged my boney frame tightly and declared, "You are not allowed to leave home ever again."

A year later, I left Israel for Canada and a journey south that would take me as far as Brazil.

The End

CPSIA information can be obtained at www.ICGtesting.com
Printed in the USA
LVOW06s1220230114

370539LV00043B/649/P